EVERY LITTLE THING

CHAD PELLEY

EVERY LITTLE THING

A NOVEL

P.O. BOX 2188, ST. JOHN'S, NL, CANADA, A1C 6E6
WWW.BREAKWATERBOOKS.COM

COPYRIGHT © 2013 Chad Pelley
LIBRARY AND ARCHIVES CANADA CATALOGUING IN PUBLICATION
Pelley, Chad, 1980-
        Every little thing / Chad Pelley.
ISBN 978-1-55081-405-7
I. Title.
PS8631.E4683E84 2013   C813'.6   C2013-901004-1

We acknowledge the support of the Canada Council for the Arts which last
year invested $24.3 million in writing and publishing throughout Canada.
We acknowledge the Government of Canada through the Canada Book
Fund and the Government of Newfoundland and Labrador through
the Department of Tourism, Culture and Recreation for our publishing
activities.

PRINTED AND BOUND IN CANADA.

  Canada Council Conseil des Arts   Newfoundland
                      for the Arts   du Canada   Labrador

Breakwater Books is committed to choosing papers and materials for our
books that help to protect our environment. To this end, this book is printed
on a recycled paper that is certified by the Forest Stewardship Council®.

For,
      Everyone who had a kind word about the last one.

"Open your mouth and fill it with food or rage.
The same leaf that turns to the light shies from the blaze."
—FROM "LULLABIES" BY GEORGE MURRAY

"I want to believe our love's a mystery,
I want to believe our love's a sin.
I want you to kiss me,
like a stranger,
once again."
—FROM "KISS ME" BY TOM WAITS

SHAKING
THE BED

HE'D CLOSE HIS eyes and thoughts of Allie would pinball around in his head—thudding and dinging and keeping him awake. He'd recollect her, bit by bit: the dart-hole dimple in her cheek when she'd smirk at her own wit. The artichoke dip she'd make for book club, and how she'd shoo his hungry hands. *You only get the leftovers, double-dipped and half-stale!* A kiss, a sorry. That smell, more clover than cinnamon, of a bath product, or her DNA.

He'd open his eyes and she'd be gone. Nothing but darkness, cement walls, iron bars. The floor in his cell was so cold, it felt like broken glass when he'd step on it barefoot. Most nights he was drawn to his window, if you could call it that: thick glass, no bigger than a textbook, so dense it blurred everything he could see into blunt-edged objects. He'd stare at the hypnotic sway of trembling aspen in the distance and think of the boy: the pacifying, perfectly spaced beeps of his hospital machinery. All those white hoses latched onto his body.

It was lights out long before he was tired in that prison and that was half the problem. Being locked in a cage, alone with his thoughts, and miles away from the people who could answer his questions, like where Allie was now, and how the kid was doing.

He'd lie there on his back, eyes closed, body restless, rocking an ankle back and forth; his toes scraping across bedsheets drier than paper. It was strange the way silence worked after lights out. New sounds would emerge from the quietness, one by one, in an ordered hierarchy. At first it was a guard's footsteps and the tossing and turning of inmates in their beds. Within fifteen minutes he could hear the heavy breathers and what thirty years of smoking had done to their lungs: the cliché rattle, the constant need to be cleared of phlegm. With everyone asleep, he'd hear the waspy buzzing of distant bulbs. And then the whispering crawl of water through old pipes; the drips from faulty plumbing as constant as a ticking clock. In time, they'd all start snoring—a rhythmic orchestra of rattling lungs. People would grunt as they came to, gasping for air, and roll over; their part in the orchestra now gone, the song changed by one less instrument.

The rusty springs in his prison cot—the *screech* and stab of them—would get him thinking about his and Allie's first bed. It had a lamp built into the headboard and the bulb would burn until two or three in the morning. Her taste in books had left her tired every morning. *Another marathon, this one's so good!* But they all were. They'd all keep her up. And every morning she'd climb over him, drunk with fatigue, blindly hammering a fist at the snooze button, and fall down over him like a third blanket; her heart beating like a bird trapped between them.

The nights he *could* sleep in prison, he'd wake early to the purple glow of dawn. It would punch through his thick window and lay a perfect mauve rectangle on his bedsheets. Like a book he ought to pick up and read. There'd be a faint birdsong, but the glass in his window was so thick, the bird sounded ten feet under water. It might have been the same yellow warbler, every morning. He'd look for it, through his window, but the window was too narrow to see anything not directly in front of him.

In the mornings in prison, the wake-up call's blare was worse than an alarm clock. It was more urgent. More insistent, like a military warning. And that didn't make sense: they had nowhere to go, nowhere to be. He'd snap the sheets off himself and sit up, disoriented as he came to. His vision dissected seven or eight times by the black cylindrical bars of his cell—the guard on the other side like a man in two halves. His body was getting stiffer than the bed he'd been sleeping in. His spine with no give to it now, an iron rod, rigid, running from his neck to his legs. And that toilet smell that clogged his nostrils every morning: like bright steel and mould. His toilet hissed incessantly, always filling with water, but there was never more than a puddle in it. He'd sit on the edge of his bed, staring at his feet, dizzy from another sleepless night. Or he'd lie back down and stare up at the ceiling's cold, porous cement. There was one solidified drip in a corner, like a stone icicle.

He'd stopped trying to convince himself that Allie would come and apologize, explain herself, because too many weeks had passed since the night he went looking for answers and got taken by the police. Three months. Twelve weeks ago. He'd lay there calculating the math of time passed. Two thousand hours, it didn't *sound* long enough. It didn't add up to all the distance between them now. Twelve weeks. *Ninety-four days.*

One night—one misunderstanding and a sloppy trial—and now he wakes to the sound of metal bars unclamping, sliding open, so he can follow a herd of hard men to the cafeteria. Choke down dry toast. Concentrated orange juice. Burnt scrambled eggs that smelled off.

He could never recollect that night as a whole; it was a smashed vase he saw in pieces only. He doesn't remember what sentence, exactly, got her crying, but her eyes were so wet with tears they must have been kaleidoscoping her vision. He can picture her strangling a crumpled tissue in her shaky hands. It was his last image of her. Crushed. Remorseful. Love and anxiety, guilt and compassion—she could never handle two emotions at once without getting the lines crossed and going off like a bomb. He couldn't put a colour to the walls of the room they were in. What time of night it was. But she was wearing the watch he'd given her. She'd always worn the thing so loosely that it swirled around her wrist in circles whenever she'd move her arm too fast. Like when she pointed to the door that night. *You need to leave, Cohen, he's upstairs, he'll hear you!*

He asked her questions, but he doesn't remember her answers.

The officers had reduced everything to guilty or not guilty. They weren't concerned with the context of the three-way argument they'd walked into, just, simply, which of the three had crossed a line and broken a law. There were cracks and pops of walkie-talkies going off like gunfire, making far too big a deal of things. All that guilt caught in Allie's throat, stretching it, until her voice was a wheezy, punctured balloon. Every time she nodded her head to the police that night, it was another dull blow, until Cohen's whole body felt like a thumb struck by a hammer. They made Allie clip the *but* off of every *yes but*, until she panicked at how simple they'd made it all sound. *Yes or no, ma'am: Did Cohen Davies enter your home without your consent?*

They dragged him down over her staircase, gripping his arms so tightly he could barely turn and face her. The male officer's grip was firm and contemptuous: his fingers pinched deep between Cohen's bi- and triceps. The female officer's grip had been less judgmental. Four thin fingers and a dry thumb, like a butterfly at his elbow.

There were no sirens going off as they walked him to the car, but the lights were flashing and it seemed so needless, such an exaggeration. The red and white lights poked him in the eyes as they tucked his head into the car. He sat in his seat, watching the lights bang off the trees in the yard: brown bark to red bark, to white bark, to brown. He looked up to Allie's window and she was staring down at him. Her eyes in his, *I'm so fucking sorry*. And that's what kept him up at night. That she really was sorry and had so much to be sorry about.

Every night, he'd lie in that prison bed, restless, running a finger around the puck-sized metal implant above his heart. His idle hand was drawn to the rough feel where the metal pushed, from the inside out, against his flesh. Raising it, just a little. It felt like a big bottlecap sewn under his skin. He'd gotten used to having that chunk of metal in his chest, *mentally*, but his body never did. It throbbed, wanting Cohen's hands to pluck it out like a splinter.

The first time Allie took his shirt off, it was dark and she never saw the thumb-sized scar below his collarbone. Surgical, but with a vicious edge. They were both on their knees, in the centre of her bed; his hands tucking her hair behind her ear, to kiss her neck. The soft mattress was bending under their weight, so they were leaning into each other; her hard nipples soft scrapes against his chest. She slid a hand up his thigh, past his hips, over his ribs, and when she felt it there, she went still as a statue. Took a deep breath with a cutting noise.

"Cohen! You've got a...it's a lump or something!" Her eyes so wide he could see their whiteness in the dark.

He laughed, "I...was born with a broken heart."

She shrugged both shoulders, "So, it's a pacemaker or something?"

"Something like that."

She reached out to touch it, hesitantly, like it was a button she shouldn't press. "Can I?" she nodded to her fingers, an inch or two from his chest.

He nodded back.

She rubbed her middle finger over it, like she was applying a cream, to feel the outline of it under his skin. She brushed another finger, her forefinger, along the glossy scar, once, and looked him in the eye. "Tell me about your broken heart."

"There was this girl I loved, and she left me for a man with money."

She shoved him, hard, her palms clapping off his shoulders, and she bounced back like she just shoved a wall. They tumbled onto opposite sides of the bed, laughing. "I'm serious!"

"You know those paddles doctors shock peoples' hearts with in the hospital?" He waited for her to nod. "I have one in my chest."

"*Fuck off!*" She covered her mouth like the words were a sneeze. "Really?"

He shrugged his shoulders. His eyes looking where his hands wanted to be. She was sitting there, crossed-legged in bright orange underwear, topless. Gorgeous.

"I dunno, I'll be out shovelling, or something like that, and it can feel like my heart is a bird trapped in a space too small to flap its wings. But it's trying anyway. That's what this implant thing is for. To shock my heart out of a, I dunno, a bad rhythm."

She reached up and touched it again. The backs of her fingers this time. Gently. He'd never seen that look on her face before. But she read his body language. That he didn't want her that far away. Or that look in her eye. Like he was a movie and things were going wrong.

HE'D MET ALLIE in his mid-twenties, just after his heart surgery. There were still stitches in his chest. The muscles they cut through in the operation were the same ones that his left arm needed to move. So it felt like someone had swung an axe at him and his left arm was dangling by a thread. There were painkillers and times he'd lift that arm too high in putting on a shirt and he'd wince from the hot stab of pain. He was all right hand for a while. He'd right-hand a cigarette into his mouth, and use his right hand to light it.

The night they met, he'd stepped outside his house for a cigarette. He'd do his smoking in a deep, dark, cement stairwell out back. The house next door had been empty for months with the same mannish, unlucky real estate agent showing it almost daily. Her jacket was two sizes too big and it flapped like a flag in the wind; he'd hear her out there, wooing potential buyers, sounding like a plastic bag caught in a storm. The place had been vacant so long that seeing the lights on had snagged the corner of his eye. He had a cigarette poked between his lips and the lighter in his hand ready to go. He looked up and Allie was leaning into the patio railing, facing him, hidden behind a puff of smoke. Their eyes banged into each other, locked, and seconds passed without either of them speaking.

"So," she said. "Safe to assume you're my new neighbour? If not...if you're about to burgle that house, I'll keep my mouth shut for the toaster." Her sly laugh was a soft blade in his gut. "I'm just moving in here," she said, nodding her head back at the house, as if it wasn't obvious which house, "and I forgot to buy myself a new toaster tonight. I remembered everything but the toaster. I'd much rather a cooked bagel to a raw one in the morning. I mean, butter won't even melt into a cold bagel, you know? Like, real fresh butter." She flashed a sad face.

He scuffed a foot, a nervous tic. "Sorry, but I'm just the neighbour, not a burglar. Although I do have a toaster. And your pending breakfast tragedy has me willing to lend it to you. Really. It's a good one, it's got a bagel setting and everything. High-end Black and Decker." He snuffed his cigarette out. "Stainless steel. Digital display. You couldn't get a loan of a better toaster."

She honked out a laugh and its unrestrained volume took him off guard. "I'm the kind of girl who'd take you up on that, you should know." She looked at her cigarette, her first cigarette smoked on that patio, and she didn't know what to do with the butt.

Cohen scooped up his mug-as-ashtray and walked up the stairs. He stood beneath her, holding it up like a bouquet of flowers. "Just...try and shoot for the mug and not my head."

"Well, it would be funny, wouldn't it?" she laughed, "the first time we meet, you make this chivalric ashtray gesture and I set your hair on fire—"

An oversized U-haul truck pulled up in front of her house, loud as an old bus, and cleaved their conversation. Her boyfriend, he imagined. A fuller head of hair. More charm and wittier.

"Well, there's my stuff." She tossed the butt and it landed in the centre of his mug. There was a soft *sist* of it being extinguished in the collected rainwater. She pumped a fist, said, "Guess who should join the basketball team?" and he liked that. "Nice to meet you..."

"Cohen."

"Cohen who...Leonard?"

"Davies." He laughed. "You?"

Her hand was on the sliding patio door now. "Allie Crosbie. And that's Allie as in Allie. It's *not* short for Allison. And you can't call me Al, either." She laughed; he raised an eyebrow. "Like, the song, you know? Paul Simon?" She started strumming an imaginary guitar, trumpeting the tune with her mouth. "*You Can Call Me Al?*" But he didn't know the song.

She shook her head and disappeared into her house, leaving him all alone with that dumb smile on his face and the filthy mug-ashtray in his hand.

But she came back out before he'd finished his cigarette. He heard her patio door slide open. In the quiet of the night, the sound of that door wasn't far off a subway car stopping on rusty rails.

"Hey, Cohen Leonard?"

He turned around. "Davies. I'm Cohen Davies." He pointed to himself.

She raised an eyebrow, shook her head, almost embarrassed for him. "I'm fooling around, you know, *hah hah*. I'm mocking your name. It's a weird name."

He had a sense of humour and it was exactly why he was drawn to her, immediately, but there was something about her, like when you shake an Etch-a-Sketch and it all goes blank. She had a look on her face—a smirk—like she knew she had that effect on him.

"My father," she said. "He's out front. I think you know him? Any chance you could give us a hand with a bedframe? Just the bedframe, I promise, not everything. It's just that it's oak: an awkward, heavy lift. It needs three people."

He wanted to say, *Sorry, I'm not supposed to lift anything right now.* He wanted to say, *I can barely get my own shirt on,* and explain about the surgery. And he wanted to know why she'd said, *I think you know him.* But she'd slipped back inside before his tongue came unknotted. He figured he could manage one quick lift, using his right arm, the good arm. If only to spend another minute with her.

He walked around to the front of the house and a man named Matt introduced himself. A bit too enthusiastically. They had something in their DNA, Matt and Allie, and Cohen pictured it as a charge, buzzing at their core, that kept them wired, and 110%

alive. "It's Cohen, right? You're Gordon's boy?"

"Yes, yeah, how'd you know?—"

The man grabbed his hand and shook it, hard, the way men of that generation do. It was his left hand and the vigorous shake burned the wound on his chest. A flash of fire along the edges of the cut.

"We're old friends. Your old man and me. He hasn't mentioned us moving in? Kinda weird, since it was him who turned us onto the place. Or your mother did." They were standing on the front lawn and it was in need of mowing. The grass was so tall it was awkward to stand in as they waited for Allie to reappear. And she did. She burst through the opened front door.

"Told you he wouldn't mind," she said. "Roped him in." She posed in a cowgirl stance and swung an invisible lasso.

"I guess...why would Gordon mention it, right? But Allie here, she needed a place by the university. She's doing her PhD. Chemistry of all things." He patted Allie on the back and she flinched like she's a bit too old for a proud father. Cohen pegged her as pushing thirty: the swagger, the confidence, the effect she had on him. They started walking towards the truck and Matt said, "Your father mentioned the place next door to his son." Matt tossed a hitchhiker's thumb at Cohen's house.

"And he just bought the thing," Allie said. "We didn't even come see it. He looked at pictures online, trusted an inspector. Fucking crazy."

Matt hauled open the back of the truck. "Just this one bed frame, kid, and you're off the hook. We can manage the rest by ourselves." And that was the point when Cohen was supposed to say, *No, don't be silly,* and offer to help. Or better yet, explain about his arm, the surgery.

They all grabbed the bedframe and lugged it to the front porch. But a third body was one too many. A third body was only in the way when rounding corners, doorways, climbing stairs. "You guys got this," she said, nodding her head like they should be proud of themselves. She let go of the frame and it felt no heavier in Cohen's hand. "I'm gonna grab a few of my boxes, speed this up."

She scurried off, leaving them to chat through the awkwardness of not knowing each other. They mounted the stairs and made a turn for one of the bedrooms. "Any reason you're only using the one hand there, tough guy?" He laughed.

"I've...just had surgery. It's fine, I'm fine using just this hand, but—"

"Jesus Christ! Lay it down!" Matt stopped walking as he made the demand, but Cohen wasn't expecting the sudden stop, so he kept walking forward. He'd butted his incision into the bedframe, winced, and laid the oak frame down.

"You had that heart surgery, like your father? The...the *thing* put into your chest? The shocker thing?" Matt looked panicked, repentant. He'd been tapping his own chest, over his heart, while he struggled to find the right word.

"ICD, yeah. Like father like son—"

"Why didn't you say anything, Jesus!" He was definitely concerned but kind of laughing too.

COHEN STEPPED BACK into his house that night, banished by Matt on account of his useless arm, and his phone was ringing, tinny and distant. It rang at least ten times before he'd found it in the cupholder of his treadmill. Ten times it rang, so he knew it was his father. A patient man. The only man Cohen knew who'd let a phone ring until someone answered it or until that blaring *give up!* signal cut in.

"Cohen?"

"Obviously. I live alone. You dialled my number. Were you expecting Oprah?"

"Yes, very funny, ha hah."

"What's up?"

"Your mother. You know what she's like. She's still processing this ARVC thing. She says the doctors are downplaying it."

"We're invincible. We're robots now. These ICDs make us immune to heart attacks."

"Yes, but, she's still working through, *What if the doctors installed them wrong,* and, *What if the battery suddenly fails,* and, *what if these machines slip loose and puncture our hearts?*"

"What if a comet is coming? What if spontaneous combustion is real?"

"Don't bust my chops, kid. Save it for her."

"I will." Cohen flicked his kettle on; eyes darting indecisively from a box of Earl Grey to a red tin of Rooibos.

"Anyway, she's insisting on a family trip to the cabin this

weekend. To *take it all in*, whatever that might mean. She hasn't been sleeping at all since we were diagnosed. She's been tossing and turning and keeping me awake too. She throws her legs around under the sheets like heavy logs. There's bruises on my shins, swear to God, Cohen. Big ones. She worries, you know. I mean, when you got the chicken pox, you were only one. She thought that was it, her first born, *gone before he'd learn to walk*. So, just, I know you're busy with the PhD and all that, but come to the cabin this weekend, hey? All four of us? Won't be so bad."

"You wanna pick me up?"

"Will do, and thanks for playing along. In fairness, this all happened very fast, me getting diagnosed, then you. She just wants a weekend together."

"I'll go, I said." Cohen took a mug out of the cupboard and almost dropped it when he heard a knock on his door. It sounded gentle enough to question whether he'd actually heard someone at his door. He walked towards it.

"So, how's the PhD coming along? Still playing with dead birds all day long?"

"Yes."

"Sounds *lively*."

"Very funny."

"Get it? Dead birds, and I'm saying it sounds lively."

"Yeah. The joke's funnier every time you say it."

He got in view of the door and saw that it was Allie knocking. "Dad, I have to go. Someone's ah...someone's at the door I wasn't expecting." He clicked the phone off, halfway through his father's *See you Fri—*.

"Hey," she said, stepping into his porch like she'd been there before and had her own place on the coat rack. He had to stop himself from widening his eyes like, *Why are you coming into my house?*

"Sorry, I didn't cut off your conversation did I?" She pointed to the phone.

"No. It...ah...it was. No." He laid the phone down on a window ledge.

She raised an eyebrow at his fumbled sentence. "Geez, man. What are you, CIA? Top secret phone calls?" She poked him in the chest, twice, a playful accusation. She pushed past him. "Sorry, I sort of invited myself in didn't I?" Palms up, like, *Whatever.* "I feel like, since our fathers are friends, we know each other by proxy or something. And I'm here for your toaster." She smiled. "Any chance you were serious about lending me this stainless steel beauty?"

"Sure." A smile tore his face in two.

"And so you know, I know it's weird I still live with my father. It's a long story."

Cohen nodded his head, still wondering why she'd just walked into his house. "I'm not judging anyone. I didn't even think it was weird. He seems like an ideal roommate." He was about to laugh, pry, but she said, "It's just, he's a real sad and lonely bastard right now." Her voice wobbled and her eyes twitched defensively, like her body was begging him not to pry.

"Come in, I'll grab you the toaster." But a quick look around and he wished he'd just fetched it for her and left her in the porch. The hardwood needed to be swept. Mopped even. And there was a pair of socks curled up like napping snakes on the living-room floor.

He walked her to the kitchen and she took in his house like she was being rushed through a museum tour. And as they walked back to the porch, his eyes followed her like puppies every step of the way. He liked the backs of her legs. Even the way her skirt dangled. She had the toaster cradled in her left arm like a baby— little crumbs falling out the bottom of it with every step she took— and she apologized for each one of them.

"Get me a broom. Really. I'll sweep them up."

ONE O'CLOCK THAT night, the lights were on in Allie's room. He was pulling his bedroom curtains closed and she didn't have blinds up yet. She was splayed across her bedsheets in pajamas that were two sizes too big. Purple, matching. She was crying her eyes dry, belly in and out like she was skipping breaths, and it was weird to see the desperate pain of crying, stripped of its sound. She grabbed a framed photo off her nightstand. Threw it across her room.

As he pulled his curtain to, afraid she'd see him there, he saw Matt walk into her room. He sat on the bed with her, said something Cohen couldn't make out. She curled into him, to put her head on his shoulder. And then Matt cried too. Harder.

SCREAMING UNDER WATER

HIS PRISON CELL window was so thick that the nights it rained he could barely hear it falling against the glass. There was just a hint of something happening outside, just a hint of the world out there, carrying on without him. The sound drew him to the window. It was glass, like any glass, but the water had a way of clinging to it and blurring his view of the duck pond in the distance. It was a pacifying view.

His whole life, he'd been prone to getting hungry around midnight, but jail didn't accommodate that. There were four meals a day and no food allowed in cells. Because food was just one more thing that inmates could barter or fight over. Curling into a ball, in bed, did little to stave off his panging for food. It was a desperate ache, deep in his belly, and his body wanted it answered. The hunger made the sheets chafe and the pillows flatter and the bed smaller.

Somewhere down the hall, the prison left a few lights on after midnight. The light itself didn't keep him awake, but it attracted insects. The sound of houseflies and moths and mosquitoes, or whatever it was zizzing around the glowing bulbs out there, kept him awake. The buzzing was incessant. Desperate and annoying. So he'd kick his sheets off. Go to the window. Stare.

The cold blue pond reminded him of the last time his family had gone to their cabin. In a way, that weekend was the moment he could trace it all back to—he could think of that Saturday morning as exactly when and where his life had gotten twisted and turned.

It had been a long drive to his parents' cabin, for his mother's *taking it all in* weekend. Three hours of never-changing scenery on the highway: an endless wall of spruce trees blurring past them. Cohen took breaks between chapters of his novel to watch the trees whir by: brushstrokes of green on the bottoms of clouds. The sun flickered through the tree tops like panic, disappearing, reappearing. Easy on the eyes and then blinding when the tree-line shortened.

They were twenty minutes from the cabin when he asked his father, "I've got a new neighbour. Someone Crosbie. Matt or Mark or something. How do you know the man?"

"He said he'd bought the place!" He turned to Cohen's mother, "We'll have to pop in on him, see how he's doing?" She nodded.

His father's eyes found Cohen's in the rear-view mirror. "How'd you make the connection?"

"His daughter. She's like—" He couldn't put her into words, she was like a vacation; you just had to be there. "She came over for...a toaster. Said you mentioned the house next door to her father—"

"A *toaster*?" he laughed. "Sounds about right. They're a wild lot, the Crosbies. All jacked up on life, you know? They've got no boundaries, no one's a stranger. Not in a hippie sort of way, just, I dunno." He shrugged his shoulders. "Me and Matt, we worked at the university bookstore, when we were first years. We wound up roommates for a semester and everything. We've always kept in touch, drinks at Christmas and that sort of thing. Which is probably why he ended up a client of your mother's." He took a sip of coffee from his travel mug, laid it back in a cupholder. "His wife passed away in January. Cancer."

Cohen's brother sneezed and it scared Cohen enough he jumped.

"Bad. It was *bad*. She'd been battling it for quite some time. Long enough that his daughter moved back home to help him care for her. You know, to help her *die*. Comfortably. Horrible stuff."

His father clicked his indicator to turn into a passing lane. He checked his blind spot three or four times and it looked like he was shaking his head for no good reason. "Your mother and I were at the funeral and a few months later we went out to Grayton to have supper with the guy. Just to see how he was holding up. He mentioned his daughter was moving here, into town, to do her PhD. Your mother wasn't having that."

She closed her eyes slowly, shook her head. "Can you

EVERY
LITTLE
THING

19

imagine being left alone in the house your wife *died* in? It's just, not right. You move. You do."

"He's semi-retired, working from home." Another sip of coffee. "Your mother planted the seed of the house next door to yours, so his daughter could be three minutes from the university, in a neighbourhood we could vouch for. I guess they're after moving in together by the sounds of it? She's got a science degree of some kind."

"Chemistry," Cohen said, like he was proud of her.

His father shrugged his shoulder, cracked a few knuckles. "Poor girl was a mess at her mother's wake, that's all I know. I mean, she sat outside in the rain like something from a heart-breaking movie. She couldn't even look at the casket. I think she went home early. Twenty minutes in. I think it's a nice thing they're here together. Still living together I mean. For both his and Allison's sakes."

"Allie."

"What?"

"You called her Allison. Her name's Allie. She seems big on the distinction."

A wink in the rear-view, "In love already, are you?"

His brother said something about having chemistry with the chemistry graduate. A lame joke for the sake of it, but their father busted his gut over it, and Ryan rolled his eyes.

They pulled into the driveway just after nine. Unpacked and unenthused, they were all in bed by 10:30, after a few games of poker. They had no idea, as their heads hit the pillows, that they were about to become the kind of family you see on the five o'clock news, looking stunned to be there, getting ravaged by senseless questions like *What really happened that day?* and *How did it make you feel?* and *Do you think you'll ever get over it?* A spotlight shinning deep into their eyes, hoping to scour out tears for some *exclusive, heartbreaking footage.*

THAT SATURDAY MORNING, he and his brother woke to the snapping scent and sizzle of bacon and scrambling eggs. Ryan in the top bunk, Cohen beneath him. Ryan was eight years younger than Cohen and he'd joked once that *Nothing says accidental child like having a brother eight years older than you.* But they clicked.

Got along. By the time Cohen was twenty-five, the mental distance between them was minimal. They'd show up at the same concerts or they'd show up to family dinners wearing almost-matching outfits. They were twins born eight years apart.

They woke that morning and laid there until Ryan said, "Yes, it's pretty up here and that bacon smells great, but what are we supposed to *do* up here for the next thirty-six hours while Mom wraps her head around the fact that you and Dad have broken hearts?"

Cohen launched himself upright, his feet bouncing off the cold hardwood, "How about a dozen beer this afternoon? We'll take the boat out, pretend we're fishing. Or, we could fish. Let's fish?"

"There's no bait, no beer."

"There's a store, not ten minutes down the road."

"Are you sure?"

"I said there's a store, not ten minutes down the road."

So they bought beer, at the store down the road, and worms for their fishhooks and batteries for the stereo. In the car, Ryan took the lid off the Styrofoam container the worms were in and sniffed it.

"What the fuck?"

"Smells great, man. It does."

Ryan brought the container to Cohen's face, "Sniff," and Cohen took his eyes off the road one second too long. Almost rear-ended someone. Ryan didn't even react. He put the lid on the container and changed the song on the stereo.

The walk down to the wharf from their cabin was steep and the path was crowded by lush spruce; their branches were cool against Cohen's flesh. It smelled like they were walking through an air freshener as they used their arms like machetes to clear a path to their private wharf. *The shittiest one on the pond*, according to Ryan, but it was enough to tie a boat to or bask on. A splintery thing, if you weren't wearing shoes. It was a big pond or a little lake—no one in the family knew the difference between the two and they made fun of Cohen, a biologist, for not knowing.

Cohen stepped into the boat to attach the outboard motor because the slot at the back of the boat had always been too skinny to really take the thing and there was a trick to it that only

Cohen and his father knew. Ryan arranged batteries in the stereo ten different ways, swearing as each configuration denied him audio. When the stereo kicked in, shockingly loud, Ryan jumped back like the music had punched him in the guts. The song was up so loud that Cohen could see, but not hear, Ryan laughing at himself.

The water was always choppy on that pond—*bucks you like a bronco*—and the pond itself was shaped like a horseshoe, studded with cabins. It took them five minutes to pull out around the bend and get drinking, out of sight of their cabin, because Ryan was still a year shy of nineteen.

He'd gotten drunker than Cohen had anticipated. His words were mashing together in his mouth and coming out without commas, periods; parts of one word entwined the next. "Dawn worry about, man!" and threw his hand up in the air, "I'm good. But what about the empties. So's you don't get busted fer intoxicatin' a minor?"

"Just, dunk them under water, so they fill and sink."

"What! Litter them, and you a biologist!" he laughed.

"It's not bad, really, the bottom dwellers will use them as shelter."

"The *bottom dwellers*," he laughed. "You make it sound like thur's zombies down there or something." Ryan let out a fit of reckless laughter to alleviate Cohen's concern and looked around, through drunk-enthused eyes, at moss-entwined trees and then the splash of a trout. When he stood again, to take in the view, Ryan was wobbly, pale. Knees like pivots. "Turn around and keep the boat going. A man's gotta piss if a man's gotta piss!" He reached to turn the volume up on their stereo, but he knocked it off the bench and waved a hand like, *Fuck it*.

Cohen sat at the back of the boat staring behind him as Ryan relieved himself. His hand going numb from the vibration of the throttle.

"Hurry up, man! We're not headed for a wharf or anything are we?"

"No. And slow down a little. Jesus, I'm gonna piss on myself here!"

There was a flying V of ducks overhead and Cohen watched it shoot like an arrow through the sky. He felt the lever of the throttle torque his wrist up, like the propellers had snagged on vegetation or struck a rock. But it didn't feel right. It didn't feel like the grinding halt, or the slight tug, that his hand had felt a hundred other times in running that propeller into stone or vegetation. He cut the motor. "Ryan?"

Before he'd even turned around, his jaw went numb at the thought of the propellers biting into his brother. He let go of the throttle and refused to turn his head and be sure. Some force, some invisible set of hands, pushing against his head as he turned, slowly, to look at the front of the boat.

And it was empty.

Ryan wasn't on the floor of the boat, but Cohen took a stubborn look behind a bench. He looked in the water behind him and Ryan wasn't swimming towards him. He wasn't swimming towards shore. Cohen hauled the outboard motor up and out of the water to check for signs the propellers had struck his brother.

He cut the stereo and a curtain of silence fell all around him. A stillness. He heard no thrashing, no panicked screaming, no reckless laughter. He shouted his brother's name into that silence. Filled it. Shouted like his screams would yank Ryan to the surface. Fish him out of the water.

He didn't think to close his mouth or take a breath of air as he dove into the pond. He was in the water and his chest stung—the wound from his surgery still not closed. He was screaming his brother's name and it came out bubbly and muffled; the murky pond water gurgling in his throat whenever he yelled Ryan's name. The taste of it thick in his mouth. Like cow manure and grainy dirt.

He couldn't see a thing. A million flecks of brown were suspended and bobbing calmly up and down in the water. A ballet of silt; such a stark contrast to his panic.

He came to the surface for air. Gulped. And his lungs felt like torn bags. He submerged and swam for the bottom: the water getting more and more visually impenetrable as he descended; the spaces between suspended dirt closing and closing until it felt like he was swimming through mud. And darker still as the sun's reach petered out. The silt felt like microscopic claws at his eyes. His legs kicking furiously and eventually his palms hit mud. Sank inches deep into that mud. His lungs begging for air, tightening, or threatening to burst. He felt around. His throat

EVERY
LITTLE
THING

23

ready to pop; an urgency for Ryan overriding an urgency for air. Buoyancy yanking him towards the surface. He fought against that pull, the need for air, kicking his feet, scraping his hands off God knows what on the bottom of the pond—the mud cool enough to soothe whenever something tore his flesh. The incision on his chest had stopped stinging or adrenaline had him feeling invincible. Like he could punch a hole in the bottom of the pond to drain it and find his brother.

He rushed to the surface for a refill of air. He was shovelling his arms through the water and the water felt like a gel. He dug deep and hard into that water, but his limbs weren't moving as fast as it felt like they should've been. And he hated his lungs for needing more air.

He was gulping pond water as he swam to the surface, like maybe he'd drown too, but the light was getting brighter and brighter and he made it. He yelled meaningless guttural panic as his head broke the surface; pond water gurgling out of his throat, rattling in his left ear drum, and stinging as it leaked from his nose. Deep breaths. He screamed Ryan's name as he bobbed at the surface.

The sound of no response was the sound of a hundred things that weren't Ryan. Buzzing insects, cars whizzing by on the highway beyond the pond. The panic had two hands around his throat. His heart thudding and thumping. It felt like his ribs were caging an agitated bird. He swam along the surface, farther away from the boat, where he assumed Ryan had fallen in and gotten struck by the propellers.

Deep breath. Conviction. But the fight against the water was getting harder as his muscles weakened. The rush to get down to the bottom. Faster than this.

His hands were back at the muddy bottom, wrist deep in mud, elbow deep in places. He felt something solid and thick as an arm and his heart stopped. His whole body stopped, but the object was loose and weightless. Attached to nothing. It was a beer bottle. One of theirs maybe and that was cruel, the bottle having belonged to them. It was cruel that they'd just been together, above surface, drinking and laughing and this seemed impossible. Them separated and searching for each other below the surface. That his brother could die. That Ryan could die. Not exist. That the water could be so goddamn murky, so visually impenetrable, that Ryan could've been *right there*, within reach, without Cohen knowing.

He kept going. Up and down. Long after it made sense. His body acting, his mind just needing to. Up and down. Mud at his hands, water tugging him to the surface, too soon, every time, and dunking him back under.

The boat a little farther away each time he came up for air. Until it was a dot in the distance.

The sun a little dimmer each time he emerged, the air a little cooler. And then he couldn't even get to the bottom anymore. His limbs like solid blocks until he couldn't feel them there at all. All torso.

His eyes felt like all the dirt and water in the pond had seeped in behind them and were pushing at his eyeballs from behind, trying to thrust them from his skull. His vision blurry as he floated there at the surface. Up and down with the incessant rise and fall of the waves. His soggy shirt twisted, almost choking him, and so what. He stayed there for a while, his first break in over an hour, scanning the surface for his brother's body, thinking, *Things float.* Thinking that maybe Ryan had made his way to dry land and found his way back to the cabin. Thinking maybe Ryan was looking for *him.* That Ryan was on someone's wharf and peering out at the empty boat, perplexed. The boat now well out of Cohen's blurry field of vision. He gave up. Exhausted and in shock. Confused. His body and his mind disconnected as he lay out on the water's surface, crucified.

The water was heaving him around like driftwood, slowly, over and over, clapping against his ears. His tongue pushing bits of dirt off the back of his teeth. He turned his head to his right hand. Went half deaf from the ear submerged under the water. The flesh along the entire underside of his thumb had been torn clean off and yet he felt no pain.

A faint echo of his name registered. He looked back up to the sky and with his ear now out of the water, he recognized his father's voice yelling over the sound of an outboard motor. His father was coming around the bend, from the direction of their cabin, in a bright yellow boat he must have borrowed from a neighbour. He got close and cut the motor.

There was a shakiness in his father's voice he'd never heard before. Like, if Cohen worded this wrong, his father would

EVERY LITTLE THING

shatter right here in front of him. There was hesitation, but a desperate need to know in his father's voice. "Cohen!"

His father was right there in front of him and yet sounded so far away. When his father stood—the sun like a yellow globe resting on his left shoulder—he looked impossibly tall. He was close enough for Cohen to see his legs tremble, like his bones were giving out, turning into sand. And it was the first time he ever really noticed the colour of his father's eyes—a black-flecked pale brown that connoted motion, waves—and he knew he'd forever equate the colour of his father's eyes with the murky pond water he'd stared into for an hour, or two hours, or maybe it was three.

"Cohen. Your brother, Cohen. Where—*Where*?"

Cohen spoke so calmly he sounded insane and emotionally disconnected from the situation. "Ryan fell over. I can't find him. He must have swam ashore. I can't find him." Waves still breaking against him, clapping at his ear, lifting him up and down.

His father tore his shirt off, buttons popping off, and Cohen stopped him. "It's been more than an hour, Dad. He's...not in this pond," and something about that line, something about sharing this search with his father, brought Cohen back into his body. His chest went concave and his lungs emptied as he wailed.

His father went whiter than a swan. "G-give me your hand, Cohen."

"No."

He had to pull Cohen from the water, his ribs—each one of them—rippling off the side of the boat, one after the other, as his father fished him out of the pond. He laid Cohen in the centre of the boat and he dove into the water. Because a man needs to try.

EVENTUALLY THERE WERE other people out in boats, yelling, looking. Red and blue lights flashing in the distance. The water black as the night sky. Everything, somehow, a shade of black: even the trees. The stars shining like they always do, like this night was nothing different. Cohen was sitting on a wharf, alone, watching out over the pond. It wasn't even his wharf. He could hear more than he could see, but Search and Rescue had the pond lit up like a night-time sport's event was about to start. Yells, motors, and meaningless, wordless sounds. RCMP. Premature ambulances.

A body doesn't just disappear. And it wasn't that big a pond. And the fact they hadn't found his body yet, meant there was a sick pulse of hope, a one percent chance Ryan was still alive. Cohen had to cling to that or lose himself right there on some stranger's wharf.

That one percent chance felt more like a five percent chance because this was Ryan they were looking for, so it could've been another one of his sick pranks.

But it had been too long.

That one percent chance felt more like a twenty percent chance, because it had to.

THE POLICE, OR Search and Rescue, or whoever those men were: they wouldn't let the family look at his body. Just his father. Two men held his mother back. Three men held Cohen back, yet he managed to push through them. He'd knocked one man to the ground and that man had grabbed another two and they all went down like bowling pins. But a moment of hesitation slowed Cohen's pace—a moment of not wanting to see Ryan and be *sure*—and they restrained him in that moment of hesitation.

There were flashlights etching shaky yellow zigzags all along the ground. There were mad dashes of red and blue lights hitting his father's body in different places. They unzipped a black bag and his father threw up all over it. Threw up all over Ryan's body. He fell to the ground, into a sitting position, bawling wordless desperate moans, backing away from Ryan's body like it was a train coming at him.

"Sir."

"No! Just—" And he was crying and Cohen had never seen him cry. Every bit of air in his lungs, gone, like they wouldn't fill again.

They went to help his father up off the ground, but his father shot up and grabbed the bag, unzipped it, looked again, and when he absentmindedly leaned into the stretcher, or collapsed, or fainted, or something, it tipped the stretcher over. A thud of Ryan's body on the wet ground. From a distance he heard his mother yelp in shock and saw her try to run to her son's body, in the bag, knocked off the stretcher. But the men held her back, righted Ryan's body, and put him back on the stretcher.

Crackles of radio and walkie-talkie static popped in the distance. The sound of his mother's eyes, exploding, and dripping down her face. All of it had felt too much like it was Cohen's fault, and he felt stabbed full of holes of pain. All of this meant: no more Ryan. Inconceivable. Ryan didn't *feel* gone. Because eighteen years can't just be undone like that. Or because there were parts of his life his brother had filled and they didn't feel empty yet.

His father came to his mother, but Cohen walked away and they didn't follow him, or they didn't notice. There was a crowd, maybe twenty people, in a small space, boxed in by trees, darkness, so it was easy to slip away. Because he couldn't stand the pond colour of his father's eyes; couldn't be near his parents without guilt bullying him.

He walked back to his cabin the long way. Took detours. Kicked sticks and cried once, briefly. He'd sat down and forced himself to cry, like that might help it sink in. It didn't.

He got up and walked back to the cabin, afraid his parents would be there and he'd have to say something to them. And he didn't know why he was afraid of that. His mother was in a rocking chair when he walked into the cabin. Back and forth and back and forth. Creaky hardwood. Crumpled tissues, like swans with their necks wrung. Cohen sat on the couch. There was a silence between them that no words could have penetrated. It would've been like shooting arrows at a cement wall.

THEY WERE SUPPOSED to go back home Sunday night. But it didn't feel right. Or it didn't make sense. Or they just couldn't.

Six a.m. Monday morning, Cohen was sitting on their sun-bleached wharf. Legs crossed. Palms flat back against the splintery wood. The light drizzle was refreshing and it had fish jumping as they mistook stray raindrops for winged insects on the water. He sat staring out at the pond. Watching ripples. The indifference of the water to the life within it. Fish leapt out at flies and birds tried to snag fish and everything just carried on, like his brother didn't die here two days ago. Their boat was knocking against the wharf, tied on with a frayed yellow rope. The bag of garbage Ryan had put the battery packaging in was snapping like a flag in the wind, stuck under the weight of the stereo.

He thought about taking an axe to the boat, in a juvenile fit of rage, to vent his anger and loss, but mainly to hear the violent sound of destruction; to drown out all the quietness around him. He felt like he should be crying and pissed off and putting a fist through something, because *that* was reaction. To bust his knuckles off something, to cry, to watch the blood spill, to yell. But he just sat there, at a loss for how to cope, and it never felt like reaction.

He blamed his mother, for making them all go up there that weekend. Because this wouldn't have happened. She'd blame him: the drinking, no life jackets. The decision to go out fishing that morning. And they'd both be right.

EVERY LITTLE THING

EVERYTHING
OLD AND NEW

NO ONE SPOKE the whole ride home. The stereo wasn't on and no one was reading. There was only the sound of rolling tires, and after so long, Cohen could hear friction at work: the rubber tires pulling at the road to thrust the car forward. And at the Irving station: the clugging sound of gas filling the tank. There was never silence, just the kinds of background noise he'd normally not notice—like the sound of his father's breathing or the wind whistling through the window—and it all emphasized the absence of Ryan. Cohen couldn't turn his head to the empty seat beside him; turning and not seeing Ryan was like seeing a ghost. So he stared out his window the whole way home: his eyes riding along the tops of trees, squinting into the sun.

When Cohen's father pulled onto his street to drop him off, he saw Allie and her father unloading a pile of stuff from a pickup truck parked parallel to the curb. They were laying stuff on the sidewalk: a floor lamp, a coffee table, some boxed appliances with yellow Walmart tape across them. A toaster. They'd stopped and stood still when Cohen and his father opened their car doors and stepped out in unison.

They knew and Cohen knew they knew. They had the wet gloss of sympathy in their squinted eyes. They were too eager to make eye contact. It was in Allie's upside-down smile—her lips puffed out from her face. Matt shook his head back and forth, slowly, *Unbelievable.* It was a city with less than a hundred thousand people in it, so Ryan's death had been all over the local news: it was front page in the papers and it got a ten-minute spot on the five o'clock prime time. *Local boy, drowned. Family getaway gone wrong.* They sensationalized it and oversentimentalized it. *Will never attend university. Will never marry. By all accounts, a big-hearted kid, the class clown even teachers cheered on.* But they didn't. They'd suspended him once, earlier that year, for the pranks. And one newspaper had gotten his name wrong, called him Bryan Davies.

Matt and Allie were carrying a coffee table, Matt on one end, Allie on the other, and they didn't lay it down when Matt opened his mouth to speak.

"We've heard, Gord, and we're devastated."

Cohen's mother opened her door, muttering that she wanted her purse out of the trunk. "I have a full casserole in the oven and there's only the two of us." Matt nodded at Allie, and took a look at his watch. "Really. It'll be ready in ten minutes. You guys—"

His mother had been rooting through the trunk for her purse and then she dropped a bag onto the driveway; the whack of it hitting the pavement had cut Matt off. She'd made a quick, frightened sound, like she'd been stung by a wasp, and they all looked at the bag, Ryan's bag, on the black pavement. A black bookbag, white straps. A Canadian flag sewn onto the strap and Cohen could remember the day his mother had sewn it on— before Ryan's grade nine trip to Greece. She'd stuck her finger and said *fuck* and Cohen had rarely heard her swear at that point.

Cohen stepped towards the bag, scooped it up off the driveway, and slung it over his shoulder. "I...I packed up his stuff. So you wouldn't have to."

She looked away from the bag, ignored Cohen. "That's very nice of you, to offer us some supper, Matt, but we've already eaten." A lie, and Cohen was starving, his stomach dancing at the thought of supper. She turned to his father, "Can you f-find my purse, Gordon?" She sat back in the car with her lower lip bit between teeth.

Matt, again to his father, "Gordon, let's cut to the chase. This is devastating...with Ryan. And we're here for you. I'll drop over that bite to eat at six, okay? I know where you live, if you haven't moved." Matt turned to Cohen, his eyes waiting for eye contact, "And Allie'll bring a plate over to you, okay, bud?"

His father's voice was lifeless and unintentionally insincere, "That's very kind of you, Matt."

Every moment since Ryan's death felt crystalline and ready to shatter. Cohen looked at Allie, and when their eyes met, she didn't look away like he thought she would. She didn't look at a loss for words or like she felt awkward about all the dramatic tension. Instead she held his gaze, held all the weight in his body, and she kept her eyes in his until he looked away from her, back to his bag in the trunk.

A reporter, microphone in hand, no older than thirty, stepped out of a car that had been sitting across the street. She was pressing her blue plaid skirt with one hand and motioning to a reluctant cameraman with the other. Cohen saw his father pretend not to notice her as he thrust his suitcases back into the trunk and jumped into his car.

Cohen dashed to his front door because it was enough to be silently dealing with it for now. Talking about it, with her, with this woman, this *stranger*, was just too much. Too real. But it was too late; she had her metal-mesh-topped microphone in his face. "Cohen? Cohen Davies?"

His mother was rolling her window down, screaming, "Get that microphone away from him, you soulless wretch!" but his father was backing out of the driveway like he couldn't handle it. Like he'd been through enough. And it was the first time in Cohen's life that his father hadn't been there for him. It was the first time his father had let him down, and those were two separate shocks. And now here this woman was, with her microphone in his face, and the camera was rolling.

She had a look on her face like there was something Cohen should say. And she wanted to be the one who got it on film. She had a look on her face like there were words for this, and he owed them to the world.

Cohen opened his mouth, mindlessly, like some reflex would puppeteer his mouth and do the talking for him. Give her what she wanted to make her go away. He never heard Matt coming, but saw his hand grabbing the guy's camera, pulling it out of his hand. The woman was shocked. "Sir!"

Matt walked over to their car, camera in hand, tugged at the handle of a locked back door, and walked around to the passenger seat. He threw the camera in through a rolled-down window.

"Get the fuck off this street. Now."

HE DIDN'T KNOW where he was headed, didn't even think about it until he rolled up to a stop sign and watched two sisters playing hopscotch in their driveway. What he needed wasn't time alone. He lived alone. What he wanted was to blare out the silence, to drown out life's background noise; the noises he'd only noticed since Ryan died: wind, ticking clocks, his own breathing. He wanted a bar with a band that could make his ears ring with just one, loud sound.

It was getting dark and he headed for The Avian-Dome because he worked there, had a key, and knew the passcode for the alarm: 8889. There was access to the roof and it seemed like the right place to go. The roof was flat, but its coarseness had been scuffed soft by the pacing of staff over so many years. A stone wall fenced it in, making a patio of the rooftop. There was a duck pond at the back, close enough for staff to throw feed over the edge into the pond. There was a picnic table, but he laid in the centre of the roof, stared up at the starless sky. Blue was bleeding into black, so the cloudless sky was a temporary and tender purple. A bruise-coloured blanket covering the world. He stuck in earphones, pressed play, closed his eyes.

By the fourth or the fifth song, he heard a knocking, weak but deliberate; unmistakably knuckles on glass. Startled, he hopped up, tearing his headphones out, hauling wildly at the cords dangling at his chest. He thought of hiding and didn't know why or what from. He looked over the side of the wall: no police cars or his boss's blue sedan with the dented passenger door. He walked to the front of the building, peered down, and it was Allie. Knocking. Waiting a few seconds. Knocking. Tugging at the door handles. Tucking some hair behind an ear. She looked at her car like maybe she should leave or maybe she should try one more time. And then she looked up, almost as surprised as he was, like she wasn't really expecting to find him, and definitely not up on the roof.

"Um. Hi!" She laughed and reeled it in, no room for laughter in the situation. The building was only two storeys high, but she had to raise her voice a little. "Listen. I can go back home, if you want. It's up to you."

He stared down at her. His eyes feeling heavy enough to fall out of their sockets. "I asked Dad to go after you, but he said men need time alone. That's bullshit. So I followed you here. I don't know. I just...I followed you." She shrugged one shoulder, looked from his eyes to the door, like *Are you going to let me in?*

"I can go or I can stay, but I wasn't going to sit home wondering if you were alone or with someone or okay or not. I can go back home or you can let me up there with you. You can tell me anything. How it happened, how it wouldn't have happened if a million things had gone differently. Whatever. Because trust me, it helps just to speak and shout and cry and burst wide open, it does. I won't tell you everything is going to be okay because it's not. Or we won't talk about Ryan at all. We can just hang out. I've got a book. I have a few books, one for you too if you want to just sit around and read." She tapped her purse as a question mark. "I took a few novels out of a box. Before I left. We can just sit and read a little?"

He liked that she'd come. How she was new and unpredictable and how that kept his mind divided between thoughts of Ryan and thoughts of her and what she might say next.

She looked in through the glass doors with binoculared hands over her eyes. "Or you can give me a tour of this—"

"Hang on a second." He walked away from the wall, out of her sight, whispered *Fuck*, shook his head, kicked his Discman across the roof. He hated himself for not being cold enough to ask her to leave or to shut the fuck up about Ryan. He hated the part of himself that was glad she'd come. It was Ryan's death he wanted to feel overwhelmed by, and pinned under, and the way she could lift him out from under that weight made him feel cheap, guilty. As if mourning meant feeling pain as intensely as he could, all alone, not sharing it with a stranger.

He peered back down over the wall. "Give me a second. I'll be right down." He went towards the door, but swung back around. "Do you wanna to come up here, you mean, or go somewhere else?" She clutched her chest; he'd startled her. She looked a little anxious, like *What am I doing here, what do I say to the guy now?*

"Up to you, Cohen, but…I like the idea of being up on that roof tonight. I bet it's…pretty?" She shook her head, like *What a stupid thing to say.* She had a shy smile she was trying to fight off.

He descended the stairs, walked across the open foyer, the claps of his feet echoing off the tile floor. He pulled open the door and she tucked some hair behind her ears and smiled shyly again. "What *is* this place anyway?" And he filled her in as they walked towards the door that led to the roof—that the mandate was all about protecting, promoting, and preserving the avian wildlife of Atlantic Canada, and that the three theatres were simulated ecosystems. He put a hand on one and said he'd personally stuffed all the auks in the puffin and razorbill display.

She was stutter-stepping, amazed by the place, a child-like awe about her. He liked that. He liked that all the stuff had caught her attention, and how she could be that interested in birds hanging from wires. He'd always equated intelligence, or intellect, with curiosity.

He reached behind him, turned a volume dial on bust, and pressed play on one of the displays to scare her. She jumped backwards, kicking into a number four, like a flamingo standing in water, and a booming voice, speaking over the sound of waves, and cawing birds, explained the mating habits and diet of the Atlantic Puffin, *Fratercula arctica*. She slapped him on the chest for it, for scaring her, as she walked past him and up the stairs.

She'd jumped again at the gunshot sound of the steel door slamming shut behind them in the stairwell. She'd clung to him, instinctively out of fright, and apologized for scaring so easily. He liked the softness of her voice in his ears, her body pressed into his elbow. He tapped in the keycode. 8889.

She burst out onto the roof, spun around once in a circle, like she wanted to say *My God, it's beautiful up here!* but those words would seem too cheery. She turned and leaned into the front of the building, palms flat against the wall. Looking at the city, from that distance, the streetlights looked like sticks with stars on their ends. She walked to the back of the building, cupped her hands to her mouth. "Oh My God!" She flung her purse on the picnic table. "Look at all the fucking cute ducks!"

Watching her was perfect. Minus the fear of awkward silences or forced conversations, like *it wasn't your fault, you know.* Because it was, and he'd want her gone if she even insinuated that it wasn't, in some trite conversation. He just wanted to watch her watching the ducks. Maybe tell her there's a barrel of feed in the stairwell and that, sometimes, the ducks come up on the roof.

So he surprised himself when the words came out. "Ryan was drunk, Allie. He was drunk, and eighteen, and I was drinking, and I never even *thought* about life jackets until he was dead. He was drunk, and that's why he had to piss, and that's why his legs fucked up, and that's why he's dead. Because he was drunk, and I

EVERY
LITTLE
THING

35

might have been too, and I thought life jackets were a fucking joke, for people who can't swim, you know? Because he could swim? Who can't swim? But. A life jacket. He would've floated. I would've found my brother."

She nodded, like she knew how to have this conversation. She nodded, like *Go on, you're not done yet*, and Cohen said, "I mean...it was a *pond*, not the fucking ocean. Who just...*drowns?* The life jackets. I mean," he shook his head. "I bought the beer. We were in this piece of shit wobbly boat, and there I was, thinking it's funny he couldn't stand up straight."

He looked at her like he was done, and she said nothing, and he said, "What if they do an autopsy? And I'm the guy who got his kid brother drunk and killed him? It's how it happens, you know. People hear the facts, and someone sounds like an asshole. It wasn't like that—"

"There isn't going to be an autopsy, okay? Or, I mean, there wasn't one. I mean, he...he's waking tomorrow night. They had no need to do an autopsy. Okay?" She kept saying *okay* until he acknowledged it with a nod of his head.

She sat at the picnic table but he didn't join her. He stayed where he was, staring out at the ocean. The palms of both hands on the ledge of the stone wall, arms straight as poles like he was pushing the wall.

"...and things like this are never anyone's fault, Cohen, even when it feels that way."

A sardonic laugh, and he shook his head, like *I should've known you'd pull this shit*. But she countered, almost offended. "Do *not* shake your head at me. Unless you kicked him overboard and held his head under water, do not shake your head at me!" And he appreciated her sudden sternness. "I said, I can stay here or I can go. It's up to you. I won't be offended if you want me to leave, or if you want me to shut up about Ryan. I just... felt...compelled to come. To be decent. To say things that needed to be said, like *this really isn't your fault*. And get ready to shake your head again, but I know what you're going through because my mother recently passed away, too, you know."

He kept staring at the sea, lulled into pacification by the sound of waves off land, over and over. Rocks rolling over each other, jostled by the sea.

"And now you're thinking, *It's not the same*, right?"

About ten seconds of silence, and he said, "It's not. I mean, I'm very sorry. About your mother. But." He shrugged his shoulders, looked out at the sea again, the fog.

"Of course it's not the *same* same. With Mom it was slow and painful." She looked down at the picnic table and drew little ovals onto it with her middle finger. "Cancer. There was less life in Mom's eyes every day, until her eyes were just these glass... *spheres*." She waited a second, like maybe there was a better word. Globes. Balls.

"And then the weird smell, like she was literally rotting away. It was slow for me and fast for you. You weren't expecting it, whereas I was waiting for it, and feeling guilty for that. I mean, she was shitting herself in bed, and she stopped recognizing Dad and me. That's brutal too, okay? In its own, different way. And that's my last memories of her now. Bloated. Fragile. Kind of gross, really. She was something to take care of, not the woman I'd relied on my whole life. At least, for you, you'll think of Ryan with nothing but fond memories. No gross ones like I have in the bank." She tapped her head with a finger, trying to act tough, but her glossy eyes gave her away.

She stopped talking for a second, to get back on track, or because it still hurt to talk about her own side of the story: the wounds still fresh and best kept under bandages, pulled back a little at a time. "You blame yourself for Ryan, right? So no, it's not the *same* same. You get to replay a thousand ways things could have gone differently, I'm sure, and I'm sure that's torture. It's all different, all of it. Of course it is. But from this moment on, it *is* the same. From the day *after* we lose someone, how we lost them doesn't matter. All that matters now is that they're gone, and there's absolutely no more interacting with that person. There's just the memories. And those memories will come pelting at you at random for a while, before you realize it can be beautiful to let them run through you."

"*Beautiful?*"

She nodded her head, once. "Don't get me wrong. I feel Mom's absence, every day, like a brick in the face. Every day. You're going to find yourself shocked sometimes, that he's gone, because you're so used to him *being here*. You're going to find yourself in places where some primitive part of your brain will expect to see him. That's the worst. Their absence feeling so...*physical*."

He couldn't think of anything to say, and he didn't want to.

"Listen," she said. "You didn't shoot your brother in the head. And you need to stop acting like you did. Because, straight up, answer me, yes or no: did you push your brother off the boat? Did you hold his head under water? Or did you almost drown yourself, looking for him? Did you swim until your muscles starting snapping off your bones?"

She waited.

"Just answer that one question, and I'll shut up. Say yes or no, and we'll both get in our cars and drive home. Did you drown Ryan? Did you push him off the boat and hold his head under water, or did you spend *hours* in the water looking for him?"

Silence.

"Did you push him off the boat, Cohen?"

Cohen broke like a doll. His limbs and torso fell to the ground in five different pieces. His throat tightened. If he blinked, tears would have fallen out. So he didn't blink.

She came to him. Sat next to him. Put her hand on the side of his head to coax it onto her shoulder. "It's okay. All of it." Neither of them were really sure what she meant.

"Thirsty? I brought a few bottles of water with me. I'm always thirsty. I'm thirsty right now. Or we can go home. But it's pretty up here, and I'd like to stay if you are staying."

Absentmindedly, like a distressed kid, "I was listening to music before you knocked at the door." He wiped an eye with the back of his finger, expecting tears there, and pointed to his Discman. "What kind of music do you like? Shitty music?"

She laughed and fetched his Discman for him. She pulled a mixed CD out of her purse, put it in, and handed it to him. "Listen to at least half these songs before you judge me?"

He put his headphones on. He felt closer to her because he wasn't embarrassed to come undone in front of her. Felt close to her because he *could* cry in front of her, if he wanted to, but not even his own mother. Crying in front of his parents would've been an admission of guilt or a way of pulling them down even further into their own grieving process.

But Allie—and not knowing what she'd say or how she'd react to him crying, not knowing what books she'd brought, or how much she loved ducks, that unpredictability, her newness— was stirring some life into his world.

She walked over to the picnic table and cracked the spine of a yellow book. Plucked out a bookmark. She looked perfectly content to be there. Cohen shimmied over to the corner, where two walls met, and reclined into it. She took the cap off a bottle of water, took a sip. He watched her. She looked up, plucked another bottle out of her pumpkin-orange purse, and threw it towards him like a football, but she didn't say "here" until the bottle was in the air, and it thudded him in the chest before he could stick a hand out to catch it. He let out an almost-audible laugh, and Allie had her hands over her mouth, laughing out an apology, "So sorry!"

He smiled at her animated body. He was comfortable enough around her now to go back to the centre of the roof and just lay there, looking up at the stars, as he'd been doing before she came knocking at the door. He was squinting one eye, then the other, then the other. The stars looked like jewels on a black blanket. It started raining, lightly.

"When Ryan was a kid, he had all these crazy, almost poetic theories about things."

From the base of his eyes, he saw her lay her book down to listen.

"He was a kid, I mean, there was eight years between us. One night, me and him and Dad were out back barbecuing chicken or something, and he just looked at us. He looked up at the stars, and then he looked at us, and he said, startled almost, like he'd just discovered it, *Stars are the twinkle of the moon, reflected off peoples' eyes, back up into the sky!* He said it like it was the truth, you know?"

She giggled, warmly, like she liked the idea of that. Or the way kids' minds could spin the world however they wanted. "That's beautiful. Really."

Neither of them said anything for ten, fifteen seconds. They just looked at each other. "It's raining," she said.

"Yeah."

She walked towards him. Threw her sandals on the right side of him and lay down on the left. Only two or three feet between them: a formal yet casual distance. They both had their head back against the roof. Eyes full of stars. At the very base of his vision, he saw Allie's bare toes—painted pink—poking up to the sky like fleshy flowers.

He didn't move his head; he pushed his eyes as far left as they'd go, without making him dizzy. Her shirt was waterlogged. It clung to her, defining her breasts: a second outjutting where her nipples poked at her shirt. The cold, the rain.

There was a divot, where her black tank top, wet, had sunk into her belly button. There was skin exposed between her tank top and her skirt, and there was nothing in the world like her.

He took his eyes back up off her. She rolled over, facing him, and closed her eyes. "That was really cute, what your brother said, I mean. About the stars. And that you've always remembered it."

They lay there on that shingled roof, two or three feet apart, and that distance was too much.

ALLIE SAT WITH him at the funeral service.

He was sitting in the very back of the church with four rows of empty pews between him and the nearest person. A smell of cedar or incense. A dead wasp at his feet. His father occasionally peered back at him, over his shoulder, with a look on his face somewhere between being perplexed and embarrassed. *What are you doing back there?*

He heard the chunky church door creak open—a splash of light on his right shoe—and he looked over his shoulder to see Matt and Allie poking their heads in; mild looks of guilt on their faces for being a little late. Allie's eyes were two flies buzzing around until they found Cohen. She sat with him; her hand tapping his knee, twice, as a silent greeting. And then she let it rest there. Matt kept on walking, up the aisle.

Sitting in the back of the church made the priest's words sound distant, and that made them more surreal. He'd never been around that much of his family without Ryan being there too.

At the graveyard, Allie had put her hand on his back the very second his breathing changed. Just barely, her fingers, tracing the outline of his shoulder blade. He had a dry, tight throat, indicative of impending tears. But when the priest started talking about God's plan for young men like Ryan, it all turned to anger. He wanted to break the man's jaw to shut him up about it. Ryan had fucking *died*, at eighteen, and the priest was putting a positive spin on it, and he saw his grandmother nod her head, like yes there's a God, and yes, he saw it fit to hold Ryan's head under water while

Ryan choked and gasped and panicked and died. And he pictured himself in Ryan's body, under water: his lungs exploding or his brain shorting out or his heart popping like a balloon, exactly like a balloon.

Allie leaned in, whispered into his ear. "Some people need to believe that. In something more, in divine reasons for things. In gods that have plans." Her voice soft and warm enough on his ear to calm him.

THE FOLLOWING WEEKEND, there were plans for supper at his parents' place, and he wanted Allie to come. He wanted to put something between him and his parents. A distraction. Something to fill the empty space of Ryan's seat or something to fill the silence, and Allie could have been that thing. But he never asked her to come. They ate lasagna, and there was too much quietness between the forced conversation: clicks of forks off teeth, knives against dishes. Gulps of wine or water. A comment about the weather, maybe. Three sets of eyes like empty glasses.

He'd let himself in. He'd come over a little earlier than they were expecting him, maybe, and he'd let himself in. His father was sitting on the couch—hands behind his head, elbows pointed left and right—staring at a TV that wasn't on. "Supper's in the oven," he said. "Be another hour though. Beer in the fridge if you want one."

Cohen pulled a sweater off, laid it on the couch, and headed for the washroom. It was like he'd caught his father off guard and his father needed a minute, so Cohen pretended he had to go to the washroom, to give him that minute. He walked passed Ryan's bedroom, and the door had been open, and he felt like it should've been closed. He stuck his head in, looked around. Why or what for, he didn't know. That feeling of sand in his throat.

It was a strange thing to have thought, but he thought it immediately upon seeing his brother's guitar: those strings would never be changed again; they'd sit there until they frayed into razors. There was a fish tank, and he wondered how the things weren't dead yet, who'd been feeding them. How hard it must be for his mother or father to step into that room and keep something of Ryan's alive. And how long would they leave those sheets on his bed. Those clothes in the closet. And how long until this room was a spare bedroom, not Ryan's, or converted into a computer room or an exercise room or somewhere for his mother to sit and knit socks and sweaters. Long after the day they did convert it, an item of Ryan's—a guitar pick or a note in his flippant handwriting—would fall out of nowhere, maybe the top shelf of a closet.

He shut the bedroom door behind him as he left.

Heading for the washroom, he walked passed his parents' room, and the door was ajar. His mother had been lying on her side, her body kinked into a Z; her shoulder blades bucking like clipped wings flapping. She had a light blue pillow, but there was a wet, navy, perfect circle, the size of a CD, where her eye met the pillow.

He went downstairs, asked his father if one of them shouldn't be in there with her.

"She's upset." He pointed to the kitchen table, visible from the living room, and there was a smashed plate on the ground in four perfectly equal quarters. "She'd set a place for Ryan. About ten minutes before you walked in. Just...give her a minute."

Cohen cleaned up the broken dish. He grabbed two beers from the fridge and brought one to his father. "Are you sure one of us shouldn't go in there?"

"Cohen, I can't—I can't deal with this myself" he said, sitting up and taking the beer. "So what am I supposed to say to her? *There, there?* I'm not getting snappy with you. I just..." He shrugged his shoulders and took a swig of beer. "This is taking a toll." His father's eyes looked loose, soft; the flesh around them saggy. "She's not making this any easier on me, placing blame. Throwing it around. And having to worry about her on top of it. Sounds selfish, doesn't it? But it's all my fault, she says, that I let you go out in *that rickety old boat* in the first place. Or that I owned that boat and taught you two to drive it. Or that I didn't go after you sooner." He clenched a jaw. A big swig of beer, and he'd hit the bottle off a tooth.

"It's what people do, Dad, that's all. They go over everything that went wrong until they're buried under the weight of all the things that could have prevented what went wrong."

"It's not something you think through out loud. It's *indecent.*"

CHAD
PELLEY

So Cohen stepped into her room. He sat on the corner of her bed, and it sank more than he'd expected. His toes pressed into the carpet, to keep him from sliding onto the floor. She stood up immediately, looked down at him. She was in a bathrobe, unshowered, a wreck of a woman: the hair on one side of her head grease-flattened into her scalp, and the hair on the other side frizzy and jumping away from her. She stood up, looked down at him. Her face went sour and she slapped him. It caught him on the ear and his ear was ringing. And instead of reacting, he closed his eyes and listened to the buzzing.

"People wear *life jackets*, Cohen. They wear life jackets so they don't *drown!*"

When he opened his eyes, she was leaning into her dresser, balancing on her knuckles. She was staring at herself in the mirror, perplexed, like some part of her was missing or something new added on.

She wasn't crying, but there were black icicles of mascara hanging down from her eyes. Too much of her breasts falling out of her robe, and she was too unaware of that. She took her hands off the dresser, tightened the terrycloth belt. "I mean, did he hit his head? Why did he just sink? It doesn't make any *sense*." She sat on the edge of the bed, beside him, and apologized for slapping him. She had laid a hand on his shoulder when she apologized, like maybe she really was sorry. "It's just, not lining up? I don't think he could have hit his head hard enough to knock himself out? I don't under*stand* this!" The thought of the motor's propeller biting into his brother still made Cohen's stomach weak. He'd felt that motor strike something that day, and he'd never know what.

His father pushed the door open, "What's going on in here! Jesus Christ, Anne! Stop grilling your son—" and she ran from the room, pushing passed his father, saying she had to check on supper. But there was a thud, and Cohen walked out into the hall. His mother was on the ground, clutching her foot; a toenail cracked from a badly stubbed toe. She was looking at the heater, like the heater had done it on purpose.

EVERY
LITTLE
THING

43

PULL

IN PRISON, THE toast was always burnt, and he hated that. It was like a sponge, sucking his mouth dry. The grit would get on the backs of his teeth, scour gums, agitate his throat. There was juice, to wash it down with, but never enough. The glasses were tiny and the juice was the fake, tangy kind. So he'd save it all for the end: he'd eat the toast, the papery scrambled eggs, then chug all the juice as a palette cleanser. The only drawback to his routine was it meant leaving his glass full, long after everyone else had finished theirs, and that made his juice prey for the scavenger hands of thirsty, impatient inmates. Maybe once a week, someone would walk past him and snake his cup. It was important to let them take it. Most violence happened in the cafeteria. It was equally important to crack a defensive joke: to call the guy an asshole and laugh. Or say, *Tastes like shit anyway*.

A lot of the tables were on wheels, and it irritated everyone. Someone would sit down, jerk the table, and it could be enough to set the wrong man off. A gangly redheaded man accidentally jostled a table one day, and knocked over Truck's orange juice. Truck speared his thumb into the guy's eye. A quick, senseless jab. The man yelped, fell backwards out of his seat, and cracked his head off the concrete floor, hard. Hard enough for his teeth to bang together. Nip his tongue. And that one incident had plagued the man as everyone's target for weeks. Surprise kidney punches in the shower, for kicks. A leg out in the cafeteria to trip him, for a gag. Some people were bored in there and never meant any harm by that sort of thing. Other people needed a target for their pent-up anger.

If someone had a dietary restriction, they'd be called a fag for it. Given a hard time by the rougher crowd. To be lactose intolerant, a celiac, a diabetic—anything that got you served a red tray instead of the standard blue one—singled you out. And prison was a place to be transparent. You did not sit alone in the cafeteria, you did not eat from a red tray with a special order, and you sat with your head down next to a man with a blue tray.

If it weren't for the colour-coded trays, Cohen would have lied, faked a gluten allergy, to avoid the toast, and get the yogurt or the gluten-free English muffins instead. Because they were thicker, the gluten-free English muffins took longer to toast, so they wouldn't burn. The one time he'd seen them on a man's plate, they were a perfect golden blonde.

He'd thought of Allie the day he craved that gluten-free English muffin. Allie had once bought a new toaster because of a poor gradation between settings on the one they owned: if she'd use setting 3, it would leave her bread *hardly even toasted*, and setting 4 made it *too toasted*. He'd come down for breakfast one morning, caught her unplugging it. Explained why the toaster had to go to the goodwill, that very day. *Come to Walmart with me*, she'd said. And he did. He bought an electric razor for himself that's still in his medicine cabinet at home—an ornate, two-hundred-dollar teak cabinet that Allie had seen, fallen in love with, and bought while shopping at a Christmas craft fair one year. It had deep shelves, requiring it be sunk into the wall. It took Cohen a whole Saturday to hang. She laid in the bathtub—not in the bath, naked, but in the empty tub, fully clothed—reading him short stories from a battered old *Journey Prize Anthology*. He had to borrow a jigsaw from Matt and pretend he knew what he was doing. Getting it into the wall wasn't too hard, but securing it was a matter of botched improvisation. Trial and error, with a lot of errors. Allie had read most of the book.

The walk back to his cell from the cafeteria only took a minute or so. It was two lefts and then a right turn, in a hallway that trapped sounds and sent them bouncing off the walls. After the second left, someone's cell was plastered with surprisingly beautiful photographs. A woman, back on, stood under a street-lamp, like she didn't know which way to walk. A moonbeam, spread like butter across a violent, black ocean. They were all night time shots. Striking. And looked the way longing feels. He didn't know why, but he didn't expect a man with that kind of artistic taste to be in a prison cell. He expected only photos of ugly wives and violent children. Or he expected pages torn from a

EVERY
LITTLE
THING

45

porn magazine, taped askew to the cement walls. But porn was eradicated as quickly as drugs in that place. Anything the part-time doctor thought might *excite or render violent an inmate* was part of the frequent cell sweeps. And they'd always come at the exact moment Cohen was enjoying a nice nap or a moment alone at his window.

Allie had been a photographer when Cohen met her. Not long after his brother died, Cohen was out back, smoking. Daydreaming. He felt heat at his fingertips and looked down at his cigarette. Two or three puffs left. And then he heard glass shatter; heard Allie's voice next door, *Shit!* and he walked up the stairwell, peered around the side of his house, and saw her looking down at a pile of busted picture frames on the sidewalk. She was holding a grey plastic bag—the bottom torn open, blowing in the wind. She looked up, saw him, and made her sad face: lips turned out and down.

"That's...too bad," he said.

"My favourite frame broke too! What a *fucker*," she said, looking at the bag, still in her hand, and laughing. She put the broken, empty bag in her purse. "Any chance you've got an old broom and dustpan?"

He nodded, went to fetch it.

When he came back out, she was knelt down and separating good frames from broken frames, jiggling the good ones to shake off any bits of glass, and stacking them beside her. She was wearing a blue dress. White polka dots. A soft black cardigan. There were places on her body his hands begged to hold.

He got to sweeping the glass, and she snatched the broom from him, turning her body into his as she did so, so that he couldn't fight her on it. "I said *do you have a broom*, not *can you deal with this glass for me*." She laughed, both to thank him and set him straight.

He smiled back and hauled a bag out of his back pocket. He held it open, "Do you want to hold the bag yourself too?"

"No. No you can hold the bag, thanks." She smiled at him without looking at him. He noticed that. What it means to smile at someone who isn't looking at you. He tied the bag off and looked into her trunk. "Jesus, who needs, like, forty picture frames?"

"Me. I do. Clearly."

"Clearly."

"I sell photography, sort of."

"Sort of?"

"Long story." She had five bags of picture frames in each hand, struggling a little with the weight.

"I can...ah. How about we take five bags each?"

"How about it," she said, face lit up as she extended a load of bags. Opening the passenger door, she exclaimed, "This one's for me," and stuck a huge, child-sized photo frame under her arm as she kicked the car door shut.

She stuck her belly out and said, "Lock that car door for me? My keys are in the left pocket of my cardigan. And then you can open the front door for us too." She slung her head, in the direction of the house, as she said *front door*, as if he needed to know which house was hers.

Sliding his hand into her cardigan pocket felt intimate, it implied some bond between them or a familiarity. He wondered if he was reading too much into it, with the back of his hand against her belly, fishing the keys out, enjoying the effect of her body on his.

He looked at her keys, titling them in his palm, noting what she'd written on them. "Did you write H for house and C for car on your keys?"

"Yes. So what. I like to be clear on things."

"You only have two keys. One is clearly a car key."

She kicked him in the shin, lightly, playfully, for mocking her. "Well, someday I'll have a third, won't I? And then we'll see who is stumbling for the right key when a mugger is a few feet away from catching her, as she runs to the front door, won't we?"

"What?"

"Oh, go open my door!" And he did.

He followed her up the stairs to her room. Laid her frames on the end of her bed. Thought of the night he'd seen her, wailing, from his bedroom window.

Everything was pushed to the centre of the room. Her bed was in the very middle, surrounded by dressers and nightstands and lamps and then a fence of boxes around all that.

"Nice layout with the room. I like it. I mean why put your dresser or headboard against a wall, right?"

She kicked him in the shin again. This was her thing, her

reaction to sarcasm, and he liked learning these things about her, one by one. "It's all in the middle of the room so I can paint, Dipshit. And if you're a real man, this is the part where you tell a damsel you'll help her paint her room tonight."

If she was trying to help him, trying to distract him from Ryan's death, it didn't matter anymore. He wanted to help her paint that room. He wanted to see paint dripped across her hands, splattering in her face, making her laugh, as she stepped back and second guessed the colour.

"Sure. I'm a top-notch painter. What colour?"

"White."

"Really? Who paints a room—"

"Well, *Computer Paper* according to the paint chip. And head's up: the white walls might mean three coats? I thought I'd have you committed before I mentioned that, because I am clever."

She winked at him. *Who winks?*

He turned his head, saw a stack of 8x10 black-and-white photos on her desk. The one on top was a photo of a bedridden woman. She had the kind of face that implied breathing was hard, and smiling was a long-lost luxury. There were bottles of pills all over the nightstand beside her, looking lost in a maze of crumpled tissues. She was in a loosely fitting gown that hinted at sudden weight loss.

"Is that your mother? Sorry if I'm being—"

"Yes. Shit. I didn't mean to leave them there like that." She walked over to the stack, grabbed them all, opened a dresser drawer, threw them in. Closed the door with a hip. "My father gets livid with me when he sees those photos. I—You might find this weird, but I took a photo of her every day, for what turned out to be the last sixty-two days of her life. Kind of morbid, maybe, but I was capturing what was escaping her, day by day. A photographic study of...death." She shrugged her shoulder and had a shy, awkward grin like maybe he was judging her.

She was side-on to him as they peered down at another stack of photos, their hips locked into each other. A breast at his elbow. She was too liberal with her body against his. It was just her nature, he knew that by now, but it flared desire in him. And there was a bed, right there behind them.

"It's why I live with my father, still, by the way, if you're wondering. I moved back in with him to help him care for her.

And to be with her. And I just...didn't move back out. Yet. We both wanted to move into town here. And your lonely dad makes for a good enough roommate when you don't know anyone in town." She shrugged her shoulders, *that's that.*

"What's weird about living with you father?"

"When you're pushing thirty? Nothing, I guess. Just making sure you know I'm not a weirdo. This stack of photos is less depressing," she said, pointing to a pile of glossy pictures. The way the light was bouncing off them, he couldn't see the image until he tilted his head. "They're the ones for the photo frames. Photos of touristy landmarks that sell pretty well."

They were vibrant images, obviously colour-manipulated in Photoshop, but confidently composed. Interesting angles, subjects, and ways of framing things. "These are great. Really great. This one's my favourite, though. The abandoned house, with the goat in the window."

She plucked two cans of paint from a bag in her closet. "Thanks. FYI: this is fancy paint. It says it only needs sixty minutes between coats. I think we can have it done by midnight. You don't have to stay for all three coats, though, okay?"

But he did. They watched a movie between coats. They shared popcorn; two hands, one bowl. Quick little fights, like *Go ahead, no you go ahead,* until they found a rhythm and stopped reaching for the popcorn at the same time. Cohen sat on one end of the couch, and Allie lay sprawled on the remaining two cushions. Sometimes her toes rested against his leg or she'd plunk a heel down on his knee and rock her foot back and forth, like there was nothing to it. Like she didn't know what her body did to his. Or like maybe she did.

Matt joined them for the second movie, after the second coat of paint, and said sad things like, *Meryl is your mother's favourite actress.* Matt said *is* not *was* when talking about Kristen. Cohen knew Allie wouldn't leave her father alone in that house until he could say *was.* There was something profoundly empathetic about Allie. He'd noticed it in her right away. How she could suffocate in sadness, so she took steps to eradicate it wherever she detected it. As much out of her own need for a copacetic equilibrium than out of compassion alone.

MEN IN JAIL could be divided into men who took pride in what they'd gotten caught for, and men who were ashamed to admit to what they'd done. He'd expected more people claiming innocence. Or to have the kind of convoluted, fucked-up story he did, about how he got six months in jail—a slim sentence for a man pegged as being a *conspirator to murder* in the initial police reports. But it all made for a good story, and that, somehow, got him respect in there. *You could write a movie about all that, and get rich! Won't have been for nothing then!* It was almost like they were jealous of all the twists and turns and characters involved in his story, versus their more commonplace ones: attempted burglary, drunk driving, aggravated assault after too many drinks in a shady bar.

Cohen's story ended with an accomplice being locked away in a place much darker than where they all were, and that was a nice detail in the eyes of inmates who loved a good *So, what'd you do?* story. As one inmate told another about Cohen's story, and then another, each person exaggerated or changed a detail, until one version of the story had Cohen's name, and Cohen's part in the story, swapped with Lee's.

Lee Brown had been a close friend of Allie's. An atypical friend: he was an elderly, American war vet turned sidewalk vendor. And Cohen couldn't hear his name now without thinking about the trajectory of it all. He thought about what domino had struck what domino first, to set things in motion: how he wouldn't have known Lee Brown, if he hadn't fallen in love with Allie, and how he'd fallen in love with Allie, partly, vaguely, as a reaction to Ryan's death, and how his brother never would have drowned if his mother hadn't of insisted on a trip to the cabin, and how she wouldn't have insisted on the trip to the cabin if his family hadn't gotten plagued by a genetic heart disorder. And even that trickled back decades, to how his grandfather's DNA took on ARVC, against its will, almost a hundred years ago. Because his father choose to marry a *Candice Heffernan* instead of a million other women. Screwy genes and all.

But if he stacked those dominos back up and knocked them back down in the reverse order, it's the same series of events that had led him to Allie. Minus Lee. And how Lee fit into Allie's life was simple happenstance.

Three mornings after the night Cohen had helped Allie

paint her room, he met Lee for the first time. There was a knock on his bedroom window. His room was below ground, and his window was behind his headboard, so he had to look at the window upside down; his body awkwardly held in a backwards-crab posture. It was Allie, awake, showered, wearing a black skirt and a bright purple tank top. The sun barely up.

He'd notice something new about her every time he saw her. The way she blinked slower than most. The way some words caught in her mouth; an over-lingering on the letter F. *Fffine. Fffuck.*

She was knelt at the window, her legs pressed together, and she plunked a framed photo against the glass. "Look! For you, for helping me paint the other night!" She said, "It's the one with the goat, in the abandoned house," as if he couldn't see for himself. "You said you liked that one, right?" She nodded her head, widened eyes. "Right?"

"Yes, thanks." He laughed as he looked at his alarm clock. "So...like...you knock on people's windows before eight in the morning, hey?"

"Well. Not everyone's. I have to know the person."

"And what if that person valued sleeping in on Saturdays or sleeping naked?"

"Well, yeah. Okay. I never thought of that. But you're not naked, are you? And you're under a comforter. And I don't judge." A wink, a shy smile. "I'll put the goat picture down by your back door, where you smoke. I have some errands to run. Sort of. I'll be back by one or two, if...if you want to do something this afternoon? It's nice out. I don't really know anyone else around here to call, but you'll do, for now, until I meet some other people!" She laughed at herself so easily. It was a different kind of laugh, less graceful than when she laughed at someone else. She was like Ryan that way. And they both had dart-hole dimples in their cheeks when they smirked at their own wisecracks.

"Yeah. Yeah, okay."

"Nice! Okay. I'll meet you out front. Two o'clock sharp?"

He laughed at her in a way that said *Yes*, and she waved before spinning and walking away; her skirt tornado-ing around her legs. A flash of orange panties.

"Allie!"

She was back at the window. "Yeah?"

"Where…where are you off to at eight in the morning? And do you want some company?"

She smiled. "Sure."

"Give me twenty minutes to shower and that?"

"Okay!"

"Okay?"

"Okay."

"Okay. So where are we going?"

"I have to drop my photos off somewhere. About an hour away. Hour and a bit. Out in Grayton, where me and Dad just moved from. Know it?"

"Of course," he said, kicking off his bedsheets. "It's nice out there."

"I thought you slept naked," she said, nodding at his pajama pants.

"What?"

"Never mind. Twenty minutes. I'll be out front with the car running. And I'm driving. I don't like being driven. I'm a… very paranoid driver. And I don't know you well enough to be all backseat driver on you, yet."

Yet she'd said. And they both paused at the utterance of it. Yet. The implication.

"And, Cohen?"

"Yeah?"

"Nice pajamas. Very manly."

She winked and walked away. *Who winks?*

He looked down at his pajama pants like maybe real men don't wear pajama pants.

ALLIE REALLY WAS a paranoid driver. *Did you see that! That son of a bitch just cut me off!* She'd slap the wheel and swear even though a school bus could have fit in between her car and the man who'd passed her with ample berth. Her driving anxiety was something a long-term partner, a husband, might grow sick of, but he loved it. Found it endearing: her so harmless, but uttering such well-articulated threats.

"Someone needs to tie his hands to his feet and roll him down a mountain!"

"What?" He laughed. "They need to do *what* to him?"

"You heard me. A mountain!"

She drove as if driving a fighter jet, and all the other cars were missiles. Even in the city, she imagined a moose might just jump out of anywhere. And kids, she'd told him, were *death-wish fearless*. She reduced her speed by 50% if she even *thought* she saw one.

"The problem is, kids think they're invincible. But a quick game of Car Versus Kneecap would prove otherwise, am I right?"

He laughed. "Yeah, you're right all right." He paused. "Have you...been in a bad accident or something?"

"No, why?" She had the wheel gripped so hard her knuckles were popping through her skin.

"Just wondering."

"So what, I'm a melodramatic driver. We all have our flaws. There are worse things, Cohen, like halitosis and...I dunno. Gambling addictions!"

"Okkkaaay..." He put up his hands like, *Don't shoot!*

"And I hate this stretch of the drive. It's the worst. I mean, why have an *undivided* highway? That's just *asking* for trouble. Some dipshit in the other lane nods off or speeds and hydro-planes, and ka-bam, it's all over for *me!*" She shook her head at the injustice of it. "You've got to wonder about a world that builds undivided highways."

"Absolutely. You do. I mean, what kind of world!"

"Are you mocking me! I'm serious, think about it. Chunks of metal, flying past each other, going more than a hundred clicks an hour!"

He was still smirking. "What?" she said. "What?"

"You should've seen your eyes when that squirrel ran across the road. It was like your brain slingshot your eyes from your skull."

She slapped his knee, *Shut up!*, and he was shocked she'd taken a hand out of the 10 and 2 position.

They'd made it to Grayton, and the town was in a state of evolution, and Allie hated it. Densely packed subdivisions were being built; the kind where you could see into a neighbour's window through your own, and they made the more traditional saltbox houses look cheap, not practical or quaint. The old, abandoned, unbountiful farmland now housed a Walmart, and an old merchant's house was, as of that summer, a two-theatre cinema. "One that doesn't even play good movies," she'd added as they drove past it.

EVERY
LITTLE
THING

Her eyes followed a ballet of litter blowing in the wind. "It's the litter—the McDonald's burger wrappers and Tim Hortons' cups—that bothers me the most. I mean," she pointed to a sidewalk, "it's everywhere."

She was scanning the street for fearless children and other potential driving hazards as she spoke. She'd swerve from potholes like they were land mines and look at him with her cheeks puffed out like they'd just dodged an explosion. Allie had definitely gotten her license on the first try.

Downtown Grayton was one main street, called Main Street, with a strip of restaurants and retail stores on one side and a stony beach on the other. When she pulled up at the curb of Main Street, she told him to wait in the car. That she'd only be a second. So he did. He could see the wharf, stretching out from the beach like a strip of brown carpet, and he could hear boats knocking off of it like wooden wind chimes. She was pumping some change into a parking meter when Cohen noticed an older man sat at a collapsible vendor's table on the sidewalk. The old man had been eyeing Allie from the moment she'd stepped out of the car. He wore thin black dress pants and a white V-neck shirt: his chest hair visible and grey. White really. Cotton-white. Fluffy like a cloud. He'd been carving wood, with a tool-like knife, into what looked like a lighthouse; his hands almost too shaky to get the job done. He laid down the block of wood, but kept his fist tight around the knife, and he stepped toward Allie.

Something was off about him. He was skinny, and yet his skin sagged from bones: there was a lizard-like flap hanging down from his chin and droops of flesh flapping off his elbows. Both jiggled when he moved, like a rooster's throat wattle. His body looked frail, finished, but his bright blue eyes and animated facial expressions were full of life. When he started walking towards Allie with that knife still in his hands, Cohen got out of the car, defensively. He felt like a fool when he saw Allie walking towards him; her arms thrown wide open for a hug. She held him close, it was a *been-too-long* kind of hug. She was rubbing his back and calling him Lee.

"Little Allie Crosbie! Don't tell me you braved that big ol' highway just to visit me?"

After a few good-natured insults back and forth, the man fell into his seat as if standing too long had weakened every bone in his body. He wore black combat boots, scuffed white in places. His cheap black dress pants were tucked into his boots.

"Cohen, this is Lee."

Lee. Casual, yet formal enough an introduction to rule out grandfather.

"Nice to meet you, Lee."

A handshake, and Lee cracked a joke about her driving. "So, how many near-accidents did she have on the way out?"

"I counted zero, but she got up to a dozen before we hit the highway."

Lee flung his head back and hacked out a laugh. Allie changed the topic. "Lee and I have an arrangement. He sells my photos at his table on Saturdays and Sundays, and we split the profits at the end of the month."

Lee was nodding along. He nodded a lot. He was staring at Cohen, and his eyelids were a crusty and sore-ish shade of red: he had vulture eyes and they were picking Cohen apart. She had a hand on Lee's shoulder, the other hand arranging photos on Lee's table, taking so many at a time from a box at her feet.

Cohen, taken off guard by the way Lee was visually dissecting him, turned to Allie for an escape route, "Do you want me to grab the rest of the photos out of the trunk?" Allie shot him a look, widened eyes, and shook her head, once, quickly, while Lee wasn't looking. Cohen took the cue to play stupid.

"No, this is all the photos. And listen, Lee, you don't mind if this Cohen fellah joins us for lunch, do you? Because I can leave him in the car while you and me eat if you want?" He loved how Allie could be around people. Her humour and compassion never separate from each other.

"We'll make that call at lunch," Lee told her. "He's not too chatty or anything, is he?" He looked at Cohen, nodding again, "I swear I literally stuffed a sock in her last boyfriend's mouth once, to shut him up. A dirty sock too, right off my foot." He laughed and tapped at his right boot. A sprinkle of dust fell to the ground. His shoelaces untied. "Kidding, of course. But her last boyfriend was so boring I had to call an ambulance one time; I told them to come quickly because I was being bored to death." He paused, waiting for them to laugh at him. He was that type. "Jesus! I mean, who dominates lunchtime conversation with the details of some chemistry thesis he's writing?" He waved a hand through the air and Allie laughed, almost embarrassed for having exposed him to her ex. "You don't talk science, do you, Colin?"

He didn't know if that was a joke or if he was being asked, and he didn't know if he should correct him about the name. *Cohen, not Colin.* "No. Not as a rule. Or at length. And I'd use layman's terms and not be boring about it—"

Lee looked at Allie with faked shock, "Did he just call me a lay person!"

"No, I meant if—"

"He's joking, Cohen."

Laughing, "Tell him to work on his sense of humour and he can join us for lunch. Now go on, get, you're blocking off my table!"

"Okay, we'll get, but make sure you sell at least one of my photos, so I can buy some lunch, hey?"

"Ah, go on, your boyfriend is buying lunch for us. Isn't that right, Colin?"

"Cohen."

"Wha?"

"Never mind."

"Just kidding, kid. Lunch is on me. Any days you two come out and visit my lonely ass." He nodded a lot as he said it. Always nodding as if someone was constantly asking him *yes or no* and he hated to disagree.

"So what is it you do, Colin? You're not a *boring-job-for-the-good-paycheque* kind of guy, are you?"

"He's a birder, like you! He works at a bird...museum. You're like, best friends, and you don't even know it yet! Cohen wrote a masters' thesis about seabird conservation." Allie turned to Cohen then. "And Lee here has protested against the gillnets set out for fish. Because they kill deep-diving seabirds." She turned back to Cohen, in case he didn't understand. "The birds dive deep for fish," she enmeshed her hands together, "and then get caught up in the nets and drown. They never come back up for another breath of air."

"Good man," Cohen said.

"I don't know about that." Arms crossed, looking down, shaking his head diagonally. "No one listens to me bitching. And the frustrating part is no one should have to protect a supposedly *protected area* like Bird Rock. Anyway, like I said, go on, get, you're blocking off my table." He waved his hand around to insinuate a mob of people were trying to get a look at his goods. The street was empty. Entirely empty. Tumbleweeds in Western movies empty.

"C'mon, Cohen." She tugged at his arm. He went soft whenever she touched him. He felt pathetic about that. Like she could sense that inner trembling. He bent to tie a shoelace as Allie stepped into her car.

With Allie out of earshot, he said to Lee, "We're not actually together together, Allie and me."

"Wha?"

"You keep calling me her boyfriend. A little awkward."

Lee raised an eyebrow. Just one. His eyes were the colour of blue Bic pens. "I think she's waiting for you, kid." And when Cohen turned around to walk away, Lee said, "You mean to tell me you'd say no to a girl like that?" He nodded to Allie in the car, buckling in.

"Well, no, just that we're not, like...we've only just met—"

"What are you, five years old or something? Do yourself a favour and win her over, Colin. It can't be that hard. Like I said, her last boyfriend was a dimwit, dull as beige. And her bright as yellow. She clearly doesn't expect much from a guy. And that dipshit boyfriend she had left her when trying to console her about her mother's cancer got old and boring. Like a proper dickhead would. Now go on, kid, she's had the car running for two minutes now. I'm choking on her exhaust here, and you're blocking off my table. Go!"

"My name's Cohen, by the way. Not Colin."

"Whatever. You know who I'm talking to, don't you?"

He picked a knife back up off the table and started whittling a fresh block of wood into another lighthouse.

COHEN GOT IN the car, and she apologized.

"People around here sort of buy things off Lee, like his little carvings he does, to help him out. He's tried stained glass too. He doesn't *need* need the money, but he sort of does. Half the time, people don't display what they buy off of him. In their houses, I mean. He pretends not to notice when he visits them."

She was talking with her head down, afraid Lee was a lip-reader. "I pretty much *give* Lee a bunch of photos to sell every month. There's a lot of sales to tourists in the summer, and he needs the money more than I do. But the rest of those photos in the trunk are for The Craft Shoppe."

She lifted her head back up, looked at Lee, and put it back down, fastening her seatbelt. "Anyway, if Lee offers to buy lunch," she said, rooting a hand around in her jeans pocket, "tell him it's on you." She stuck a twenty and a ten-dollar bill in his hand. "That's for my and Lee's lunch. He'd never let me pay, but he'll take your money no problem." She laughed about that, staring back at Lee in the rear-view mirror as she drove towards The Craft Shoppe.

"He's an interesting guy. Sweet and witty. He, ah…He was also a prisoner of war. For *years*. In the Philippines. Can you imagine? *Years*. Starving and wasting away like a stray cat. Malaria and everything. Watching your friends die or be killed. Besides all that, when it was over, and he came home from the war, he couldn't find his parents. His father's job had him moving around a lot by necessity. He says he figures they assumed he died, but I assume they were never that close. That there was some tension there. A story I'll never know. I mean, sure, it wasn't like these days where you can find people online, but still. You'd try hard enough, and you'd find them, wouldn't you? No one loses their *son*. After the war, Lee ended up here, in Grayton of all places, even though he's from The States."

She'd finished her story and looked at him like he should be impressed by it. A slow nod, pressing her chin into her chest. Neither of them spoke for a few minutes. He looked out his window, following the sagging U of power lines between telephone poles as Allie drove down the street. She was so intent on the road when she drove, so alert and paranoid, that he wanted to yell *boo*.

"There's a fantastic hike up by Bird Rock. Wanna do that, once I drop these photos off? Before lunch?"

"Yeah. Sure."

"There's petrels and razorbills out there. And those cute little dovekies. And I saw a cormorant out there once too."

"Must have been a double-crested—"

"Aren't you impressed?"

He looked at her, waiting for an explanation.

"I mean, aren't you impressed that I like birds so much?"

His face folded into sarcastic grin. "Cormorants, hey? Why

are women so impressed by big birds?"

"Grow up," she said, and she hit him. "But. Did you know there's actually a bird called a blue-footed *Booby*? I mean, *booby*, c'mon, right?"

"Actually, there's three boobys, in the genus *Sula*, and the term, *booby*, is innocent. It means clumsy, in Portuguese or something, because boobys look clumsy on land."

"Who the *fuck* knows something like that?"

"Now who's immature?"

It was a forty-five-minute walk out to Bird Rock from the parking lot, but Allie said she knew a shortcut through the woods. Five minutes into her shortcut, the spaces between the trees were getting closer and closer until they had to sidestep through crusty and closely spaced spruce. The pokes from serrated sticks weren't far off jabs from knives. Sometimes they'd have to duck under immoveable branches. They played limbo under one branch, and Allie won.

Every couple of steps, he'd turn around and see her taking a picture of something. Sometimes him when he wasn't looking. The snaps of her shutter. He liked the way she'd point the camera at something like it was the only thing on earth. And the way she'd pace around a thing, trying to find the right composition and light. Her tongue sometimes bit between teeth. At one point, he turned around and she was knelt into a patch of bright pink wildflowers, her camera in them like a bee. Without turning to face him, she shouted out an inquisitive, "Are these ones rare or anything?" not looking at him as she snapped the picture.

"Bird's eye primrose. Not common, not uncommon."

"What kind of answer is that," she said, turning to face him as she launched herself up from her kneeling.

The army of branches had already hitched Cohen's shirt twice, as warning, before a third one took action and cut the back of his neck deeply enough that Allie winced when he showed her and asked her how bad it was. No words, just a wince, and she offered him some tissues from her purse.

EVERY LITTLE THING

59

"Are you *sure* about this detour? I mean, maybe we should turn around. Unless...you have a machete in your bag and want to clear the way." He put a hand up, *Look at all these trees*. He turned around and Allie was right there; she brought her lips to his. Put a hand on his face to make the kiss count.

She pressed her body into him, leaned hard, so he'd know to lay down on the ground, and she crawled on top of him. There were tufts of lichens crunching under his head; twigs like dull forks in his ass and elbows, and she was wrestling his pants off, impatient with his belt. She left his shirt on, and scooped a hand up her skirt to shed her underwear.

Her skirt curtained over his knees and belly, rising and falling, up and down. And then she took it all off: all of her bare there in front of him. His hands on her hips. She fell forward, planted her hands on the forest floor; her hair dangling over him like a tunnel blocking out everything but her face. That smell of cinnamon or cloves: the first time he'd been close enough to notice it. She reached down and put one hand to use on her clit, finished first, everything tightening, that infinite exhale, as her hand, under his armpit, grabbed a fistful of dirt. She laughed, as she rolled over, like there was something funny about it. She knelt beside him, naked still, and did something fast with her hands, something practiced and to the point, that finished him off in a minute.

There was nothing awkward about it as they dressed, and she was surprisingly nonchalant about being naked in broad daylight: the shadows of tree branches flickering over her body like TV static. She stepped into her orange panties; let the elastic snap hard as she took her thumbs away. He had his arms wrapped around her before she'd gotten her bra back on, for a waltzing, swaying bear hug. He ran a finger up her spine, ran it back down. The bumps and ridges of her backbone drumming through him.

She laid her head sideways onto his shoulder. Whispered, "What?"

"You're...I mean. That was...I—"

"Shh!"

"That last bit. What was—"

She was smiling when she broke free and tossed him his shorts. "Let's not talk about it."

They hiked back to the trail and walked out to Bird Rock with their arms slung around each other like they'd been together for years.

FILLING
SPACES

THREE MONTHS IN that jail and Allie hadn't visited. Called. Sent a letter. There was supposed to be that much. A phone call, after the trial: her on the other end fidgeting with the phone cord. Sorry as hell and blubbering with remorse. A good person would have set the record straight with the police that night, and every night, that kept him awake.

The judge had sentenced him to six months, and he wondered, as the gavel cracked down, if six months in prison meant 180 days or 183. And if he'd get out two days early because February was part of his sentence, and February only has twenty-eight days. Being sentenced that day in court, hearing *guilty*, sitting on that stone-hard stool, had felt like standing in freeway traffic and seeing a transport truck barreling towards him. Except the truck never hit him, and that unique split second of panic lasted longer than a split second. Longer than a day.

They weren't allowed pens in their cells, but a calendar was fine. He'd scratch the days off the glossy pages with a cracked bit of cement, small as a penny, he'd found in the corner of his cell. It was a satisfying midnight ritual that gave some small purpose to his day. Then he'd go stare, out that tiny window, at that tiny pond, waiting to be tired. And by the time he was tired, he was more hungry than he was tired, and robbed of another night's sleep on account of the aching hunger. Rocking back and forth, tossing and turning, worried about mortgage payments now that he was out of a job. His RRSPs could only get him through a year.

There were two or three nights, when he hadn't even fallen asleep before the wake-up call, and his cell door slid open, to let him get in the line of men that would file him into the cafeteria. Human cattle, in orange jumpsuits, always tired and hungry, and always bored.

In jail, there was nothing to distinguish one day from another, except the arrival of a new inmate or spotting something or someone he'd never noticed before. Like the time, in line at the cafeteria, he saw a man with a red tray and got jealous of the contents. Those golden gluten-free English muffins and how they weren't burnt and how they came with a side of yogurt instead of papery, poorly cooked eggs. The man holding the tray looked too much like Allie's father. But with big, plastic-framed glasses. A hipper, younger Matt. Before the greying eyebrows and the cynicism and the bad decision that ultimately landed Cohen in jail.

Cohen stared at this new inmate, and it wasn't so much that the man looked like Matt because he didn't really. And he had an amazing caricature of Johnny Cash tattooed on his forearm with a quote Cohen couldn't make out. This man had a guitar-shaped scar on his left jaw, and he didn't bite his nails or make excessive eye contact when he spoke to someone like Matt had always done. But the guy whistled like Matt did. When idle, like waiting in line for food, this guy whistled without realizing he was whistling. Like Matt, he'd stop abruptly whenever he caught himself. A quick look around like, *I hope I wasn't annoying anyone.* Minutes later, his lips were pursing again.

When Cohen and Allie had gotten their first apartment, half the thrill of it was watered down by Allie worrying about her father, alone for the first time since her mother died. Matt was a warm and loving man, but in a way that made him prone to loneliness. He was like a kid that way: he needed people seeing what he was doing, and sharing in the joy of it, and if no one was there to share in the fun, the bottled-up joy festered into loneliness. He was the kind of man who'd laugh harder at a movie if there was someone sitting next to him. The kind of man who'd say, *Did you hear that?* And if there was no one there to say it to, he'd feel painfully alone.

Allie wished he could've admitted that. She wished he could've said, *I'm bored, visit more.* Or, *Don't leave me here.* Cohen had offered to move in there, with the two of them. For months he basically lived there anyway. Allie cooking for them as Cohen tried on the role of Matt's new best friend, in the yard, helping him build a new fence, at the Saturday matinée, sharing the combo #2 as if on a date: *Two root beers and a large popcorn.*

What bothered Allie was Matt's bad acting and his overeagerness to make comments about how okay he was. She phoned him to check in, the Sunday after she'd moved out, and Cohen overheard it all because she'd had him on speaker phone. "Hi, Dad, how's life? How's having the place to yourself?"

"Great!" he said, enthusiastically enough for her to hear the exclamation mark. "I've bought a build-it-yourself greenhouse package. Really looking forward to getting it up and running. It'll give me something to do, and you two are welcome to half my tomatoes!"

When they visited him a week later, the build-it-yourself greenhouse was still in a box. In the porch. In a shopping bag.

The day Cohen and Allie had moved into their apartment, he and Matt were walking boxes and furniture from Matt's house to a U-haul truck. Allie was in the back of the truck arranging things as they plunked them in to her. *Tetris-ing things into position* she'd said. She loved order, organizing things, labelling things. Each box had a letter scrolled on all six faces to indicate what room they were destined for: K for kitchen, NE for non-essential items. When he and Matt each laid a box down, labelled *Cam Gear*, with little drawings of cartoony cameras all over them, she said, "That's it, except for two boxes of photo mats in the storage closet." A big smile like, *What's two more boxes?*

"One each?"

"Sounds good."

They were walking through the kitchen to the storage closet at the back of the house. Matt ran a finger along the handle of a pan filled with leftovers from supper, as he passed by. Some kind of stir fry: vegetables and chicken covered in a brown sauce and sesame seeds. "She sure can cook, that one. Almost as good as her mother."

There was nothing accusatory about the statement, but it was in no way about Allie's culinary skills. It was about him having to dine alone now. Cook for himself. Lay one plate of food at an empty table. Every clink of a fork off a plate, every gulp of water, would be a sound that no one in the world would hear but him.

Matt opened the storage closet door and handed Cohen the

lighter of the two boxes, the half-filled one. All day long, Matt was silently concerned about Cohen lifting things, because of his heart. *Careful now. Slow down. Let's take five, hey?* Matt could never wrap his head around the vagueness of Cohen's genetic heart disorder. It wasn't as easy to understand as diabetes or hemophilia—because those things were as simple as not feeding a man sugar or cutting him. So Cohen had fun with it: they were lifting a mattress down over the stairs, and Cohen laid his corner down. He clutched his heart and feigned a heart attack. Just for ten seconds, but long enough for Matt to panic.

Matt punched him on the shoulder and had a stern look on his face as he walked down over the stairs, shaking his head. When he turned around he was grinning too. "I'm laughing, Davies, but that joke's only funny once. The boy who cried wolf and all that."

Cohen was scanning all the random stuff in the storage closet as he waited for Matt to grab the other box of mats. He saw a chess board on top of a Monopoly box. The chess board was all stone: granite. The white pieces were marble and the black pieces looked like onyx. Matt saw him looking at it.

"Nice board, hey?" He ran a finger over its smooth surface. A line parting dust. "I got it in Mexico, on my and Kristen's honeymoon. You play?" He flicked off the light and edged past Cohen.

"Well. I know how to play if that's what you mean. But no, haven't had a game in ten years. I could kick your ass, though, if that was a challenge."

"I could beat you using all pawns, Davies!" He laughed before saying, "Doesn't work, does it? Chess and smack talk?"

Cohen, laughing a little in agreement, looking down at Allie's stir fry as they walked through the kitchen. "No. Not quite."

"What's the point of a game where you can't smack talk your opponent? Ever play Scattergories or Balderdash? Allie and I, we love those two."

And that's where it all started. Right there, in Matt's kitchen, talking chess like two budding best friends. It took Cohen ninety-something sleepless nights in a prison cell to trace it all back to where a fuse got lit. And it should've been something more caustic and explosive than a friendly, innocent competition, and how bonding over board games led to them spending so much time together.

If Cohen hadn't learned chess, off his crush in grade four, or if he'd never made that comment, that promise of a game of chess with Matt, his life might have gone differently. Matt wouldn't have come to trust him so much. Matt wouldn't have asked that favour.

Some nights, he'd think: *if I hadn't met Allie at all.* Or if his brother hadn't drowned, because what a fucked up thing to have brought two people together in the first place: death. His brother's, her mother's.

But things had gone the way they did, and the first Wednesday of every month, he and Allie would go eat supper with Matt. Play Scattergories. Matt would make homemade pasta with his new pasta maker. His house was filling with gadgets: palm pilots and telescopes and specific-use things like pasta makers and tomato dicers and plug-in apple peelers. He was becoming a shopping channel addict. Filling empty spaces. Filling time. Because an idle man is haunted and a busy man is not.

One night, Allie couldn't make it. A baby shower. And the phone rang that night. Two rings, Cohen answered, and someone hung up. Five minutes later it rang again. It was Matt.

"Cohen?"

"No, it's Allie."

"*Har har.* Listen, what are you doing for supper? I know Allie is out, but I figure you gotta eat something anyway. I got the pasta maker out, and I have some Bocconcini, straight from Italy, the package says, for my tomato-basil salad. You'd have to be quite a fool to say no and miss out, but hey, some people are fools. And I thought we could crack out that chess board you admired that time?"

"I can be there in fifteen?"

"Take your time. I'll be another twenty minutes slaving over this. Bring some red wine, of course."

"Okay."

"Grab a...I dunno. Something Italian."

"I'll go all out. I've had my eye on a pricy Barolo for some time now."

"Yes. Yes that'll do it."

FROM THAT NIGHT on, Cohen never declined an invite from Matt to a game of chess or a visit to check out a new gadget he'd ordered: a homemade ice-cream maker or a new digital camera. *There's no film. I don't even understand. Come over and check it out.*

I read about them on Canon's website while I was looking for a new telescope. They're calling them digital cameras! It was Canon's first model on the market. He was probably the first one to own one.

If Cohen had plans with someone on a day Matt called, they'd always understood why Cohen would break those plans, to fill Matt's loneliest moments. Especially Allie. Cohen had adopted Matt's interests, one by one, to spend time with him. He'd feigned the interest, as a rule—golf, Scrabble, Roman Polanski films—but more than once he'd actually come to like some of Matt's hobbies, like astronomy.

Through Matt's casual, backyard lectures about astronomy, the night sky was becoming a nightly show. Most people looked up and saw the same thing every night—a moon, stars—but it only took a couple of nights with Matt to see something more. That the world looked like a different place every couple of days. And a man like Matt needed to see that, and feel that way. To separate the days. Matt thought maybe he was teaching Cohen about astronomy, but Matt was really teaching him about love. That love was the dent you'd put in someone's life if you left them behind. And Cohen could only hope, in thirty years, that he'd miss Allie, the way Matt missed Kristen, if Allie died of cancer too, thirty years from now.

They'd sip beers and chat, and Cohen got it now, astronomy, and why people gave a shit about the stars. How every night was different if you'd just look up. So they'd look up at named patterns in the sky, constellations that were there some nights and not there others.

"The stars are like a million bright mysteries, you know, because no one agrees on how the things even form. Some nights I come out here," he'd told Cohen one night, "and I can get so lost in the stars that I forget I'm even rooted in the world. Does that sound crazy? A grown man like me, lying on his picnic table and looking up at the sky?"

"No. That's what a hobby is, isn't it?"

"No. A hobby is an interest; a way to waste time or relax. This is something more. For people like me, it's an exercise in longing. Or proof there's…something more."

For people like me?

"Some of the stories behind these constellations are half-interesting," he'd told Cohen one night, drunk, lying on that picnic table. "The Greeks say that Gaia sent a scorpion to kill Orion, after Orion tried to force himself on her, and now, at the times when the Scorpio constellation shines the brightest in the sky, the Orion constellation is the dimmest it gets. It shines less brightly. Like Scorpio is jabbing the bastard full of poison."

Cohen pulled the lever on his lawn chair. Leaned back. Took the sky in. "So, what else we got up there tonight, Matt?"

"Cancer. And Lynx too. But those are harder to see. Especially Lynx. It's one of the faintest constellations. Hevelius named it. He named it Lynx because you'd need a lynx's eye to see it."

"Well, bring on the Cancer then, point it out!" And Cohen's enthusiasm snagged on that word. Cancer. Kristen had been dead for years now, but Matt clearly had no intention of replacing her absence with another woman—just stars and telescopes and gadgets he didn't need.

"Cancer means crab, in Latin or Greek or whatever, right?" Cohen stepped up to the telescope. "Am I looking for a crab?"

"Well, no, just pincers, actually. Just the crab's claw. And it's more like a tuning fork, really."

"Oh, c'mon!" he teased, "first Leo looks more like a lollipop than a lion, and now this? All these constellations a rip-off?" and Matt threw an astronomy book at him, both of them laughing.

He liked Matt right from the start. Right from the day Matt had turned that reporter away, the week Ryan had drowned.

A
BROKEN WING

THE DAY OF Cohen and Allie's fifth-year anniversary, Cohen's parents had him, Allie, and Matt over for an afternoon barbecue. Matt saw it as the right time to try out the mesquite he'd ordered from channel four one night. He showed up waving the bag of mesquite, a big grin on his face, *I thought we'd try this, to spice up the chicken?*

He'd not read the directions and threw too many sticks in the grill. A cloud of smoke, too thick to see through, billowed up from the barbecue and clawed at his eyes. He ran from the thing like it was an angry beehive, and his eyes were red as boiled lobsters. They were spilling water, like cracked aquariums.

The smell was too much for Cohen's mother. She excused herself, breathing only through her mouth, so that the pitch of her voice was weird, claiming that she had to add a few dressings to the salads. Her salads were restaurant quality. They always were. She had a thing for Thai cuisine—peanut sauces, sesame seeds, and the texture that coconut milk imparted on meats. Allie had always left with her recipes. His mother loved that. As they'd put on their shoes before leaving, she'd ask, *You got your recipes, Allie?* and Allie would tap her pocket, say yes, and Cohen would watch his mother nod, beaming a smile. *See how much she likes my cooking?*

Matt's overly mesquite chicken tasted like a mouthful of forest floor. "Well, I had to try it once, just to see?"

A round of laughter before his mother interjected. "A toast to the cutest couple in town, on their *fifth* anniversary!" She ran a hand through Cohen's hair before resting it on his shoulder. Five cups clinking together, not one of them the same: a glass of white wine, a glass of red wine, a beer bottle, a bottle of water, and a can of ginger ale.

There was the toast, and then there were the questions, right away, a blitzkrieg. A guillotine of a statement. "So. You're both thirty now. You've been together five long years."

Allie raised an eyebrow, and shrugged one shoulder. *Yer point?*

Matt chimed in. "Any talk of wedding bells and children?"

Cohen's father, "Because no one has ever gotten any younger. No one."

Allie dove headfirst into the question. "Of course, yes, it's just, there's an order things go in. Career, house, wedding, baby number one. I mean, we need to do Europe first, while we can, and..."

They were all exchanging smirks as Allie talked, to mock her need for order and having the next five years all charted out in daily planners. It was a running joke. Cohen and Matt apologized every Christmas Day that neither of them could find daily planners for years beyond the coming year. *Can you believe they won't make a 2005 daily planner until late 2004! I mean, what about people who are thinking 2005 in 2003?* One year, 2003, Cohen and Matt got together and handmade her a 2006 agenda for a joke.

"...babies are expensive, hence wanting the student loans and car paid off. And how many parents can flee to Europe, backpacking it for a month?..."

But Cohen's eyes were on Matt now. As his daughter talked about her future, Matt shifted uncomfortably. Not awkwardly—he was smiling and laughing along, louder than anyone else—but uncomfortably. Someone would have to have known Matt, as well as Cohen had, to see the fidgeting. It was like a lie was trapped in his body and bouncing around in there. Creaking in his skin. Itching. The further into her future Allie got, in explaining why they weren't married yet, the more Matt's face tightened, and the more he stretched his toes up, off his sandals, and plunked them back down, over and over, like he did whenever he talked about his dead wife. Cohen looked at Allie, to draw her attention to her father's odd postures, but she wouldn't have noticed it anyway. She saw what she wanted to see.

Later that day, Matt was waiting outside the washroom when Cohen came out. He put a hand on his shoulder, his warm breath smelled like peanuts, and he whispered. "This is the engagement ring I gave Kristen."

EVERY LITTLE THING

He was being secretive, occasionally looking over his shoulder as he uttered, "It would mean a lot to Allie, I think. Though maybe she'll want her own, something more fashionable or contemporary or whatever, but I—"

"My God, no. She'll love it! She will. She's already said she wants one just like it, honestly. This ring is right up Allie's alley. Very thoughtful of you—"

"Yes, well...she'll recognize the ring without you having to tell her. I know that much. When Allie was eight or nine, she used to steal her mother's engagement ring, this one," Matt looked at it in his hand, "off our dresser. She'd tuck tissues between her bony little finger and the ring so it'd stayed in place. She'd wrap herself up in silk scarves and pretend she was a princess. Had a name for herself. Delilah, or Danine or something." He got lost in thought and looked a little upset that he couldn't be sure of the name. "I thought I'd give you the option of giving her this one, instead of buying one."

"No, this is great, saves me a few grand!" He laughed. He laughed the way men do, to water down emotion in a sentimental conversation. And normally Matt would have laughed at his comment. Instead he laid the ring in Cohen's open hand, tossed it there really, and turned to walk down the hall.

Cohen speed walked after him. "Matt, wait up? You know that was a joke, right? This will mean the world to Allie, and it means a lot to me you've put this ring in my hand."

When Matt turned around, he was more himself again already. Just like that. Smiling. "Yes, well, it's great you think she'll like this ring."

Cohen said, like he'd seen a ghost, "Of course, Matt. Of course."

Matt kept walking down the hall, towards the patio door.

Cohen watched Matt through the open blinds, as he put his hands on Allie's shoulders. He stood behind her, re-joining the boisterous conversation. Allie making his parents laugh, slap the table. They loved her as much as Cohen did.

Allie put her hands on Matt's hands and turned to look up at him. "Tea or Coffee, Dad?" She nodded to the kettle and coffee carafe on the table.

Cohen's cellphone went off in his pocket. He jumped in fright, before realizing it was just his phone. Everyone turned and looked at him. Standing there in the window like a stranger.

It was Lee on the phone. For a man his age, his voice could rattle and boom in a way you had to brace yourself for. Cohen wasn't ready for it, so he let it ring a few times, taking a deep breath, like he was getting ready for a marathon run. Lee would call Allie, once a week, to hit her up for more photos, and Allie wouldn't need to put him on speaker phone for Cohen to hear him from across the room. His deep voice busting out of the receiver as if it were his own bullhorn. *You're my hot seller this week! I'm fresh out of your photos. The table's scant, can't have it!* Allie would always offer to bring out a month's worth, but Lee liked seeing her, and she him, so there were weekend runs, and Cohen often joined them. They'd eat lunch, insult each other, laugh.

His phone had rung five times, as he stared at Lee's flashing number, and his father shouted, "You gonna answer that or what!"

He pointed to the phone, shouted through the window. "It's Lee!"

A collective Oh! from the table. Understanding laughter. Allie looking at him, laughing, but watching to make sure he'd answer. Her eyes had always gone soft for Lee—her vintage war vet BFF, fifty years her elder—and he loved her for it.

"Hello?"

"Cohen. It's L-Lee. Need your help."

"What, you? You don't say!"

"I'm serious, and this favour's not optional! I have a bird. It's been shot. In the wing. But survived. A murre." There were sounds of panic going off in the background, like thumping and helicopter blades. "I found the sucker washed ashore on the beach. Like a wrecked ship. I scooped it up. How soon can you come? *Jesus!*"

"What?"

"It's poking at me!"

"No, I mean *What*, like, are you serious!"

"I figured you'd know where to bring the poor thing? Hold on a sec!" Lee covered the receiver with the palm of his hand. Everything sounded muffled. He heard, *Calm down you stubborn bitch, or I'll break your other wing!* and then the scratches and muffling were gone and Lee was back. "It's in my bathtub. I just tossed it in my bathtub and ran for my life! One minute, it's calm as anything, the next it's trying to bust through the walls. I dunno what to do here! Bring some sedatives and take this psychotic bastard away!"

"It's Sunday! I'm at my parents' place, with Allie, we're—"

"Try telling the bird that. The fucker is the size of a penguin, and it's all riled up and scaring the shit out of me. Have you ever heard one of these things agitated? It sounds more like dog—"

"And it's not like. You don't get it. Every time you call. It's not like I can just go and steal sedatives from my employer's lab every time you rescue—"

"Fuck ya then! And hang on a sec, I'm going back in..."

There were more sounds of struggle, like Lee was choking the bird: it squealed like a gull and then growled like a cat, and then Lee hung up. He hung up knowing Cohen would come deal with it. Like he'd dealt with it the last two times this happened. The last time, a few weeks before this call, the bird, a boreal owl, was lying dead in Lee's tub by the time he got there. It had been attacked by *some hiker's dog*, Lee figured, and he convinced Cohen to bury it out back. *I'm too old to be out digging in that half-frozen earth. You came all the way out here,* he handed him a shovel, *Make yourself useful!*

So Cohen went to help Lee, again. He rang the doorbell and heard Lee stumbling towards him. Cursing and swearing and kicking things out of his way. "Coming!"

He opened the door with a panicked but playful grin on his face. "Well, thank Jesus you're here!" He had the bird tucked under his left armpit so it couldn't get free. "Jab the bastard, quick!" He turned his head away as he stuck the bird out towards Cohen.

"Lee. Relax. There's no jabbing, no needle." He showed him a capsule in his hand.

"What's...are you *kidding* me? No needle? You brought *pills?*"

"I brought sodium amobarbital. It's enough to knock out a duck, and I'm hoping it'll do the trick here."

"Hoping?"

"Just. Take the bird back into the bathroom. Lay it down. It's freaking out because you're handling it. You've got your goddamn arm around its neck. What do you expect?"

"It bites when I let go! What do *you* expect?"

Laughing, "I grabbed some feed. I'm gonna lace the feed. Go put the damn bird back in the bathroom. We'll lock it in there with the drugged feed. It'll eventually eat it. I hope. And the drugs take about fifteen minutes—"

"You *hope?*" Shaking his head. "You should've brought a needle-administered drug. Something we could've jabbed it with. Get the job done." He stabbed an imaginary knife into the bird's neck, to emphasize how easy it would've been.

"Lee...that's not how it works. And I'll probably get in shit for taking what I took from the lab, by the way. It's not even legal, really, what we're up to here. These are *controlled substances.* I have no legal right to have this on me. Do you get that? I have stolen a controlled substance, and you're pretty well strangling an injured bird. We're up to no good here."

"What do you mean, *up to no good*! I'm saving a poor fucking animal's life here!" Lee looked down at the bird and laughed a little. "You're a good man to have come. Sorry I ruined your—" The bird started jerking around under Lee's arm again, yelping, sounding more like a growling cat than a bird. It swung its neck back and plunged its beak into Lee's belly. Lee winced like he'd been shanked. "See! See that! One minute it's fine, the next it's a madman! *Go!* Do your thing!"

"Sorry you ruined my what? My five-year anniversary?"

"No I didn't, did I?" He was running off to the bathroom, cradling the panicked bird. "Drug the food! Get to it!" And then he stopped and turned around, stopped walking. "Is this son of a bitch gonna attack me when I let go of it, to lay it in the tub?"

"I dunno, but it's not like you can keep it in your arms forever, right?"

COHEN DISSOLVED THE sodium amobarbital in water, mixed it in with the grainy feed, and laid the bait in the bathroom, hoping it wasn't too much sedative. He wasn't going to bury another bird in Lee's backyard. Two was enough. Three would be an unsanctified graveyard.

When he came back into the kitchen, Lee was buckled over in pain and leaning against a wall: one palm flat against it, the other arm dangling like it didn't know where to be. And then that arm clutched his back, like a ghost had swung a baseball bat. He steadied himself. "Been getting these quick blasts of pain in my back. Brutal. I'm falling apart. You want a cup of tea?"

"Lee, I don't know about that."

· "What? Tea? The bird's going to be a while isn't it—"

"No, the random back pain."

"I'm eighty-odd-years old. I'm lucky I'm not senile and pissing myself."

"Doesn't mean you shouldn't go to a doctor. How long's that been happening?"

"Drop it, Mom. I've been a little under the weather. Fevers and that. It's nothing. Yesterday, the flashes of pain, they were all over my lower back, and now they're not. Whatever it is, it's getting better. Do you want tea or what?"

"Yes. And for God's sake, leave the bag in longer than you usually do. Just as well you drank hot water, the way you make tea."

"Whatever." He put the kettle on the stove.

"You know you can buy plug-in kettles these days, right? They boil the water faster."

"The water doesn't get as hot. What's wrong with your generation? Everything has to be faster, sooner, now! What's wrong with pausing the day, and making a big production about a cup of—" And this time the pain was bad enough to hurt, to shut him up. It cut his words off and sent him running in circles around the kitchen table, swearing his head off. He had one hand pressing into his back and the other flapping like he was trying to take flight.

"Lee, c'mon. I'll go grab the bird and we'll head back to town. You should get to a hospital."

Banging a fist off the countertop. "It's just something passing through."

"Through what, *your spine?*"

"It's not my spine. It's...*Jesus!*" And he fell into a chair clutching at his back. "It's right here."

"That's your kidney, not your back. This isn't good. You need to get to a hospital, or I'll tell Allie, and she'll come take you there herself."

He put a finger to his lips, took it away, and started rocking in his chair. "No offense, but shut up. I can't take hearing someone's voice when I'm in pain. Go check on the bird!"

Cohen shook his head, and walked off to the bathroom. The bird was unconscious and still breathing. He sat on the edge of the tub and gently picked it up and laid it in his lap: the wings falling open and unfolding like decorative fans. Its neck slung backwards and spilled over his knees, slowly rocking back and forth like a pendulum. Its chest bulged out, rising and falling. He scooped its head up as Lee appeared in the doorway.

"To be honest, the pain never really goes away. It just goes between bearable and really bad. Yesterday, I sat upside down in a chair because it was the only position I could get into that made the pain go away. And when I go to piss, it's like my tubes are all tied up. Don't know how else to explain it. It's like I can feel—"

Not looking up at Lee, and running a knuckle between the bird's eyes. "You've got kidney stones."

Lee went silent. Winced. Knew what that meant. Birthing stones through his dick. Cohen looked up and saw Lee processing the pain to come. "Just because you can sedate a bird doesn't mean you're a doctor. And what the hell are you rubbing its eyes for?"

"I'm aging it. Mature murres, they have a bony ridge between their eyes, and this guy doesn't. This one's immature. It takes years for a murre to mature, and that slow rate of reproduction is what makes them susceptible to getting wiped out in..." He looked up and Lee was entirely not listening. He had his hand on his back, staring at his toes, his face flushed with a fever. He had a look on his face like maybe Cohen was right, he should head to a hospital. A look like a man who really didn't want to piss kidney stones.

"Lee. If you don't go and get those stones blasted with one of those sonic blaster machines at a hospital, they're going to be even more excruciating to pass. Pack a bag. Come into town. Crash on my and Allie's couch, before and after the hospital is done with you. I'll call Allie, to meet us at the hospital. I'll drop you off, and I'll go deal with this bird. We both know that's what Allie is going to arrange if I pick up the phone and call her, so don't fight with me about it. Don't end up pissing out a kidney stone the size of a grape when the hospital can blast them up into," he laughed, "something more...manageable. Like a grape *seed*."

Lee nodded his head. "I can handle a few grape seeds, but definitely not a whole fuckin' grape."

RISE
TO A FALL

THERE WAS ANOTHER weeknight phone call to come watch the stars with Matt. Decipher them. Except it wasn't that at all. Matt opened his front door, to let Cohen in, and almost fell into Cohen's arms.

"Come in," he said, and he walked them to the back door. Matt pointed to a cupboard as they walked through the kitchen, "Take a glass. I have some wine poured. Bunch of stuff poured. Whatever you want." He felt around for the door handle like he was blind and trusted his hands more than his eyes. It took him three tries to grab hold of it. "I'm going to need your help with something. I'm going to need, n-need you to say yes."

He took Cohen out back and there was a bottle of Jameson's, a bucket of ice, and a bottle of red wine, but it was empty. He waved a hand over the top of the bottles, *Take your pick*, and he fell into the chair like he wanted to break it. Cohen wanted to leave before he knew why; before Matt said something Matt couldn't take back. And Matt was too drunk and distressed to gently ease Cohen into the news.

"This. I—I mean—" Matt stopped talking to pour a drink, even though he'd just laid a full one by his chair, and forgot about it. Didn't even notice when he knocked it over with an errant foot.

"Are you..."

"No. I'm not okay. Not at all. Are you? Are *you* happy?"

"Yes—"

"And what does that mean to you, Cohen? That you're fucking *happy*? What does that take?"

"I don't know, I don't feel like there's anything missing in my life. I'm content that way, but what's—what's going on, Matt?"

Matt stood up, grabbed his telescope off its stand, and swung it like a golf club at a can of beer in the grass, driving it into a neighbour's yard.

Cohen got up and grabbed Matt by his wrist, yanking him back to his chair. "What are you doing? What's going on here?" He sat Matt down as a light came on above the neighbour's patio door. A woman turtle-headed her face out of the doorframe and looked around.

Matt looked at Cohen, steely, "Can you *guarantee* me you'll make her world feel right? My daughter's? Don't crap out on her, the way men do, years into a relationship. She's—"

"Matt, c'mon. Back up. What's going on?" For some reason, Cohen imagined it having to do with Allie. Something she couldn't bear to tell Cohen herself: that she's got Lou Gehrig's disease now, something degenerative a man might run from, or that she cheated. "Is Allie alright? Are you?"

"Everything's wrong!" He grabbed at his drink again. Big, consecutive gulps, and his throat looked like he was guzzling baseballs.

"Give me one specific thing—"

"One, *hah!*"

"Yes. One. Let's start there."

"How about pancreatic cancer? How about esophageal cancer? Or is that *two* things? I'm sorry, is that *two* things, or is that the same thing?" He was throwing the words at Cohen like buckets of cold water, like stones. "I'm dying. I've got cancer. Bad. My pancreas. My esophagus. It's...everywhere." He rubbed a hand up and down his chest, tracing the warpath of the cancer treading through him.

A tear dangled from Matt's chin, but Cohen hadn't seen it form, never saw it slide down his face, and Matt's eyes weren't red. His voice was not shaky, it was notably steady. So maybe it wasn't a tear.

He was coldly certain and matter of fact about his plan. "I'm dying and you can't tell my daughter. We went through this shit, together, with her mother, and she won't be going through it again. Not with me." He shook his head, determined, settled on it. "Matt, statistically, we...cancer is how most people...it's not...I don't...want to be—"

"*Sta-tis-tically, hey?*" Matt batted the word away with a hand. He reclined in his chair, shaking his head more than necessary.

"She saw her mother *die*, slowly, day after day, night after *fucking* night, and I watched her watch every bit of it. Buckling knees and eyes wet with tears, and you're talking statistics? Have you watched a person you love do that? Die a little more every day, for half a year? Allie could take that pain once a day, but after twenty days. After forty slaps in the face. Sixty. Ninety." He stopped, let out a big sigh punctuated by a drunkard's belch.

"Fuck your *sta-tis-tics*, Cohen. I'm talking effects here, emotional damage. I'm talking about how her mother was a bottomless hole, and pieces of Allie were falling into Kristen as Allie stood over her crying." Matt tapped his chest three times as he said *pieces of Allie*. "Or it was like her mother needed to take some of her daughter with her, wherever she was going." He looked up at Cohen. "She's not the same now. You don't realize that, because you never knew her before her mother died. Her eyes dried out, I dunno. There's less life there now. The glow's gone, the sheen's been rubbed off." And he wiped his own eyes with the palm of a hand. "She used to paint too, did you know that? Always going around with globs of paint matted into her hair and her clothes and her face and everything. It was beautiful, somehow, seeing your daughter so passionately lost and engrossed in something, that she'd skip meals or she'd run out for food not caring how she looked. But...*Pfft.*" He threw his hands up in the air like an explosion.

Matt straightened up in his chair. Unnaturally perfect posture. "It'd be too much for her to lose both parents that way. That's what I'm saying. I won't watch her watching me go. I won't do that."

Matt was too drunk or he was desperately sad. But he wasn't Matt Crosbie. He wasn't *there*. A harder man was. A clumsier man: waves of his drink splashed from his glass and over his jeans whenever he moved.

"If you're sick, Matt...she...she has to know. She *will* know. You'll be in hospital and she'll be camped out in a chair next to you. Or you'll be at our house, and we'll be there for you, with you. You're scared, and you're worried for Allie, and that's perfectly natural."

Staring at the fence, not Cohen, not even the fence really, just staring. "Not the case. She has to see me die, but she doesn't have to see me die of cancer, not over the course of however long this takes."

Cohen was heartbroken. Words were catching in his throat like sticks, choking him. He was trying to keep up with the conversation on top of processing Matt's cancer: that Matt was going to *die*. His jaw felt like a struck bell, and the weight of the news made him realize how much he'd come to love this man. "What are you saying, Matt?" His throat was dry in the way it gets before tears. "And how long have you known? I mean, *Jesus*." Shaking his head, not knowing what to do with his hands, freefalling still. "How long—"

"Look. I have a plan. I've thought it through. It's best for me, and it's best for my daughter." He looked away from the fence and poured another drink, missing the glass at first. Puddles all over the tabletop. "I've made up my mind about this. You're going to have to help me. For me, and for my daughter."

"*Matt!*" Cohen leaned forward and waited for Matt to look him in the eyes, and their eyes crashed. "If you're saying what I think you're saying, no. You don't get to kill yourself." He wiped his palms on his jeans. "She won't understand suicide. She won't understand *why* you did it. She'll spend forever grappling with that, not understanding that, and I'll fucking tell her why, Matt, that you had cancer, so you killed yourself, so what'll be the point of...of—" He just shook his head, *no. Don't.*

Matt looked up at Cohen like a handful of salt in the eye. Cohen blinked and one tear fell out of each eye, racing each other down his cheeks.

"Because she won't have had to sit and watch me die. That's why. And I'm not talking suicide. I'm talking about an accident."

Matt slid up in his chair and said, "You can tell her what you want after it's done. But if you tell her before it's done, and I love you, Cohen, I do, but if you tell my daughter beforehand, it's a war between us, do you understand? Are we clear on that?" He glared at Cohen until Cohen nodded yes. "I don't want any trouble between us, and I don't want this to be any harder than it's gonna be. Allie wouldn't understand. She'd want me to fight it, fight the cancer like it's a bad flu. All throughout Kristen's struggle I watched the look on Allie's face, like there was still some hope, even after her mother's eyes had sunk back into her skull. Even when she stopped eating and food had to be pumped into her. But you don't know that. *I* do. There are parts of my daughter's life you'll never know like her father does. Things about her you won't understand. She'll believe I can fight it. I can't. There's nothing to fight, just a mess of pain. She'll say, *but we can go through this together*, spend those last few weeks together, and I don't want to feel like an asshole for denying her that."

"But you're okay with putting me in this position to lie? To live with keeping this from her? To know I helped," he waved his hands around, at a loss for words, "with this?"

"Look. Sorry. And it's not all about Allie here. I don't want to die slowly, painfully. In agony, waiting to go. That's my choice to make. I'm asking you to respect *that*. And yes, I'm asking you to trust that I know what's best for my daughter. You have to trust that. You'll have your own kid someday, you'll understand. This is too much, I know, but I'm gonna tell you my plan and you're role in it...."

Cohen had his face held in one hand, and tears were piling up along the fingers he had spread across his face. Matt couldn't look at him once the tears had started. Their eyes were opposing magnets. And Cohen's hand felt like it was sinking into his face. No plan Matt was about to share was going to feel any less harsh than jamming a shotgun down Matt's throat and blowing a hole in the back of his neck.

HE PULLED HIS car over, halfway home from Matt's house, under a tortured-looking oak tree on someone's yard. He turned off his headlights and the windshield wipers. There was rainwater on every window, and the wind was blowing it the way a carwash does. Streetlights splashing yellow across his dashboard, and sometimes a passing car would spray his with the red of brake lights. He was cold and he liked it. Puffs of air when he breathed out. Condensation on the windows, and he was drawing in it: thoughtlessly, mindlessly, circles.

He couldn't go back home that night because he wouldn't know how to look at Allie or what to say when she'd ask, *How's Dad?* He couldn't look at her without thinking about *how* he was looking at her. He wouldn't be able to talk to her without considering the tonality of his words. Matt's news, and his expectation of Cohen's compliance, had flatlined his voice and his facial expressivity. Allie would see and hear that, ask what's wrong, and he didn't want to lie. Not right to her face like that. It

y

CHAD
PELLEY
80

was the first time he had to keep his thoughts so far away from her. The only way he knew how was to physically distance himself. Parked there, by the curb. Teeth chattering. He sat in his car, alone, with thoughts of Matt's death, and how it might change everything. He pictured Allie at the wake, crumbling in his arms, wondering what parts of her she'd bury along with her father. What parts of her would go out like busted lights.

The rain was falling harder now; galloping horses on his bonnet. Violent claps. He went to drive home, but he couldn't. The car was running, his foot on the pedal, gently pressing it to hear something other than his thoughts. A mild revving of the engine. Soothing, somehow. He pulled his cellphone out of his pocket. Opened it and closed it. Laid it on the dashboard and picked it back up. Dialled her number and talked too formally. "Allie, sorry to wake you up. Hi. Listen. Matt and I, we had a few more drinks than I realized. I should sleep here."

"Drinks? It's a Tuesday night."

"I know. It just...happened."

"But I need the car, to get to my eight o'clock meeting, remember—"

"I know, sorry. Just happened. I'll be home. In the morning. In time for you to get to work with the car. Promise. Sorry. Then I'll get a cab to work."

"Are you all right? You're talking weird, and you sound like you're crying. Are you two watching sappy chick flicks again?"

"No, just whispering. Your dad's asleep. On the couch. Don't want to wake him."

A soft, warm giggle from her tired body. She could alter his temperature with that laugh. "You two are so cute together. Goodnight. Love you. Set an alarm so I'm not late for work!"

He closed his cellphone and shook his head. No one there to see it shaking. He'd been with Allie more than five years, and that was the first time he'd felt awkward talking to her.

He turned his car around, went banging on Matt's door, and then he did get drunk. Too drunk. They were standing in the hallway, Cohen refusing to "join him out back," but not leaving either. So it was a heated standoff in the hallway. He'd looked at Matt—his eyes so wet, the lights behind Matt looked like stars—and he said: *You're a fucking idiot.* And he meant it. He'd screamed it. He was clutching a wine bottle so tight his fist tingled and went numb.

He had to have loved that man, to have, in that moment, hated him so thoroughly. This man who'd given him Allie, and lessened the loss of Ryan, all those years ago. This man who'd enlightened him, all those nights he'd come over, for years, shaping Cohen in ways maybe his own father hadn't shaped him. That hate was sorrow: resentment at the thought of losing him. That hate was having to lie to Allie.

THE NEXT MORNING came. The alarm clock on the coffee table like a drill doing damage. A red digital display flashing *7:00, 7:00, 7:01*. The smell of coffee and the sound of it percolating. Lying on the couch, staring straight ahead, he saw Matt's scrawny bare legs go by. Matt fell into the loveseat across from him. His bony knees pointing at Cohen like accusations.

"Got time for a coffee before you go?"

"I'm not sure I have much to say, Matt, other than you're asking too much of me. And Allie needs the car, pronto. This isn't happening. Not the way you laid it out last night." He sat up, threw the blanket off himself, and rubbed the side of his head that ached the most.

"Fair enough, but I think we owe each other some apologies, and my clock's ticking. I have cancer. Best say our sorries before it's too late?" And maybe only Matt Crosbie would make that joke at that moment, at a time like that, and maybe only Cohen Davies would get it, and take it as apology.

"That was just you drunk last night, working through it in your head, right? You're not serious about this plan of yours?"

Matt got up, walked away.

COHEN BROUGHT THE car back to Allie. He walked towards the front door with his head down, dragging legs heavier than barrels, afraid of how visibly Matt's news had altered the set of his face.

She was waiting in the porch to greet him. "I made you some breakfast," she'd said, and she hooked an arm around his neck, kissed his lips. "I love you. I love how good you are to my poor old father."

He kept his head down as she hugged him. He kept his eyes away from hers. His tongue felt clipped, numb, so he said nothing back to her. He held her close enough to feel her pulse bouncing off his cheek. She smelled like caramel in the mornings. A hair product, or a bath product, he was never quite sure, but that smell was always gone by noon.

He ran a hand up the back of her shirt to feel her skin and ran a finger down her rocky spine, letting the bumps of her spinal cord drum against his fingertips and course through him. It was how he calmed himself, that motion. He went to kiss her, but she got shy. "Lee's here! The kidney stones, remember?" she whispered, slapping his hand off her breast. "He's in the kitchen. Go get your breakfast!"

ALLIE WENT TO work, but Cohen called in sick from the phone in his bedroom. Turned out it wasn't the kind of day he could: nineteen five- to ten-year-olds had their lunchboxes packed, expecting a man to take them on a hike and talk about birds and bugs and wildflowers and how pitcher plants grew near bogs, but irises grew near fresh water. No one else at the Avian-Dome could do that the way he could. The kids' parents had already paid.

"Cohen. How bad is it? I mean, can you come in for the two-hour hike and go back home? Please? Never mind the rest of it today, Justin can take care of the COSEWIC presentation this afternoon. But, the kids, that's, I mean, some of them are already here for Christ's sake. Their little hiking boots on, all laced up. Suzie Gardener's kid bought new hiking shoes *just* for today. You know? She *just* showed them to me."

So he went into work. Had to. Had to smile and pretend and educate. He was even a little jealous. They'd all seen a blue jay, and that blue jay would be all they thought about for the rest of the day. Excitement at something so small and trivial. One kid claimed he saw a parrot. Entirely impossible for Atlantic Canada. Just as well he'd said he'd seen a gorilla, riding an elephant. Normally Cohen would have explained that, explained that parrots only lived in warmer, tropical places. Some days, if the kids were bright enough or interested enough, he'd even explain *why*. But he left it alone. He let the kid believe in something impossible while the kid, being a kid, still could.

EVERY LITTLE THING

WHEN HE GOT back home, noon-ish, Lee was asleep on the couch. Snoring. Snoring like there was something wrong with his lungs. The history channel blaring about Vietnam, "...*the gruesome, decades-long aftermath of Agent Orange.*"

The hospital had dismissed Lee, but Allie wanted to keep him overnight. Just in case. Ever-precautious. Ever-caring. Tender. Ever-loving. All traits that one too many emotional blows could beat right out of a person, and he was getting worried about that. About how Matt's sudden death might change her, the woman he loved and didn't want changed in any way. It seemed selfish, like his thoughts should be with Matt, not Allie, not how his death might destroy something about the way she laughed or put her clothes on in the morning.

He went upstairs, into his bedroom, sat on his bed, and called Matt.

"Look. We were both drinking last night. We said some crazy things. You can't *possibly* be serious. About. Suicide—"

Matt hung up.

Cohen called him back.

"I'm serious, Matt. I'm not sure if this is right or wrong... what we're doing behind her back. She can handle the truth—"

"Some things don't get to be right or wrong."

"She can handle the truth. Are you listening to me? She's a goddamn rock, stronger than both of us combined—"

"I'm not going to lay in a fucking hospital bed, rotting into a corpse, while Allie snaps those morbid photos of me like she did with her mother. That was...*sick*. See. You think she's strong, and she is, but I'm her *father*, don't you *get* that? There is no...*being strong enough* for that."

"No, there's not, but every day, everywhere on earth, hundreds of people watch loved ones die of cancer. I don't mean to be insensitive. I mean to be frank."

"I'm not talking about hundreds of people. I'm talking about Allie, and what's best for my daughter. Fuck. For me too. This is not how I'm going to die, and that's not up to you."

"But your plan is—it's sick, man. You can't expect me not to tell her, the second she comes home today. I'm giving you a choice. You tell her, soon, or I do."

Matt hung up again. Cohen called him a *fuckin kid* and threw the phone to the foot of his bed. Laid down. Put an arm over his eyes to block out the sun that was punching through the window.

The phone rang again, and he thought about not answering it. "You weren't there when her mother died. That's the part you need to understand. Allie spent days, in her bed, un-showered, not eating. She cried until she threw up. Her last boyfriend left her when she became a woeful chore, did you know that? She stayed in her pajamas all day. She lost her job. Her grad work suffered. She came around, but not all the way around. I mean, fuck, she sat outside the funeral home, on a park bench in the rain, crying so hard it was all anyone could hear."

"I get it, Matt!"

"She sat in her car during her own mother's funeral, Cohen. Did she ever tell you that? That she left me sitting next to an empty plastic chair?"

"Yeah, because her mother died. Not because her mother had cancer. How do you think finding you hanging from a fuckin noose is gonna be any easier on her!"

"I told you. It'll look like an accident. Me driving off the cliff, some rainy night. I've scoped out the section of the road. I can get in behind a guardrail. I've told you this. Sudden. Boom. Gone. No extended, belaboured heartbreak."

Minutes passed without either of them talking.

"I'm very sorry I've dragged you into this, Cohen. I was weak. It was a weak moment. But it's too late now. This is between me and my daughter, and my dying wish is that you keep your mouth shut. Because this is none of your business anymore, and I'll not forgive you, and I'll do it anyway, and your telling Allie won't have changed a thing except causing her more torment. I'm talking like a villain here, a real asshole, but I'll be that villain for my daughter. That's my point. That I'm doing this for her, and it's between me and her, and I'm sorry I filled you in, drunk, last night."

Cohen sank his toes deep in carpet. Speechless. He slid his feet back and forth over the carpet until the friction burned. "Did it...help. That you told me? Did it help, serve some purpose, for you?"

"Yes. It did. It was a lot to keep to myself, and I don't have a lot of people in my life. And I love you, kid, I do."

Cohen spent another speechless minute curling his toes in

and out of the carpet. "*Cancer*. I mean...c'mon. How cliché."

A joke, but neither of them laughed.

THAT NIGHT IN bed, he watched the elastic flick of the clock's arm jutting from one second to the next and the long pull of the minute hand from 57 to 58 to 59 to midnight. Allie was asleep, her head nuzzled in between his shoulder blades, her arm tossed over his torso and tucked under his ribcage like a seatbelt.

When she'd wake throughout the night, she'd trace little circles on his collarbone before drifting off again. He'd feel little puffs of air on his back because she breathed through her nose when asleep, but through her mouth in those moments between sleep. When she wasn't there, if she was away for work, or if he spent the night at Lee's or Matt's, he found it hard to fall asleep without the weight of her on him.

He slipped out from under her that night, and turned to look at her before stumbling down the hall to the bathroom. More asleep than awake, he'd forgotten Lee was in the house, and he jumped at the sound of rustling cutlery in the kitchen. He found Lee at the table with a cup of tea in his fist, steam puffing out, and two pieces of toast with blueberry jam.

"Shit!" He ducked as he whispered it. "I didn't wake you, did I?"

Cohen shook his head and grabbed a mug for himself. He put it back and grabbed another one, a bigger one. He had an odd habit of looking inside a mug for collected dust and then rinsing the mug out, whether it was dusty or not. He checked the kettle, and it had enough water left in it to pour himself a cup of Earl Grey. He popped two slices of bread in the toaster.

"I can't sleep some nights," Lee told Cohen. "Most nights, really."

Cohen took his tea to the table and fell into his chair. He rested his forearms flat against the table and encircled the base of his mug with his thumbs and forefingers. He stared at the mug for a minute and said nothing.

"You...all right, kid?"

He looked up at Lee, and with no lead-in, asked him, "The men you've seen...go. Back in the Philippines. In the war. Like, in the prisoner camps. Before they died, were they...thinking clearly, near the end, once they...*knew?*"

Lee was jarred by the question and scrunched up his face. "I'm not sure what you're asking me, kid."

Shifty eyes. Both of them. And Cohen felt rude, or bold, for asking Lee to go back to the war, mentally, and think about it.

"I'm asking you if you think a man facing death can think clearly or if his judgement is clouded?"

A sip of tea each and Lee said, "He told you, didn't he? Matt, I mean. The cancer."

"You...know about Matt?"

Lee's head slung down like Cohen's question mark had cracked his neck. He shook his head and he bit his lip. Hard. "I fucking told him to leave you out of this shit. I told that son of a bitch that if he dragged you into this mess, I'd kill him myself." His head, lowered now, was still shaking.

Cohen's toast popped up and he left it in the toaster. He sat there, staring at Lee.

"...he showed up at my door a month ago. His eyes burning red and too much alcohol on his breath to've been driving, if you ask me. He..."

Cohen stopped listening. He tuned out when Lee said Matt had shown up at his door a *month* ago. He wondered what it was that had festered in Matt for a month—*a month*—that made Matt feel the need to tell Cohen about his plan as well. It could have been uncertainty, like he needed someone to talk him out of it after, Lee gave the plan a thumb's up. Or maybe fear and loneliness had him rambling. His guess was that Lee had not given Matt the reaction Matt had wanted, so Matt told Cohen too. And now Cohen started wondering if he had reacted the way Matt needed. If not, Matt had told him for no reason.

The mug was thin and hot against the palm of his hand. He squeezed it harder. To feel the burn. He thought about getting up to get the toast; if he even wanted the toast. Since the night Matt had told Cohen about the cancer and his sick plan, Cohen was constantly aware of all the trivial things people mentally process in the run of a day: what kind of jam to use, what pair of underwear to put on, whether or not to run the yellow light. It made him aware of how much of his days were littered with trivial thoughts that really didn't matter.

DRIVE-BY

COHEN WAS GAINING weight in prison. The sedentary lifestyle and the lack of sleep made it easy. Outdoors, in the recreation area, there was a cluster of tubular exercise equipment that looked like a child's playground. The equipment was bright blue, and the paint looked like it should have been chipped more, to be in a prison yard. It sat outside in a town that rained and rained but the equipment looked brand new and free of rust. The machines were all one piece, with no detachable parts that inmates could use as weapons. If no one was using one of the stations, Cohen would.

There was something called a hack squat, and it took watching someone else use it, to figure out how it worked. It was a flat platform, at forty-five degrees to the ground, with weights on a sliding mechanism. He had to scrunch down, get under those weights, then thrust upward, over and over, until his abs turned to steel, threatening to buckle, or until his legs turned to water. He liked the motion of it, up and down, with a relaxed sense of purpose. And because it was at a forty-five degree angle to the ground, he saw nothing but sky. Calm birds, content clouds. Up and down, up and down, like the whole world was moving with him. The routine thrusting motion forced him to breathe the same way that psychiatrists tell their patients to breathe when they're having an anxiety attack. It was a calming push and lift, push and lift.

All the men around him would grunt and spit, almost getting off on torturing themselves with the equipment. Plunked there among criminals, hard men jailed for theft and violence or some other broken law—DUIs or cheating the taxman—Cohen thought more than once on how betrayal ranked so lowly in the eyes of the law. No one went to prison for adultery. And you could lie to someone so long as it wasn't to defraud them of money. Yet nothing in his life had burned Cohen more than Matt's betrayal. And eventually, Allie's. Betrayal was a mental wound; it had no clean way of closing over and healing well. Betrayal was a fire, burning, stoked by questions that had no answers. There was a daily need for a *why* that he'd never get, but always need.

"We'll go to this nice cabin B&B I know, just west of Grayton," Matt had said. "Just me and you and Allie."

"And why will we do that?"

"Me and you, kid, we need a nice weekend, to put all this arguing behind us. Plus, I want a weekend with my daughter. I never see the girl anymore, for any longer than a quick meal like tonight. I see you more than her, I'm sure of it."

It was a Sunday night and they were barbecuing at Cohen's place, waiting for Allie to get back from a deli with salads and dessert and wine.

"We've been arguing, going on two weeks now, and I'm tired of it. And I'm sorry." He grabbed Cohen, putting his hands on each of Cohen's shoulders to steady him and demand eye contact. Matt had a tong in his right hand, and it had clapped together with a metal ting. "You were right to talk me out of it. What I was going to do. And I owe you for that. For talking some sense into me. I'll pay. The weekend's on me. Food, booze...cabin rentals." He let go of Cohen's arms. Flipped the chicken breasts on the grill. Slathered on more honey. "And nothing settles tension like a weekend away."

The B&B that Matt had oversold them on was a dingy little place in the woods with hokey charm and poor water pressure. You could blare music and not worry about the neighbours. There were owls at night, hooting as they slept. They laughed and drank expensive wine, and when that ran out, they drank cheap rum. He remembers the weekend in isolated flashes and actions. In before and after.

They'd gotten to the bottom of the rum, and Cohen was drunk enough to be waltzing around a kitchenette with Matt to "After the Gold Rush." He remembers Matt twirling him around, and he caught a look at Allie laughing so hard that rum and Coke were shooting out of her nostrils. The fizzy burn had tears streaming out of her eyes.

Dabbing her eyes with her knuckles, "You can't waltz to that

89

song. It's not a waltzing song!" So Matt pulled him closer, to defy her logic. He was a wild drunk, in an endearing way.

They kept on waltzing, to put on a show for her. Intoxicated and uncoordinated, with their knees knocking together, they were stepping on each other's toes and laughing about it. They were trying to sing over each other, in terrible channellings of Neil Young. *I was thinking about what a friend had said, I was hoping it was a lie.*

And when "Only Love Can Break Your Heart" came on, Matt pushed Cohen away. Hard, in an exaggerated way, for fun. He stuck his hand out and said, "Can I have this dance with my daughter?" as if they were in a formal setting. She stood up, and he said, "Isn't she a pretty one?" and Cohen said he was going out for some air anyway. To cool down. And he'd made it outside just in time. His ribs tingling, his belly going in and out. He plunked down on the patio steps and dried his eyes with the bottom of his T-shirt. His belly exposed to sharp blades of air. He could hear Allie's laughter blending with Matt's, and he'd miss that. The sound of them together. The purity of Allie's laugh that Matt's death would steal or mar somehow. They were singing, belting it out, *Yes only love can break your heart, What if your world should fall apart?*

Matt had wanted this one last hurrah before the bad news broke his daughter's heart and changed the way she'd look at him. *Sit down, Allie. It's cancer. Too far gone.* They'd decided they'd both be there—for her, with her—when Matt told her he was dying. But they hadn't nailed down the date yet. *After the weekend getaway*, he'd promised Cohen. *Some night that week.*

As Cohen sat outside, listening to them sing and laugh and pour another drink, he thought that maybe the next half a year could go like this night was going, until Matt got too sick to sing and dance like they were doing now. It could've been a beautiful, prolonged goodbye. The three of them celebrating every day, that wasn't his last, until it was.

More cackles of laughter broke through the window. Each successive echo through the trees sounded gentler. They'd forgotten a line, in a verse, or one of them did, or they were arguing about who was right. Cohen cracked his throbbing jaw. Every day, since Matt had told him about the cancer, had felt like walking through sniper-filled streets. He was talking suicide, and they were talking about Allie never being the same again. Death, coming one way or the other, had strapped him with a free-floating anxiety that put firecrackers under his feet, every step he took, and it distracted him at work. He'd left a dissection kit out on a table: a bloody scalpel in reach of children. The kids would have to say *Mr. Davies* two or three time to get his attention and snap him out of a daydream: picturing Allie at the wake.

ALL NIGHT LONG it had been *drink up, drink up*, so that the hangover, the fatigue, kept Cohen and Allie in bed that Sunday morning. And waking up next to Allie, in her underwear, with an arm around her gym-disciplined body, in a bed that wasn't their own, made him see Allie in a different way than he did when waking up next to her in their own bed. It set off an instinctual lust for the half-naked woman beside him. They fucked, quietly, laughing, like *Don't wake him*, and, *This is wrong*. They'd gotten down on the ground because the bed was too noisy. It was fast and hard and to the point; her teeth sunk into her own fist to keep herself quiet.

They snuck out of their room, quietly, the giddy afterglow on their flush faces, hoping Matt was still asleep. Or down at the pond catching a trout. The night before, Matt had promised to catch them all some trout for breakfast, and they'd laughed it off as drunken promises. "I'm dead serious," he said. "You've never had anything like my bacon-wrapped, herb-stuffed trout for breakfast! Breakfast of the champions." He'd pointed to the counter. "What do you think I bought those lemons for?"

Cohen and Allie rounded the corner to the kitchen that morning, and saw that Matt had lived up to the promise. They came out, and there was a casserole dish, and in it: one big trout, slit down the middle, lemons and rosemary inside, the outside wrapped in bacon. A yellow sticky note, *Just re-heat! You're welcome. I'm outta here, left bright and early, to give you two the place for the day.*

"Jesus," Cohen said, concerned. "You don't suppose he heard us in there and took off?"

"Relax, tiger. That was hardly a marathon, no offense." She touched the fish with two fingers like she was taking its pulse. "Besides, the fish is cold. Not warm at all. He left a good hour ago, and like I said, that high-school shaggin' you just gave was

EVERY
LITTLE
THING

five minutes, tops." She laughed, grabbed two plates. "I've got shit to do before work tomorrow. Wanna just eat and run?"

"Well, no, actually. But, fine. We can leave right after I eat and shower."

She set the table, kissed him, said, *thanks*, and grabbed his dick, squeezed it once to get his attention. "Whatever got into you this morning, let it happen more." She let it go. Winked. Grabbed the orange juice and two glasses.

On the drive back home, he watched Allie, half napping, half taking in Grayton. The town she grew up in. The closed-down diner she used to work in as a teenager. The place where Lee usually set up his vendor table. "That's weird, that he's not at it today. He's getting too old for it I guess?"

"Maybe."

They rounded the mountain that took them to the highway, but had to slow down. An ambulance, two cop cars, a transport truck pulled over; its engine still running. There was some kind of red emergency vehicle with its lights still going.

Cohen knew. It was right where Matt had told him he planned to kill himself. His whole body felt like a struck gong. His stomach tied into pulsating knots, and his vision gone to TV static. Allie had just opened a pack of M&Ms and offered him some. He didn't answer. She looked up, and started patting his leg, *Pull over, pull over!*

Cohen's heart was beating too slow; he was too aware of his own heartbeat and heard it in his ears. A vibration throughout his body. He was rolling to a stop on the shoulder of the road, and Allie was panicking like somehow she knew too, "Stop! *Fucking* stop!"

She was too frantic to get her seatbelt off. When she opened her door, to run to the guardrail, it wasn't completely off and the blue seatbelt tugged against her, cutting a sob in half. Her squeal interrupted. He watched her, from the car, before getting out. His body feeling like a thousand pounds he couldn't lift. Allie's eyes went over the cliff, and he knew it was Matt's truck she saw down there. Cohen got out of the car as an officer approached her.

She fell into Cohen's arms, wailing. Her screams sounded so far away. "It's Dad! It's a black truck, Cohen, it's Dad!" and she went back to the cliff's edge, to watch two men being lowered down to the ocean; to the beach where Matt's truck lay upside down. An officer got to asking Cohen to leave the scene, but he switched gears when he heard Allie screaming, *It's Dad!*

The officer was asking Cohen questions, but Cohen was watching Allie and still feeling like a thousand pounds or a struck gong or like he had something to do with shoving Matt down over that cliff.

Allie was too close to the edge. Roaring, ripping her throat sore. *Dad!* Pause. *Dad!* Pause. *Da-had!* like maybe he was shouting back, but she couldn't hear him. The tips of her shoes were poking out over the edge, resting on nothing. Cohen went to her, leaving the officer's questions unanswered. He got to her and the look on her face was a knife in the guts. Desperation had ripped her face into a mask Cohen didn't recognize. There were lines everywhere, a topography of pain, and her whole body was shaking and red, especially her hands. She turned back to the cliff, took another step, and now half a shoe dangled over the cliff's edge.

Dad! Da-had!

He grabbed her by the elbow to haul her back to safety, but she fought against him, and he worried that if she broke free, with him pulling her back, she'd slingshot herself out of his grip and over the cliff.

"Allie, stop, if you break free—"

And she turned and grabbed his neck, nails like knives. She fell dead into him, all of her weight, and she weighed twice as much as the 130-pound body he'd held so many times before. Her body was ricocheting off his with breaths so fast no oxygen was getting in. Her hands were sliding all over him like she was swimming and he was a pond. Her howling into his ear felt like sticks thrust into his brain.

He wanted her pain. All of it. A thousand knives worth of it, sinking into him, so that she could at least cry slower and breathe right. Cohen peered over her shoulder at Matt's truck, eviscerated and struck dumb by the lie he'd bought. *We'll tell her, right after the weekend getaway.* He looked down at Matt's truck, and it was upside down with the ocean lapping its hood and windshield. From that height, the truck looked like a toy. The men, who'd been dangling from those bungee cords, had gotten to the truck now.

Allie couldn't talk to the emergency response unit. She went back to their car. She didn't get in front. She crawled into the backseat and lay there, in the fetal position, face down in the seat. Cohen wanted to curl into her, spoon her, but there was no room. He checked with the officers, and they needed nothing more from him or Allie, and Matt was confirmed dead on the scene. A necessary statement of the obvious. *Closure.* Just like Matt had wanted. His very word. *Allie will need closure. I've scoped out that section of the road. I can get in around that guardrail.*

She'd made no attempt to see his body. Or be the one to identify it. Cohen had to do that. He'd said *I'm the son-in-law, and she's his only blood family, and she doesn't need to see this.* He'd spared Allie that much, and he'd been living with the image of Matt's bashed-in chin: the splayed flesh dangling like icicles. The colour of fresh human bone nothing like he'd imagined. Dull, dirty. The sickest detail: Matt's left nostril was torn open, exposing a deep, cavernous hole.

Those men were only doing their job, Cohen knew that, but it seemed indignant and heartless of them to open a body bag and expose a man in that condition. To show a cracked shell of a man to a person who had loved that man. Even a photograph, to have shown Cohen a photograph instead of the real thing.

HIDDEN
SHOULDERS

COHEN'S MOTHER, NOT Cohen, played grief counsellor to Allie, and it didn't go unnoticed. Every time she'd start crying, his mother was there with a hug or some hands through her hair. *Tea? Can I make you some lunch?* One day in the kitchen, out of Allie's earshot, she asked Cohen what was wrong. She could tell something beyond Matt's death was bothering him. He shrugged his shoulders, *Nothing*. She eyed him judgmentally about that. There were two or three loose ends at work for Allie to deal with, before she could take some time off, and somehow, his mother found a way to sort that out for her too.

His mother had dealt with the funeral arrangements as well, because Cohen said he couldn't. She never questioned it. She nodded her head, *Leave it with me*. But part of him wanted her to pry, ask why, force a confession, draw the words from him. *He had cancer, that wasn't an accident, and he shouldn't be dead.*

The night of Matt's wake, he sat with his father at a small, two-seat table. He wanted to tell his father what he'd done, or helped get done, but he didn't. The hesitation, his wanting to tell his father, distracted him from being there for Allie. He wanted to tell his father, and he wanted his father's face to look appalled. He wanted his father to turn on him. Or he wanted someone to understand and reassure him that it was Matt's decision to make. That he'd made it, lied, and it was horrible of Matt to have wrecked Cohen like that, as part of his sick plan.

Matt's suicide had been too much to keep in, but now that days had passed, too much to share as well. The day of the funeral, as they lowered Matt into the dirt, Cohen cried harder than anyone. Too hard. And people stared.

They got in bed that night, and Allie knitted herself into him. Their body heat warmed the sheets as a window let in a shatterably crisp air. She cried hard once, but it was enough to soak the pillow, so they flipped it. He ran the backs of his knuckles up and down her ribs, and it soothed both of them. When he'd stop, she'd arch her back, *Don't stop*. Morning came and they did not go to work. Noon came, and they did not get up to eat lunch.

But months passed, and Allie healed far faster and better than Matt would have predicted. Her reaction to Matt dying so suudenly left Cohen wondering if Matt had been right about the sudden accident being easier on Allie than the weight of a prolonged, painful goodbye—watching her father bleed and vomit and hurt. Needing more help than she could give him.

In the months after his death, Allie would mourn her father, often, but she'd cry like he'd been a beautiful man she'd never forget, not like her life was missing something now, or there was a hole in her world she kept stepping in. She'd welcome the fond memories as they came to her. She'd pause for them. Re-live them. When they came, she might close her eyes to feel more there with him. Matt's death had cracked a fissure in her, but only in a way that let more life in. She took nothing for granted now: the taste of honey—not sugar—in her morning tea; the feel of an extra ten bucks for a more expensive pair of pajamas.

It was Cohen who found himself restless at nights, watching infomercials at 3 a.m. or spacing out at work. One night he watched back to back infomercials about the same set of kitchen knives until he could repeat the lines along with the blonde-haired bimbo selling them. Trying to sleep was fruitless, so he'd spare Allie the tossing and turning. For weeks, his dreams were about him missing something: Christmas dinner, the first day of school, stopping Matt's truck. And his brother was in his dreams more than ever. One night, he dreamt he was staring over the cliff at Matt's truck, and out of the corner of his eye, he saw Ryan walking along the guardrail as if it was a tightrope: his arms straight out like airplane wings to keep his balance. He knew that if he looked at Ryan, Ryan would tell him that Allie was in the truck with Matt.

Everyone at work noticed the black U under each of his eyes, but said nothing. Most of them shot sideways glances at him with pity in their eyes; some with worry and one with disdain, *Get over it*. He'd pour a coffee in the lunchroom or slice open the sternum of a dead bird at the dissection table, and he'd notice the sixth sense: someone watching him on the sly.

It hadn't taken long for Allie's confusion about Cohen's distance and state of mind to fester into resentment. Some nights he'd wake up, and she'd be back on to him, like they each owned halves of the bed and she was sticking to hers. She'd confronted him one night. *Are you even listening?* They were in a restaurant. She'd started crying when a friend of her father's came to ask her about her father. How he was making out. If he was retired yet. She told the man her father had died in a car accident, punctuating her story with a few sobs and tears, and when the man walked away, she said, earnestly, *I need you, more than ever, and you're miles and miles away.*

FOR YEARS, THE favourite part of his job had been the once-a-week hike when he took a batch of kids along a trail and showed them the natural world. His stories, his lectures, they'd peel back a curtain and expose all the wonder that was hidden in the forest. He liked seeing facts fire off like popcorn in their skulls; the newsflash jangling around their brains and lighting up their eyes. Even something as simple as how every bird's beak is tailored perfectly to what it eats: the hook of a hawk's bill that lets it tear through flesh; the scissor-shaped beak of a crossbill, so it can pluck seeds from pine cones; the needle-like bill of a hummingbird, so it can act like a syringe and draw the nectar from a flower. The nectar that other birds, with shorter bills, couldn't reach.

He'd start the conversation by saying, "If you were a plant and you didn't want anyone stealing your berries, what's one way you could stop people from eating your berries?" and then they'd understand why some plants had poisonous berries. He'd tell them all about how some plants *wanted* their berries eaten, so they could spread their seeds farther across the forest, and they'd always laugh at his bears-and-blueberries example. He'd kick at a blueberry bush in front of them all and say, "The bear eats the berries here," and then he'd point off in the distance, "and then he has to poop later, so he poops out blueberry seeds a hundred yards away. The bear gets a meal," he'd rub his belly, "and the blueberries get their seeds dispersed!" They'd all laugh at the story because they were young enough that poop was a funny word. And he played that up, the way he said poop.

But in the weeks since Matt died, he hadn't told that story. He just kept a watchful eye around patches of deadly nightshade and made sure everyone knew the plant with the purple and yellow flowers was poisonous. He didn't even tell them its name until a copper-headed kid asked, and then he felt horrible. Stopped, explained. Told them that nightshade was a distant relative of the potato. *Like a cousin?* The copper-headed kid said. *Yeah, like a cousin. A lot of the same family traits. Plants are kind of related the same way you and your aunts, uncles, cousins, and parents are. Some more closely than others.*

It went on like that for weeks until one day a kid, Lacie Decker, got a blister. Her parents had bought her brand new hiking shoes, and they were a size too small. Lacie had tugged at his pinky finger and said, *I think I've got a blister. Like my dad gets from hauling up lobster pots in the summer. He says fuck when he gets them!*

He smiled at Lacie, bent down on one knee, and tapped his lap, offering it up as a bench. He made a big, funny ordeal about plucking off her shoe and taking a look—he plugged his nose and said *Pew!* and she giggled and said her feet don't stink, and he said *Try telling my nose that*, and she laughed again. She had little cookie-crumb freckles drawn out by a day in the sun. She had a blazing smile and a laugh like only a kid can have and blonde hair that turned white whenever the sun was in it. And she did have a blister. The size of a dime on her heel. He offered his back, tapping at a shoulder, "Hop on! Free ride on the Cohen-mobile. C'mon."

He piggybacked her, and they had their own private conversation.

"Mr. Davies! What's your favourite kind of bird!"

"Ducks! Any kind, all of them! What's *yours*?"

"I don't know yet. I like polka dots!" She stuck her socked foot up in the air and pointed at the red and white circles all over it. "What's the most polka-dotted bird in Canada? That'll be my favourite!"

"When we get back to the Avian-Dome, I'll show you some pictures of a northern flicker. It's a kind of woodpecker. Its chest is *covered* in polka dots!" He tapped his fingers all over her shins, polka-dotting them as he said *polka dots*. "We have them here in our province. So you can keep an eye out for them or even put out a feeder with their favourite grub."

"Okay!"

They were doing this thing where she'd squeeze his shoulders and then he'd squeeze her dangling ankles, and then she'd squeeze his shoulders and he'd squeeze her ankles. She'd laugh every time.

"Mr. Davies! What's the animal you're the most scared of?"

"Scorpions! They've got pincers, poison, *and* a dagger-tail. *And* they've got a hard body, like a crab's, so you can't just squat them. What's *yours?*"

She laughed about the playful way he kept saying *What's yours*, like it made her feel special that he'd asked, and sounded so interested in her answers.

"I don't like spiders," she said. "They got too many legs and they suck your blood out!" She made a wet slurping noise, pretending she was sucking blood, and he laughed at the effort she'd put into it. "Both of those are creepy facts! Are spiders scary, Mr. Davies?"

"Why don't you ask the one on your leg?"

She panicked and flailed her legs like she was running on air. She was bucking around on his back so much that he'd almost dropped her. "Right there!" he said, and he pinched her leg, and she honked out a frightened laugh.

Walking back to the Avian-Dome, with Lacie on his back, he'd felt like he wanted one of these himself: a little Lacie Decker of his own. Him and Allie. It would *fix* things somehow. To co-own something with untied shoelaces and a lunchbox and endless questions that needed answers. A child would be some-where to pour the better aspects of themselves and see what grew. Allie's child; he loved the idea of her as a mother. She had all the right traits, and a child would make them shine in her. He wanted to see her belly balloon, and he wanted to see her eight months pregnant and struggling with her shoes: her feet fattening up and her belly too big to see over. The two of them, needing each other again. And someone needing them too. The way Matt had. The way a kid would. He wanted to see Allie, flying a rubber spoon towards their daughter's mouth like an airplane, and know they were building a life together.

He got home that night, and there was a look on Allie's face like he'd brought someone home with him: a new puppy or the man she'd been missing. There was a way she greeted him in the porch some days, a way her arm bent into a hook and caught him around the neck, for leverage, to half-hug him, and kiss his forehead. But on this day she stepped back and looked at him. She pointed to the couch and said, "Take a load off, Co-Co. I'm making your mother's Pad Thai recipe. Call you when it's ready."

"Did you just call me Co-Co?"

She shrugged her shoulders like, *Yeah, I dunno where that one came from.*

"My little Co-Cohen-nut," she said, calling out from the kitchen.

He laughed as he spread out over the sofa. "I've got a new favourite kid at work, again."

It wasn't solely the ghost of Matt's death that had been haunting their relationship. Not exclusively. His death and the toll it took had only exposed the fact their relationship wasn't as solid as they thought. Five or six years together and they'd started taking each other for granted. They were in need of renovation. Of meeting again as strangers.

ALLIE HAD ACCEPTED a job offer, as a Chief Environmental Impact Assessment Officer with a brand new firm. "Chief Environmental Impact Assessment Officer, hey?" Cohen said to her jokingly, "Maybe you should tack five or six more words onto your job title and be the first person, ever, whose job title runs two lines on their business card?"

Her new office was halfway out to Grayton, forty minutes away, and she had to be there for 8:30. Their little morning routine of leaving for work together, after coffee and a crossword, was gone. For years they'd rotated, daily, who got in the shower first. Now it was always her. There was no more time for him to slip into the shower and surprise her anymore, to feed the hunger in his hands for her soapy body. Tactile bliss: sometimes he couldn't help himself. She'd never objected. But now she'd bat him away like a buzzing insect.

It was Cohen who had to start taking public transit to work, so she could take the car. There was a witchy-looking kid with wild eyes on the bus who smelled like a cat's litter box, and she was sitting closer and closer to Cohen every day. Smiling at him, too long, after saying hello, with her gunky, yellow, wooden-peg teeth. Frizzy hair and dirty jeans.

In an ongoing joke, Cohen threatened Allie he'd leave her for the witchy busgirl if they didn't get a second car. She laughed about that, but one night, out of character, she'd reminded him he'd "make way more money working directly for the government, you know," if he'd kept his eye out for a job.

"Yeah. Bird biologists. Hot commodity. Right up there with tradespeople and chartered accountants."

A quick shrug of her shoulders. It was a Friday night when she'd told him about the newest job. She'd picked him up from work, and they were too lazy to cook, so they got take-out. She wanted flowers for the table, so they stopped for Gerber daisies. He took the burgers out of the bag and set them on the table. He stuck the straws into the cups and watched her throw out the old, wilted flowers with hesitation. She stared at them in the bottom of the garbage can for a minute, like maybe they had a day or two left in them, and she'd been hasty.

"So, like, on these oh-so-important environmental missions you'll be travelling to. Will you be travelling alone or with hand-some gentlemen?"

Setting the flowers on the table, sitting into her chair, "Yes. I will, from here onwards, be surrounded by dozens of dashing men. Many of them will make wild advances on me. Be advised that I won't be able to help myself, with these dozens of dashing men. I hope you understand?"

He threw his straw at her, like a dart, and she dodged it, laughing. She took another sip from the bucket-sized root beer. "I'm not going to work in a brothel, Cohen. What the hell?"

"Oprah says most affairs happen with co-workers."

She laughed. "*Oprah*?"

"Yeah."

Rolling her eyes, "I'll be traveling alone, or with Leslie, or with Keith, or, with both Leslie and Keith."

"*Keith*?"

"What?"

"That's a boy's name!"

"A man's, actually."

"A gay man, who in no way likes women? A gay man who is strikingly ugly. Is he hideous? So hideous cabs won't stop for him?"

She shook her head. "Keith's definitely not gay, but why are we having this—"

"Is he a happily married man, with an excessive number of framed photos of his wife on his desk? I hope so. I hope he's married and he calls his wife something sickeningly sweet. Like *My Princess* or something. And he talks about her too much. Does he talk about her too much?"

"Having an insecure partner in your thirties. What a turn on."

"I hope Keith is an entirely unavailable *older* man. Like, tell me he's so old people don't know why he hasn't retired yet. And they're trying to bump him out. Is he in the *Guinness Book of World Records* for being so terribly old. Does he have a walker? Emphysema?"

She rolled her eyes, playfully, and reassured him. "Keith's a bit...cavemanish. He openly hits on waitresses and coffee shop girls. It's tacky when guys aren't funny in their flirtations. Keith is...predictable." Her face looked more like she was thinking of Keith than the topic at hand. "He's one of those types of guys who's sweet, under a showy shell of wisecracks and stuff." She was looking at a napkin in her hands, not at Cohen. He'd noticed how she couldn't talk about Keith and look up at the same time. Wondered how she knew so much about the guy. How he was with baristas.

"How'd you two even meet, anyway?"

"One of his current clients was a client of Berkley-Dempster's when I was there. Apparently they were name-dropping me and explaining how they liked my *meticulous* way of doing things. He told them maybe they'd hire me, as a joke, and well, he followed up." She gave him a look like she was patting herself on the back. Punctuated it with a cute grin, *Ain't I Sumpthin'?*

"And you're confident some joke-cracker caveman is starting a firm good enough to leave your government job for?" He could feel his eyebrows bumping together.

"It's a pretty well established firm already. It's not *new* new. It's, like, I dunno, two or three years old now. I'm not *dumb*, Cohen. I've met with him. And Leslie. A few times. For lunch and that."

She'd been meeting people at lunch and not telling him. That's all he heard.

"...I asked to see details on their most recent projects, and you should see their current client roster, Cohen. This is a *great* opportunity. It's kind of a dream job, really. I'm not jumping into something here, you should know me better than that. It's been two months of back and forths. I even took a vacation day once, to go see their office—"

"A *vacation day*? You woke up one day, acting like you were going to work, and didn't tell me you had the day off, so you could—"

"I—I dunno, I—"

"I just—I don't know how you could be out there, meeting with some guy and not telling me about it. It's...weird."

"I'm not meeting with *some guy*. It was about a job, Cohen."

"I know it is. That's not my point. I'd have told *you* if *I* was interviewing for a new job—"

"At first it was nothing. Some email from a guy feeling me out about a job, just after Dad died. I mean *just* after he died. I...explained my situation, that my professional life was hardly a priority at the moment, but thanks for thinking of me and all that. You know?" She took a daisy out of the vase. Petting its petals, "But he turned out to be super sweet and understanding about it all—"

"Or he was just adamant about acquiring you."

"No, Cohen, *Jesus*. And I'm just answering your questions here. He opened up to me, about how his own father died when he was young, and it was sweet and honest and open of him. He didn't need to do that. I don't care what you say, it was… nice. He sent me details about the job, said it was an open offer, and to get in touch with him when I was feeling ready to get back to work. Or, to think about the offer, or whatever." She shrugged her shoulders. "So I back-burnered it and didn't think to mention it. It was the last thing on my mind at the time. You can understand that much, right?" She looked at him. "My father had just died."

Neither of them spoke.

"But he emailed me again, a few days later. He sent me this totally useless and corny article on ways to grieve a loved one in a positive way. It even had a cheesy epigraph and a cheesy poem at the end of it. I thought it was sweet, so what? To be honest, it's why I agreed to meet with him. A small-staffed, family-feel of a work place might be nice for a change, you know?" She paused. "Why do you look mad at me? This is a good thing. It's a better job."

"I'm weirded out. You're out there," he threw a hand in the direction of a hypothetical location, "meeting some guy about a job, over the course of a few *weeks*, and this is the first I'm hearing about it? Are we really this detached from each other's lives now?"

She groaned and got up from the table, bringing their trash to the garbage bin. Violently throwing it in there. "So what. He sent me some kind words after Dad died. It was more than you could muster at the time, wasn't it?" She turned to face him, leaning against the counter by the sink, arms folded in an accusatory stance. "You were a cold shoulder when I needed you the most. Do you know that? Do you know how that made me feel? The whole time I was mourning Dad, you were so weird and distant, all I could think about was how there for you I was, when your brother died! Can you really sit there and fault Keith for being kind when I needed kindness?"

"That's not what I'm doing."

"I don't care what you're doing." She walked out of the room. "I'm getting a bath and I've got nothing to apologize for."

BUT SHE DID apologize, that night in bed. Cohen had gone to bed before her, and that was weird, rare, that they didn't go to sleep at the same time. He could kick a foot across the bed, leave it there, like he was in a hotel or another life. She'd slipped in at some point. Tapped him on the shoulder to see if he was awake or to wake him. "I think you might have been right." A girlish warm grin on her face. She reached over him, grabbed her bedshirt off his nightstand and pulled it on. It was his green t-shirt she'd been sleeping in for a year. "So...I'm sorry. I am. You were right. We need to communicate more. We've been together long enough we need to remind each other of things like this. But please don't sour this exciting job opportunity, by being mad at me."

She kissed his forehead. Pushed her glasses back up the bridge of her nose with a thumb knuckle. She wore glasses, hip plastic frames that slid down her nose, and he loved the way she'd push them back up with the back of her thumb. It was unique and kid-like. She'd smack them back into place with her thumb knuckle, not a forefinger like everyone else. It spoke to her lack of patience, because half the time she'd bonk her nose, say *Ah!*

"And I didn't mean to talk like Keith, some stranger, was more there for me after Dad's death. I know you and my father were close. I know you were hurt too. I know you mourn, in your own withdrawn way, like you did with Ryan. And your relationship with Dad is a big part of why I love you so much."

He had nothing to say, just a few things to mull over. The jolt of her father's death had given her pause and, with it, a chance to evaluate her life, her next steps, whether she was really happy with her job, her surroundings, the person she was with…and so goddamn used to it ached.

"You weren't wrong though, that I was distant, when you needed me."

"Shh. Let's get some sleep."

"Really. I got past Ryan's death…*through* you. I could've been more there for you."

She was back on to him. Laughed like it had been a weird comment. "What do you mean you got through Ryan's death *through* me? What, like I was an escape route? And here I thought it was my pretty face that made you want me years ago." Another laugh. "Goodnight. I'm dropping here."

So he had his own conversation in his head. A prediction. Or a pragmatic rationale—the mystery of a stranger is the most potent pull anyone feels. The promise on the other end of those emails from Keith had to have been pulling on her. Some guy she hadn't figured out yet, the way she had Cohen figured out. She had no more questions about Cohen, for him, and he had none for her. To most people that's what being in love means: but Allie was a romantic, who'd rather be falling in love. Curious and exploring that curiosity.

She took the job. And it was nothing for her to be out of town a week a month. She'd started taking longer in the washroom in the mornings; she was wearing eye makeup now, there was a plastic case devoted entirely to housing eye makeup: liquids, powders, something that looked like a pencil. They were eating supper later so she could go to the gym after work. A choppy new haircut. A calculated wardrobe: there was a collared shirt she wore exclusively under a blue sweater vest and never alone. She was looking better than ever, but in a way that made her a different woman.

There were new priorities.

April 23rd was Keith's birthday and she'd asked Cohen to come to his party, but she'd asked like she *had* to ask him, with her eyes staring at the tips of her toes and muttering the words like it wasn't a big deal if he didn't come. And he said yes like a man who felt obligated to go.

Keith had been calling her at home more than Cohen felt he needed to be. It's natural for someone to answer the phone and take the call in private, in another room, so that never bothered him. What bothered him was that the paranoia felt warranted. Her muffled words would come through a door, or a genuine laugh would push through a wall, and it felt like Keith was in the house with them. And fighting to ignore it made him feel pathetic. Replaceable. The idea of being replaceable never bothered him, the *don't-take-it-personally* aspects of the dynamic. It was more the thought of waking up one Sunday morning, throwing an arm in her direction, and finding her missing. He imagined the weight of his arm falling from where her body should have been, to the empty mattress. That extra quarter-of-a-second drop of his arm would be the loneliest moment of his life.

His mind could roam, throughout his days. And did. He cut his finger with a scalpel at work one day because he wasn't paying attention. Cut it deep.

Allie was playing along with Keith's flirtatious nature, innocently, because it benefited her. Cohen would complain about Keith's forwardness, and she'd say something cute-ish, like "I'm an anchored boat, and you're the entire ocean," kiss him on the forehead, say goodnight. But there was a wedge, and it was between them, and if Keith wasn't the wedge, he was at least hammering it into place.

In time, the sex was less vocal and more to the point, like she was doing him a favour. She may as well have been reading a magazine. And that made him not want it at all. A month rolled by, the longest they'd ever gone. And then six weeks. And then the sex was awkward again. There were suppers at the coffee table instead, in case something good was on TV.

Keith wanted to teach her golf and Cohen couldn't understand why. He was happy Allie declined his offer.

She shouted up over the stairs at him that night, from the porch. "You don't have to come to Keith's party, but if you are coming, we need to leave. We're late enough already."

He was hauling on his jeans as he walked to the staircase. She looked up at him coming down the stairs like she wanted to say something.

"What?"

Hauling on her jacket, "Nothing."

"What?"

"You're wearing jeans?"

"Dark denim is the new dress pant!"

She laughed. "C'mon then! Hustle hustle." She swung her new purse towards the door, like Cohen was a fleet of school-age kids and she was a crossing guard. She fixed his collar as he walked past. "That shirt makes me proud to own you!"

"It was a gift. From my girlfriend."

It was something they did: talk about each other, to each other, in third person.

"Well, she has impeccable taste!"

"Yes. You should see her boyfriend. A stand-up guy."

Clicking the car doors open, she said, in a tone played-up to sound more funny than serious, "Behave yourself tonight, please, even if Keith's...drinking and pushing your buttons for fun."

"Gotcha. He can be a prick to me, but I can't be a prick to him."

"Just...be tolerant, for my sake? That's all I'm asking. Don't try to outwit him or make him look like a fool?"

He sat into his car seat, a smirk on his face. "Like last time?"

She laughed as she turned the key in the ignition. "Yes, asshole. He doesn't have your ability to laugh at yourself."

"*Asshole?* Who, me or him?"

"Well, both of you. Men are...ridiculous."

"Men like *him* are—"

"I have to work with...work *for* him, rather. Forty hours a week. We travel together. So we kind of have to get along, you know? And he's honestly a good guy. You two just have the wrong impression of each other."

"Allie. Your last staff party. C'mon. No one likes this guy, it was obvious. If he wasn't belittling someone, he was bragging about himself. That's no one's favourite kind of person."

She rolled through a stop sign, and another car beeped its horn and she ignored it. "Yes, he can be a total prick to some people, but never to me. And he's talking about giving me a

EVERY
LITTLE
THING

raise. This is important. Tonight is."

He shouldn't have said it. A man knows what not to say. "Isn't being so friendly with a sleazy guy, for financial gain, a bit like…"

"Like what? Say it."

"Nothing."

She hit the brakes. Right in the middle of the road. The car behind them slammed on their horn. She pulled up along a sidewalk. "Maybe you shouldn't come tonight?"

But he did. They walked into the restaurant rented out for Keith's birthday, and there were hors d'oeuvres on all the tables with descriptions in front of them like nametags. Votive candles in red glass holders made the place glow the colour of exit signs, and flicker importance.

Allie handed Cohen her jacket—like he was a bellboy—and walked towards Keith, waving and smiling. Keith opened his arms, clearly belligerent and drunk, and she hugged him back. He held her too long. Rocking her back and forth with his chin on her shoulder and his eyes in Cohen's. Like salt. Allie's arms went limp and dropped away from Keith's body to signal, *Enough*, and he let her go. She walked to the bar and after Keith had peeled his eyes off her, she cast Cohen a look, like, *What was that all about?* Her eyebrows raised like she was surprised he'd held her that long.

Keith made his way towards Cohen at a coat rack as Allie stood at the bar waiting for the bartender's attention.

"So, you're Cohen, right?"

"Yes." They'd met before. Three or four times.

"I'm Keith. Allie's boss. She tells me you play with birds for a living. That must be…something? An adult playing with animals for a living?"

A dozen confrontational responses piled up on Cohen's tongue, but as he cycled through them for the best hit, he saw Allie eyeing him from the bar. *Please, you're better than him.*

Keith drained the glass of whiskey in his hand. Crunching ice cubes, "Did she tell you I'm tryin' to jack her salary up another dozen grand?" He widened his eyes like Cohen should be impressed. Thankful.

"Yes. Yeah, great news."

"She'll probably be making more than you then, hey?"

"About thirty grand more, actually. Imagine that, a woman making more than her man. If this was the seventeenth century, I guess I'd have to be ashamed of myself?"

He gave Cohen a strange look, and said, "She's worth it."

Keith turned and looked at her. Too long. She looked great in that black dress and green malachite bracelet and he didn't like sharing the view. Keith turned back to him. "Yeah. All those nights on the road, away from her man. Gotta be rough on a relationship, hey? Deserves a raise?"

He tipped the empty glass to his mouth again—something black where gums met teeth—and said, "We take my car when we go out to lunch. She says her car doesn't even have air conditioning."

"Yeah, well, point A to point B, right?"

Keith sized Cohen up, another mouthful of ice cubes as he did so. He said, walking away from him, "There are two kinds of men, Cohen. I'm one and you're the other."

Keith and Allie crossed paths as Keith walked away from Cohen. Keith turned, sharply, like his shirt had gotten hitched on her, and took her in as she walked by. So that Cohen would see. He tipped his empty glass to him. Allie came over, stuck a glass of red wine in his hand, and said, "I'm sorry. He seems really drunk and idiotic. It's just the way some people get with liquor in them."

"Allie—" He shook his head. "It's the way *he* gets, not *some people*. Saying *some people* forgives the guy for being a fucking idiot."

"Look. The way he is with you, it's not really him—"

"Do you know what you sound like right now? One of those abuse victims, *Oh, I know he doesn't really mean it when he hits me and calls me a dumb bitch*—"

"Wow. That's." She shook her head. "I've got to work with this man, okay! Can you try and deal with that for me? You take it all so personally." Her left eye was glossing over with a tear. So he shut his mouth.

"Look, I'm being a bit extreme. I know you're just trying to get along—"

"No! No, you don't know. And you don't understand. It's my fault he's a prick to you. I never told you this, but I confided in him, that you were strangely distant when Dad died. So, he... he has the wrong idea about you. You as a partner, I mean. About your...character or our relationship or something. I don't know. But it's my fault he's an asshole to you."

THEY STAYED LATE that night anyway. And the drunker Keith got, the less he could defend himself when Cohen turned his jabs and insults around on him. They played a game of pool, to keep the conversation to themselves, and make Allie think they were getting along. Allie sat on the opposite side of the bar with Leslie and some other women Cohen didn't know. Laughing louder than anyone, and a drink or two ahead of them.

From eleven to midnight there'd been a raunchy stand-up comedian cracking dirty jokes about his latest European adventure—pitching *Speedo tents* on nude beaches, feeling self-conscious "with reason" in no-clothes spas in Denmark, and his unforgettably educational cunninglingus session, with a "demon-possessed Parisian, who knew exactly what she wanted, and how I was failing her...barking orders like that mean boss you'll never forget, except here, I wasn't allowed to quit! Here, I was in the clutches of a demon who wanted the best orgasm of her life."

They left after the comedian because Allie was tipsy enough to feel too tipsy to be at a staff function. They left their car and hailed a cab. Halfway home, she laid her head on Cohen's shoulder, and he liked the idea of her napping there. The comfort, familiarity. He had that much over Keith.

She kissed him that night in bed like she meant it. Hands on his face, legs wrapping around him. Something at the party had lit a spark in her—and even though he hated the impersonal nature of it, he screwed her from behind that night. Her face in a pillow. His hard thrusts throwing an echo into her panting. She had her eyes closed, her breathing disconnected from his. He was about to come when she twisted around and kicked him off her with a foot to his chest and ran to the bathroom. He flicked on a lamp, and there were wet streaks on her pillow that might have been tears.

CHAD
PELLEY

110

ROUNDTABLE

KEITH, ALLIE, AND Leslie had a convention to attend in Halifax. They were going to capitalize on their time there, to meet with and loot new clients for their company. Allie had suggested Cohen come along: it was a long weekend, and if he took that Tuesday off as a vacation day, they could *make a mini-trip out of it*. So he did. And Cohen was happy Keith wasn't on his flight. But they checked into their hotel, and Allie looked delighted when the woman at the front desk said, "A Mr. Keith Stone upgraded you to our beautiful penthouse suite."

"Oh, very well, thank you, Madame." She was trying to act debonair, but the clerk never caught her sense of humour. Allie turned to Cohen. "Be sure to thank him."

They had tickets for a Josh Ritter concert that Saturday night, but she was out to supper with Keith, Leslie, and a client, and he was starting to think she wouldn't make it back in time. But his phone buzzed, jangling the keys and coins on the bedside table. A text message: *Almost done here, Sexy Face, see you in 15! ;) Josh Ritter!* He'd just released his album *The Animal Years* and it was all that played in their house since it came out.

Cohen had been sprawled up against the headboard of the hotel's king sized bed, the most comfortable bed he'd ever been in, finishing the last few pages of the best novel he'd ever read. He was reading the last page with a glass of pinot noir when he heard a splash of laughter from the hall. Allie's delicate laugh, tucked under, and overwhelmed by Keith's obnoxious, hear-me-roar laugh. Keith sounded like a choking horse when he laughed. Like a man demanding a room's undivided attention.

He tucked a bookmark into his book because he didn't want to ruin or rush through those last few paragraphs. He'd savour them, later, undisturbed. But sitting on the bed, idle, he felt like he was eavesdropping on them. They were talking. Too long. Her hand on the door handle. The door handle rattling, but not opening. Two minutes. Three. Muffled conversation. Four minutes. Keith's jackal laugh. And then the click of the keycard in the door.

She came into the room with a phosphorescent smile, her face flushed the way it gets after a few glasses of red wine and a big meal—eyes like sun-struck jewels; Kool-Aid red cheeks.

She threw her jacket across a chair and dove onto the bed with him. Dove like it was the sea. She swam over and curled into him. They'd been together so long that it was effortless for their bodies to comfortably interlock, without thinking about the physics of their embrace. She was more drunk than he'd thought. Her body loose and clumsy. Warm.

"Ready for the show?" She looked at her watch. "We should leave in like, fifteen minutes?" But she caught sight of his face. "What's wrong?" But she'd said it like, *What's wrong this time?*

"Just, wondering, what's gonna happen to a girl, between the elevator and her room in a five-star hotel, that Keith felt the need to walk you to the door? It's like he thinks that was a date you were just on. Not a work function." He paused. "And that fucking laugh. Like he owns the world."

"Let's not let this ruin another night okay. Let's just go to the show? It's Josh Ritter, your favourite. It's why you're here, right?" She slapped his knees playfully to freshen up his sour attitude. She stumbled a little as she stepped down off of the bed, giggling at herself, her slightly intoxicated self, and disappeared into the bathroom.

He yelled to her from the bed. "It's too early yet. We should wait another twenty minutes?" No response. He got up off the bed and went to shout at her through the bathroom door. "Allie?"

"Yes, I heard you. Too early." She shouted through the door and over the bathroom fan. She opened the bathroom door, topless, her tits pointing right at him, a giddy drunk smile on her face.

"I've got this wild idea!" she said, grabbing at the button on his jeans and falling to the floor with them. Her knees in the puddle of denim around his ankles. He leaned back against the wall, and she did that combination of pace and actions she called The Fast Way, as he clutched the bathroom's doorframe in one hand and the corner of a wall in another. Breasts against his thighs. Her tiny hand on his hip.

But her cellphone rang. He could see it on the edge of the table behind her. The digital display flashing *Keith Stone, Keith Stone*. And he banged his head back against the wall. He almost laughed about it. "What the *fuck* does he want now?"

She leaned back away from him, freeing her mouth. Looking up at him playfully, "*This!*" she said, and they burst into laughter. Her breasts such a sharp angle from that view.

They walked downhill to the bar holding hands. Their favourite musician. A night in a town not their own. The afterglow of intimacy. They were reading every shop and restaurant sign they walked past, making mental notes of places to check out before they went back home. Allie was a little tipsy, her knees would knock into his whenever he walked too fast. It was May, and mild, but there were cool gusts of wind, and they made a tornado of Allie's skirt. And a flag of her hair.

"Maybe I *should* start looking for another job?" she said.

He opened the pub door for her, a big black door with massive brass handles. She gave the man on the door their tickets. "I'm not saying quit your job for me. You love it, you earned it. I'm saying, Keith, I don't like the guy. But I'll get over it."

She shimmied into a booth. "You'll get over it? Really? Is this one of those situations where you feel obligated to say you'll get over it, even though you won't get over it?"

A woman came over to their booth, offering to fetch them a drink. Cohen didn't respond until the woman had taken their order—a pitcher of a local microbrew they hadn't tried before and two glasses of pinot noir—because Cohen didn't like strangers hearing his conversations. Allie had always found that weird.

"Maybe the whole situation will get old and normal. I mean we already joke about him. It. The situation. I'll get over it."

The blonde-haired lady came back and laid their order on the table. She had a tight ponytail that was hauling her face back along with her hair. Her features were harsh and time-worn. Her lips were so chapped they looked like shredded computer paper. She had a tattoo of a daisy on her neck, and it didn't work for her. It didn't even look like a daisy. She asked for money, and Cohen laid two twenties on the table and got up to go to the washroom.

On his way back to their table, he saw Allie looking at him and laughing like he'd missed something while he was gone. There

EVERY
LITTLE
THING

was a tray on their table now, with four shots on it. Shooters, bright colours, the kind of stuff kids drink to get drunk.

"What's—"

"Those kids," she said, still a little surprised and laughing about it as she pointed to them at the bar. "They're, like, sixteen years old. The bargirl with the intense ponytail said they bought them for me! I looked up, and they were smiling at me like eager little fratboys! Aren't I a hottie on the town!" she said, flattered.

"Hottest hottie in the bar, look at you."

"I told her to take them back, and she said *They're paid for m'dear. May as well drink em'* and I said I don't do shots and she said, *Then give em' to yer man.*" Allie laughed and echoed it, "Give em' to yer man, she said!"

He laughed and waved at the kids. They couldn't have been more than nineteen or twenty, still in their first year of legal drinking age: giddy on shots and pints and twirling barstools and live music and beautiful women.

"I kind of wanna try the blue one," he told her. "Blue alcohol. What's that all about?"

"You can't do that!"

"Why not?"

"If a man sends you a drink in a bar, and you accept it, it suggests you might indeed sleep with him later. That boy is *so* not your type." She laughed at herself. Always laughing at herself. The three frat boys were still staring over. At her. He could tell she didn't like it. So he dragged the tray towards him, bits of liquids sloshing up over the shot glasses, and he shot one after the other. Heat. His whole upper torso on fire. Salty eyes. Fire-filled nostrils. He hid the pain well and raised the last shot glass to them like a toast, to say, *Thanks* or *Fuck off*, and they all turned around, pissed off and embarrassed.

Allie looked appalled. "*What* was that? What are you, sixteen too?"

He wanted water. His eyes burned. "I have no idea what that was! I mean...*fuck*, my chest is still burning!" He rubbed it for dramatic effect, a plea for sympathy, and she laughed. "I thought it was pretty bad-ass though, you?"

She rolled her eyes. "We're here trashing *Keith* for being a macho jackass? And look at you. I hope they've roofied you. It'd serve you right."

Everyone clapped and the band took to the stage. The show about to start. A sharp cackle of feedback as Josh's lead plugged his cord into his guitar; the drummer taking a sip of water from a bottle, his two sticks in his other hand.

She looked away from the stage and back at Cohen. "Dad wouldn't like this situation with Keith much either. A—he loved you, and B—Keith has become disrespectful." She still talked about her father a lot, and what he would think about a situation. It fit with her character that she still thought of him to that extent: what he would say to her in certain scenarios. Cohen's thoughts of Matt had died with him. Except when Allie would say something about her father, positive traces of Matt would spark in Cohen's mind. He'd think of a soft black sky, a case of beer at their feet, wet with condensation, and a chess board on a patio table with a king left in checkmate. Or he'd think about the lie. The way Matt looked him in the eye, *Thanks for talking me out of this.*

After Cohen's brother had drowned, Allie would encourage Cohen to talk about Ryan still. They were at a record shop one day, and she turned to him and asked what kind of music Ryan had liked. As if he was still alive and she'd like to buy him a gift. It didn't work that way for Cohen. It felt like thinking of the dead as alive. It was sweet, he envied her for it, but to him it was like digging up peoples' bones and expecting interaction.

"Disrespect was criminal in Dad's eyes. He took it personally that his neighbour's dog pissed in his flowerbeds."

Cohen grinned at the thought of that, of Matt always taking things personally. "There was this time your dad and I were driving back home from the mall." Cohen had forgotten all about it, so he smiled as the memory came back to him. "A bunch of kids threw snowballs at his car. I mean, they were just kids throwing snowballs at cars and running away, so it could have been *any* car, but your father had this look on his face, like he took it personally. Why *my* car? You know? *Why me?*" Another laugh as he let the memory run through him.

"That was weird."

"What?"

"You said *your dad and me* instead of Matt. Like you didn't know the guy or something." She sipped her wine, eyeing him. She laid her glass down to clap along with the crowd. The end of a song and the start of a new one. "Why do you have such trouble talking

EVERY LITTLE THING

115

about my father?"

"I don't have trouble talking about your father. It's just…it's like summoning something. It takes a little effort. Some warming up. I dunno." He shrugged his shoulders.

She was peering into her wine like a crystal ball, swirling the glass by its stem. "Sometimes I don't understand what happened that day. The day Dad went off the road."

A kick in his throat.

She had the stem of the wine glass pinched between two fingers, sliding them up and down. Her eyes searching for something in that pool of red. "I went there last month, to that part of the highway. I was on my way home, from work, and I slowed down. I pulled over. I really took a look at where he went off the road, in behind the guardrail. It doesn't make sense…"

Cohen had been holding his breath, tighter, with every word she spoke, until his lungs felt like rocks, and then an avalanche in his chest. The music suddenly quieter or more distant in sound. He was afraid that if he looked at her, she'd see panic in him, but deserve attentiveness.

"…I assumed he was tired, hungover. That he'd fallen asleep or dozed off. But I took my car onto the shoulder of the road that day, and I would've had to *steer* my car, I mean, I really would've had to pull it in around that guardrail. It's a weird angle. You'd have to see it, to know what I mean. And the cops never questioned that? So I was sitting in my car, wondering if I'm crazy to be thinking that. Noticing that. And it's not like he was swerving from something. The police report showed no signs of him swerving from a car or an animal or something…"

If she asked his opinion, it would be the difference between lying to her and withholding the truth. A fine line, but one he'd never cross. It would make his actions twice as unforgivable.

"…I'm parked there, car idling, sitting on the hood of my car. Wondering why I'm even there…" She was doing all the talking, but he'd need words, soon. "…all these months have gone by, yet I felt like his truck should've still been down there, for some reason. Like, the world couldn't possibly have moved on from that moment…"

He owed her a perfect sentence. But he was nowhere near it. He was feeling sloppy from the shots and the beer.

"…are you even listening to me?"

He felt caught, arrested, the cops at the door.

"*Cohen?*"

He nodded, *Yes, go on.* To buy time. He wanted a distraction, a glass to smash in the distance, a fight. He wanted a drunk kid causing a scene.

"…I got off my car and sat on the guardrail and I just stared down at the sea for a while. There were cars passing by and staring at me. One woman stopped and asked me if I was all right, like I was going to jump or something. I need you to tell me that it's okay I did that. That I stood there that day and wondered."

"It's…sort of beautiful, in a way. It's okay, yes, of course it is. It makes sense. It's what graveyards are for."

He knew his response was disconnected and gauche, but she hadn't really heard him over the music, and kept going. "Thing is. Like I said. You'd have to see the guardrail to know what I mean. I want to show you someday. So you can tell me I'm being crazy. That it doesn't make sense."

He couldn't say, *Really?* He couldn't say, *Matt fell asleep, Allie, so the car did whatever it wanted.* He couldn't lie to her the way the police report did. Shifty, eyes in his beer, the truth rattling around inside him. Trying to find the best way out. "A-Allie?"

"What? What's *wrong* with you?"

Cowardice, hesitation, a lie: "I have to run to the washroom again."

Her heart sank, like, *You fucking bastard.* She was visibly hurt that that had been his response to her confession. It was in her voice and the subconscious shake of her head. "I'm coming too. Those shooter kids at the bar are staring and creeping me out. Wait outside the bathroom doors for me?"

He nodded and they left their booth for the washrooms. He went into a stall, put the cover down, and sat with his legs shaking back and forth in wide, anxious swings. He stabbed an elbow into each knee and laid his chin on the knuckles of his hands.

He couldn't stand the idea of her, parked at that guardrail, questioning the physics of her father's death. Him not there to hold her. This day was inevitable, but the timing was all wrong because he was drunk, and they weren't home, and that meant a taxi to the airport and a plane ride with this news throbbing between them. She'd need some distance, some personal space, that the hotel room couldn't provide.

The harder he searched for the right words, the less sense it made he'd never told her the truth until now. Because Lee had reassured him there was no use, but what did Lee know? *Your father's idea. I was dragged into it. I was betrayed, to my face.* He wanted to offer that as an excuse. For sticking with Matt's plan A and the suicide he was duped into being a part of.

There was a kid throwing up in the stall next to him. Allie was probably outside the bathroom door already, waiting for him, watching over her shoulder for those kids at the bar. She worried easily.

He should have been putting those few sentences together—the truth, well-worded—but an anger at Matt kept rising to the surface. He'd want her to know Lee knew too. To share the resentment, spread it over two people. He felt callous for thinking that way. And it wouldn't work to tell her Matt had threatened him, *If you tell her, there'll be a war between us, understand?*

He'd been in that stall way too long. He thought of Allie out there waiting for him. Looking over her shoulders at the guys at the bar. He got up off the toilet. Went out to meet her. They walked back to the booth without saying anything to each other, until sitting in the booth. She asked him again, "What's *wrong* with you? Are you okay? You look pale, and you took forever in the washroom."

"Lineups. At the urinals."

"No there wasn't! I could see in. Every time somebody walked out of the washroom, I peeked in, because I thought maybe you'd come out and I missed you. There were no lineups at the urinals. There was no one at the urinals. Why are you acting so weird? Do you want to leave? Did the shots make you sick?"

"Allie. Your father."

"What? What about him? *Say* something. Jesus Christ!"

"A—" He clenched his jaw. Took a sip of beer. Looked away from her to the stage.

"Cohen, what the fuck?"

"A month before he died, he went to Lee's house." Cohen stopped, wanting to, but not needing to drag Lee into this. She was still as a statue, waiting for his words. "A few weeks before your father died, he called me to come over. When I got there. Something wasn't okay." He looked up at her and quickly looked away. She had a face like a beating heart. "When I got there, something was wrong. He wasn't okay. He was drunk. He—He had cancer, Allie. Terminal, *definitely* terminal cancer. He told me all about it. His esophagus, his stomach, it was bad. He only had months. And didn't want to die that way, in a hospital bed. He was talking suicide. So I..."

Allie deflated slowly. Her arms tucked into her body, her stomach concaving, her tailbone sliding into the groove between the seat and the back of the booth. She clutched her big white purse with two hands and held it like a shield to the words. She motioned like she might get up and run away. But fell back into her chair.

"...He didn't want you to see him, go through it, like—like you had to with your mother. I told him that wasn't okay. I—I did. I tried to stop him. And he fucking lied to me. He looked me in the eyes and promised, with his hands on my shoulders, that he'd tell you at the cabin that weekend or later that week. I had no idea, but he thought he knew what was best for you. He didn't want you going through it with him, day after day, like you had with your mother. He wanted to spare you that, and himself too, I guess. He—He. He made me part of his plan."

"He *made* you?" She'd howled it so loud that the bartender's head turned to their booth. "You sat there, in the car with me, by the guardrail, and you fucking knew? And you bit your tongue?"

"I was shocked. Crushed. Hurt. I did *not* know he was going to do that."

"Then how do you know it wasn't an accident!"

"Because he told me. The night he told me he had cancer. He told me. How. He'd...do it."

Her face was swan white; her eyes pinched half shut. There was a thick tear in one eye that had to be blurring her vision. She slammed her eyes shut to block it all out, and one tear ran quickly and then stopped altogether on her cheek. She let out a moan that sounded out of context. She was supposed to cry, to yell, but the moan was un-gaugeable and unexpected. A whimper really. A slight trembling in her lips and then her hands.

She put one hand straight out in front of her—an open palm at first, and then a closed fist—and slammed it down on the table. Unwritten sign language.

She grabbed her purse and dashed off, he'd assumed, to the washroom to be alone. He swallowed the rest of his beer and walked across the bar. He leaned against a wall to perch somewhere he could see both the washroom door and their booth.

He waited there, for twenty-one minutes, and she did not come back to the booth.

She did not come out of the washroom.

He waited another minute before walking into the female washroom, and he apologized to three shocked women applying makeup or drying their hands. "Emergency, sorry. I'm looking for someone."

He peered under all the stall doors, at shins and shoes, and not one combination was Allie's.

No black and red shoes.

He ran back out and looked over to the booth they'd been in, and she wasn't there. Three fat men in matching baseball jerseys were there instead. Boisterous. Laughing. Almost drowning out Josh's music. Slapping their hands off the table so that their beer bottles wobbled. They'd pushed his and Allie's pitcher of beer to the edge of the table.

He combed the bar, quickly, thoroughly, and went outside. Looked up and down the sidewalk. He saw a woman on a park bench in the distance, and he wanted it to be Allie, even though this woman was taller and wore a white coat. She in no way resembled Allie, and yet he stared, squinted, to bend her shape.

He called her.

No answer.

He called her back. Nothing. Her voicemail. "Hi, you have *not* reached Allie Crosbie. Better luck next time."

He was there when she'd recorded that message and laughed at herself. She was painting her toenails, on the corner of their bed, and called him into the room. She said, *Listen to this, my new voice mail message!*, and she threw him her phone, laughing at herself.

He walked along the outside of the bar. It was attached to other pubs and shops and restaurants, so he walked the whole block. He walked up and down every little alley between the buildings, dialling her phone number over and over. Each time she didn't answer was a separate panic.

He tried calling their hotel room, and she didn't answer there either. She wouldn't do that to him. Disappear like that. She would at least answer his call and then hang up on him.

She liked the Public Gardens, at the end of Spring Garden

Road. So he went there, poking his head into every pub along the way that looked like a place Allie might have been drawn into for a drink and a dark corner. She was in none of them, and she was not in the Public Gardens. He had not randomly seen her, on a staircase outside of a hotel or shopping plaza or walking aimlessly along a sidewalk.

He went back to their hotel room, and she was not there. And had not been there. There were no signs of her: her purse wasn't on the bed, no half-drunk glass of water on a dresser. Her suitcase had not been hastily packed and taken out of the room.

Hours had passed. Too many hours. He peered through his hotel window—forehead flat against the cold glass—eyeing Halifax like a hawk; waiting for the red dot of Allie's jacket.

He knew she wasn't okay. She wouldn't do this to him. She was rightfully in need of space, but she would've called to say she was okay, after storming off like that. Hours ago. It was who she was to do so. Naturally paranoid, always checking in, empathetic. And she would have reacted by now, said her piece, expressed herself. She couldn't keep emotions to herself. She'd need to express the words in real time; articulate the frustration while it was still fresh enough to word well.

Prying himself from the window pane, it had occurred to him that she was probably two floors up with Keith. Keith, not Leslie. Leslie had flown back home that morning.

Allie had used Cohen's cellphone earlier that week to call Keith. She'd left hers back at the hotel room. So she asked to use Cohen's phone at lunch one day, to tell Keith she might be ten minutes late for a meeting. A meeting she hadn't seen the need of attending, but Keith had wanted her there. *Yeah, to stare at*, Cohen said. *Probably*, she confessed.

He grabbed his phone and searched through sent calls until he found the only number he didn't recognize. He assumed it was Keith's and dialled it.

Keith answered. He sounded groggy and a little pissed off, "H-hello?"

He didn't want Keith to have been the place she ran to that night, and yet he desperately wanted him to say yes. "Keith, it's Cohen. Davies. Is Allie...there? With you?"

"Um, no."

But there was a long pause before Keith had said no. Like

EVERY
LITTLE
THING

maybe he was lying. Maybe she was there, waving her arms like a traffic director saying, *No no no!*

"Are you *sure?*"

"What the fuck, man? It's...three a.m. What's going on? I've got shit to do in the morning, man."

"She's...missing. We fought. She ran off. It's been five hours, and she's not answering her phone. I don't know—"

"Have you called the hospitals?

A long pause. Keith said the word *hospital* and a storm of visuals silenced Cohen. He shut his eyes. "I. No. I can't do it, man. I—"

"What room are you again?"

"Three-o-two."

"Look, I-I'll be right down, and we'll start calling some hospitals and police stations."

"No, look, listen. You have my number in your phone now. Let me know if you find something out."

"It only makes sense we stay—"

Cohen hung up the phone. Irrational. He took off to the nearest hospital.

No one here by that name, sir.

And the police hadn't heard the name either.

A young cop, younger than Cohen, only said, "We can't do much until it's been a little while longer, bud. But I'll take your name and call you if, God forbid, anything comes up about...," he squinted at Cohen's desperate scribbling on the back of a business card, "Nellie Crosbie."

"Allie." He took the card back. Fixed his writing. "Allie Crosbie. Something's wrong. We're not even from here!"

It was five a.m. The city was still asleep and so quiet he could hear himself breathing. There was a lack of bustling city activity around him, to drown out his panic, and that amplified his anxiety. He'd dial her number every couple of minutes, and it would ring until he hung up. He was sitting on the bench he and Allie had picnicked on earlier that week. Slices of smoked gouda and a tub of pecans and prosciutto. Red wine in coffee cups. That memory like a ghost there beside him.

KEITH CALLED. "WE'RE at the QEII Hospital." And Cohen's cab driver wouldn't drive fast enough.

When he finally got Cohen to the hospital, Cohen handed the man too many bills, rushed to the sliding doors, frustrated at how slow they were to open. Keith was waiting in the lobby, and then he was shaking his head, trying to hold Cohen back.

"Wait, man. *Wait!*—"

"For what, Keith? Where is she? What happened?"

A family in the foyer was staring.

"She's been hurt. Mugged from what I can tell. But something's not lining up. I'll take you to her. Just calm down. She's saying something about kids in a bar you two were at tonight?"

Cohen took off down the hall, with Keith trailing behind him. "You're going the wrong way! Calm down." A tug at his elbow.

Keith took him down the right corridor, "Right here," he said, "but I don't think you can go in yet. The police are—"

He burst in through the door. Her left eye was swollen shut. It was black; apple-red where the lids were fastened together. She shot up in her bed and shrieked that they take Cohen out of there. And they did. They grabbed him and walked him backwards out of the room. Her reaction was disorienting, shocking, and he never fought against them. He was too tired for that, too scared, hurt. Two police officers and a male nurse engulfed him like a net, and gently, respectably, dragged him out of the room and onto a bench across the hall.

"I need to know what happened. You don't understand. I'm her partner. She's just...shocked. We had a fight, and then...*this* happened. What is this?" he pointed to her room, perplexed.

The two officers looked at each other, unsure which should do the talking. "Sir, you need to understand she was not distressed until you came into the room. She was relatively calm. I understand you two had had a quarrel, before she ran off. I understand the grave nature of your quarrel. I understand you're shocked at seeing Allie here. But you need to understand Officer Rose is not done taking a statement from Allie, and it's important that her statement is not interrupted. She's trying to help us catch her offenders. You don't want to impede that, do you? By distressing her?"

He waited for Cohen's response, like Cohen was a dumb kid and the man needed to know he was being clear. Cohen nodded yes.

"She's banged up, yes, but not in a critical way. There's no concerning medical issues to worry yourself with."

"Where?"

"Sir?"

"Did this," he pointed to Allie's room, "happen?"

"She was headed back her hotel room. Three intoxicated males confronted her. She feels they were the three males you had a confrontation with, in the bar, earlier tonight—"

"Confrontation?" He was still drunk and the word had come out as *con-fron-ta-ta-tion*. "Those guys. They sent her drinks. I implied they should cast their attention elsewhere. That was all!"

"Confrontation was her word, buddy, not mine. Should I keep going?"

Cohen nodded.

"There was some name-calling and what she believes to have been allusions to you making a show of their gesture, in sending her drinks. They were handsy, rough, and ultimately, wanted her purse and belongings and to rattle her up some. But this story is for Allie to share, Owen."

"Cohen."

"I'm sorry?"

"Never mind." Cohen got up to peer in her window again.

"C'mon, now. Let's, just, sit back down. You also need to consider your actions. Assisting a suicide is a possibly indictable offence in Canada. It's at least grounds for a civil lawsuit. You need to tread lightly."

"Her eye. What, they punched her? Her jaw, the cut there?"

The cop was being coldly informative, and Cohen wondered if the man had been trained to be sensitive or to be painfully clear when talking to people. "They became physically abusive when she tried to retain her purse. There was a ring leader, goading the others along. When one of them tried to convince them to leave Allie alone, the ring leader also become physically abusive with him. They wore masks, but she's been very intelligent here, very helpful. She's told us one of them had raised moles on his neck. Another one of them stuttered. These are good details. These will help. Mainly, she tailed them to their van. Not a bright bunch. It had a company name on it."

"What company."

He eyed Cohen. "That's our job, to worry about such details." But the report was right there. On the edge of Allie's bed. When he'd gotten up to peer in the window, he'd seen the yellow pad of paper there, three thirds of a page of details. He'd make a dash for that detail.

He looked at Keith. "She called *you?*"

"No, man, the hospital did. I'm hearing this for the first time too." Keith peered through the window, shook his head. "I mean, Jesus Christ. Who pounds the face off a woman? Fucking animals. And why'd she fight back?"

Cohen opened the door and made a run for the police report. He stood at the foot of her bed, started a senseless apology, with his head down, so no one would notice what he was really doing: scanning that report for the company name on the vehicle. And he'd found it, *Tulley's* something or other, before another pile of men tore him out of there and escorted him to the nearest exit.

He let the police watch him hail a cab. Told the cab driver, *I've forgotten my briefcase, sorry, don't wait for me*, and hopped back out of the cab.

He went to the cafeteria and texted Keith to let him know where he was. And he sat there, pouring two packets of sugar into a coffee he didn't want. His eyes lost in a maze of rain on a cold window pane.

Keith came to find him. "What the fuck, man. It's best you leave, don't you think? What kind of purpose do you think you're serving here?"

He handed Keith a tub of vanilla yogurt, with chunks of apple and cashews stirred in. Allie's comfort food.

"What's this?"

"It's for Allie. She'll want it."

Keith took it and stared at it like it was a mystery. "Are you sure. I mean. What's wrong with a muffin or something like that?"

Before Keith had come down, twenty minutes after Cohen texted him, Cohen was cutting up that apple, wondering if Keith would take the time to get to know a woman the way Cohen knew Allie. If he was that kind of guy. If he would go to two different checkouts—one for a tall tub of yogurt and another for an apple—and then go to a vending machine for cashews. Would he find a plastic knife and cut up that apple or would he just get her *a muffin or something like that.*

"Bring that to Allie, and come right back? We need to talk."

"I don't know that we do, not right now." He looked down at

the tub of yogurt in his hand, still perplexed by it.

Cohen was going to ask Keith to come with him. To confront those kids. To get her purse back. He'd found a place called Tulley's using his phone. A locksmith place. A father and son operation. They had a website, and there was a photo on their *About* page. It was labelled, *Three generations of family ownership!* A caption: *Left to Right, Aaron Tully (grandfather), Aaron Jr. (father), and our young apprentice Nathan (son).* The son of a bitch wasn't even smiling for the camera, the way his father and grandfather were. Nathan was listed in the phone book, halfway across Halifax.

He told the cabbie, "Here's fine," at a stop sign at the start of the street, but there was no house for thirty paces in either direction. "Whatever," the cabbie said. "Twenty-three fifty," and he hit the farebox.

Number 58. There was a black truck parked two doors down from Nathan's house and a fire hydrant two doors up. He bounced back and forth between the truck and hydrant like a pinball. There was a white van in their driveway with *Tulley & Sons Locksmiths* written on it. He thought of Allie's sealed-shut black eye; apple-red in the centre. Her cut jaw. The cop's descriptions. More adrenaline soaked his brain and lengthened his gait every time he walked past that house. And it was this kind of macho bullshit that had gotten Allie into the mess in the first place. But he was drunk and pissed off and needed a place to put it and it was more than revenge that put him in that cab. He wanted those kids to feel the way Allie did about the attack. Gross, wrong. And she didn't need to go through the process of getting a new SIN card, hospital card, credit card. He pictured her standing there in line, in a sickly hospital or a stale-aired government building, staring at their out-dated flooring, waiting in queue, wondering if they'd ask her how she'd lost her card.

The house was rundown: one shutter missing on the left side of a window, cracks in the pale yellow siding, and the lawn was knee-high weeds tangled up with litter: silver flashes of pop cans and a torn-open chip bag. There was a smell of mould as he walked up three cement steps to their front door. He didn't knock: he pounded the door with the underside of a clenched fist and still had no plan for when two or three drunk kids threw themselves at him. Through the living-room window, he saw them, all three of them, plus one, playing video games. And then the door opened.

They recognized each other immediately from the bar. The guy who'd opened the door went to slam it shut, but Cohen got an arm in. Just an arm, elbow deep, and the door was a vice. Each time they rocked the door against each other, it was another blast of pain: an intense pain that splashed from his arm, to his chest, in angry waves.

"*Nathan!*" and the kid sounded like a kid: twenty and terrified and almost ready to cry. He was shrieking for Nathan to come plough against the door with him because Cohen had gotten a leg in the door now too.

It was about *not* breaking his arm now, that was all. But the door was a snare around his arm and leg. Vicious rivers of blood were getting dammed up, where the door met his knee and elbow.

"*Nathan!*, it's *him*...from—"

Nathan charged the door like a bull, pinning Cohen's thigh and forearm tighter in the wooden frame. Cohen shrieked, pounding on the door, but he still heard the guy. "Shut the fuck up, Travis! You don't know this guy, okay? You don't know this guy, remember?"

Cohen's hand had gone entirely numb. It was being pricked by a hundred invisible needles and ballooning with trapped blood. Travis and Nathan had no plan beyond pressing hard against the door. They were panicked, and each time they shifted, he inched himself out a little more. "I just want her wallet back. Her purse! Throw it out the fucking window, I don't care!"

A third person slammed against the door, and the door was a guillotine at Cohen's arm. This guy was vicious. He grabbed Cohen's hand and squeezed so hard it felt like his knuckles were grinding each other into dust. The guy squeezed harder, and the bones of Cohen's fingers were being rearranged.

Cohen was slapping at the doorframe, yelling: begging them to let go. He saw one of their hands. Claw marks. Like a cat had taken a swipe at the guy. Except it hadn't been a cat, it'd been Allie, defenceless but trying. Those three cuts, puffy and pink, started on the back of the guy's hand, and then became two pink lines instead of three as they ran down his thumb.

"Throw her purse out the window!"

There was whispered discussion, a conference. "We don't know where her goddamn purse is now!" And he sounded like he meant it. Like they'd chucked it after looting it.

He managed to tear his leg out of the door and it had gone too numb to stand on. It rested on its tippy toes, useless. And now his arm was taking all the pain, all of it: three men, pushing one door, against one arm, and now there was acid fizzing under the surface of his skin.

His foot regained feeling, and he started kicking it against the door, *Fucking let me go!* but they weren't listening. They were drunk or stoned or both, and they were 100% panic. He turned his back to the door and pressed against it with everything in him: his toes crunching up in the ends of his sneakers, and his sneakers squeaking as they slid across the pavement steps.

"We don't have no one's purse, man! Will you piss off if we crack the door and let you go? The goddamn neighbours— My sister's baby. You need to fuck off."

"I'm *trying* to get my arm out of the door! Fuck! I'm *trying* to!"

Panicked slaps at their door, and then he saw one of their faces through the slit of the open doorframe. The guy's head was pressed up against the wall; he saw his left eye, blinking madly, and half of his mouth, but mainly that one blinking eye. And it was Nathan.

Without thinking, Cohen reached into his pocket, hauled out his keys, and jammed a long car key into his face. It hit a tooth, made a sick scrapping sound along his gums, and Cohen cringed as the door swung open. They all stood there, watching Nathan on his back, on the carpet, wailing, with his right hand covering his bloody mouth. His limbs flailing around like an overturned beetle. Cohen was stunned still, holding his arm, looking at Nathan. He felt everything but satisfied with himself.

The door shut and a deadbolt clicked. He heard them all yelling *Holy fuck! Holy fuck!* One of them poked a head out a window. "We don't have her purse. We panicked. We threw it in the harbour, off the MacKay bridge."

He walked back up to the stop sign, where the cab had dropped him off, to call another cab. While he waited, he watched a vicious, snarling dog. It was tied to a thick tree trunk. It was a hyena of a dog. Marbled and angry. Every time it lunged in Cohen's direction, its body snapped itself midair as the leash restrained it, temporarily muting its barking as the collar tightened on its throat. The dog didn't even know what it wanted.

GAPS

THEIR FLIGHT BACK home was only half filled. There were vacant seats and Allie *thought it best* to sit in one. Three seats behind Cohen. Every now and then he'd hear her turn the page of her magazine, the sharp *snap* of a page turning. Or she'd clear her throat or sniff, and the plane was somehow quiet enough to hear all that. He watched clouds pass the window, whiting out the blue. The flight attendant came by and asked if he wanted a drink, and he'd instinctively turned to Allie, who wasn't there, to let her order first.

"No thanks. I'm fine." Except, he wanted a drink, and caught her in time. "Actually," an apologetic laugh, "I'll have a glass of anything red."

"I'm very sorry, but we're fresh out of red. And that's a first! White?"

At the luggage corral, Allie suggested he sit in front of the cab. The hefty cabbie had an impossibly thick moustache. He shifted uncomfortably as he drove, biting a fingernail to fill the quietness with action. Even a rough-looking man like him—with rolled cigarettes and a bottle of Brut in his cupholder—could sense something wasn't right between Cohen and Allie. He'd turned the radio up a little too, like the uncomfortable non-conversation between the couple in the backseat was worth drowning out with a bad pop song.

When he got in bed that night, he lay right at the edge, with an arm dangling over the mattress, to emphasize the distance he could offer: eighty percent of the bed could be hers. Lying there, he heard her brushing her teeth: the scrubbing, the water running, then clinks of her toothbrush falling into a ceramic holder. She walked passed their bedroom door with an extra pillow and blanket tucked under her arms. The blanket trailing behind her like a tail.

Minutes later he got up, peered over the staircase railing, and shouted, "You can have the bed. I'll take the couch."

"I'm shorter than you. The couch isn't very long. Just...go to bed, okay?"

"Can we talk about this? About us?"

"I have to work in the morning. It's going on one. Tomorrow night, okay?"

"Keith won't care if you show up late for work tomorrow."

"Can't we just go to sleep?" She wiggled into the couch, trying to find a comfortable posture.

At three in the morning, he felt her sliding under the covers. He felt the sheets lift, and then he felt a warm breeze across the mattress. The comforter grazed his chin as she settled in.

"Should I go down on the couch?"

"No."

Silence. Minutes worth of it.

"Listen. We. We were having issues before. All of this. And I'm not overwhelmed and I'm not confused. It's. Just. We've been expecting the past, to keep us stitched together. Hold us in place. Memories." She brought her hands together, interlocking her fingers. "I need some space. Just to...see how that'll feel. I might stay with Lee. Maybe. Just...for a while."

Silence again. Withheld tears had a way of making her eyes look twice as big. She rolled over, away from him, and the sheets started moving as her shoulders bucked up and down.

"C'mere," she said. "Just. Put your arm over me. Spoon me." And he did. "Just rock me, back and forth, like this. Yes. Like that." And she cried harder when he kissed the back of her head.

He woke up the next morning, and sun had filled the room. Allie was sat against the headboard, his arm laid in her lap like a book, and she was smoothing her fingers over the car-shaped bruise on his arm, as if it was a story in Braille.

"What happened?" They both looked at her fingers, skating over his bruise.

"I was trying to keep a door from closing."

IT WASN'T JUST the bed that got bigger. The house felt bigger too. Like there were extra steps in the staircase now, and there'd be echoes if he yelled. The hall closet looked needlessly spacious with all of her shoes gone, and seeing only one toothbrush in the toothbrush holder made him feel like he was traveling. Half bags of spinach were going bad before he'd eat it all. He was tearing banana bunches in half at the grocery store, understanding now why *some people* did that.

Lee had a spare room, and he was lonely and kind enough to agree when Allie asked for it. But his guilty conscience had him calling Cohen more than he normally did. *I'm rooting for you guys, you know that, right?*

Lee's house was closer to her work, and there was less traffic heading to her office from Grayton than from their place in town. She also wouldn't have to pass that guardrail twice a day. He wondered if that had factored into her decision. All she'd said was, *It makes sense for me to stay at Lee's, for now, until I clear my head.* He gave her that space without pressure or an argument because him wanting her to stay wasn't the same as her wanting to stay.

First she packed a few changes of clothes and a toothbrush. Then he'd come home from work and her bathrobe would be gone from the hook on the back of their bedroom door. Or one of their DVD players would be replaced by a note, *Sorry, but you always watch movies on the couch anyway. We never used this one, right?* There was a thief erasing her presence—every day he'd come home from work and she'd be a little more gone.

By mid-August, the hall closet was gutted: her jackets and winter boots moved to Lee's house months before any signs of winter. By September there was never any mail for her anymore. He missed browsing the magazines she'd subscribed to. The cooking ones, mainly. One day, late August, he'd come home to their bookshelf looking lonely and hastily gutted. Books toppling into each other; some of the shelves needing book-ends now. She'd stripped her photos off the walls, and nothing had made their home feel as half-vacant as seeing those nails, still in the wall, and her photos, their decor, gone. Eventually the memories were eroding too: he couldn't gauge her height now, if she'd come up to *here* or *here* against his body.

His mother came by one day. She'd bought a Tassimo coffee maker, but didn't like it as much as "normal coffee." She wanted Cohen to have it instead of throwing it away. It was a Saturday, so she asked him where Allie was, and he didn't know what to say. She hung her jacket up in the porch, noticed the lack of jackets

EVERY
LITTLE
THING

131

and the emptied shoe rack.

"She's been...living at Lee's, for a while now."

She looked at him like he was crazy. "You—You didn't tell us?"

He shrugged his shoulders, put a hand in his pocket. "I thought she was coming back."

"She's not?"

"We haven't talked in a while now."

"It was mutual, or she left you, or..." her words trailed off as her eyes took in his emptied home.

"It was mutual in that...I don't want her here if she doesn't want to be here."

DECEMBER. THICK SNOWFLAKES blowing through the air like angry white wasps. Some clung to his kitchen window as he threw scallops into a bed of fettuccine. He hadn't seen Allie in months.

His phone rang and it was Lee. "Kid, it's none of my business, but there's things going on here, with Allie, you need to know about. That you deserve to know about. Things she's sworn me to secrecy about. Let's just say, you need to *see* her. You need to take a *look* at her. And I'll say no more. Except the fact that she just left here looking radiant. She got picked up by a fucker who shook my hand too eagerly. He said all that bullshit, you know? *So nice to meet you. Heard such good things.* He's a prick, Cohen. Men can spot a prick when they see one. I don't like the guy. Not for her. And I don't need a good reason why."

"His name Keith?"

"Yes, but that's not the point of my call. Remember, you need to make an excuse to meet with her, to see her in person. That's all I can say. Or she'll cut my tongue out and turn on me."

Cohen dismissed it.

CENTRIPETAL

FOUR MONTHS HE'D been in that prison. Four. And he was supposed to be used to the place now. Or the days weren't supposed to be passing slower. And slower. And slower.

Four months had been long enough for him to watch some of the familiar faces get released. Releases happened on Tuesdays and Fridays at eleven in the morning. He could watch Friday's releases from the yard because Friday at eleven was part of his Yard Time. He'd be sitting in his hack squat machine. Pushing himself up and down, pushing his body to burn, feel alive, ache, but he'd stop to watch when someone got released. Got greeted by their family. Bear hugs. A kiss. A kid clinging to someone's leg. He'd wonder about those kinds of families. The ones who brought their kids to greet Daddy on release day. But they were always so goddamn thrilled to see each other that Cohen longed to be in someone else's shoes. Longed to be elsewhere, over that fence, in another life.

He'd realized, in prison, after all those days breezed by him, indifferent and undifferentiated, that, in the years since Allie first left him, his days needed something he wasn't giving them. There were shots at women he never took, an opening for a promotion, vacation time he did not spend in the places he'd always wanted to go. Nothing significant had punctuated the years as they rolled by. Just a leak to fix in the attic, some dishes to wash, a movie that sounded good.

His friends were all married now, and on nights out, he'd hear the clink of their wedding rings against beer bottles. It was the sound of missed opportunities. He was nearing thirty-five, and something had gotten away from him.

He met Julie Reid on a day life made him look up. Two dimples and pure sincerity whenever she smiled. They'd shaken hands and introduced themselves, and her smile never really went away. She had electric blue eyes, like if he touched her face, he might get a shock.

The lease was up on his car, and he went into the dealership to buy it out, and it was Julie's first week on the job. She had a cellphone in one hand and an office phone in the other, and her hair was a cartoon drawing of a flustered and overworked employee. He could almost see the radiating waves of anxiety a cartoonist would've drawn, beaming from her head.

"I'm very sorry," she said, and she meant it. "I've never done this process before, this paperwork. But bear with me. I have notes." She had two sheets of paper in front of her with red stickers hanging off the sides of them. There were little arrows drawn on the red stickers as if the stickers weren't enough.

He laughed. "Sure. Take your time. I'm not in a rush. Honestly. Take your time."

As he reclined into his chair, she looked up at him. Those electric blue eyes. She could taser someone with those things. "It's my first week, and one of the managers left, *quit*, before my training was over. And this place is a *madhouse* of people coming and going without appointments. I like appointments. I *love* appointments. I like daily planners and punctuality and schedules, you know? Marking things on a calendar." She etched a big X in the air with an invisible marker. There was a scribble-filled calendar on her wall. *Twelve Months of Monet.*

"Yes. Organization. Keeps life on the rails."

"Anyway, sorry. Back on track here. I need the exact kilometre count on your odometer and your insurance policy number." She was looking through what he'd provided her. "I, um, do you have it on you?"

"I can run out to the car and get both."

"Thanks so much!"

She pulled a pen out from behind her ear to hand it to him. Then she looked at it like, *Is it weird to give you a pen from behind my ear?* He took the pen, and she rooted around her desk for a piece of scrap paper he could write his kilometre count on: her hand like a foraging mouse, searching under forms and prodding through drawers.

"My God. Sorry. I'm just, I'm so. Ah! You know? Here." She pulled a balled-up receipt out of her pant pocket. "Write it on the back of this for me?"

He looked at the front of her receipt on his way out to his car. Some movie rentals. A sucker for romantic comedies where everything works out okay.

He came back into her office, handed her the insurance card and odometer reading, and her stomach roared. "*God!*" She clutched her stomach. "I'm sorry. But I'm *starving!*" She lowered her voice and looked around to make sure no one was in earshot. "Third day on the job and I haven't taken a lunch break yet because no one here seems to stop and eat." Then she shook her head, *Why am I saying all this to a customer.* "Anyway, sorry. Back on track. Can I see your license and registration?"

"I, ah. I already gave it to you—"

"Right." Quick shakes of her head while she looked around her desk for it.

It's always what he fell for: someone a little off kilter with a dozen endearing traits to fall for, one at a time. Like the way she got all animated when she was rattled. Her two-finger typing on the keyboard.

He read her nametag. "Julie, hey?"

She looked down at her name tag and back up at him and then back at her computer screen. "Um, yeah. Julie Reid. And that makes you the first person, ever, to have validated the use of nametags."

"If you could have anything to eat right now, what would it be?"

"Oh, a chicken Caesar salad. Easily. *Mmm*, right?"

"I can go buy you one. If you want?"

She wasn't taken off guard, and he liked that. He liked that kind of girl. "If what? If I accidentally write in that you owe us four grand instead of six?"

All that chemistry crackling there between them. Her eyes like a net she'd thrown at him.

"If nothing. I hide a chicken Caser in my manbag here," he tapped it, "and sneak back into your office and everyone thinks you are selling me a new minivan or something. You've got to eat. I know how awkward a first week at a new job can be. Settling in. Skipping lunch. All that stuff. Do you want a chicken Caesar or not? I'm not being boldly and awkwardly flirtatious here. I'm just offering some lunch to a hungry woman. Because I'm that kind of man."

She eyed him playfully, but said nothing.

"Just let me buy you a chicken Caesar and sneak it in to you. Like a customer, turned delivery boy. Just one, I won't even join you. I'm a very important person as you've probably gathered in looking at me. And I have some very important places to be."

"Are you being funny or arrogant?"

"Funny."

"Then you need to work on your schtick." She laughed and said, "You know what I like as much as the thought of eating? Talking to you about something other than two-doors and four-doors and licences and registrations and gas mileage and minivans with TVs on the backs of headrests for the kids on the long drives to the cabin. I'm hungry. I could cry just *thinking* of the tang of Caesar dressing on my tongue. I'm mentally crunching croutons right now."

The crook of her arm and the M of her top lip and the wet vivacious gloss in her eyes. The little things. They added up to everything that had left his life, along with Allie Crosbie, two years ago.

Before long there were dinners and movies and he'd seen the vicious scar on her right shoulder blade—white around the edges and cotton-candy pink near the centre—from when a hunter, *a poacher*, had accidentally shot her when she was a kid, camping on Labour Day weekend. She'd missed the first week of grade twelve because of it. The scar was the shape of an upturned beer cap. It was raised as if the bullet had shot out of her. He'd asked her about it, after the first night they made love. And she'd asked him about his scar, the one above his heart.

She made pancakes for lunch sometimes, but never for breakfast, and she was big on pepper. Especially on her eggs. He liked the taste of her lips. Whether it was natural or some product she smeared on, it was like biting into an apple. He liked the husky they'd had, for two years, before it fell over a landing, down a staircase, and had to be put down.

But in the end she needed too much. She'd beg for more sex after he'd come and going down on her wasn't enough. She wanted to be out five nights a week, but once a month was enough for him. He was always up for a hike, but she'd pack the tent because they *may as well make a night of it.* He'd have to assist in making a fresh meal every night even if he was dead tired, on a

Monday night, and a frozen pizza in the oven would have done the trick for him. Yoga, jogs, lame TV shows: she couldn't do these things alone.

One year into their relationship, he didn't know why he was trying to keep up with her. And then he stayed with her for two more. Because it wasn't all bad—knowing when she'd laugh at a movie and how, three years into a relationship, she still kissed him like she meant it. Intimacy, sharing the mundane details of his day with someone. This he liked. To be connected to someone made him feel connected to life. Alive. Even if she felt like a substitute for something, or someone, that had already happened. Or was yet to happen.

He dreamt of Matt a lot, still, in those years he spent with Julie. All of them together again. Glimpses of Allie and the way she looked back then. In his dreams of Allie, they were always about to get married, but Allie herself was seldom in the dream. It was always Matt, and there was *talk* of the wedding. But never a wedding.

One night he'd dreamt that he was lying in his bed with his eyes closed, knowing that if he opened them he'd see Matt standing in the corner of his room and staring at him. Shivering, blue with cold. Panting, in a tattered suit, with beads of water dripping off of him. Like he'd just climbed out of that upturned truck in the ocean. Ragged purplish skin. Cohen shot up in the bed when he woke that night, and Julie jumped awake too. She whispered tiredly, rubbing at her eyes, "Nightmare?"

And it was that night he realized there was so much about him she never knew. Too much, for a woman he'd spent three years with. She knew he had a dead brother, but she'd have to struggle to recall his name was Ryan. Julie was with a *version* of him. She was occupying select roles of a partner, but was never the whole package.

AN INVITATION HAD shown up in his and Julie's mailbox one day. *Longing: An exhibition of contemporary photography by local artists Allie Crosbie and Cynthia Nash. Saltscapes Gallery. Tuesday, May the 13th.*

It wasn't Allie reaching out. It was a flyer everyone on that street had received, maybe everyone in that town or on that gallery's mailing list. But he thought, maybe Allie *had* tracked him down. His address. Gotten it off Lee or something. He and Lee still kept in touch a little over the years. Phone calls during the Christmas holidays and quick visits on birthdays, but not much beyond that sort of thing. There was a night or two, in the years since they'd broken up, that Lee'd called him and said, "We were just doing some reminiscing, and I thought you two should say hello to each other. For old time's sake." And he'd hand the phone to Allie. Awkward *Heys*, awkward *Hellos*, awkward *How are things?*

But the sound of her voice had always reset something in him. He'd hear the way her voice snagged on Cs. The little things he'd forgotten about. Then he'd hang up the phone and remember a whole lot more about her.

He hadn't seen her in years, and then the invitation. He always took his mail into the kitchen with him and stood over the recycling bin with it, throwing out envelopes and then their contents after reading them. But he took the invitation upstairs with him and sat on the corner of his bed with it. She had shorter hair now. At least she did in the artist photo on the invitation. A smile like someone had told her to smile. Say cheese. She was all pose and no glow.

May 12th, midnight, the night before her show, his phone rang and it was Allie and she was drunk. "Maybe...maybe you shouldn't come tomorrow night? I don't know."

"Are you...okay?"

"Yes. Drunk is all."

"Are you talking about your show, at the gallery?"

"Of course, what do you mean?"

"I, ah. I dunno why...you'd think I was going."

"Well, Je-*sus*, mister. Sorry I invited you!" He laughed, but kind of shocked by his answer.

"No, no. I assumed it was a flyer, not an invite!"

"Hah! When was the last time an art gallery sent out invitations for a show? You've always been really supportive of my photography. Or you were. You seemed let down I got out of it. When I stopped taking photos. I started getting back into it recently. Got my first show. Put some thought into who to invite. You know? It's."

She said nothing after saying it's. Cohen waited a few seconds. "It's what?"

"Sorry. I'm drunk. In the bad way. Rum and wine and pints,

and all of it mixed up in me. Gross. It is. Gross. I feel...gross. The bed's spinning like I'm a teenager. Remember that ride we were on, that time in Toronto? And the lady in the bucket in front of us threw up, and it sprayed back and slapped all over our bucket? It got on my shoes. You bought bottles of water to wash it off, and I couldn't even watch—"

And then he heard Keith's voice enter the room. The phone muffled, like she'd put a hand over the receiver or hid the phone under a pillow. After five minutes, he decided it was the latter, even though he felt someone in their thirties needn't hide a phone call to their ex, *an old friend*, about an art exhibition. He waited out ten minutes of white noise, until the phone clicked off.

He put his phone back on the cradle, doubting he'd go to her show now. The drunken dial. The forty-five minute drive and all that awkward silence that would linger after the, "Hi, how are you, how have you been? Congrats on the show."

And yet, before that phone call, he'd even thought about what he'd wear and had conjured up some ideas for small talk. Jokes about Lee, mainly. About the bird rescue missions and if he was still up to that sort of thing.

Maybe you shouldn't come tomorrow night. He wondered why she'd even called in the first place.

His phone rang again a little later that night. But just once. There was no one on the line when he answered it. But the call display had been the same number she'd called from earlier.

The next morning he read the email she'd sent him, drunk, at three a.m.:

> *Hi there! Where to start. I'm sorry, maybe? Keith came in and I buried the phone under my pillow, without thinking. I don't know why really. I'm drunk, maybe that's why? I don't know why I'm sorry. I don't know why about a lot, you know? Remember when I took this job? I didn't think I'd be in it forever. I like the job still. That's not my point. I don't know what my point is. Or why I am typing. I just mean, I'm not far off forty, and that happened too fast. Do you know what I mean?*
>
> *What I mean, really, is that I can recap the last few years of my life in a paragraph. That's what I mean. I don't mean I can, I mean anyone can. That's sad. Life goes too slow and then too fast.*

D'you know what I've noticed? I've noticed that time doesn't always feel like it moves forward only. I mean, it's like it can just orbit around certain moments for years. It's hard to explain. I'm doing hand motions that would help, if you were here to see them.

Anyway, I should go. I'm feeling nauseous. Nauseated. Whatever. (There's a difference right?)

I just wanted to try and explain a little. You know me, with the over-explanations. I think that's why we got along. Everything was always on the table with us. Everything was always off our chests. Oh, except for that one thing. Yeah. Except for that.

A couple of new things about me: I have discovered this: buttering toast and sprinkling cinnamon on it. I'm gone back to using bars of soap in the shower, over body washes. There's something thicker and more purifying about it. The smell lasts longer.

Did you know we never had any pets? Me and you. Weird, right? Keith's allergic to cats and dogs. So he and I don't have a dog. A Boston terrier, I'll never have a Boston terrier. Can you really be allergic to both? I looked into it. Fun fact: it's cat's saliva people are allergic to. Not the fur. The saliva in the licked fur.

I'm really just drunkenly rambling now. Like a kid or something. The dam is busted and the words are flowing. I should go. Goodnight. But it's okay to be a kid sometimes. When it feels right.

By the way, Lee is doing good. He says you two talk still. Sweet. Both of you, sweet as hell. I always liked you two together. It was like a comedy skit. The Bird Rescuers. And what an unlikely duo. He probably shot and maimed those birds as an excuse to get you out to Grayton! (Kidding.)

It's great you two keep in touch. We should. You and me. I guess that's what I am saying. Good friends are few and far between. Lee's okay but lately in some ways he isn't. He talks about the war a lot now, and it scares me because it's not something he ever used to talk about. So why now? He's getting a little slow and repetitive lately. A little nasty, even.

I'm into yoga now. "Wheel Pose" and "The Side Crow" and shit. I've got all the moves. Or I will. I'd like you to say something back to me. Maybe you've had cinnamon on toast too, who knows?

I'm working on the ultimate yoga move now. "Little Thunderbolt." You should Google it. Keith makes lame jokes about taking the bendy yoga moves into the bedroom. Keith sort of ruins everything. In that high-school jock sort of way. Like, unintentionally, I mean—thinking he's being funny. What I mean is: I think yoga poses are beautiful. Women contorting into those impossible shapes. It's what got me back into photography, weird as it sounds. I wanted to do self-portraits of me in my poses. Is that weird? Black and whites. As I master each pose. I've done a series of other women. There's something so primitive or empowering or elegant about a woman in a yoga pose. I've framed my friend Melanie doing the "One-legged King Pigeon" and "Scorpion" poses. She's amazing, graceful. (Why am I putting the poses in quotation marks?) I asked Keith to photograph me, from above, while I was in the Bow Pose. He laughed and rocked me like I was a rocking horse. He didn't even take the photo before slapping my ass and walking away.

I did something, years ago. Four, five? I kept a secret from you. I'm very sorry about it. I have less of an excuse than you had. About Dad. We're even now. It's that big of a deal. Or it might be, I am not sure, and that's how I justified keeping it a secret. It may or may not have been relevant to you. About you, involve you, whatever. I tell myself it likely isn't, but someday I'll tell you all about it. But not now, in some drunken email, about yoga and cinnamon toast. I'm babbling. I should go.

I dream of your dad a lot. What's that all about? Never you, never your mom, just your dad and me (or your dad and I, which is it?), and we talk about you. But indirectly. I Googled it, of course, and it's a phenomenon. People commonly dream of their ex's parents, but seldom the ex. What's up with that, right?

I wanted you to come to my art show and see my work and catch up and put the past behind us. Be friends, you know? We got each other. If nothing else, I miss that. Two people

EVERY
LITTLE
THING

shouldn't throw away a kinship that took years to build. True friends are hard to find and all that. You can't force time to pass and bond you and your new friends, do you know what I mean? The past friends are the ones you have a history with— the more significant life moments the merrier. And being known like you know me was nice. We were best friends as much as anything. You're fun stuff, pal.

I saw you at Dad's grave once, by the way. I sort of watched you, standing there. You looked like you didn't know how to interact with a headstone. It was windy and your unzipped jacket was a blue cape because of the wind. Like you were super-sorry-man. It was sort of beautifully sad. You there listless and biting fingernails. And I forgave you, that day. You had him to think about, too. I sort of understood that, that day. Watching you there. It wasn't all about me, and you were caught in the middle. But I should have mattered more. And my father shouldn't have left me so suddenly. You did things wrong, but unintentionally wrong. Here's my forgiveness. Eons later. Via email.

Look. Me and you, let's talk more regularly. Okay? But, after that phone call and me hiding the phone, and this email—and how embarrassed I'll be about it tomorrow morning—scrap the photo show tomorrow. Don't come. It'll be boring as hell anyway. They even made me write an artist's statement. That's not me, as you know. But call me sometime, okay? Let's catch up. For all I know, you've got three kids and a wife by now. And it seems like I should know their names.

I mean, I know you're not married. But you know what I mean?

It's been fun acting like a drunk schoolgirl and typing non-censored blabbering, but it'd be even more fun to catch up over a coffee. And hear you talk back.

Best, really, all of it, Allie. Allie Crosbie. Remember her? That cute little thing who followed you up to the rooftop that night? Hey Birdman?

P.S—I met someone with your heart disorder recently. A woman. ARVC. There's herds of you out there now, apparently, going around with robot hearts! Got me thinking of you. That and the show.

HE RESPONDED RIGHT away, but if he had his time back, he would have thought out his response a little more. He would have asked more questions. Flirted a little. Pried, subtly, to see if she was okay, happy. All he typed back was, "Allie, Allie Crosbie. Yeah. The name rings a bell. The coffee sounds nice, or a drink. I'll even buy the round. P.S.—You made Keith sound like a real catch in that email. I think you chose the right man after all. You?"

And she'd typed back "A drink sounds great, moneybags."

But the drinks never happened. The passing of time and all that. Hectic schedules, things to do, a fear of awkward silences. Because what would they say, really?

Not long after that email, he got up out of bed one night, half-asleep, half-awake, and sat on the edge of his mattress with his hands holding each other in his lap. His shadow on the wall looked like a toppling building. The light coming through the window was a shade of purple he read as four, maybe five in the morning. Minutes later, only slightly more awake, he wandered into his spare bedroom, to the computer desk, and opened the top drawer. There was a tin can full of things he didn't know what to do with: a copy of the first article he'd published in a scientific journal and a photo of him and David Suzuki shaking hands at a benefit that the Avian-Dome had hosted in 2004. There were some old photographs, his birth certificate, and the engagement ring Matt had given him and made him promise Allie would get.

He took the ring out of the tin and laid it on his desk. The ring cast a shadow beneath itself like a donut until a car drove by his window and its headlights hit that shadow, dragging the top of the donut down to make a temporary heart-shaped shadow beneath the ring. He Googled where the tradition of proposing with an engagement ring had come from and couldn't get a clear answer.

He put the ring in an envelope, with a note, and sent it to Lee. *Make sure Keith gets this? It was her mother's, and I promised Matt that she'd get it one day. Feel Keith out about whether or not he's ever going to propose to her and, if need be, give him this ring? (But only if you know for sure the moron is going to propose.)*

Thanks, best, stay in touch,

- Cohen.

EVERY
LITTLE
THING

143

OFF AND ON, Julie Reid would stumble back into his life, between relationships of her own. They were friends, but sometimes she'd spend the night. She had a thing for sex in the shower and unbearably hot water, even in the summer. She liked the steam and slippery stall walls and the way he pressed her against the wall. She'd tuck her head into his neck, and her wet hair would cling to his chest. Her hands like hawk claws in the backs of his arms, and her heels squeak-sliding along the basin's edge. And then always, after they were done, *Take a bath with me?* All that steam and heat and passion had his heart flickering like a wasp trapped in a jar. But only ever with her, in the shower, did sex shock his heart like that. It was the heat and steam or it was Julie Reid or it was both.

She'd pour the bath, turn off the light, get in first, and ask him to lay back-on into her. She'd drape her hands over his shoulders and slide a finger over the glossy scar on his chest. She'd run her fingers over the hard chunk of metal below the scar, pressing hard enough to feel it there. She'd ask him to explain what ARVC was all over again because she could never remember what was wrong with his heart, and then she'd joke as she re-remembered. "So, you got poor rhythm? Can't keep a beat? *Hah hah.*"

Julie would meet someone online, or she'd give in to a neighbour's forward advances, or a customer buying a hatchback would pick her up, the way he had, and he wouldn't hear from her for months. And then one night she'd knock on his door. A distinct knock. *Tap, tap…tap. Tap, tap…tap.* She'd spend a night telling him that all men are inane or insane. It didn't count as a relationship, and yet their periodic flings—three times after they'd broken up and never longer than a few weeks—were enough for Cohen. Whatever that meant about him.

She'd comment on that, with an arm around him, lying in his bed, skating fingers around his chest. *Don't you want something permanent and meaningful? A wife to take to staff Christmas parties? A kid to throw baseballs at?*

She got knocked up by a high-school physics teacher named Pete. He met her baby once, in a coffee shop. *My little Charlie Man*, she'd called him, reaching down into the stroller to pinch his cheeks. And then he never saw her again.

SEEING AND NOT KNOWING

IT STARTED WITH a casual conversation at the staff coffee pot. "You like kids, right, Davies?"

"Depends where you're going with this. But yes, as a rule, more than adults."

"And they like you. You have a way with relaying information and making learning fun." He tapped his skull twice, "Learning only sticks when it's fun. Or at least, interesting."

"It's not hard to make plants and animals exciting to kids."

Clarence laughed as he poured then handed Cohen a cup of coffee. "Tell that to any other adult who takes thirty kids on a hike in the woods. Your patience is a virtue."

Cohen took the mug from Clarence and took a slow, temperature-gauging sip of coffee, wondering where Clarence was going with this because the man never spoke a sentence without reason. He started every conversation like a persuasive essay.

"I have a proposition," he said, "not that you can say no, really."

Clarence grinned and pointed to his office door, but he'd pointed with the hand his mug was in, and hot coffee sloshed out of the mug, down across his fingers, and onto his shoes. "*Shit!*" He shimmied his mug to his other hand and shook the burning fingers like he was strumming a banjo. "Go on, take a seat in my office." He took a handful of napkins and soaked up the brown puddle of coffee on his black shoes. "I'll be right in."

Clarence came in the room, shut his door, and sat behind his desk with a sigh, laying his mug on a coaster. "Fine way to start a rainy Monday, hey? Spilling your goddamn morning coffee all over yourself?" His office was all things nautical: a silver ship as a paper weight, framed photos of his boat on the walls, and blue curtains with a sea shell design. He was the only man Cohen knew who smoked a pipe and owned a yacht.

"So, what's up, Clarence? You looking to pawn your son and daughter off on me or something?"

Clarence laughed and looked at a framed photo of his two children on his desk. "There's days you could tempt me to pawn Jane off on you, no doubt. Fucking junior high!" He shook his head. "Half her friends are spoiled brats and she has to play the part, you know?"

A couple of nodding heads and a few sips of coffee and Clarence explained, "We've had great success with the Nature Adventurer hikes in the summer, in terms of registration and parent feedback. So, to bring in a little more cash and added community value to the Avian-Dome, *year-round*, and to avoid becoming a tourist trap, I want to do an after school program. I want you to be my man and educationally entertain the kids from three to five thirty, on weekdays. And well, to be blunt, having an afterschool program like this would also open up a whole new batch of grants the Avian-Dome could be eligible for."

"Is this for sure?"

"Supposing I can get enough elementary school kids enrolled, and other such considerations, yes. Do you have any reasonable objections to being my man for this?"

"Yeah. No. Sure. I mean, I'm your man."

Clarence nodded, once, and took a big sip of coffee into his grinning mouth. "It'll mean you work until five thirty, Monday to Friday, but in exchange I'd be willing to give you a month off in the summer...like a teacher. Do you like the sound of that?"

"I love the sound of that."

Clarence got up to pull his curtains open, and it was so foggy it was like they were in a tall skyscraper shrouded by clouds. "The two or three hours a day you spend with the kids will mean you'll be doing less sample analyses and raw data crunching. Less research projects in general and seminar hosting. I'll take on a few more honours and graduate students from the university to pick up your slack. I'm willing to bet that's not going to bother you?"

"That's not going to bother me."

Cohen got up to leave the room, and Clarence said, "I'm not

sure yet, but you might have to take some kind of childcare course or something. First Aid maybe. Not sure, but we'll pay for it, of course. Strange PD for a scientist hey?"

"Stranger things have happened."

THE NATURE ADVENTURERS After School Program was like any other daycare, except they drew dinosaurs instead of pictures of families standing in front of houses. They played *To which bird does this egg belong?* instead of hide and go seek, but they played hide and go seek too.

There was a kid he took to right away, a favourite, and he couldn't deny it. Years ago, Allie's best friend had been a teacher, and she confessed the same. *It just happens. Sometimes you click with a kid, but it's the same with any friendship, right?*

The first day the bus pulled up in front of the Avian-Dome, he guided the fifteen kids inside. The sixteenth kid, Zack, had been sitting alone on the bus, drawing comics in the condensation on a window. He wouldn't get out until he'd finished his master-piece—a Tyrannosaurus rex. He got out last and hung back from the crowd. He wasn't shy so much as disinterested in being part of the group. His imagination, or drawing on that window, was entertainment enough for him. What Cohen noticed right away, and found endearing, was Zack's pride in his mental catalogue of random animal facts and how he'd only share those facts with Cohen if none of the other kids were nearby. Cohen wouldn't even see him coming sometimes. There'd be a quick tug on Cohen's pant leg, and then, "Hey! I know why all the dinosaurs died."

"Do *you?*"

"It's because a giant meteor smashed them!" and he banged a fist into an open palm: one hand the earth, the other a meteor.

Most days, Zack was the last kid to be picked up. As they stood in the porch with their shoes on—Zack weighed down by his blue and red bookbag and clutching his Buzz Lightyear toy by its thick arm—he'd say something like, "Whales can't breathe under water like fish can," and smile about knowing it. "They gotta jump out of the water to gulp some air down. But they can hold their breath for a crazy long time, so it's all okay. Don't worry."

Sometimes Cohen would act surprised about what Zack had just told him. He'd say, *Really?* and Zack's neck would pop off

EVERY
LITTLE
THING

his shoulders like a jack-in-the-box. Eventually, Zack's father would show up: a cellphone clenched between his ear and shoulder. His voice was always exhausted but stern with whoever was letting him down on the other end of the line. He'd smile and nod, but unlike all the other parents, this man never greeted Cohen. Or Zack.

He never bent down and rubbed Zack's head and said, *Hey little man*, the way Cohen, for some reason, wished he would. He wanted this kid's father to be the best father of the lot, but the man would just snap his fingers and hold out a hand for Zack to take.

By October, Cohen felt overly close to the kid. So it was a punch in the guts when he noticed how Zack's father would hold Zack by the wrist, not the hand, as he guided him back to their car. Zack tripping up on his own little feet as he tried to keep pace with his father's hurried gait.

By November or December of that year, he could be tossing a spoonful of coffee into a percolator on a Sunday morning and wonder what Zack was doing. Same with a Wednesday night at a grocery store if he saw parents talking to their children in the cereal aisle. Because it had always bothered him to see a parent answer their child's questions with a *Shh!* And he had Zack's father pegged to be that kind of dad. The shushing kind. And that bothered Cohen to his core for some reason. It could've been that Zack was a dead ringer for Ryan. Not only in his face and bony little body, but in the way he was so full of questions and curiosity and thought Cohen had all the answers. Or it could've been that Cohen was halfway through his thirties and had always wanted a son and had always imagined that son would be exactly like Zack. Independent. Eyes held wide like everything was amazing. A big, breakable heart.

Zack's father was one of six parents—doctors, nurses, chefs—who dropped their kids off on school holidays. The Avian-Dome had kept a few snacks laying around for the kids: granola bars, yogurt, apples. Some of those mornings, Cohen would notice the way Zack gorged on granola bars like he hadn't eaten breakfast. Two granola bars at 8:30 a.m. didn't sit well with Cohen. It spoke to a missed breakfast. He wanted to pick through the kid's bookbag to make sure his father had packed him a lunch.

He mentioned all his concerns to Clarence at a staff Christmas party. They were at the drink table, a makeshift bar, shoulder to shoulder with their elbows plunked down, waiting for the bartender's attention. All he got was a dismissive, "We're not in the business of child welfare, and to be curt, it's none of your business until the kid says something to concern you. Something *specific*, Cohen. I can hardly call up Child Services with what you're giving me. And it would be drastically inappropriate for me to have a one-on-one with Jamie Janes because my employee thinks he's *too cold* with his kid. Give me something concrete if you expect me to overstep my bounds."

The bartender came their way and axed the conversation with an inquisitive nod, "What can I get you?"

Clarence asked Cohen what he wanted, bought the round, and said, "Look. Maybe the guy isn't the father of the year, but you've got no right to say so, unless the child's health and safety are on the line. Come to me then. And for fuck's sake, Davies, lighten up. It's nine days before Christmas!" He handed him his drink. "We're all half-drunk and trying to have a good time, aren't we?"

Over the Christmas holidays, his mother casually asked Cohen how work was as she scraped bits of turkey and vegetables into the garbage. He found himself telling her all about a kid named Zack, and it simply fell out of his mouth, unexpectedly, like he'd dropped a glass of water. "He reminds me of Ryan, actually."

She looked at him like he'd said something wrong.

But the fact was, since he'd met Zack, Cohen had been thinking a lot about Ryan because it was when Ryan was that age that they'd spent the most time together. Shared the controller for video games, stuff like that. On the first day back from Christmas vacation, it was the only time Zack had burst out of the bus before the other kids. Zack came running towards him with a high five, his feet stamping fresh prints in the snow, and Cohen knelt down to greet him. He was well aware by now that he'd unfairly separated these kids into Zack and the other ones.

There was the high-five—Zack's mittened hand a muted slap off Cohen's bare hand—and then Zack said, looking over his shoulder before the other kids caught up, "Guess what I know?"

"What do you know?"

"Not all owls sleep in the day and hunt at night! The snowy owl is different like that! It's awake in the day!"

"I know, buddy, I know."

"Oh."

The other kids had caught up, and they all walked into the building and down the hallway, near single file.

"So how was Christmas, buddy?"

"It was good. I saw my nan. She lives in the United States of America. Not Canada. She gave me a book about birds and read me a bunch of stuff about owls. There's, like, two hundred and something of them, you know? And owls got special feathers that don't make a sound when they fly, so that their prey can't hear them coming." He made one fist an owl and the other a shrew and smashed them together. It was a hand motion he made to explain just about everything. "She gave me a microscope too, but dad hasn't put it together for me yet."

Walking into the boardroom, the boardroom that had become the kids' rec room, Zack hauled a cheap plastic lantern out of his bookbag. When he pressed a button, the centre lit up yellow and a frog on the top lit up green. "I got this too. I turn it on when I'm home alone, if I think I hear something scary."

"What do you mean, when you're home alone?"

"If Dad has to run out or work. He locks all the doors and leaves his phone number by the phone. But still, sometimes I worry someone scary was *already* in the house *before* he locked the door. Sometimes Tanya can't babysit, see."

Cohen urged Clarence to do something about that. A kid being left home alone. Six years old.

"Do what, Cohen, citizen's arrest?"

"No. Put in a call to Child Services. I'd hate to see the day come that I'm put in the position to tell someone in Child Services that I told my superior that a child was being left alone, and possibly neglected in other ways, and that my superior ignored—"

"Watch it, Davies! D'you hear me? Cool off. Get out of my office and get back to work."

"That came out wrong." Cohen laughed. "I wasn't threatening to call them."

But Clarence stayed firm. Eyed him curiously. "You bring

your concerns to me and then you're done with the matter, you hear me? I take action on this stuff. Not you. And I do as I see fit. Do *not* overstep me on these matters. That's an official warning," he said, making a note on his computer. "And I've just sent you an email, so the warning is on record. I like you, I like the kid, but I'm concerned with what your worry might do to us all here."

MAY SEVENTEENTH. A call from the hospital. Zack's father had badly burned his hand at work.

"I don't know what to say, I'm really sorry, I'm still in the waiting room, and what time is it?" a slight pause while he must have checked a watch. "It's after six. Shit."

"Shit is right. We've been waiting in the porch for an hour!"

"Listen. I'm injured. I've been held up here, waiting forever. I'm sorry, but I can't think of anything to do, about getting Zack looked after."

"What about that girl who picked him up a few times last month?"

"Tanya?"

A harsh sigh, "I don't know her name, man."

"We're...we've broken up. Like. Listen. I know you've got some kind of problem with me. I see it on your face every day I pick the kid up—"

"See, man, it's the fact you just called him *the kid*, not *my* kid or Zack—"

"Listen, I'm in a hospital waiting room. I can't have this...confrontation right now. But I know you think the world of Zack, and I need a favour. I need someone to watch him until I get my hand taken care of here. He talks about you, you know. At home. This will never happen again, but I'm stuck. Can you just...take him back to your place maybe? I'll pick him up there?"

"That's. I mean. I would, but my employer will have my head. These days, you don't...take kids back to your place. Liabilities, perceptions—"

"Are you saying you can't or?"

He gave Jamie his home address and hung up without saying goodbye.

In the car, on the way back to Cohen's, Zack seemed really worried about his father and that much made Cohen happy. Worry stems from love.

Zack had a tiny toy dinosaur pinched between each thumb and forefinger, making them fight on his left knee. "Is my dad gonna be okay?"

"Yes. He hurt his hand is all. But he's got two of those! And we can always buy him a new one if he needs it."

Laughing his head off. "You can't buy a new *hand*!"

"I know. I'm kidding. Everything will be all right, I promise."

"My dad's a chef. He always hurts his hands."

"Oh yeah?"

"Yeah. Burns and cuts. He makes really good desserts. Sometimes I help."

"So your dad is fun, good to you?" Zack stared at him, like he didn't understand the question. "You have fun with your dad? You two play a lot?"

"Well, he's on the phone a lot and says he needs time alone to think. He's always thinking. I guess that means he's smart, right?"

Cohen laughed at the logic, sad as it was. "Yeah, I guess so. I wonder what he's thinking about? What's your guess?"

"Things to cook."

Cohen laughed again.

"Hey, Mr. Davies, did you ever see how short a Tyrannosaurus rex's arms are?" He held the toy up. "I bet if one bent over, to pick something up, its nose would poke off the ground too—"

"Who's he talking to, on the phone all the time. Do you know?"

"My nan. She doesn't live here. She lives in Florida. It's warm down there and they have lizards. All the birds with long legs. And long beaks. He always talks about Lynn. That was my mom's name. He's still really mad at her. Just been gone a long time. And doesn't give him money."

He wanted to pry, but he didn't know where to start.

"...or he tells Nan about how I've been fainting. Like he's mad about that too."

Cohen pulled the car over, against a curb, and turned around to face Zack in the back seat. He laid a hand on Zack's knee, looked him in the eye. "Zack, I promise you, no one is mad about you fainting. And certainly not your dad. But how many times has it happened, buddy?"

CHAD
PELLEY

152

"It happened in my backyard and then twice at school in gym class. Everyone thinks I'm afraid of sports now. I'm not. I'm actually really good at basketball." Cohen took his hand off Zack's knee and turned around. He was looking out his windshield and processing the news when Zack asked him, "Am I all right? Does everybody faint?"

"Your dad's figuring everything out. Don't you worry."

"I know. He talks to Nan, and they think I should move to Florida with her. But I might not be allowed for some reason."

"Is your dad moving to Florida?"

"No. Don't tell him I know that. I listen to them on the phone from behind the couch."

Cohen didn't know where to start, and he said, "What did the doctors say or how did your father explain it to you, about why you're fainting?"

Zack shrugged his shoulders and accidentally dropped the red dinosaur. It bounced under the seat, and he complained he couldn't reach it. The seatbelt snapping him upright every time he'd lunge for it. So Cohen got out and fetched it for him. And he stopped interrogating him.

He took him home, fed him, and they played hide and go seek and tag and watched a show about crocodiles. Within a minute of the show coming on, Zack had blurted out, "Crocodiles and alligators are different. They live in different parts of the world. And alligators got fatter snouts than crocodiles!"

Zack fell asleep before eight. Cohen didn't know much about kids his age, but that seemed strange. Jamie knocked on his door, his bandaged hand was a white cannonball. Instead of letting him in, Cohen stepped outside and closed the door behind him. Jamie took a step back, wary, ready for confrontation. Like he *wanted* Cohen to provoke him.

"Is it bad?" Cohen nodded to his hand.

"Yes, actually. Second-degree, down to the nerves, but it won't need a graft or anything." He shrugged his shoulders. "It'll heal. I appreciate this, man. It's a one-time inconvenience."

"Thing is, Jamie, it wasn't an inconvenience. Zack's great company. But I'm concerned it was me you had to have look after him. He should have a...I don't know...a next of kin or whatever."

Jamie's body tightened, his face went twitchy. "Look, man...Zack likes you, and the Avian-Dome is a convenient place

EVERY
LITTLE
THING

153

to drop him off and pick him up on weekdays, but I'm sick of...you. To be blunt. I mean, Jesus," an angry laugh, "Think about it."

"And what's up with the fainting?"

He shook his head. "Just go in there and send out Zack."

"Yeah, of course, but I mean, c'mon. Someone at the Avian-Dome should know about any medical conditions? It's called responsible parenting—"

"The doctors are looking into it. What do you want me to say? They don't know, so I don't know. I'm doing the best I can with this kid, and it's really...it's goddamn bold of you to be grilling me."

"And what's up with shipping him off to Florida?"

Shifty feet, a shaking head. "You want the full story? To shut you up?"

"I've got a few legitimate questions, that's all."

"Why I'm *shipping him off to Florida*. You call that a legitimate question from some daycare worker?" He looked him up and down. "I adopted that kid because Lynn wanted to. My... ex. It wasn't even my idea. Kids. *She* wanted kids. I just wanted Lynn, and if that meant us being parents, fine. But the adoption process was all sorts of bullshit. It was years of our life, waiting, being inspected, renovating the goddamn house to be up to the most absurd codes. But along came Zack, just as Lynn and I are going through a rough patch. Zack was three when we adopted him. Two years into motherhood, Lynn up and runs off. Runs out on us. I haven't seen her since, and I have no shot at her sending along financial support. So there you go, gumshoe. The full story from one stranger to another. And you're here judging me for trying to do the best I can with the kid?"

"You're absolutely right that I'm being an asshole. But you can understand why, right? Why I had to ask some questions?"

Jamie clenched his jaw, looked away from Cohen, but then right back at him. "I never asked to be a goddamn single father. I'm a chef. The hours are rough. I've got a lot going on in my personal life. This latest round of stress, the boy fainting, I mean fuck, what do you want me to say? First it's anxiety attacks then it's some kind of epilepsy or some other kind of fucking defect with his heart or his blood or his brain activity. And how should I know what's wrong with Zack if the doctors don't? The *child*

profile I got from the adoption caseworker says the mother's family has no medical issues, but the father's medical history is *unknown* because the birth mother was some kind of slut who checked *not certain of paternity*."

Jamie shouldered past Cohen, hard, butting him in the chest. He thrust the door open to yell out to Zack, but Zack had been standing behind the door, listening in on their conversation, and now he was on his ass, two palms up to a bloody nose. There were tears streaming down into the red mess on his face.

Jamie helped him up off the floor as Cohen ran to get some paper towels. The blood and tears hadn't stopped. They took Zack's hands away from his little face, and the tears had trailed through the blood, etching mini mazes onto his cheeks and jaw.

COHEN CAME INTO work the next day, head down about lines crossed. He was giving a tour, to a group of kids on a grade six field trip, when he saw Jamie blowing around the Avian-Dome like a hurricane. He was asking anyone who looked like staff where he could find a man named Clarence Royce.

An hour later, throwing away a banana peel, Cohen heard Clarence beckon him. *My office. Now.*

"You had no goddamn right. Now go the fuck home! Two weeks, unpaid. Janet will be taking over the afterschool program. Until I hire someone else. Actually, the Morris kid will be done his master's work by June first. Stay away until then. When he's done, you can come back and take over the lake enrichment project. Do you remember the one I am talking about?"

Cohen nodded yes.

"We need all the samples processed and the numbers crunched and analyzed. Wherever the Morris kid leaves off, on the first, you pick up. You're absolutely done with the hikes and the after school program."

Another nod. Cohen expected worse and was speechless.

"I mean, you took the kid back to your *house*? His nose is broken, by the way. The kid's traumatized about the two of you shouting at each other. Is that what you wanted?"

Cohen stood up and, before leaving, he said, "I'm sorry, Clarence, but there's some parts of myself I can't turn off."

"I'm not judging your character, I'm judging your actions,

or you as an employee. I'd fire anyone else over this, and you probably know it." To Cohen's back as he walked out of the room, Clarence added, "I'm acting accordingly, I'll have you know. You really screwed me on this."

Cohen got home and found a tiny toy seahorse on his couch along the line where two cushions met. Zack must have left it behind. He sat down, picked it up, and flipped the seahorse like it was a coin. Over and over.

A FACE IN THE MIRROR

EVEN THOUGH HE'D been off work for weeks, he'd still set an alarm. The shrill drilling sound at 7:30 in the morning made him feel like his life was still on track. But he'd take longer showers now, maybe go out for breakfast. He was in a deli when she'd called him. He had to finish chewing through a mouthful of croissant before he could utter a *hello* without sounding gluttonous. Allie sounded like there was a gun to her head or the plane was going down. He dropped his cutlery to take the call outside. The sun greeting his eyes like a handful of salt.

"I didn't know who else to call, Cohen! I'm in Montreal. I'm fucking trembling here. My hands. It's Lee. He. My *God.* He—"

"Allie. It's okay. Just tell me, and I'll deal with it. It's okay. He's alive...right?"

"The. The hospital just called me. I'm in a meeting. I was. They're all in a boardroom behind me. Waiting for me, I don't know. He, Lee, he doesn't remember anything. He's had some mild strokes this year. But that's the thing, *some.* He's been...moody, strange. I knew I shouldn't have left him, but I *had* to, to come to Montreal—"

"Allie, calm down. Are you saying he's had another stroke?"

"No. I dunno. He's had a few. Over the last year. They've left him all foggy, harsher, but he's pulled through them. It's just...it's everything." She paused, and he pictured her throwing her hands up in the air. "His eyes are really bad now too. He's half-blind and he walks funny and falls a lot. Like he's clumsy. He's got an angry edge now too, Cohen, you wouldn't know him. He gets in funks, and I'll find him in his bed, just lying there at three in the afternoon. I thought I could come to Montreal. But I just got a call. Some kids found him in a snowbank. A fucking *snowbank*. In his house-coat." She paused, like she was picturing it. "Nothing on, but underwear and a bathrobe. I mean. He's all right now. But. *Lucid*, they're saying. *He's lucid now*, as if he won't be for long. Like he's going to snap any day now. I need to get home, I…I don't like the way the hospital was talking and I don't really underst—"

"Allie."

"He's turning on people, he's not right. He laces into Keith a lot, unprovoked. One day, he lost it at his neighbour's teenager. He caught him smashing coke bottles on the street and lost it. *Lost it*. He threw a bottle at the kid and hasn't made good with the neighbour. All these signs and I—"

"Allie. It's okay. I'm going to go get Lee, right now—"

"Don't do that. Don't say my name at the beginning of every sentence because I know that means I'm panicked and you're panicked too, but you're trying to calm me—"

"I'll go talk with the hospital. You call Lee's house tonight and I'll be there and I'll explain the whole thing, okay? I'll get the full lowdown from the doctors."

"They found him half-naked in a *snowbank*. I can't shake it. I don't care if he's okay *now*, right *now*, at this particular *minute*, because what's next?"

"Allie. What hospital?"

"You're saying my name again!"

"Sorry."

"No, God, I am! Here you are trying to do me a favour. I—I'm just really rattled here."

"Don't worry about anything until you at least know what you have to worry about, okay?"

"He's at Grayton's hospital. You're sure you can go?"

"Of course. My God, of course."

"*Lucid*. I mean, isn't that what they say about people with Alzheimer's and dementia and stuff? He's not himself lately, but it's the kinds of things I could turn a blind eye to. Old age in general, you know? Crabby and speaking his mind and all that."

"He's old, Allie, and you had to go to Montreal. Neither of those facts are your fault. He's in his nineties. It's amazing he's living alone and somewhat self-sufficient. *Amazing*. Think about it. I'm actually…off work for the next while anyway. Call Lee's house later. I'll be there. I'll stay with him day in and day out until you're back, okay?"

"Thanks," she said and, after a long pause, "I—I mean, I didn't know who to call. He's got no one, you know? How sad is that? Not even Keith's in town to do this for me."

"Yeah."

Another pause. Less cry-stuttering on her end now. He could see her, wherever she was. Her face full of tears and her palms sponging them up. Radiant as always in some kind of business casual outfit that would have black in it somewhere, if only in a bracelet or her shoes. Her hair down and not up: it was always up in buns or ponytails or a hundred different things, except when she had *a work thing.*

"So you're...*off work.* What does that mean?"

"Long story. I'm still at the Avian-Dome, though."

"You're still there, the Avian-Dome? That's nice. I always liked you there. Especially with the kids."

"Yeah. We've got a new afterschool program now. One of the kids really reminds me of—"

"You should go. Get Lee. I have to go anyway. I'm outside a boardroom right now, missing a seminar, looking like a little girly cry-face. I can feel sets of eyes on my back. Like...like their eyes are the ends of taser guns or something. It's embarrassing. I really freaked out when the hospital called. I might have overreacted."

"Well, if it's a room full of men as sweet and sensitive as Keith Stone, I'm sure they—"

"Don't be a prick—"

"Ah, but you laughed a little. I heard it!"

Another laugh, though muted under the weight of her sadness. "Maybe Keith has grown into a class act over the years. What do you know about it?"

"I know enough by the way you just laughed."

"I'll call you later," she said, and it sounded like she was biting her tongue. "Call me back if things are serious."

"Okay."

"And Cohen?"

"Yeah?"

"Don't go into that hospital room expecting the sweet old man who used to rescue birds and crack jokes, okay? Truth is, he might not...I don't know...*take* to you. He's fine around me, but

EVERY
LITTLE
THING

he doesn't have time for anyone else. That's half the reason I'm reluctant to go out of town now. And I know you've kept in touch, but it's been a while, I gather, since you didn't know about the strokes. So, seriously, call me if he's difficult with you. Call me right away."

"Roger that."

"I really do appreciate this. He's been a second father to me, you know that."

"Lee would do this for me, right?"

"What, if you went crazy?"

"If they're sending him home, everything must be okay. No one's crazy yet."

She said nothing for a few seconds. Then, "Is this why we met all those years ago? So I'd have someone to call the day Lee turned up in a snowbank?"

ALL THE TESTS the hospital had run, and their presentation of Lee's case, was akin to a pack of scientists having identified an impending natural disaster. Clipboards, charts, machines, bad news, something ready to blow.

A middle-aged blonde doctor in a white lab coat sat him down. She kept adjusting the collar of her lab coat, like it chafed her neck or something. She spoke kindly, softening her truth so it'd sting a little less as she pelted it out.

She and her intern or resident—Cohen assumed resident by the guy's keen confidence—explained the whole story. The resident, in blue scrubs, couldn't have been more than thirty, but plain looked smart. His eyes held intensely wide-opened, like a guy who reads textbooks on the beach instead of novels. The doctor and the resident, sat on the same bench, turned to face Cohen. The resident leaning awkwardly forward, to peer around the female doctor: his chest almost touching his knees.

"Mr. Davies. I'm Doctor Ross and this is Doctor Langor. Are you...a grandchild of Lee's maybe?"

"I—Lee never had children. I'm here on behalf of the closest thing he has to a daughter." He stopped there, at that gauche response, and didn't fill in the blanks of his and Allie's failed relationship. "She's in Montreal," he added, as if that gave his presence more purpose.

"Well, he has you down as one of two next of kin. *That* counts." A big bright smile: red lipstick parting to expose her snow-white teeth. A mouth like a bitten apple. Cohen was touched by the news.

"Firstly, Lee is stable right now, physically and mentally. But I don't want to mislead you, nor do I want to alarm you. So stop me at any point as I explain Lee's condition, and I'll try to clarify. We also have some pamphlets for you. But I like to give a summary in person." She smiled then, like she was proud of her generosity of time. Like she was repulsed by how curt and uncaring some doctors could be.

"I like to use a plumbing analogy when I explain this disease. Picture pipes instead of arteries and water instead of blood. Now, picture things like cholesterol as tissue paper, clogging up those pipes. There's tissues, or cholesterol, blocking the flow of Lee's blood, so it can't get to certain parts of his brain. These blockages are interrupting the flow of blood—and there-fore oxygen—to parts of his brain. When tissues are deprived of blood, they die. These areas of dead tissue are called infarctions. Do you understand so far?"

"Actually, yes. I'm a biologist, so..." He shrugged his shoulders. He didn't mean to sound la de da, but didn't want her talking in analogies.

"Oh. Perfect. Lee's strokes have caused what we call multi-infarction dementia. But Doctor Langor noticed abnormalities in Lee's workup that indicated a rare type of multi-infarction dementia. A distinct disease known as Binswanger Disease or BD. We ran a CAT scan and there were definitive signs of BD." She smiled over at her resident, proudly, and Langor beamed pride.

"Everything you need to know about Binswanger Disease is in this pamphlet." She handed it to him. "I'm afraid it's irre-versible. And I'm afraid it's incurable and progressive. You'll need to look into palliative care for Lee as soon as possible," she said, standing up and smoothing her lab coat. "Things will deteriorate and I would advise you to avail of the care services detailed in this pamphlet—"

"But, for now. Should I take him back to my place or his?"

"His, certainly. He'll do much better in familiar surround-ings. As we all would. Also, is there a washroom and bedroom on the main floor?"

EVERY
LITTLE
THING

He had to think about it. A washroom yes, but Lee slept upstairs. "There...could be."

She nodded, smiled again with her bitten-apple mouth. "It'll be best to move his bedroom to the main floor. Staircases might become a challenge. Impaired muscle movement and subsequent clumsiness are common. I've already noted odd posturing. But in any case, unrelated as it is, his vision is very poor. We see far too many senior-related slip-and-falls as it is. Particularly down stairs. But mainly, you need to be thinking about a long-term facility care that can accommodate your loved one. I can vouch for the ones in the pamphlet you have."

She took her prescription pad out. Scribbled furiously. "Abixa might help offset dementia, and this other pill will lower his blood pressure to reduce risks of further strokes." She tucked the prescription into the BD pamphlet then nodded her head to Cohen as if to say, *Okay, we're all done here.* Langor the sidekick followed her, walking in her shadow.

Cohen sat there for a few minutes, absorbing the details in the BD pamphlet. There were diagrams of the brain, with explanations of strokes and quick-fact textboxes in the margins, like *What does "Executive Cognitive Functioning" mean?*

It was too much text to take in, knowing Lee was waiting in that room alone. But a quick scan of bolded words and headlines was enough for now: irritability, inappropriate behaviours, difficulty concentrating, forgetfulness, depression, changes in personality, impaired thought processes, *mental capacities will diminish.* Memory could deteriorate as well as a sense of time. A likelihood of additional and more frequent strokes. Possible incontinence.

It was a small font and the list went on and on. The symptoms were so numerous and free-standing they were to be treated separately with a new personal pharmacy of pills: anti-depressants should they become depressed and so on. He closed the pamphlet and heard an echo reverberating through the hall before realizing it was the sound of his own shoe tapping off the floor. *Should've been a drummer*, Allie had always said to him. *You're always tapping. Always.*

HE WALKED INTO Lee's room not knowing what to expect. Because of Allie's warnings and the doctor's bleak news, Cohen approached him like Lee was a delicate vase he didn't want to knock over. He'd have felt bad about it if Lee had noticed Cohen's softened gait, but Lee's vision was as bad as they'd all implied it was. He *heard* Cohen before he saw him. Heard the claps of feet on the floor, craned his head towards the sound, and then he titled his head back and up; staring at Cohen through the bottom slit of his bi-focals. It was a weird, slow, bat-like echolocation. The left arm of his thick, black, plastic glasses was taped back on: a cocoon-shaped bundle of grey where arm met lens.

Lee was sitting on the edge of a bed with only the tips of his sneakers touching the floor. He looked older, terribly old. His eyes sunk so deeply into their sockets that it had to have cost him peripheral vision. There were too many bones visible under his skin. His jaw was shaky, like he was muttering to himself, but he wasn't. His eyes were all crunched up like he was angry about something, and Cohen was worried about Allie's impossible warning that Lee might not *take* to him.

"*Cohen?* Cohen is that you, Cohen?"

Cohen nodded. But he wasn't sure if Lee had noticed. "It is. How are you—"

"Allie's not with you?"

"No, she's—"

"Why not?"

He waited a second before answering. "She's…still in Montreal." He didn't know if he should say *still* because he didn't know if Lee would remember that she was in Montreal.

"Right. Allie's out of town. Right. Montreal."

There was something almost childish about the way he spoke and put his thoughts together. And something disconcerting about that wobbly jaw. It looked like Lee was trying to say something else, and Cohen waited to be sure he wasn't. "Yeah. She sent me to get you. I'm happy to be your pick-up service. It's been a while."

Still adjusting to this new Lee Allie had spoken of, he grabbed Lee's jacket off the back of a chair and stepped in really close to Lee so he'd see him. He held Lee's jacket open for him, and said, "I told her I'd get you home, and then she stationed me at your place until she gets back. Looks like we're roommates for the next five days, buddy ol' pal." He patted Lee on the shoulder, but with a little malaise because of the way Lee had put his arms

EVERY
LITTLE
THING

163

into his coat. His arms wouldn't bend any more than they had to at the elbow. It was like putting a coat on a scarecrow.

Three minutes and not a single wisecrack. His feet were gliding along the floor, never leaving it, as they walked out of the room. He was skating instead of walking.

In the hallway, on the way to the elevator, Lee said, "Not surprised she sent you. Her shithead fiancé and I have never gotten along."

"Fiancé now, is it?"

"I'm afraid so. And he used that ring Matt gave *you*. Hopefully he'll get hit by lightning or choke on a chicken bone before they tie the knot." Cohen laughed, but Lee glared at him, lips in a snarl, *I'm serious*. "I wish Allie had of come for me herself. No offense."

It hurt like a thrown rock; caught him off guard. There was nothing *old friends* about him and Lee anymore. And shaking it off wasn't as easy as blaming the disease. "So Keith hasn't won you over in all these years, hey, a charming man like him?"

"It's not even funny. So don't make jokes about it." Lee stopped walking when he talked, like he couldn't do both at once. "I've seen the guy with his mask off and it's ugly stuff." He shook his head, but started walking again. "Allie, she's too, I dunno. It's sad, really." He stopped walking again and said, "She's got this warmth. But that guy. Too many years with a guy like that. Taking and taking and taking, never stoking her fire. I wonder how long until he's taken all the sticks out of her fire, you know?"

"Sort of." And he meant sort of. Lee's fire analogy either showed a deep cognitive ability or it hinted at the kind of screwy thought processing the BD pamphlet warned him about. "If she's happy, she's happy—"

"If I had enough life left in me, I'd run the son of a bitch over or I'd knock him in front of a bus."

Cohen went to laugh then because there it was: the extremist Lee he was waiting to hear a trace of. But when he looked at Lee, Lee was all anger. His face a mouthful of lemon.

"It's almost like I owe it to her to get that son of a bitch."

"*Get* him?"

Lee had nothing more to say, and Cohen needed time to recalibrate how he'd expected the next five days to unfold. What made Lee seem so foreign now couldn't have been as simple as a lack of wisecracks and humour, and yet it was.

They got to the elevator, and Cohen stepped in. He pressed the main floor button, but Lee was still standing in the hall, looking into the elevator. Cohen had to stick an arm out to keep the doors opened. That much time had passed. *Delayed psychomotor response. It was in the BD pamphlet. A delay between a patient thinking and his muscles acting.*

HE PULLED INTO Lee's driveway, and Lee thanked him for the ride as if they were saying their goodbyes. Cohen had told Lee at least twice he'd be staying with him until Allie got home. And driving home, there'd been a stretch of five minutes where Lee looked totally lost in a daydream. And then he balled up a fist and slammed it down on the dashboard. And then he did it again. Cohen almost sideswiped the car next to him.

"*Lee*, my God, man! What's the matter!"

And Lee only shook his head. Cohen had been expecting small talk on the way home. Some catching up.

It felt like the doctors at the hospital had misled him about how stable Lee really was. What stable even meant. How many degrees of stable there were. He pulled into Lee's driveway, and Lee said, "Well, kid, thanks for the taxi ride," and he grabbed the door handle to open the door.

Lee had a new gesture that spoke to his agedness. He tilted his head back, excessively, when he looked at anyone. It was so he could look through the lower half of his bifocals, Cohen figured, but still. It was an exaggerated gesture.

"No, no. Allie has me stationed here until she gets back from Montreal." He wanted to say, *Remember?* but he didn't. "I've got a suitcase in the trunk."

Lee said, "Oh," and he looked away from Cohen, staring straight through the windshield at his house. He nodded once and opened the car door.

Oh, he'd said, and less jovially than Cohen would have liked.

Long seconds ticked by between Lee opening his car door and him stepping out. Following Lee up the steps and into the house at that snail-crawl of a pace, he saw what a challenge a few stairs were to Lee now.

They made it into the kitchen and Cohen caught himself

shout-talking to Lee, slowly, like Lee was dumb now, like he might not understand, and Lee looked a little embarrassed about it. "All right. I've got a suitcase and some boxes out in my trunk. Make yourself useful and get some coffee going for us?"

He turned to walk out to his car, and Lee finally spoke. "So you're here to prevent me from diving into another snowbank, so to speak? I don't care if everyone's talking about me. Not in this town."

"No one's talking about you. Get the coffee on. I'll be right back."

Cohen left the room without a response and fetched his suitcase and a few boxes of work stuff. A microscope and some pond samples. He laid it all down in the living room where he'd sleep and work until Allie got back in town, sizing up the couch like it might be too short to make a decent makeshift bed.

When he went back into the kitchen, Lee had his head titled up like he was looking where the walls met the ceiling. His chin pointed out. Even with those googly glasses, Lee had to move his head the way an owl does to see anything. It was like there was something wrong with the bones in his neck.

There was a wet disc radiating out from Lee's crotch. He was pissing himself, and Cohen didn't know what to do about it.

ALLIE PHONED AT six. In place of a hello, she said, "Go into another room."

"What?"

"Go into another room where he can't hear you. Or go outside or something and tell me when you're there."

So he did. He went outside without putting any shoes on and stepped on a small, sharp rock and screamed about it.

"What?" she said, concerned.

"Nothing, I," hopping on one foot, "I stepped on a pebble or something."

She laughed. "A *pebble*? Man up, Cohen. Toughen up a little bit."

"It was a sharp one. Like a tack!" He got into his car and slammed the door shut. "Okay, I'm out in my car, out of earshot."

"What'd the doctors say? How is he? How are you two getting along?"

"We're fine, but you're right. He's not Lee anymore. It's sad as hell. He's a fucking prick now, actually." Cohen laughed so she'd know he meant it in a sad way, not a harsh way. "He's a bore. I don't think he even likes me anymore." He reclined his chair, leaned back, and put his feet up on the dash.

"Don't take it personally, Cohen. My God, you're smarter than that. We're all just a sack of blood and organs waiting to fail."

"Jesus! That's a little depressingly pragmatic of you. Don't tell me you're a bore now too? I just want the guy to laugh a little, that's all. Lighten up. He's like hanging out with Frankenstein."

"I know. Trust me. The doctors, what did they say?"

"Well, that's the thing. I don't know how different he is now compared to last week, before the latest stroke. He's irritable. Bitter. Flat. Nothing's funny anymore. Movement seems like such an effort. When he walks he doesn't even lift his feet. I don't know how he does it. It's like he's moonwalking forward. Is that what it's called, moonwalking? That thing Michael Jackson did, where he slid around without lifting his feet?"

She laughed, "Shut up about Michael Jackson, but yes. Keep going. This is nothing new."

"Well, he started punching my dashboard out of the blue on the drive home. Scared the shit out of me. I almost hit another car. His eyes are gone, you're right. He, ah, pissed himself, but dealt with it himself, after I got him up the stairs. Is *that* new?"

"Well. No. But. That's a rare one, don't worry."

"The doctor suggested I set him up on the main floor before he can't do the stairs anymore or before he falls down over them. So I'm going to move all his junk out of the den and move his bed and bedroom furniture down into the den."

"Wait. Until I get home. I'll…help you. Or you help me or whatever. Can you? Help me? Move the stuff?"

"I…just told you I'd do it, didn't I?"

"Thanks so much."

"So I'll wait for you to get home and help me?"

"Yeah. I'd get Keith to help, but since you're already there, you know? Lee doesn't stand for it when I take Keith along."

"Finally: me and Lee still got something in common. I'd rather Keith not come along too."

"About that. It's a little awkward I called you to help me out here. Keith's not very happy about that."

"Keith needs to worry a little more about Lee and a little less about who is looking after him?"

"Truthfully, Lee's been the unreasonable one there. He threw a potted plant at Keith last time he came over. And then he threw it at Keith's car—"

Cohen laughed, cutting her off.

"Don't laugh! There was damage, scratches anyway. So, like, just trust me. The situation isn't funny. There's nothing funny anymore when it comes to Lee. You've seen that, right?"

"More or less. I'm still waiting for him to yell *gotcha* and start cracking jokes."

"Not gonna happen. Now what else did the doctors say happened?"

"I don't know. I've got pamphlets here and places they suggested he be...checked into for proper care. *Long-term care* or whatever. The way I understand it, all the strokes are causing or maybe are caused by—I dunno. It's like a vicious cycle between the strokes and the damage they are causing because the damage causes more strokes. It's called Binswanger Disease. BD. It's Alzheimer's-like, but without the severity of memory loss—"

"Holy shit! He's actually *got* something. I'm coming home. I—I'll call you later. Stay there, okay, like you promised? Stay there?"

He shouted *Allie!* into the phone, but she was gone.

JUST SHY OF midnight, Cohen had finished brushing his teeth and heard evil snickering coming out of Lee's room. He snuck up the stairs like a burglar, tiptoeing, knowing that if he kept quiet, Lee couldn't see him. He watched Lee, on his side in bed, muttering like a character possessed in a horror movie. That jaw wobbling around. It was eerie. Spooky. And Cohen crept away.

He went out to his car with shoes on this time to avoid the angry tack-sharp pebbles. He took out his phone and punched in the number Allie had been calling him from.

"Look. I don't want to scare you. And like I said, I don't know what Lee was like before you left, and the latest stroke, but

I think he's worse off than the doctors thought. Mentally, I mean. He eats when I cook something and all that basic shit, but when he's alone. I don't know. He's talking to himself. Or. To someone that's not there. And he talked to the news on the TV earlier, like the anchors could hear him. Like he thought they were listening or being rude for talking over him."

"I got a ticket already. I'm coming home early."

"Like I said, I don't know what's *normal* for the man anymore."

"I'd have lost my mind by now, if you weren't there. You know that, right? And the TV thing. That's nothing new. The doctor said it was harmless and common and not to upset him by making him feel strange about it. I'm gonna figure everything out when I get home. Long-term care, all that. I've been reading up on Binswanger Disease all night."

"You there alone, in your hotel room?"

She paused, like he'd said something wrong. "Yeah. And I might have to let you go, so I can call room service. I'm looking through the menu right now. What's Cod au Gratin all about anyway. Can you believe I've never had it? Maybe tonight's the night?"

"You wouldn't like it. Trust me. Too many greases for you. Cheese, fish—"

"They've got a pizza here with caramelized grapes and pears on it. Yum."

"Remember how Lee would always take us out to supper and tell the waitress that *it's my son's birthday* so I'd get a free piece of cake? *One less dessert I have to pay for*, he'd say, and I never had the heart to tell him the bland birthday cake was the last thing I wanted to eat on the dessert menu."

"Yeah. All I remember is being a little jealous he pretended you were his son, but never that I was his daughter. He liked you right from the start. I remember that. Most women have a dog, and when their dog bonds with a new man, she knows *he's the one*. I had Lee, instead of a German Sheppard, and he took to you *almost* right away."

"He called me Colin for like, months." A little giggle on her end.

"Probably on purpose," she said.

Cohen was fully reclined in the car seat and gripping the

steering wheel with his toes. Smiling in a way that made his face warm. "Little Allie Crosbie."

"Let's…um…not do this nostalgic, memory-lane flirtation thing, okay? I'm engaged, and I'm hungry. I've got room service to order. I'll call you when I get back in town. Maybe you can come pick me up at the airport?"

"Sure."

"Or. No. Maybe I should get a cab."

"I don't mind picking you up."

"No. See you soon and thanks again."

But neither of them hung up.

"*Hello?*"

"It was nice talking with you. You're an okay guy."

"You're half-decent too."

"*Half?*"

"Fully. Fully decent."

"G'night."

"K."

HE HUNG UP the phone, but didn't go back in the house. He thought about how she was always putting on hand lotion. How she'd take a long sniff at her wrist. Honey or vanilla or something like that. It was odd what memories came. They were minor, trivial things. Like the way she ate ice cream right out of the tub with an ice cream scoop and not a spoon. A big ball of ice cream that took ten or eleven bites and licks, and that was the point, she'd said, of eating it with a scoop and not a spoon. *Less double dipping.*

CHAD
PELLEY

FALLING BACK

COHEN EXPLAINED THE situation with Lee to Clarence and asked to work from home for a while to look after him.

"Just while Allie's looking into...*homes* to register Lee with."

"I don't care where you analyze these samples," he shouted into the phone, crunching through his daily dose of salt'n'vinegar chips, "just hurry up about it! This project's behind schedule. That Morris kid we had working it was slower than a sloth. About as bright." He laughed.

"I'll tear through this in under a month."

"I've missed you in the lab, kid. Cheetah quick, wiser than an owl." Clarence finished a mouthful of chips. Added, "Ugly as a boar."

So Monday mornings, Cohen would drive into town to fetch more pond samples to analyze and to punch the previous week's stats and notes into his work computer. Clarence stumbled onto Cohen in the lab one day.

"How'd you make out last week?"

"Two weeks' worth of pond samples, processed in one week, *check.*"

"Flash Lightning over here," Clarence pointed to Cohen as if addressing an imaginary crowd that should be impressed. "But don't let me hear you're getting too attached to the pond samples and roughing up their fathers, hey?"

"I didn't rough anybody up—"

Clarence clawed a hand through the air. "Drop it. Too early to joke about it anyway. I shouldn't be making light of the Zack Janes incident. Just saying, it's behind us. I don't like tension in the workplace." He tapped the Bob Marley CD case on his desk, said, "All about zee good vibes, mon," and laughed at himself. "I'm happy to have you back on projects like this anyway. You're so on the ball. Kids these days, man, the ones we're getting from the university. You take away their textbooks and ask them to think for themselves and they're deer in headlights."

Cohen nodded. "I'm fuckin' brilliant. Einstein with better hair."

"Hardly, Einstein was too much of a hippie to go around roughing up peoples' fathers."

"I *talked* to the man, Clarence. That's all."

"Seriously, enough joking about it. Was what it was, whatever it was."

"So, how's the new hire working out? My replacement? For the kids?" He didn't mean to sound so sheepish.

"Her name's Jenny Lane." Clarence looked at Cohen to see how he'd take the news. "She's working out. I even checked her background for violence against single fathers."

Cohen shook his head, laughed. Clarence said, with raised eyebrows, "I thought you'd be irreplaceable for a while there. Even your precious Zack likes her."

"That's…good I guess."

He said it sternly, "You know you're not to even *look* at that kid's father again, right, if, God forbid, you two cross paths in this building? And I'd like you to steer clear of the kid. We don't need Zack going home to Jamie, dropping your name. We've got less than twenty kids in our program. Every loss would count." Cohen nodded, but Clarence said, "Nod harder. I'm dead serious."

Cohen's phone rang. So he gave Clarence the solid nod he needed to see and excused himself. He found a chair in the empty staff lunchroom and answered the phone.

"Hey, it's me, Allie Crosbie. Any chance you can come get me at the airport? Save me the cab fare? Keith's in Ottawa until Sunday night."

"Sure thing. I'm not far from the airport now, actually. I'm at the Avian-Dome—"

"Why aren't you in Grayton…with Lee!"

"Relax! It's eight thirty in the morning and the man sleeps until noon! It seemed like the right time to run out. I'm doing my best not to leave him alone, but I do need to occasionally pop into work—"

"Sorry. God. I'm so sorry."

"I got up and over here early, so he'd still be asleep while I was out."

"Look, I'll get a cab. You picking me up is…too weird."

"Is it?"

"I still need to get my luggage, maybe some breakfast. See you ten-ish."

She hung up. He took the phone away from his face and stared at it, shook his head, put it back in his pocket.

He purposefully walked towards the front exit, so he'd pass the kids and try and gauge this Jenny girl's character. He poked his head in the door and looked around, but Zack wasn't in there. Just Erykah, Bryan, Kaytee, and Jennah. No one spelled their name normal anymore. Jenny saw him and approached him.

She had a voice like she'd just sucked in a blast of helium. "Hi! Are you…one of the parents?" A ginger, five foot five. Freckles thicker than cookie crumbs.

"No. I'm Cohen Davies." He extended his hand and she shook it. "I work here. I used to do the afterschool program, actually." She had tiny hands. So tiny he had to leave two fingers out of the handshake.

"Oh." She said it in a way that meant she knew exactly why he'd said *used to.* "Well! Nice to meet you! I better get back to the kids! Such a handful! These aren't natural curls!" She laughed and pointed to her hair, "I'm just that rattled!" She couldn't do more than three words without an exclamation mark slowing things down.

"Yes, take care, Jenny." He looked down and saw she was wearing real moccasins. Instead of waving, she flashed a quick peace sign.

He was walking towards the front exit when he heard Zack calling out to him, running, like he'd spotted Santa out of season. "Mr. Davies! Mr. Davies! Hi! Hi, Mr. Davies! Hi!" and he wasn't going to stop greeting Cohen until they were face to face.

Cohen bent down to get on Zack's level and stuck his hand up for a high five, but Zack came in with a bear hug. His two little arms like sticks around Cohen's neck. A reek of cheap gummy candies. "Want one?" and he stuck out a bag full of shark-shaped candies. Their spongy white bellies looked like a different texture than the gummy blue tops.

"No thanks, buddy. I don't want a blue tongue like you've got there!"

EVERY LITTLE THING

173

"I know! I was just looking at it in the mirror. I like having a blue tongue! It's cool. Did you know that there's blue octopuses?"

"Is there? I don't know much about octopuses."

"I know something you didn't know!"

"You're getting smart, buddy!"

"Mr. Davies?"

"You know you can call me Cohen, right? We're friends, aren't we?"

"I like saying Mr. Davies."

"Okay, that's fine too, whatever you like, Mr. Janes."

"Why'd you leave daycare teaching? Was it because I eavesdropped on you and Dad that night? I'm sorry. Dad told me listening in on other people's chats is a bad thing to do. I didn't know. I promise I didn't know—"

"No, buddy, no! That had nothing to do with it, okay? Say yes. Say you understand that that had nothing to with it."

And Zack's little head was bouncing up and down like a dropped ball as he said, "Okay, good. But I was just going to ask you if you wanted to be my best friend. Then you stopped being our afterschool teacher." He shrugged his shoulders, a little embarrassed at the statement. "Jenny is okay."

"Did you hear us that night, though, your dad and me?"

"No. Just muffles, but Dad sounded mad at you."

"He wasn't. Okay? The traffic was really loud, so we had to shout to hear each other over the traffic, that's all. And, about daycare, my boss needs me doing other things now, that's all."

"Forever?"

Jenny came out of nowhere. "*There* you are, Zack Janes! I was getting worried! What did I say about going to the bathroom and not coming *right back*? You don't want me to have to wait outside the door, do you? You're a big boy, aren't you?"

Cohen butted in, "It was my fault, really. I distracted him. Sorry."

"No, no! This little boy is a wanderer, aren't you? Always off playing by himself somewhere, this one!"

Cohen got up and stuck his hand out for Zack to take, and Jenny shot him a look. "C'mon then, let's get back." Zack took Cohen's hand. They got back to the room, and Zack hugged Cohen's left leg goodbye then scurried off to the toy chest.

"He's a sweet kid. I see you two really hit it off?"

"He reminds me of my brother, actually. And he's a fire-cracker, bright." Cohen motioned to say goodbye and nice to meet you, but she said, "Very sad about Zack though."

"What's that?"

"His health."

"Yeah, the fainting you mean?" And here was his chance to pry. She nodded yes, and he said, "It was still a new thing when I was told about it. Are things any better or worse?"

"As of this week, the doctors have him taken out of gym class until they figure out what's happening. I've got to keep an eye on him, make sure he's not up to much. His episodes are linked with physical exertion, every time. They've ruled out all the epilepsies, low iron, the basic stuff. They think it's a physical exertion thing. Poor little guy. They had him in an MRI machine last week, and he was crying his eyes out. Claustrophobic, I guess. He told me it was like *being trapped in a tiny rocketship so small you can't move your legs and arms*, and he mimicked the banging noises the machines made. This week, he's had a barrage of EEGs and EKGs."

He couldn't talk to Zack's father or to Clarence about Zack's health, but chatty Jenny Lane would do the trick. So he laid his second hand atop their shaking hands, and patted her hand too affectionately. Like, *Hey, let's talk again soon.*

Jenny walked on, and Cohen watched Zack bang two dinosaurs together; the Tyrannosaurus winning the battle. He thought of Jamie sending Zack off to Florida. And he thought of adoption again. Since the night Jamie had burnt his hand and shared his story of adopting Zack, Cohen couldn't stop thinking about adoption as the way to fill the hole in his life. To catch up. To find meaning, purpose. But the waitlist was unreasonable. The criteria. The fact he was unmarried wouldn't help. He'd want a newborn, and those had the longest waitlists. There were codes your house had to meet—impossible codes normal parents weren't subjected to, and the renovations were beyond him. Yet he'd logged into that website a few times. Bookmarked it.

ALLIE WALKED IN the front door like a mother who hadn't seen her kids in a month. She flung the screen door open so hard it gonged off the outside of the house. And then she smacked a knee off the porch doorframe. She bent over to rub out the pain, but didn't stop walking forward. Cohen had been sitting in a chair, at the kitchen table, peering through a microscope at a petri dish full of insect larvae and pond matter. Tweezers in one hand, a pencil in another. He looked up and saw her rubbing her knee, but coming towards him in long strides.

She was wearing a form-fitting, form-enhancing black dress, and the first thing he remembered when he saw her was how much he liked to run his hands over that body when they kissed. She stuck her head in the kitchen, craned her neck left and right—her ponytail playing catch up with the movement of her head—and asked, "Where is he?"

He remembered her hair as being black, and yet it was brown, light brown, the colour of dry soil. "Lee's in bed. He sleeps until, like, noon. I never know if I should make him breakfast or lunch when he gets up. So I compromise and make something brunchy."

She nodded, not really listening, and sat across the table from him. "I guess I'll let him sleep then. So, how are you? Been a while," she said, laughing. She took an apple out of a fruit bowl Cohen had pushed to the edge of the table and bit into it. "I'm *starving.*"

"How I am is a long story. Kind of a boring one. You?"

She brought the apple back to her mouth. Chomped into it. "What's all this anyway?" She swept her apple-holding hand over the microscope, the bags of pond water, and the photos of freshwater invertebrates.

"Work."

"Duh."

"Fish research. Via insect larvae. I'm off birds for a while. Long story, again, pretty boring. My life's pretty boring lately. I've been picking dead snails and larvae out of petri dishes, counting them, and in between that, I've been getting harassed by that surly man who used to be Lee. Meanwhile, some of us are off in Montreal, sauntering around from deli to bakery, buying nice dresses like that one." He nodded to her black dress and she smiled.

Crunching her jaw into the apple, "Thanks!," she said, standing up to model it. "Kinda had to buy it, right? But seriously, why are there bags of bug-filled pond water and gross photos on the table?" She got up off the chair, scooped up the fruit bowl. "I don't want this bowl of fruit next to dead bugs for some reason." She walked it over to the kitchen counter.

"There's a few government-funded folks throwing nitrogen and phosphorus into a lake. All these bags are samples, from the last six years, of the bottom of that lake. I've gotta count and compare the number of larvae to see if fertilizing the pond increases the number, size, and diversity of larvae. Because trout and salmon feed on these things. Another guy is summarizing the number and size of fish caught in the fertilized and not fertilized lakes, to see if more fertilizer equals more insect larvae and, in turn, if more insect larvae equals more and bigger fish in the fertilized pond. It's for fish farms, I guess."

"Riveting," she said. "And what's the deal? Fish galore?"

"By the bucket. Backfires though, because loons have caught on that this pond is a jackpot. They're eating the shit out of the fish."

"Maybe," she said, as if truly contemplating it, "Maybe I missed this vicarious scientific experience you gave me. I mean, who doesn't want their kitchen full of snails and insect larvae and pond water?" She picked a bag up and peered into it. "*G'ah!* What are these spidery-looking ones?"

"Dragonfly larvae."

"Really?"

"Yes. *Cordulia*, mostly."

She laid the bag down, grabbed the kettle off the stove, and started filling it. "Cup of tea, Cohen? So you can catch me up on Lee before you go?"

He turned in his chair to face her, "That's the thing. I'm all set up here, and I don't mind staying for another while. I love it out here in Grayton. Fuck the city. Next door to me now, there's a dozen obnoxious kids. They must've pooled their mommies' money and bought the house next door. They're out on their patio 'til two or three every night. There's crushed beer cans in my yard half the time, and they've got horrible taste in music. I'm happier here, and Clarence is more than fine with me staying on this project, working out of here, until I'm done counting these dead bugs."

"Oh my God, really?" She abandoned the kettle for a minute and sat back at the table, excited. "Because I have to go to Toronto on the twelfth. Just for two days, but still, I don't want him left alone until I figure everything out. One of those live-in nurses or whatever they're called or a home maybe."

"Yeah, really. I'm all set up. I'm on vacation, in my head."

"Lee's...deterioration has gone on too long now, and he's too blind, let alone the rest of it, to look after himself. I don't know." She shrugged her shoulders. "I've been stopping in here to cook him most meals because I'm not sure that he eats otherwise. There's never any dishes or signs of him having eaten. I ask him about it and he gets testy. I've gotten too used to it. To the way he is. And he's been getting worse, but slowly enough for me to adapt, you know? He's not okay to be living alone. The doctor telling you he needs to be in a home was a wake-up call."

She picked up another bag of pond water and peered into it. "Keith said he'd like it a lot more if I didn't move in here while I figure out Lee's long-term care. Keith thinks Lee's *crazy* and that *crazy people are dangerous.*" She walked over to the cupboards to get two mugs for their tea. "Are you sure you don't mind? Because— *Jesus, shit!*" She'd opened a cupboard door and a stack of glasses fell out, shattering all over the counter and the floor like bombs going off. He looked over, and she had the edge of a cut finger in her mouth; one foot laid on top of the other foot, like a ballerina, and broken glass encircling her. The way the sunlight refracted in it made the glass look like a ring of fire. "Um. Help." She was frightened, cute, laughing.

"Okay, don't move."

"Obviously! Broom's next to the fridge."

"Got it."

He looked back to her and saw a small drop of blood at her heel. "There's some under my foot!"

He ran out to the porch and she yelled, "Where are you going?"

"Don't move!" and he wrestled on a pair of Lee's too-tight steel-toed boots. Only the first half of his feet would fit into them, so he came back into the kitchen tippy-toeing in clunky boots, walking like a man with broken knees.

Her panicked face relaxed a second to laugh at him. "What are you doing, you fool?"

He came towards her, glass crunching under his feet. He swept the countertop behind her with a dishtowel. Little clinks as glass rained down to the floor. "Okay, put your arms out."

"What?"

He motioned with his arms. "Make a T shape."

"*What?*"

"Be a scarecrow. I'm going to pick you up and sit you on the countertop." She stuck her arms out, made a T of her body. "Okay, keep your arms stiff or you'll just slide back down onto the glass. Ready?"

She panicked, dropped her arms. "No. Wait!" She hugged herself. "Say you won't drop me in this sea of glass!"

"I won't drop you in the sea of glass. Arms back up. Let's go."

He grabbed her, her warmth penetrating his fingers. His palms awkwardly close to her breasts.

"Okay, ready? One...two..." He plunked her down on the countertop, and as she settled there, a hand grazed her chest.

"Wow. That was mildly heroic! Your little outfit there: the boots, the broom." She laughed. "Thanks!"

Cohen got to sweeping the glass. Perched on the countertop, she explained, "Lee always does that. He takes dishes out of the dishwasher and just lays them in there, right on the edge. The glasses end up stacked high and resting against the insides of the door just waiting to tip over, like a...glass skyscraper. It's never him that opens the door when the dishes fall, so he never learns not to do that..."

Cohen was throwing the first batch of glass into a garbage bag and went back to sweep up the rest.

"...half the time he smashes glasses putting them away like he's not looking where he's thrusting things, but it isn't his fault, I suppose, if he can't see where he's putting them."

She put two hands up over her eyes like binoculars and said, "Can you imagine losing your peripheral vision?"

She was kicking her legs through the air as she talked to him. Her heels sometimes banging off the cupboard doors beneath her.

Cohen, kneeling in front of her, sweeping glass into a dustpan, looked up at her and said, "I think I got all of it. You can hop down." He saw her purple panties before she'd scissor-snapped her legs crossed and blushed a little. She'd kicked him in the head as she crossed her legs. Cohen got back up and swept the broom around a little more.

She stuck her two legs straight out. Nodded her head to her slightly bloody foot. "There's rubbing alcohol and Band-Aids in the medicine cabinet upstairs. Fix me up, Doc, before I get down?"

He pulled up a chair and wedged the rubbing alcohol

between his thighs. He handed her the Band-Aid, "Here, hold this," and took the top off the rubbing alcohol. Soaked some cotton balls. She leaned forward to watch, her chest resting on her thighs as he cleaned her foot. She let out a quick sigh of pain; the alcohol like a wasp at her heel. When she flinched, she'd squeezed his shoulder and kept her hand there. A finger against his neck. And maybe he leaned a cheek onto her hand. It was fighting an instinct not to kiss her wrist. He looked up and saw that she'd been staring him in the eyes the whole time. A *kiss-me-now* cue, but it couldn't have been.

She sat back up, "So, you really don't mind hanging around until I get back from Toronto?"

"No sweat."

"It's time. For proper care for him. I'm travelling more and more now, and he's not getting any better, but definitely worse…"

Cohen tuned out. Fell back through time. Every year between now and back then stopping that fall no more than a cloud could, until it was the day they'd met all over again.

He heard something at the staircase, looked over. It was Lee, sat on the steps, two hands holding rails like a man in prison. "Allie? Allie, is that you?"

"Yes, I'm here." She jumped down off the counter onto her not-cut foot.

He shouted, "Where've you been!"

She leaned into Cohen as she passed him, her soft voice in his ear, "I said he *takes* to me. I didn't say he was nice to me. Appreciated things." She walked over to greet Lee.

He wanted to ask her how long she's been slaving over Lee like this. Because he wanted her to whisper the answer, like she just had, into his ear. With her hand on his shoulder. Lips to his ear.

ALLIE CUT UP red potatoes, fried them in a lot of olive oil and fresh rosemary. "I'd bottle this smell if I could," she said to Cohen as he washed a few dishes beside her. "Wear it, like a perfume."

"What, and have men hunger for you?"

"Lame," she said, patting him on the shoulder, *Nice try*.

She laid out some flaxseed toast with real butter. Cut up chunks of smoked gouda. She was fearless with knives: the clicks on the cutting board were faster than a ticking clock.

When it was all ready, she called out to Lee, not sure where he was, and Cohen cleared all his stuff off the kitchen table. Lee came stumbling into the kitchen with his hands out, waiting to bump into a chair. Everything was guesswork now; having given up on what remained of his vision, he was all hands and ears. The top of a chair found his hand, like it was being helpful, reaching out to Lee. He sat down, jammed his neck back, and looked around the room, with his owl-head movement, scanning for Allie. He shouted at her. "Them potatoes and the herbs, is it?"

"Yes."

He nodded. "Smells good enough, I guess." He put two hands on the table, and as they fumbled around in search of cutlery, they knocked over his glass of water. Cohen jumped back in an exaggerated manner, out of fright more than anything, and went to get some paper towel.

"Goddamn glass," Lee said.

Allie sat beside him with her food. "It was only water. No biggie. Cohen's got it cleaned up already."

"I didn't want water anyway. I want some juice!" He jammed a forkful of potato into his mouth. White bits falling out of his mouth as he made his clenched-fist demand. Allie got to wiping his chin, and he batted her hand away.

Cohen shot Allie a wide-eyed, raised-eyebrow look, *Wow.* And said, "Coming right up," as he laid a glass of orange juice where he knew Lee could see it.

Lee was a fast eater: he ate as if an impatient busboy was waiting behind him, to yank the plate away. Every second counted, so he barely chewed his food before he'd swallow it.

Near the end of lunch, Allie said, "I think we're going to relocate your bedroom to the den, Lee, so you don't need to worry about the stairs anymore. It only makes sense," she said, trying to soften the situation. "I don't know why you've been taking those stairs all these years, since you don't use the den at all. May as well be a main floor bedroom—"

"I don't give a goddamn where I sleep! I'll sleep in the fucking garage!" He gulped down his whole glass of juice and wiped his mouth with a shirt sleeve. "Do whatever you want to do, just hurry about it. If you're going to move me, move me, but don't make me go around later wondering where the fuck I'm supposed to sleep tonight!" He threw a quarter piece of toast down on his

EVERY
LITTLE
THING

181

plate. It bounced, flipped over. Cohen could see perfect teeth marks in it.

Allie and Cohen gave each other a look, *Well, could have been worse, at least he agreed,* and Lee stormed out to the living room. He turned on the TV. It was blaring. Lee was shouting complaints about something or other, but the TV was up too high to hear him. "Fuck—damn…microscopes every—all of…it's for!"

"What?"

"*NOTHING!* Never mind!"

Cohen walked over to the living-room doorway and looked in at Lee. Arms crossed, face crumpled up, history channel on. Something about army tanks. Voice-over narration and black-and-white footage.

He turned back to Allie, and she was putting Lee's plate in the dishwasher. "I guess we should get to it then?"

She clapped her hands, *chop chop,* and glided over to the staircase at the end of the kitchen. "Giddy-up." Her ponytail wagging back and forth like a happy dog's tail.

Allie was already sitting down on Lee's bed when Cohen entered his room. Her facial expression was a perfect embodiment of *Hmm.* "I dunno know where to start!"

"I gutted out the den last night, so that's done and ready to move into—"

"Yeah, I noticed. Good man. I guess… let's take the drawers out of the dresser," she nodded to it. "Lay them on the bed. We'll move the dresser down and then bring these drawers down, with all the stuff still in them, and slide them back in." She'd already started yanking out dresser drawers and laying them on the bed. She had three drawers laid on the bed before Cohen got started himself.

She went over to a nightstand and hauled out the top drawer. She plucked out a photograph, held it up like she'd panned gold. "Oh my God, how sweet is this? He keeps a picture of me…" she paused for a second as she looked at it, and her tone changed a little, "… a picture of *us,* in his nightstand!" She sat on the bed, and Cohen came over beside her. It was a picture of Cohen and Allie on the pier in Grayton. One of Cohen's elbows resting on the fence-like ledge around the wharf. In the photo, Allie was side-on, facing Cohen, her face stretched into pure joy, shocked or surprised she'd actually hooked something on her fishing pole, and she was reeling it in. Cohen was mid-laugh in the photo, a hand on her hip like, *I'm here if you need a hand reeling it in.*

"Remember?" She asked him, punching him on the shoulder. "It was totally a red plaid fisherman's coat that I caught. Remember?" He nodded, and Allie said, "We shouldn't be picking through his stuff." She threw all the photos back into the drawer and gave Cohen a look, like she wanted to ask him something. Her mouth opened a little and then closed, like a fish on land.

"What?"

"Nothing." She got up off the bed and they put the last of the drawers on the mattress.

They stood at either end of the dresser, ready to lift. "Got it?" He lifted his end.

"Got it. Go."

But halfway down the stairs, him struggling under the weight of the heavy oak dresser, her barely with a hand on it anymore, she'd blurted out, "Keith's not as bad as you make him out to be, you know. He never was."

"Okay."

"*Okay?* What's that supposed to mean?"

"It means let's get this dresser over the stairs, quickly, before it steamrolls over me!"

She laughed, "Sorry," and took a bit more of the weight.

Walking the dresser into the den, Cohen said, "Allie, if he makes you happy, and all that shit, does it really matter what other people think?"

"It does. Sort of. No one understands. People not trusting my take on Keith. It's—I mean, shit, you want people to like your *fiancé*, you want them to want to be around him, so that he feels a part of you! I mean, Jesus." She put a hand up, *C'mon.* "It degrades how I feel about the relationship I'm in, and that's not fair. If someone invites me somewhere, out for dinner or to a movie or something, they seem more excited when I say Keith's out of town or he's busy and can't make it. They don't *say* anything, but it's in their voice. Or it's obvious because, like, Mel and I will go out for a drink after a movie, when it's just the two of us, but never if Keith's with me. That kind of thing."

They laid the dresser in place, but it wobbled. Allie kept pressing the edge of it, watching it wobble, and said, "What the hell?"

"Old house with sunken floors. There's levellers on the bottoms of the legs. I'll fix it later."

"May as well fix it now."

He got down on his knees and said, "Lift it up off the ground for me?" And she did. He turned the leveller a few times, and she laid the dresser down, surprised it had done the trick. He stood up, brushed a splotch of dust off his knees, and said, "As long as you can list five things, about the person you're with, then you still belong together."

"Five, hey, magic number?"

"Yes, and one's a universal freebie: the financial convenience of splitting bills."

"Would you judge me if I said that I love how Keith's still the jealous type, all these years later? That he's giving me shit that you're Lee's caretaker?"

"That doesn't count as one of your five. You could live without a jealous man. The fact that he's jealous adds nothing to your daily enjoyment of life."

"Jealousy means he still cares. Most of my friends' husbands, like Leslie at work...*her* husband wouldn't react if she spontaneously combusted right in front of him and needed to be extinguished. I swear. He'd just ask her to keep it down and be quiet about it because the game is on."

"Really, *he still cares*, that's enough for you? That's all you're after? You...*any woman* deserves a little more fireworks than *he still cares*, don't you think? That whole jealousy thing. That's just a personality trait. I bet he was the kid who never shared well at daycare, and that had nothing to do with him *caring* about his toys."

"Never mind. C'mon. Let's go start bringing the drawers down." She slapped him on the shoulder, walking passed him.

He followed her up the stairs. "How about you get the rest of these drawers down, and back into the dresser, while I start taking the headboard off the bedframe?" He hauled a screwdriver out of his back pocket and held it up like it was something to be proud of and knelt down to start removing the headboard.

He was still on his knees, half-hidden behind the bed, when he heard her giggle, say, "Still loyal to Fruit of the Loom, hey? Your shirt's halfway up your back," and she tugged it down for him. Helped him up.

They each grabbed an end of the mattress. It wasn't heavy, but it was awkward to manoeuvre. They tugged and steered it towards the staircase and were taking it one step at a time until Allie lost her footing and came flailing towards him like a skier who'd lost control. He let go of the mattress to catch her. He planted his feet to make a wall of himself. She fell into him like a bird hitting a window, and their bodies were enmeshed. He had an angle of her hip in his left hand, his other hand on her back; their necks joined the way swans embrace. They stayed that way for long seconds, like maybe the fall wasn't over. But it was. And so much can happen in a second, and they let it.

He slid his other hand to her other hip to stabilize her. She squeezed the backs of his arms before hauling herself away from him, slowly, sending a blunt-edged sigh into his neck. It felt like sex. Like *fucking*. Like something too basic and primitive to fight against. So he broke the ice, a corny joke, because no one feels what he just felt unless it's mutual. "What are you, falling for me all over again?"

She looked at him like she didn't understand.

"It's a joke. You fell and I caught you."

"It's not even funny, Cohen. It wasn't supposed to be like this. Some corny soap opera story and everyone rooting for us. I don't want to be that cliché."

"Who's rooting for us?"

She walked away from him towards the kitchen table and took her jacket off the back of a chair. She snapped it up into the air, like a matador's bull-blanket, and jammed her arms in. Tugged it tight. "I wasn't expecting this. This chemistry. Me and you. Whatever. But...it's there. And even admitting it, it's too much like cheating. I think Keith's right. It might be confusing for you and me to adjust to friendship. Considering the way things ended." And she walked out of the room.

He should've let her walk away. He shouldn't have said it, but he did. "The issue isn't *our* chemistry. It's that a happily engaged woman doesn't feel chemistry with another man, no matter who he is."

She stepped back into the kitchen. He wasn't expecting those tears under her eyes. "Yes. They can! People are attracted to strangers, for God's sake! Being in a relationship doesn't mean you stop feeling attraction, it means you stop acting on it."

"Love isn't devotion, Allie."

"Then what is it!"

"A feeling."

She said nothing, stared at him. "Our...situation is *different*, Cohen. And complicated. More complicated than what you just said. Nothing's *that* simple. Nothing is!" Her lips started trembling in a way that tore at his heart. "I have to go!" And she did.

Cohen sat down on the staircase—one hand on the rail, the other on his lap—looking at the mattress on the floor.

Lee stumbled into the kitchen and shouted at him. "What's going on! I don't want anyone in my house if you're going to be shouting all the time!"

Cohen nodded his head as if Lee could see him nodding from that far away.

"Allie? *Allie!*" His neck tilted back, owl movements as he scanned the room for her.

"She's gone, Lee. She just left."

"When's she coming back?"

LOUD,
LOUDER

ALLIE DIDN'T HAVE to come by on her lunch hour to make lunch for Lee. Cohen had to eat, so Cohen could have easily made Lee's lunches. But she'd say, *It's only fair I help out*, and, *he's accustomed to me checking in. Regularity's important here.* So she'd come by, eat lunch, feed Lee, and be formal with Cohen: hellos, goodbyes, thank-yous, and that was it, as Cohen sat at his microscope tweezing another spider-like dragonfly larva from murky pond water in a petri dish.

Bag after bag, and week after week, he'd been pouring pond samples into petri dishes and plucking out snails and larvae to catalogue and count them. He was sick of it. The results had proven that fertilizing the pond had worked, but science is based in numbers and his boss needed mathematical proof that something was working.

Three or four times a week, Allie would come by: act warmly to Lee and distant to Cohen. She'd never utter more than those *hellos, goodbyes*, or a *thanks again*, but she'd started laying plates of food beside his microscope without a word. On one of those days, just after plunking food down for Cohen, he'd turned and saw her at the fridge; her ass pointing straight at him. *Come here, right now. Grab me by the tops of my shoulders, for leverage. Get it over with.*

She'd caught him looking. A forgiving glance. She sat beside him at the table, crunching a raw carrot. "I *am* trying to find a facility for Lee, so you know. I know you can't stay here forever. And I feel bad coming and going without thanking you enough or chatting more." Another crunch of her carrot, and she wouldn't speak while chewing. He sat back in his seat and waited. "I've gone to visit two of the three places in the BD pamphlet that those doctors gave you. But I only liked one of them, and there's still a third to go see. I'll keep you posted." She tapped his hand a few times with hers, to emphasize the promise. Or to gauge the chemistry between them.

In the two weeks after the mattress incident, she'd kept her visits brief and their interactions dry and formal, but the looks they'd cast each other were a language all their own, and his eyes heard her eyes just fine.

Or they heard what he wanted them to hear.

Wait.

SOME NIGHTS SHE'D come by in the evening to *keep Lee company.* But Lee didn't want company. He didn't need it. Cohen had hooked cable up to the TV in Lee's bedroom, and that TV was the only thing Lee wanted from the world. If someone came into his room and talked during a show, he'd snarl like a dog, scratch at the air, *Get Away.*

On one of the nights Lee had cast her from his bedroom, Allie made herself a cup of tea, said to Cohen, sitting at the kitchen table peering down his microscope, "His show's over in fifteen minutes. Might as well wait it out."

"Yeah, but then another show starts: i.e., another reason to yell at anyone breaching the ten-foot radius around his TV. It's gotten to the point I lay his meals by the door like he's a prisoner. Or a dog."

"Tea?" she said.

"Sure, thanks. There's a box of Earl Gray—"

"I know where it is," she said. While she waited for the kettle to boil, she caught a look at the website opened on Cohen's laptop which was sitting on a section of the kitchen counter he'd converted into a makeshift desk.

"I'm nosey, and you know it, right?"

"Yeah?"

"Can I ask about...this?" She turned the computer screen towards him. The headline, *Adoption in Canada.*

He laid his tweezers down, caught.

"Wouldn't know where to start."

"You're...are you serious, about adopting?" She smiled, for some reason, looking very excited he'd say yes. "I've heard it's easier to fly to the moon than adopt a child though, right?"

"Basically. And being single doesn't help. But that's only the start of my barriers."

"My God! So you're serious about this!" She was thrilled. "You'd be Daddy of the Year, man! You're so great with kids. You'd raise the best little people...ever." And she was finally talking to him again. Guard down, warm, the way he liked her. She was at the table, leaning on it with both arms, to look him square in the eye. "Boy or girl?"

"You don't really get to choose. It's not like a pet shop where you point and pick."

"Take what you can get, hey?" The kettle whistled and she tended to it. "So, knocking a woman up the old fashion way is too roundabout for you?" She laughed, fishing their teabags out of a box and throwing them into their mugs.

"Long story, but there's an adopted kid at my work. We've got an afterschool program now, and I was running it for a while. The kid stole my heart, basically. Coolest little guy you'd ever meet. Honestly. His father's a dud, and he's shipping him off to Florida. To live with his grandmother. Broke my heart and got me thinking, I guess. I'm cruising through my thirties, and I've always wanted a kid. Just one."

"Sounds to me you want *this* boy. What's his name?"

"Zack."

She came back to the table. Laid their teas down.

"But like I said, you don't get to pick and choose. You just hope you get a kid like Zack."

"Or you *make* the kid as cool as Zack. That's what good parents do! Mould and shape their offspring like potters at a wheel. This is exciting, Cohen!"

She laid her hand on his again for a moment. Tapping it like, *Way to make such a big life decision.* But she went cold, fast, said, "Keith doesn't want kids. And he's not amendable on the matter."

She shifted back in her seat. Their legs met under the table and neither of them moved. Their eyes met. The look on her face softened his bones as he sat there. She started rocking her leg, against his, in a way that seemed like she was only rocking her leg.

Lee burst out of his room. It was at the back of the kitchen. "I want some food. There's a movie coming on!"

Allie shot up. "Is it something we can watch together? I'll make us some popcorn, on the stove."

EVERY
LITTLE
THING

SHE CAME BY a few nights after that. With a movie she thought Lee might like. Cohen was at his makeshift desk at the kitchen counter and recognized the way she enters a house. With patience, and grace, like taking your shoes off was an event you didn't need to rush. She'd lay them side by side out of everyone's way. And then she'd be loud about tearing a hanger off a rack for her jacket. He heard her out there that night, and he anticipated her coming into the kitchen.

She had a way of foregoing hellos and cutting right into the chase of a conversation. "I've been thinking about you adopting, Cohen. I'd be so happy for you. A little boy or girl. You building them from scratch!" She was standing behind him, an arm on his shoulder, being nosey about the email he was composing to Clarence. It was to let Clarence know he might be working from Lee's longer than expected.

Allie's beauty was something he could sense. It didn't require him turning around and seeing her. It didn't require eyes, though he'd caught a glimpse of her reflected in his computer screen, reading his email. "I'm not definitely adopting, and if I apply, there's a very slim chance I'd be considered anyway. Then there's the waiting game. Takes forever."

"Classic Cohen attitude," she said, pouring two glasses of Pepsi: one for her, one for Lee.

"You seem confident he'll let you watch that movie with him." Cohen nodded to the DVD on the countertop.

"I was talking to him earlier. We made a date. He's game. And listen. I couldn't help read your email there," she nodded to his computer screen, "telling Clarence you're going to be working from here another while yet. This is getting ridiculous, I know, and I'm sorry. I'll go meet with that other care home *A-S-A-P*." She walked to Lee's room with the glasses of Pepsi and the DVD tucked under an arm.

Cohen got back to typing his email, but heard Lee shouting right away, "Fuck off! Go on! Go, get out of here!" Lee had gotten up off his bed and chased her out of the room like she was deaf, dumb. "I know what you're up to! Trying to take my house from under me!"

She backed away from him, scared, and Cohen got between them.

"Lee, no!"

"Well Keith is. What's the difference? Keith is trying to take my house!"

"*What?*"

He went back into his room. Shut the door. There was the sound of furniture being dragged around as if he was barricading himself in there. She went to his room, pushed the door open to confront him, but he pushed back, jamming her hand in the doorframe. And she cried about that, blaming the pain for the tears as she wrapped ice cubes in a dishtowel and brought it to her fist. Lee hadn't even reacted to her yelp, after he hurt her hand. He simply walked away like he'd proven his point. Sat on his bed. Blared the TV even louder.

Allie and Cohen sat at the kitchen table, staring at her slightly swollen knuckle. Her tears like flecks of glass in that light. "He's such an *asshole* now!" And her guilt for saying so had kicked a triplet of sobs out of her throat. She looked vulnerable, isolated. Alone. So he put an arm around her. For the first time in six years. And that current, that voltage, was still there. "May as well watch the movie anyway" she said, sniffing that distinctive end-of-a-cry sniff.

"Fuck that asshole!" Cohen said. "Let's make popcorn and not offer him any!"

She laughed and offered him the glass of Pepsi she'd poured for Lee, and he took it.

They sat on the sofa together, and she said, "He's not even *there* anymore, you know? In that room, in that body. He's not even *there* anymore."

She was okay by the end of the movie. Popcorn. Two hands, one bowl.

"Keith hates these kinds of movies," she said, halfway through the film, during a sex scene, because one of them had to say something to cut through their own sexual tension. "He's a car blowing up and flipping over forty times kind of movie guy. Vin Diesel and Rambo and shit."

But Cohen referenced the scene in the movie they were watching. "Do men actually do that?" he pointed at the screen. "Rip a woman's bra off? Aren't bras like twenty bucks a pop?"

She laughed. "This from a guy who can't even unhook a woman's bra. If someone tore my favourite bra off, I'd slap the bastard and bill him for it."

All four of their feet were up on the coffee table that night. Heels plunked down, toes pointing up, legs spread so that their lower halves were Vs. Vs that made a W though: her right-foot toes resting against his left-foot toes.

When she was leaving that night, he walked her to the porch. Grabbed her jacket, held it, so she could get her arms in. "Lemme see that knuckle," he said, and the swelling had gone down.

"I know he needs to be in a facility," she said, and the first thing Cohen thought was, *But that means no more of this, us.* She bent over to grab a shoe, laid a hand on Cohen's shoulder for balance. "But I mean, he's fed, he's looked after, right? He *must* be happier here, in his own home. If he treats us like shit, I can only imagine how he'd react to a bunch of strangers, the nurses and doctors and other patients."

"Exactly."

IT WASN'T LONG before she'd started coming over for no good reason—no more excuses—and lingering longer. Keith spent half his time travelling and the other half at the office. And she never liked being alone.

Cohen got out of the shower one day and came down over the stairs, pulling his shirt on, to find Allie in the kitchen. "There you are!" she said, as if she'd been combing the whole city for him. She was holding a tomato, pointing to it, "What's *this?*"

He screwed up his face, perplexed, "What do you mean? It's…half of a tomato."

"No," she said, peeling a sticker off of the tomato. "This?"

He looked at her like she'd lost her mind, and she said, as if he'd cheated her out of something, "This is *grocery store* tomato." She shook her head and grabbed the handle of the back door. "Go get your shoes. Get mine too? Lee's got this *amazing* heated greenhouse."

Walking through the yard she filled him in. "He'd let his greenhouse go to hell, but I cleaned it up two summers ago. I got it all in order, heaters and everything. Spiders and sticky tape so it's pesticide free. It's rigged so that I can get red, ripe tomatoes by *June*." *June!* she'd said, raising her eyebrows like, *Holy shit, right?*

"Those tomatoes from the grocery store, I mean, they're so sour or tasteless or rotten because they're shipped here all the way from…Mexico, sometimes."

They got to the greenhouse and she tugged open the bulky wooden door. It caught and skipped on the ground. She had to wrestle with it as it dug into the grass. It seemed rehearsed and habitual, the way she got the door opened, just enough to get in behind it, and shoulder butt it the rest of the way open. ·

There were glass shelves covered in pots, stray soil, and white balls of fertilizer, and potted plants hanging from the ceiling. There were little strips of masking tape on all the pots with Allie's handwriting scribbled on them. Looping Ls, Os no bigger than periods. The dot on her *i* in dill was more like a sideways line than dots. Dill, zucchini, tomato, grapes (Please Grow!), mint, garlic.

She said, "Isn't this place amazing?" as if they were standing in the middle of a picturesque jungle and Tarzan might just come leaping out from behind her tomato plants. She grabbed a small and rickety wooden chair. The chair had been painted army green—at least ten years ago, judging from the state the paint job was in—and climbed up on it. She had a serious, goal-oriented look of concentration on her face as she reached for the tomatoes, tugging them off a vine and lobbing them down to Cohen. Her tongue poking out past her lips sometimes. A little rustle of leaves every now and then. There was a herbaceous smell on the plump tomatoes in his hand, like cut grass and mortared parsley.

Allie climbed down off the chair, handed Cohen a Tupperware container to lay the tomatoes in, and got to looking around for something. He had no idea what, but she couldn't find it and wouldn't give up. She was poking around like a burglar in a rush. He'd seen her look in the same place twice. Move things around. And then she smirked a little.

"What?"

"Nothing."

"What are you looking for?"

"The package the tomato seeds came in. It had a funny comic on it. I wanted to show you. They're called *Alicante* tomatoes. Get it? *Allie* Can-tay. Me and Lee, we were pretty excited about our tomato operation, the first year we got it up and running. So we started calling them Allie Can't Say tomatoes or Allie Can't Stays. All sorts of lunch-time puns. I'd say, *Sorry, Lee, I gotta go* and he'd say, *Allie Can't Stay?* Before, you know, he changed."

She took a tomato out of the Tupperware and held it like it was a baseball. She brought it to his mouth. "Here. Taste this. You won't believe it!" She got impatient when he didn't bite into it. She stamped on one of his feet. "Take a bite!"

"It's a tomato. You're acting like it's an apple. I can't just bite into it. It'll...squirt everywhere."

She stomped his toes again, out of impatience, and moved the tomato closer to his mouth: the skin just shy of his face. He tilted his head left and right and back and forth, contemplating the best way to sink his teeth in, and he did. A spray into his mouth, a burst of flavour. Pale red liquid dribbling over her hand, and she licked it off the backs of her fingers, saying, "See! Amazing right?"

And it was.

"Holy shit." Chewing it, "Best tomato ever. Honestly."

She took a bite out of the other side and more liquid squirted out. Some of it dribbling out of the corner of her mouth. He saw her throat drinking the juice down; another burst of red gushing out of the bite he'd taken from the other side. Her sucking her fingers clean.

"Oh, there it is!" And they both looked to the pack of seeds resting against the wall. Flecks of dried soil caked onto it. She laid the half-eaten tomato back in the Tupperware container. She shook her hand dry and Cohen saw a seed fly off behind her. She reached for the packet, but a makeshift shelf at her shins forced her to lean forward, lunge, and miss. Her fingertips had knocked it into the gap between the shelf and the wall. It fell to the ground, in behind that clunky wooden shelf at her shins.

"Shit."

"Goner. Looked empty anyway?"

Sizing up the situation. "No. I can crawl under there. I think."

"I—I saw one-ninety-nine written on the package. If you're that hard up for two dollars, I have a pocketful of change here. Really." He jingled his pocketful of change.

"The comic on it. Remember? I wanted to show you. It's

really cute. I think you'd get it." She was already on her knees, palms against the floor, peering under the shelf like a cat stalking a mouse. "It's, ah, it's pretty dark under there. But I think I can see it." She made a move to crawl under, but hesitated. Cohen blinked and she was on her way under. The board was not quite three feet off the ground. She looked like a mechanic under a car, except she was on her belly instead of her back.

And then her feet kicking in the air, like maybe a spider had bitten her "*Help!*"

"What?" He bent down instinctively.

"My hair! My hair is snagged in something!" He saw her try to roll over and then she screamed out in pain. Loudly. "I can't…my arms. There's no room! Help me for God's sake, man!" And she started laughing a little in between the moans of pain.

He got down and looked under. It was dim, but he saw her there, flat on her belly, one hand planted on the ground, the other triumphantly clutching the pack of seeds. Her hair was caught in a split in the plywood. He crawled under, but once he was under, it was even darker, and the limited space had him feeling claustrophobic, straightjacketed. His limbs awkward and useless.

"I need to get my right shoulder flat against the ground, in order to roll over and get your hair out."

"Then do that!"

"I can't. That's the problem. Unless. I lay my arm flat along the ground, under your chin maybe?" He flapped a hand around to make things more clear.

She shouted "*Why are you yelling?*" and laughed at herself. "Here." She lifted her head up off the ground. She put her face back down on his arm, nestling it in the crook of his elbow. Her soft cheek and chin radiating heat into his arm. Her breathing like the brush of a ghost. There, not there, there, not there: condensing on his bicep. He'd shift, and her lips would kiss his arms involuntarily. The poor lighting had him relying on his hands as much as his eyes. He had to lay a leg over her legs to get a little flatter. He had to spoon her.

"Sure. Make yourself cozy." A joke to peel back a layer of imposed intimacy. Skin clinging to skin and the feel of two bodies breathing in unison; rising and falling together. Her lips were still pressing into his bicep whenever he made a movement,

EVERY LITTLE THING

195

and then peeling away softly, like a Post-It note grip. The back of her hand at his crotch.

"I got it! Don't move at all!"

His eyes were adjusting to the light. He looked at Allie, and her eyes were in his like arrows. A look he knew. A look like quicksand. He unhooked her hair and got out from under the board.

He helped her up after she'd shimmied out. He let go of her hand, but she kept hers clasped to his. They were standing toe to toe, face to face. Breath on breath. "Just. Kiss me." She put her hands on his shoulders, and she walked him to the wall behind her. "Just kiss me until we're thirty years old again." She closed her eyes and leaned against the wall: an offering. Her hands grabbed fistfuls of his shirt. "Not on my lips. I can't kiss you back. Just, kiss me." And he did. Lingering on her neck, her pulse feral against his teeth. He kissed her along her jaw and tried for her mouth, but she'd turned away. He kissed the backs of her fingers; a frightened butterfly at his mouth. He slid a hand up her dress, his fingers sensing heat as he knelt, and she snared his hand with hers.

"I have to get back to work." She never let go of his hand as she walked away. His arm going up and up and up until their fingers snapped apart.

THE NEXT NIGHT, Cohen heard a series of thuds end in smashing glass. He ran to Lee's room—skidding on the hardwood floor—and swung the door open without knocking. Lee was sat up in his bed; his hands full of balled-up blanket.

He was shivering, staring at Cohen, taking long, slow breaths.

"Are you...okay? Lee?"

Cohen looked from Lee to the dresser and saw broken glass on top of it, by the TV. There was a dent in the wall. Little bits of white powder from a split in the gyproc. A few drops of water trickling down the wall.

"What happened?"

"I woke up. I was really thirsty. But the goddamn glass was empty." He pointed to its shattered remains.

"So you threw it at the wall?"

"It's ah-ah big production...to get up. This hour of the night.

I can't see a goddamn thing! It's like the light switches move every night. I can't find them no more!"

"You could have called out to me!"

"I'm feeling strange. Like something's wrong." Lee looked to the window, like he was ashamed to look at Cohen or he was scared someone was out there, looking in.

"Healthwise, you mean? A headache? ... Did you...Did you have a bad dream?" Cohen stepped further into the room, concerned.

"The Japanese are in my dreams now. And I don't want Keith coming around here anymore!"

"What'd you dream about, Lee?"

"I didn't *dream about* anything! It was real. Like memories. They'd fill the ends of bamboo sticks with sand and crack us with them. They'd make this gesture, asking for cigarettes. They'd put two closed-together fingers to their mouths, and they'd make a sucking noise." Lee demonstrated, with exaggeration, smacking himself in the lips with two fingers and inhaling fake cigarette smoke. "It was sign language, for cigarettes. If we didn't have any, they'd crack us over the knee. Or whack us on the back. Or a hand. Remember? Those sand-filled sticks stung as much as a whip. Hit as hard as a baseball bat. That sound and the way the men would howl. No pride or courage left in them." Lee snarled; a flash of angry white teeth.

Cohen leaned into the doorframe, crossed his arms. He wanted to say, *What?* He wanted to say, *Was that dream?* But whenever he or Allie talked to Lee like a child, he'd get more confrontational, irrational.

"Where's Allie?"

"She's not here. Are you talking about the Philippines, the camps you were in, after the war?"

"Yeah, well, she's never fucking here, is she? Keith's got her turned against us!"

"That's not fair and you know it. She has to work, Lee, and she doesn't live here. And when she comes, you're never kind or welcoming. You tell her to go away. You jam her hands in doorframes. Ring a bell?"

Lee clawed a hand through the air like an angry bear. *Whatever.* "He is! He's...*tainting* her. He'll turn her on me. Like he turned her on you."

"That was years ago, Lee. And not as simple as him *turning her* on me."

"Don't mock me! You'll see!"

Cohen turned on a floor lamp and saw that Lee was sweating, maybe even crying. He threw the blankets off himself. White, thin boxers clung to him from the sweat. He was wearing a black tank top three sizes too big. Something about that made him look sad. Sadder. His sparse, thin hair was sweat-dampened too; the perspiration doing the job of gel in his hair.

He looked at Cohen, his eyes googly and magnified by his glasses. "She's after my house, and Keith is putting it in her head."

"No one is *after your house*, Lee. Allie has her own. Nobody even *needs* your house. But I do want to hear your story, your stories, from your time in the Philippines. Let's get back to that?"

"I don't give a fuck about World War Two! I don't. That's not what I'm talking about!"

"I'm gonna go get a broom and clean this up. Do you want a glass of water?"

"Narcissco taught me how to find food in the jungle. He knew about ten words in English, but he also knew I was a scared kid. A hungry one. His weapon jammed that night they got us. They stuck him like a pig, with a bayonet, and kept running past him. I played dead and tried to plug up his stab holes with my fingers. But he still died. In my hands." Lee held his hands in the air like they were a bloody mess.

Cohen waited for more, searched for context, didn't know if that was the start or an end to a story. Lee simply held two hands out to Cohen, like they were holding a tray. He tucked them back under his thighs and said, "*That's* who I want to give my house to. Not Keith. Narcissco!"

"I—I'm sorry, Lee, but I think Narcissco...I think you just said—He died, didn't he?"

"I'm just trying to explain something. So you'll understand."

"Understand what, though?"

"So you'll understand that I saw a man's eye pop out. That I'm not shocked by anything. I'm not afraid."

"Of what, Lee? You're not afraid of what?"

Lee stopped talking. Stared at his toes. Wiggled them. Closed his eyes. Kept them closed.

"Do you want that glass of water?"

"I'm trying to tell you something. I made it out of that place and never did anything worth a damn."

"You had a good life, Lee. I know you did. I saw it happen."

"You'll see."

"I just don't. I don't understand. I don't really understand what it is we're talking about? Let's try and be a little more clear. What is it I'll see?"

"Why are you asking me that? Is Keith here now?"

He didn't know what else to say. "Do you want that glass of water?"

"You're going to tell Keith everything I'm saying, aren't you? Is he here right now? He is, isn't he?" Lee got up, put hands out like a blind mummy, and pushed past Cohen. He searched the house.

Cohen went to the nearest phone. Dialled Allie.

"My God, it's late what's wrong! Is he okay? Is everything all right?" She had a concerned but muted tone, afraid Keith would catch her on the phone with him.

"No, he's not. I'm spooked, for the first time. I actually don't know what to do here. He's tearing up the house, looking for Keith. I can't make sense of what he's saying, and it's plain fucking scary. He's all over the place here."

"Is it just a bad night?"

"I'll let you go, but in the morning, Allie, one of us needs to start looking for a place for him to live."

Lee was screaming muffled slurs, directed at Cohen as much as Keith. Something about the both of them failing her.

"Is that him?" she said. Her attention regained.

Cohen heard the cutlery drawer rattle. Walked into the kitchen. Said, "Jesus Christ, he's got a knife" and threw the phone on the table to put his hands up. To look innocent and harmless.

"It's Cohen, Lee, I'm *Cohen*."

"Who's that on the phone? I caught you! Was it Keith?" He was pointing the chef's knife like he'd use it.

"It was Allie."

"Put your hands down, this knife's not for you!"

"Lee. The knife, Lee. Let's just—" Cohen could hear Allie shouting through the phone, but the words weren't clear.

"I don't want to see Keith in this house ever again. Are we

EVERY
LITTLE
THING

199

clear?" And Lee threw the knife in the sink. It broke a plate. He walked back to his bedroom. Turned the TV on. Cohen picked the phone up and Allie was hysterical.

"Did he just threaten you with a knife?"

"I don't know. I think he might have."

COHEN COULDN'T SLEEP that night. He wanted to leave, sleep in his car. He hadn't been truly scared like that since he was a kid watching horror movies. Lee was a mystery now and capable of anything. Cohen was lying on the couch, with his eyes closed, imagining a blade sliding into his guts. Two hands around his throat. There was a lock on Lee's old bedroom door. The room he and Allie had moved Lee's stuff from, to relocate him to the den. He slept in there that night. On the floor, behind a locked door, in an old sleeping bag he'd plucked, quietly, from the hall closet. It smelled like moth balls and wet tents. And it was where he slept the rest of the week.

But Lee had been fine that week. The best he'd been in a while. And the fact he could act normal, after low points like that, was eerie. Proof he wasn't there anymore. Gone.

There was one morning, that week, when he and Cohen were eating cereal and Lee cracked a joke or two.

"Why did Mozart sell his chickens?" He was grinning.

Cohen didn't know what to say, what Lee was thinking. "Um..."

Lee dropped his spoon into his cereal like, *C'mon*. "It's a joke! Why did Mozart sell his chickens?"

"I dunno. Why?"

"Because they kept saying *Bach Bach*." He laughed. "What did the Alzheimer's patient forget to buy at the pharmacy?"

"I dunno. What?"

"Her Alzheimer's medication." Lee laughed again.

Cohen wanted to call Allie to come over, but she was at work. Lee was smiling and everything. "What are you, working on a stand-up act, Lee?"

Lee pointed his spoon across the kitchen at the TV in his bedroom. "I was watching open mic comedy before you called me for breakfast. Why'd the chicken cross the clothing store?"

But Cohen knew that one. "To get to the other size!" And Lee went sour that Cohen had answered it right. Smacked the side of his cereal bowl. And the bit of milk that was left in it—along with the spoon—landed on the table. Lee went back into his bedroom and shut the door. Cohen cleaned up the milk.

The old Lee had only made an appearance long enough for Cohen to question if that could've been called a moment of lucidity or just a man mimicking his TV. And that day, the day Lee was cracking jokes, was the very same day Lee slapped Allie. Hard. She came by around five, he stormed out of his room, and he slapped her. *I know what you're up to!*

There wasn't a handprint on her face, but there was a red splotch: an angry red shape. When Cohen looked at it under the light of the porch, he could feel the little needles of pain there. She took Cohen's hand away from her face. "I. Just. I wanna get out of this house. Now." In the background, Lee had been shouting. *You don't even care what I'd do for you!* And it was irritating, the tone and senselessness of his shouting. *He can keep his hands off my house!*

They got in his car and drove. *Bird Rock?* she said, and Cohen started the car, nodded, pulled out of the driveway even though the car was still fogged up with condensation. His headlights, like spotlights on the house, shone directly on Lee in the window, still cursing them both.

Allie propped her elbow up on the door handle and rested her chin on a hand; her eyes following power lines up and down and up and down. Eyelashes blinking slow as butterfly wings. She said, "Keith's saying you and me are using Lee as an excuse to see each other. He's saying that I haven't put Lee in a home because then I'd have no excuse to see you anymore."

"I don't really care what Keith thinks."

"You're right. This is my problem." A sigh.

"I didn't mean *that*. I didn't mean—Do you want to talk about...it?"

"About what? I mean, what's going on here, Cohen?"

She was using the side of a knuckle to etch maze-like designs in the condensation on her window. Her knuckle looked lost in the middle of it. The corner of his eye caught her looking at him. He knew the look. She needed reassurance. About something. About Lee, about how sad that was, that he'd slapped her just now. Or about Keith's grilling her, his accusations. His being right about what was or wasn't happening between the two of them. And why Lee wasn't in a home yet.

There weren't any words for that, so he took her hand. Held it. And she didn't haul hers away. She rubbed her thumb up and down over his, whittling away any unfamiliarity of touch between them. She laid her other hand down on top of their two held hands, like she was hiding something.

Her phone buzzed at a red light. It was in a cupholder, and they could both read Keith's text. *Home in the morning, Babe. Meetings with Thorne and Sons couldn't have gone much better!*

"Isn't that weird? Either you're both out of town or one of you is."

"Isn't the real question, how come my fiancé is sending texts about business, not...I dunno." Her thought trailed off. "Don't ever shack up with a co-worker. The lines get crossed in who you are to each other. Or *how* you are with each other, if there's a difference. I love him, yeah, but he's my co-worker, my boss. It's weird."

"I meant...it seems like he lives on the road then vacations in his office at home."

"You get used to it." She pointed to a Tim Horton's. "Pull in." She reached for her purse. "Why is Tim Horton's the only option for drive-by coffees in this town?"

Cohen laughed. "Drive-through, you mean. Drive-by coffees would be rollin' through a hood, tossing hot beverages at some *mofos* who *be steppin'*!"

"*What?*" She laughed. "Want a coffee?"

"Two sugars. And a box of Timbits for the table," he pointed to the dashboard.

The road up to Bird Rock was steep enough to press them both back into their seats. He told her, "So the project I've been working on. With all the dead bugs. I can't do it any slower than I've been doing it lately, and I'll be done in three weeks. Maybe less. Likely less. Clarence has been asking what's taking so long. I'll have to go back to living at my place, in town, so I can go into the Avian-Dome every day. I'll have to move out of Lee's."

Sipping her coffee, "Oh."

"Yeah. Three weeks or so."

"That's not long."

"No."

He pulled into the parking lot and it was pretty much empty. He put at least fifteen parking spaces between him and the nearest car and took his keys out of the ignition. The moonlight was a strip of white oil flickering on the black ocean—a line of white fire.

"Be right back," and he got out of the car and walked up to the guardrail, braced his shins against it. The ocean was two-hundred feet below him. There was nothing gradual about the slope of the mountain: he could have stood on the guardrail and dove straight into the ocean. There was a lighthouse ahead of him, across the bay. It was close enough to see, but far enough away that its light never illuminated him as it spun around.

He got back into the car and hauled the door shut harder than he'd intended.

"Pretty up here, hey?" She opened the box of Timbits. Laid them on the dashboard where they could both reach.

He saw the ring on her finger. The one Matt had given him to give to her. "Yeah. A real maritime cliché, must say."

"So. You're leaving Grayton soon."

"Yeah."

"You shouldn't."

"I shouldn't, but I have to. We're all slaves to bills and then we die."

"Paycheques."

"What?"

"The saying is, *We're all slaves to paycheques and then we die.*"

"Same thing. I mean, bills are what paycheques are for."

"No more hanging out, me and you."

"Maybe not, no."

Some silence, raised eyebrows. "I'll find a good place for Lee. This week."

The moonlight caught her ring again and must have folded his face up in disdain. She looked at him, curious. "What?"

"That ring. On your finger."

She looked at it like she did and didn't want to talk about it. "Well, you gave it to Keith to give to me. Remember?"

"I gave it to Lee, to give to Keith, to give to you. There's a big difference. I told your father you'd get the ring. I didn't think I'd ever see it on your finger. Us in a car like this. It's like seeing a pristine forest about to be bulldozed—"

A blast of laughter cut him off, "That's *got* to be the cheesiest thing you've ever said." She stuck a hand into his face,

EVERY
LITTLE
THING

203

laughing, pushing him away. She had her hand plastered upside down over his mouth: her pinky over his nose, her thumb into his throat. Her palm was a perfect seal over his mouth. He squirmed until she took her hand away, and then she leaned over and kissed his mouth. No hesitation. One kiss. And then another one, a slower one, to punctuate it.

"You just…"

"Yeah. I did."

He wanted to say, *Wait*, or *Maybe you shouldn't*, but he didn't say anything as she undid his jeans and slid them down to his knees. Wrestled them down to the floor. He looked around, worried about neighbouring cars. "Allie, Jesus. I mean there's windows!"

"Doesn't seem to be bothering you," she said, holding the proof in her hand. "Here," she pulled the lever on his chair so he'd fall out of sight of any cars coming into the parking lot.

She moved her head down there, but she'd hit her head off the steering wheel, laughed, said, *ah*, and Cohen shot up to see if she was okay. "Yes, dammit! This was supposed to be sexy…and you're ruining it!" She slapped a palm into his chest, pushed him back down. She took it in her mouth and he shut up; went weightless. He watched her free hand go up her skirt. It came back with a purple ball of cotton panties. Soft handcuffs around her knees.

She tugged his condom on, then put her eyes in his as she climbed onto him, like she wanted it to mean something. When she tilted her head forward, her hair fell and dangled between them: a tunnel blocking out everything but her face. And he'd missed that. That moment of nothing but her. And then her lips were on his mouth, his neck, his chest.

He grabbed her hips hard as he finished, and she swayed gently to a stop, fell down over him, and they lay there with their eyes closed.

"That was—I could—"

She nuzzled her head into his chest. "Shh."

"What? I'm just saying, if you want, I could—"

"We're good, champ." She reached a hand up and squeezed his shoulders and laughed. He could feel her grin against his chest. Like she felt awkward, shy, kind of uncomfortable, in hindsight, with what had just happened. He craned his neck down, trying to get a look at her face, and kissed the top of her head instead. He ran a finger along her jaw and she cocked her head back like a content cat. She was biting a hangnail, pensive or perfectly happy.

"I don't want to move," she said, sawing her knuckles over his ribs.

"Me either."

"But. We're kind of naked, in a parking lot."

She rolled over into the passenger seat, slid her underwear back up, and that elastic snap shook him into action. He untwisted the jeans around his ankles and hauled them back up. She'd reclined her seat and was laying there with her eyes closed. Cohen scanned her face for regret, or guilt, and saw neither. If anything, she looked tired. She opened her eyes and looked over at him. "What?"

"Nothing."

She sat up, kissed him. Wrestled her hair into an elastic.

"In a parking lot. Like a couple of teenagers. We've still got it in us."

"We're not senior citizens," she said. "And I said stop talking about it!"

"I—"

"Stop talking about it, I said! We need to go. I gotta get home. I have an early flight to Montreal in the morning."

"Montreal? My favourite. I'll grab a ticket too? Lee can fend for himself at this point."

"Used to be my favourite too. Keith hates it, so he sends me to attend all things Montreal." She seemed like she wanted to say something more. And when she did, it was, "Ever since you mentioned you're looking into adoption, all I can think about is how I travel too much to be a...present, active mother."

But Cohen wasn't listening to her, really. He was picturing them in Montreal. Almond chocolatines and bitter coffee on Mont-Royal when they got there.

He looked over, and Allie's face was a puzzle of guilt, giddiness, remorse, excitement, confusion, and calmness. Until she looked at her engagement ring. Her eyes like a car into a wall.

EVERY
LITTLE
THING

MEANING WELL

TWO MORE WEEKS and he'd have to move back home. The thought never left him. Years had raced by, changing nothing about his life, but this one slow stretch of months had the past rear-ending the present.

He was making a pizza for him and Lee, eating as much prosciutto and green olive as he was throwing onto the crust. He cut up some tomatoes with the same chef's knife he'd found on Lee's nightstand two nights back. He'd asked Lee why the knife was in his room, and Lee said, "Mind your own business. My house. My knife. Fuck off." So he did.

He was putting the pizza in the oven when Clarence phoned. "Cohen?"

"Yeah?"

"How's it going?"

"Good, you?"

"I meant...with the sample processing. How's *that* going?" He laughed. "But I'm glad you're well."

"Oh." They laughed a little more. "Good. I have about seventy bags left. I'll be done by your August eighth deadline. Maybe even sooner."

"You've obviously not started in on the 2011 bags yet. Have you?"

"Yeah, I have. This week. Why?" He popped another green olive into his mouth. Maybe his tenth.

"Well, I just found another dozen bags. *About* a dozen anyway. I don't know how they got separated from the rest."

"I'm getting sick of this, Clarence. I'm seeing larvae when I close my eyes. I'm dreaming about getting swarmed by dragonflies, eaten alive by midges. Sunday night, I dreamt that two loons were pecking at my shins—"

"Going *looney*, are you?"

"Yes. Hah hah."

"Well, if you're already losing it, another twelve bags won't kill you."

"No, I guess not. I'll see you tomorrow. I'll be in tomorrow to get them."

And when he went in to the Avian-Dome, he went in the afternoon, so that Zack would be there. He poked his head into the daycare room, and Jenny Lane recognized him, waved. She was knelt down and helping little Lacie Decker get her shoes on, and Lacie turned and waved to him.

Jenny nodded her head sympathetically towards Zack as she tied up Lacie's sneakers. Sympathetically, like *Poor Zack*. And when Cohen looked over, Zack looked like a kid at a Christmas tree who had no gifts to open while everyone else was tearing into theirs. There were kids running around, screaming and banging toys together—airplanes and plush birds—but Zack just sat there watching them. He was sat on the floor with his two hands rested on the carpet beside him. A shoelace untied. He looked like an old toy all the other kids had outgrown.

He saw Cohen and smiled, but not overly. It was weird, that lack of enthusiasm. The stony face. Zack got up and walked over to Cohen and let out a laborious "Hi." His left hand was wrapped up in gauze.

"Why the mummy hand?"

Zack lifted his hand, looked at it. Slumpish and slow. "Oh. I was washing Dad's big knives. He fills up the sink for me, and I stand on a chair. Sometimes it's hard to see through the bubbles. A big knife got me. I put my hand in the water too fast I guess?" He shrugged his shoulders.

Cohen tried hiding his anger from Zack, and bottling it up only made him angrier. He couldn't say, *Your father's a fucking idiot, do you know that?* He asked him, "How about the fainting, buddy, how's that been?"

"Worse."

"Yeah?"

"Yeah.

"How? What do you mean, worse?"

"My lungs are sick and I pass out more now. I'm not even supposed to run around."

Cohen felt a hand on his shoulder. Clarence's. "Say goodbye to Mr. Davies, Zack." And then Clarence's hand was hauling Cohen away.

Zack only waved, as if uttering the words was exhausting. He was the colour of wet tissue paper: a purplish underglow.

Walking down the hall, "You know goddamn well where the samples are, and they're not in that kid's possession, are they?"

"What happened to Zack's hand, Clarence?"

"*Don't* start in with the heroics. Do *not*."

"His father had him washing *chefs' knives!*"

"Cohen, it's not your business."

"There's got to be a fucking rule, about you reporting shit like that. But fine, I'm done. I mean no ill will. I just need to express my opinion. And *then* I can drop it."

"I'm not sure you can." They'd gotten to the storage closet, and Clarence fished his keys out of his pocket and unlocked the door. Jangles of keys amplifying Clarence's anger. He flicked a light on. Said, "Are you done yet?"

"You agree, don't you?"

"What I think, Cohen, is we've gotten too buddy-buddy for you to respect my authority when I tell you to drop something. And for that, I'm losing the high regard I've been holding you in. To be blunt." He opened the closet door, looked at Cohen steely.

"What's wrong with his lungs?"

"His lungs?"

"Yeah, he said his lungs are…sick."

Clarence put an empty box in Cohen's arms. "It's his heart, not his lungs. He's got what you got. ARVC. How appropriate. Maybe you've all got some bond that makes you irrationally protective of each other?"

"He doesn't have ARVC. I have ARVC. I don't faint and go around looking like a pale mummy. The kid looks lethargic. Half dead."

"He's got ARVC, Cohen. He's been diagnosed. Maybe he's just…got it really bad? Worse than you?" Clarence kept loading the box Cohen was holding with more pond samples.

"You're a biologist, Clarence. Listen to yourself."

"I'm your *boss*, Cohen, so why don't *you* listen to *yourself*?"

"Jokes, I was joking. I'm just saying—"

"Since you're his fairy godfather, I guess I can fill you in. It's not good. He's on a transplant list. The heart's shot, apparently."

"That's *not* ARVC! ARVC is a rhythm disorder. I should know."

"I'm sorry for your denial, but the muscle of his heart, it's turning into fat. It's a sad state. A rare case, unheard of in the province for a kid his age, but the doctors aren't lying, Cohen. Zack was supposed to go live with his grandmother, in the States, but there's specialists here. And while my heart goes out to the little slugger, that's enough on him, okay? I don't like the look on your face."

"It can't be *that* bad! People on transplant lists. They...live in the hospital while they're waiting, don't they?"

Clarence laid the last of the twelve bags in the box in Cohen's arm. "Zack's gotta wait it out. It's interfering with his attendance at school, at this point. But no, he can't just sit around in hospital. There's only so many beds to go around."

Clarence was locking up the closet door, but Cohen had already turned to walk back down the hall. Zack's father had come in to pick Zack up, and Cohen dashed off towards him, but Clarence came bustling up behind him. He slapped his two hands on Cohen's shoulders, like meat hooks, and Cohen's feet kicked forward. Cohen hadn't gotten close enough to Zack's father so he had to yell at Jamie while he waited for Jenny to lace up Zack's shoes. He screamed, "*Hey!*" and everyone turned around. "You've got him washing *knives* now?" And Zack's father, from the other end of the long foyer, peered, perplexed, with a hand over his eyes, in the direction of the shouting.

Clarence lassoed an arm around Cohen and hauled him into a nearby washroom. A woman's washroom. He pinned Cohen up against a ceramic tile wall by his shoulders and roared at him. A thud from his lungs as Clarence pushed him into the wall. "You're *seconds* away from losing your job. Do you hear me? Is the man worth that?"

"It's not about the man, is it? Are you asking me if a kid's safety is worth my job?" And Clarence thrust Cohen into the wall again, out of frustration. Cohen's shoulder blades, and then his skull, knocking off the wall. A sharp crack of pain that buzzed in his teeth.

"*What* is your deal with this kid? You're out there shouting at the man in front of visitors and staff! I can't have it—"

Cohen shoved Clarence off him. He tossed the samples on the floor, and one of the bags burst open: a shot of pale brown water squirt through the air like a sprinkler going off. He caught up to Zack and Zack's father, and Zack's father was reaching a hand up for the door; his back to Cohen.

"You've got him washing knives now?"

Turning around, knowing who it was without seeing him yet, "I've got him helping out around the house, yeah, and we had a little accident."

"Helping around the house." A sardonic laugh. "You couldn't just have him fold some laundry? Dust a coffee table?"

And it was Jenny Lane coming up behind Cohen now. She grabbed Cohen by a hand and yanked him back, like she thought Cohen might hit the man. "Cohen! Stop it! Back off! Mr. Janes, you go on! I'm sorry for this. I really am!"

He said, "Are you going to hit me, Cohen? Do you want to hit me?"

The look in Zack's eyes was a slap across Cohen's face. Fear. *Don't. Why?*

Clarence was jogging up towards them now, flinching from stabs of pain in his bummed ankle. "You go on, Mr. Janes. We'll deal with Cohen."

Cohen looked back at Clarence and then back at Zack's father. "*Hit* you? Maybe I should stick a knife in your hand?"

Too much. He regretted it instantly. Zack looked panicked and afraid, and Cohen felt horrible. Everyone shaking their heads as Zack and his father walked out of the building. Cohen looked back at Clarence.

"Jesus Christ, Cohen. I mean. *Jesus Christ.*"

Jenny walked away, still shaking her head, and started herding the other kids back into the playroom. They'd all come spilling out to watch the show. Little snickering voices like, *Is that man going to cut Zack's dad's hands off?*

"You're done. I'm sorry. But you're done here. That was it. I warned you. I warned you twice, really, didn't I? I gave you a second chance and you threw it back in my face! Finish up the samples you have out in Grayton, at that man's house, and consider it your last two weeks at the Avian-Dome. I'll pay you the full two weeks if you're done sooner than that." He shook his head again, gobsmacked, and walked away.

"I don't know where that…came from. I've got a lot going on. I wasn't threatening him, it only came out that way."

"Just go, Cohen. Just, go."

Clarence's head was still shaking. His arms at his hips like two triangles hanging off his body as he walked away. Cohen went to leave and Clarence turned around, "I never said the kid's father doesn't need a talking to. All I said was stay out of it, and you didn't. So. You're done. I—" Clarence scratched the side of his nose with a forefinger. "You're a bright guy, you're a good guy, a good worker. I'll give you a reference, depending on the nature of the job. Don't worry about that." And then he turned and walked away. Whispered, *Fuck.*

TWO DAYS LATER. Not even long enough for things to sink in, and it was his brother's birthday. Ryan. He'd drowned more than ten years ago, and Cohen's memories of him were as cloudy and malleable as recollected dreams. There were pieces missing and details blurred. But there were some moments, not murky at all through the lens of memory, like the time they were kids and Ryan found a tiny yellow worm wriggling around in his bowl of blueberries. Moments as trivial as that. Ryan, blue-toothed and terrified, pushing the bowl away. It smashed off the ceramic floor in their kitchen; little blue balls scurrying under the heater, the oven, the fridge. Ryan never ate blueberries again after that day. Not even blueberry jam.

His family never visited the grave on the anniversary of Ryan's death. They'd do that instead on his birthday, in celebration of Ryan, after a nice big lunch. So his mother called him that morning. A reminder.

"We'll see you at lunch, yes? Our place. One-ish?"

He sounded inattentive, he could hear that in his voice. So he kept his responses brief. "Yeah." It sounded like he was distracted, reading the newspaper.

"What's wrong? You sound, I don't know…is something wrong?"

It wasn't the right time to tell her about his job. "I'm tired, long week."

"You're sure everything's fine?"

"Yeah."

"Okay. Stop and pick up something for dessert, will you?"

"Some strawberry-chocolate Danishes from Deniro's?"

"Perfect."

Allie had gotten back into town that morning too. An hour after he'd gotten off the phone with his mother, she'd burst through Lee's door like someone was chasing her. She came into the kitchen as he was peeling an orange.

"Say something nice about my dress!" She was tugging her jacket off, laying it over a chair.

"It's new?"

"Yeah. And it cost *way* too much money." She swirled it a little: made a tornado of the dress. Did a curtsy to show it off.

"It's very...Montreal. Very nice. *Chic.* You are very easy on the eyes right now, *Mon Petit Bijoux.*" He feigned a laugh.

She looked at the barren kitchen table and said, "No microscope action today?"

"No." He opened the cupboard door, the one under the sink, and threw his orange peels into the garbage.

"Why not?"

He didn't want to tell her why either. Not today. "It's Ryan's birthday...my brother. I can take the day off. Something came up at work, and I'm not in that big of a rush to finish the samples anymore."

She went tender: not unlike she looked the day his family drove back from the cabin and found Allie and her father moving in next door. She scooped her dress behind her knees and sat at the kitchen table. She had her hair styled differently. Cover-girl-like. Purposefully messy. Hipster-ish. "You guys have lunch and go to the graveyard on his birthday, right?"

"Yeah."

She waited a minute, like she was thinking about it. She had her heels up on the chair and her arms wrapped around her shins, hugging herself. He sat into the table, offered her a wedge of orange. She took one and said, "Can I come? Would that be... weird? I'd like to go with you. I don't have any reason to rush back to work today."

"Okay."

She seemed surprised he never hesitated in saying okay. "I mean, I used to go with you and your parents every year, and we're friends now. Your parents won't find that weird, right? I'd like to see them. Very much."

"We're *friends* now, are we?"

She reached over and yanked the orange out of his hand. Tore off a wedge and handed it back to him. "I'm gonna pop in and say hello to Lee. How is he today? Nasty or super nasty?"

"Not bad. Earlier anyway. But be careful. I found an axe on his dresser last weekend."

She laughed.

"I'm fucking *serious*," and he laughed too. "I think he thinks someone's planning on breaking in. He keeps saying people want to steal his house, as if his house was like a purse someone could grab in the middle of the night and run off with. Foundation and all."

"What time are you heading to your parents' house?"

He looked at his watch. Shrugged his shoulders. "I might leave here in twenty minutes?"

"Okay. I'm going to say hello to Lee and rush home to drop off my suitcase, and pick up a few things for work. So I can head into the office from town. Afterwards. I'll meet you at your parents' place for lunch."

"You came right here from the airport?"

"Yeah, why not? I only live, like, three streets over."

He liked that she'd come right over from the airport. He liked the way that dress tornado-ed around her knees as she spun and walked out of the room.

RYAN'S GRAVE WAS black marble, and light grey where the words were etched in. When someone mentioned Ryan's name now, Cohen pictured this gravestone instead of the flesh-and-blood kid who was his bother. That bothered him. When his mother talked about Ryan, he saw it in her eyes that she was seeing *him* in those recollected memories. And he was jealous of that. She could see the clothes he had on, what his hair was doing. Cohen saw the headstone. Or the pond that day. Or the guitar that sat in Ryan's bedroom, unplayed, so long the strings felt like saw blades the one time Cohen picked it up and strummed it.

There was a line etched into the gravestone. "Those who leave too soon are remembered the longest." It bothered Cohen when his mother chose that line. The simplistic nonsense of it. It felt cheap; it wasn't visceral enough. It said nothing of Ryan himself.

As the years passed, the annual trips to Ryan's grave went from morose to an uplifting pleasantry. The conversations weren't even about Ryan, really, beyond a few *Remember whens* and one or two mentions of *How he always used to*. It was about not forgetting more than remembering.

His parents were thrilled to see Allie that day at lunch. She'd shown up at their house before he had. He'd planned on explaining that Allie would be joining him when he got there, but he got there and Allie had already explained. No one seemed off put. He never did ask how she'd explained her presence. She was hypnotic: the kind of person people were happy to have around, and they didn't need a reason. They only had to hear her laugh.

He came in the front door and his mother greeted him, a kiss on his cheek, and she took the box of strawberry Danishes from his hand so he could pluck off his shoes. On his swoop back up from taking his shoes off, his mother said, "Allie's here." She said it with a smile on her face, *I'm so happy for you guys*. But his father was wary. They ate their lunch and laughed and reminisced, but all the while Cohen's father would stare at Allie's engagement ring and then stare at Cohen. To prove a point.

After lunch, at the grave, Allie and his mother were still catching up. Cohen was looking down at their feet, at how close they were standing together, and how the grass was long and needed to be cut. It came up over their shoes in limp green spikes. His mother, smoothing Allie's shoulders, said, "I love your dress."

"Thanks."

"And your hair." She ran a hand through it. His mother had always needed to touch something to trust her eyes about it. Letting go of Allie's hair, "How's work?"

"Work's work. How's *retirement?*" She'd said retirement as if it was the same as winning the lottery.

Cohen and his father scurried away, towards a bench, and sat down. His father said, "I saw this coming—you and Allie getting all tangled up like this—when you said you were going out to Grayon to look after Lee." Shifting his weight, settling into the bench, he looked up at Allie and said, "So, how serious is this?"

"It's a weird topic. Let's leave it for now. I don't know, to be honest."

"She's married, isn't she?"

"No, not yet."

Allie's cellphone rang and they stopped talking to look at her, eavesdropping before they realized it.

Muffled, *Oh my God*s. A sharply toned, *I'm leaving now. Doesn't matter where I am.* An irritable, *I'll explain later.*

She hung up. "I'm supposed to be in a meeting. I entirely forgot about it. I've got to run. I'm *very* sorry! It was *so* nice seeing you both," and his mother kissed Allie's cheek, twice, carried away with the enthusiasm of seeing her again. She'd held Allie's shoulders in her hands and looked at her adoringly, and Allie shot Cohen a look of flattery over it. "Gorgeous," she said. "You just keep getting more gorgeous. You'll have to tell me how you do it one day soon, when we have more time?"

Allie came over to his father on the bench and hugged him goodbye too. She stood in front of Cohen then, and they looked around, not sure how to physically express their goodbye. She said, "I'll call you later" and tapped his knee a few times with her fingertips. He nodded.

His father called out as she was walking away. "Yes, it was nice seeing you too, Allie." She turned and smiled and waved again, her eyes fighting off a finger of sunlight, her keys jingling as she waved. Under his breath, his father whispered, "Her fiancé, that's her boss too, right?"

"Yeah."

His mother bent over to straighten the flowers she'd brought to the grave. She said, "I just love these yellow ones Allie brought along. They're soft as ears." She bunched them all together: the flowers she'd brought and the ones Allie had brought.

Cohen's cellphone beeped in his pocket. A text message. He took it out and read it. *Keith's PISSED. I told him where I was today. Why I missed the meeting. We need to talk. He's losing it for real this time. I'll call you later.*

His father peered at his cellphone. But he didn't see the message. He didn't have to.

EVERY
LITTLE
THING

215

PULLED
THREADS

HE RE-READ ALLIE'S text message as he sat in his car, *He's losing it for real this time. I'll call you later.* But she never did get a chance to call. Or she just didn't call.

Back at home, he read it again as he took his phone from his pocket and laid it on the kitchen table, and later still, after he signed Clarence's generous severance package from The Avian-Dome. He waited for his phone to ring, and every minute ticked by like a separate blast of anxiety.

He'd pour himself a cup of tea every night at eight, and Allie knew that. She'd join him sometimes, stopping by with something from DeNiro's Bakery. He'd miss her on the nights she didn't show up, smiling, cutting her piece of cake in half, as if anything chopped in two isn't bad for you. But there was no knock at the door that night, until after nine. And it was an urgent banging. Allie, she wouldn't knock.

He walked towards the porch and saw Keith there, distorted by the stained glass window: pounding on the door, trying the handle, pounding on the door. The sight of his face broke Cohen's stride, but he got to the door, pulled it open.

"Where's that crazy old man?"

"Lee?"

"Yeah."

"He's in his room. He doesn't leave his room anymore—"

"Good. You could nail his door shut as far as I'm concerned. He's hit her, you know? He's punched Allie." Keith brushed past Cohen into the living room, looking around to make sure Lee really was in his bedroom. "That crazy fuck threw potted plants at me last time I was here. Did Allie tell you that?"

"Yeah, she did, so keep your voice down or he'll come out throwing more."

Keith turned his neck, quick and hawk-like. "You think that's funny? The senile old fuck."

"No, I'm just saying. Keep your voice down. Unless you want more pots thrown at you." He laughed to make it seem like friendly advice.

Keith walked into the kitchen, so Cohen followed him. Put the kettle on. It was a long and narrow kitchen with a staircase at one end and the appliances on the other. Keith leaned into the counter near the staircase-end of the kitchen, arms folded. His head was nodding in all directions like someone was shaking him, and his mouth was getting ahead of itself, or he didn't know what order to let the words out in. "It's not you she wants. This isn't about whatever you two had before. Me and her are having a hard time, that's all that's happening here. You need to understand that and back off. For starters, let's not forget you killed her father. Or have you forgotten that?"

"I remember it a little differently than that."

"You could be anyone. That's all I mean. A guy from her gym. A client, whatever." He shrugged his angry shoulders. "This isn't an *Allie and Cohen* thing. Allie and I, we're in a rut, and you're preying on it. Do you understand what I'm saying? You two aren't having some kind of end-of-a-movie moment where you end up back together."

Cohen wanted to say, *You're talking in circles, like she does.*

"You're some kind of pathetic shit, who's been hung up on a girl for, what, more than five years?" He looked at his watch as if it were a calendar. "Six years?"

"I came to Grayton because of Lee, Keith. Lee and I have a history separate from Allie. What happened after that, well, I dunno what to say. It's beyond me."

Keith wanted Cohen's retorts to be longer, bolder. He wanted words to bite into. Or a reason to get physical. It was dark in the kitchen, but Cohen could see how adrenaline-soaked Keith's posturing was. He was a marionette in shaky hands.

"You need to pack up here and go back to your sad little life. Check Lee into a fucking home somewhere and forget all about this fantasy blast from the past you're living. And stop acting like you're here for Lee! The man belongs in a straightjacket in a dark

EVERY
LITTLE
THING

217

room, and if he lays his hands on her again, it's where I'll be putting him. That's what a real man does, for the record."

"The man's sick, is what he is. Binswanger Disease. Maybe you should read the fuckin pamphlet. He's got some neurological issues, impairing his personality, and that's what slapped Allie. Not Lee. I'm smart enough to know we're all a few chemical imbalances short of being just like the guy. And Lee's been there for me more than this one time I'm trying to be here for him."

"Fucking hero card, man. You play it so well, don't you? You've got yourself convinced you're a great guy. *Hey, sure Matt. I'll help you kill yourself. Right after I get my kid brother drunk on a boat!*"

Cohen leaned off the counter to pick the hissing kettle up off the stove. "Do you want a cup of tea or coffee or something?"

"No, man, I don't. I don't want a *fucking coffee or something*. I want you to realize you're not some kind of saviour and I'm not some kind of asshole you're saving Allie from."

"What do you want me to say, Keith? It's not up to me or you what Allie wants. And this bullshit showdown isn't going to change what she wants."

"*That's* my issue! You're acting like it's me versus you."

Cohen shook his head and poured two teas, in case Keith changed his mind. "There if you want it." But Keith came unflinchingly towards him and knocked both mugs of tea off the counter and into the sink. A scorch of liquid heat across Cohen's forearm. A splash of brown on his shirt. Keith was in his face, leaning up on his toes, pointing. "You know what you need to hear?"

"Calm down, Keith. And back up." He put a hand on Keith's chest, extended his arm to push him back. But Keith walked back in, closing the space between them, and Cohen heard Lee's TV go quiet.

"She gave away your fucking kid and never told you. Did you know that? She was pregnant when she left you to live with Lee. That's how much she cares about you, asshole. And that's how loyal Lee is to you too, by the way. He never told you a thing about it, did he?"

Cohen put his hands up and out, begging for a minute to process what Keith had thrown his way, but Keith stepped back into his face again, spit coming out with the words, "Yeah, how do you like the truth of it, asshole? Might not have been yours because her and I started in long before she left you."

"You don't just fuckin tell someone something like this, in a goddamn kitchen, shouting in their face!" He pushed Keith away and looked to the floor, to channel a moment of clarity. He went to say, *Bullshit* or, *What the fuck was that?* but when he looked up, Lee was halfway across the kitchen, charging at Keith with a knife clutched in both hands, like it was a sword.

Cohen shifted gears, from shock to instinct, lunging at Keith to protect him because Keith had his back turned to Lee and never saw Lee coming. But Keith saw Cohen lunging towards him and backed up as if Cohen was going to swing a fist at him.

The knife went in. A wet, smooth thud. It was the biggest knife in the house. The same one Cohen had been finding in Lee's room for weeks. The knife went in and Keith's face went paper-white. His mouth fell open: his chin right into his throat. Two rows of teeth, but no scream.

Lee had the knife deep in Keith's back, near his kidney, and was about to haul it up and kill Keith, but Cohen got there in time and pushed down on Lee's hand. He wedged his body in between Lee and Keith, using Keith's body as a wall to push against, to thrust Lee and the knife in the opposite direction.

Lee fell to the floor in a way that expressed his age, his mental state, and Cohen pinned him there, gently as possible, like he was a brittle bug. Keith knelt into Cohen's back, punching Lee in the face over and over, belting him, with Cohen sandwiched there between them, trying to protect them both. Lee was cowering and bawling in pain, crying and reaching for the knife way out of reach under the kitchen table. Keith kept swinging, more blood and tears bursting over Lee's face, so Cohen rolled over and covered Lee entirely, lining his head up over Lee's head, his torso over Lee's, his legs over Lee's, to shield Lee from the blows and to keep Lee from getting the knife.

But Keith kept swinging, hitting Cohen now. Knowing the difference and taking pleasure in it. It felt like Keith was hurling rocks at his face. "Call an ambulance, get out of here."

Another punch, like another thrown rock; the after-sting and the instant swelling. "Keith, I've got him. Get up, get out of here, call an ambulance." One more sharp crash into his face and Cohen started swinging back. *I could've let him kill you.*

Keith got up, feeling his back. "Fuck! Fucking Christ! Jesus fuck!" He was wiping his back and looking at the blood on his hands, over and over, panicking more every time. He took off running and left the front door wide open.

Lee sat with his back against the cupboards, below the kitchen sink, crying, wiping his bloody hands all over the parts of his face Keith had welted and left bruised. His face and hands were equally smeared red. Lee was panicked and his body was shivering like he was cold, but he wasn't cold.

Cohen stepped back, away from Lee, more alarmed than concerned for his own safety. It was too much at once. His heart like an angry wasp, and his face still stinging. He was absolutely terrified of Lee now and not sure where Keith was. He took his phone out of his pocket and dialled the direct line to Grayton's police station. Allie kept it plastered to the fridge. He was backing away from Lee as he dialled, his eyes never leaving him. Lee kept yelling. "You fucking ruined it! I was waiting weeks for that! We had him! You want Allie, don't you?" He kept a distance from Lee, who was pacing around the kitchen now, blood-smeared and capable of anything. Cohen called the police, but they already knew the situation.

"The police and an ambulance are on their way. The victim is still in your driveway, locked in his car, and waiting for us. Are you okay? Is the offender still in the house?"

Offender. Lee a criminal now.

"Sir, the yelling in the background, are you in danger?"

"I don't know. I don't know what I'm supposed to do. I know this man. I don't think he'll hurt me."

"Sir, let's stay calm. I need you to place a sizeable object between you and the offender. A table. It might be best if you join the victim in his car and wait—" But Cohen heard the sirens coming. That quickly, the police station a two-minute drive from Lee's house. He hung up on the woman and looked up. Lee was gone. Not in the kitchen. He heard Lee's TV flick on, the news blaring something about a tropical storm. He'd crawled back into bed, bloody clothes and all. The knife still under the kitchen table.

The cops came in like a small militia, shouting *Police* and pointing guns. Something in the panic of it all had amplified the wispy-crackling of static from their walkie-talkies. Cohen put his hands up and pointed to Lee's bedroom. They arrested Lee on the spot, cuffed him, brutally, his chest crashing into the floor, his left cheek pancaked into hardwood. One cop had his knee pressed into Lee's back so hard Cohen pictured Lee's ribs snapping like spaghetti sticks. A man that old, knocked down and pinned to the floor. Three on one. All that shouting and panic. The contrast between how the police were looking at Lee and how Cohen was. It was too much to feel real.

She was pregnant when she left you to live with Lee. And then the pattering of police boots derailed his train of thought. He looked over at the bloody knife under the kitchen table again.

Three officers scooped a handcuffed Lee off the floor like he was a tagged animal. His glasses had fallen off his face. One officer looked down at his glasses, stared, like he was contemplating if he'd pick them up or not. He did and he put them on Lee's face in time for Lee to turn to Cohen as they guided him out of the house, and Lee shouted, "I did this for you, and you had me arrested! I did this for you and Allie! But you just wanted my house, didn't you!" He spat.

All eyes on Cohen now. Three officers took Lee out of the house, and one stayed behind with Cohen. Notepad in hand. Cohen said, "That's not what it sounded like."

The officer licked his fingers and grabbed the edge of his notepad. Found a fresh page. He motioned to the couch in the living room. "I'm constable MacDonald. We need to vacate the scene of the crime."

Cohen sat on the couch; the constable on the edge of the loveseat. The cop's phone rang just before his mouth got started on his first question. He laid the notepad on the cushion beside him and talked for three or four minutes in *yeahs* and *okays* and *uh-huhs*. Cohen stood up. He went to go see if the paramedics had arrived and to see how Keith was doing, but the constable stuck his hand up at Cohen, *Don't move.* Through the window, he saw that the paramedics hadn't arrived yet.

Two more officers, new on the scene, walked through the living room and into the kitchen with something like toolboxes in their hands. The constable clicked his cellphone closed and picked up his notepad.

"I need a statement. What is your last name, Cohen?" and Cohen wondered how the officer knew him by name.

"Davies."

A nod, a scribble. "I need to advise you that you're entitled to

EVERY
LITTLE
THING

221

have a lawyer present."

The comment never struck Cohen as accusatory or extreme. He knew the police had disclaimers to make before everything they did; that they were required to shout *police* at potential criminals before drawing a gun and to tell everyone they talked to that they were entitled to a lawyer. Bullshit formalities, for legal reasons. Cohen made a facial gesture that that was fine and told the officer his story. He told him why Keith had come by—suspicions that he and Allie were more than friends—and he gave the details of that conversation. He mentioned Lee's contempt for Keith.

"...I know they don't get along. I know Lee's thrown flower pots at the man's car. I know Lee's been increasingly unstable, but I *never* saw this coming. I *never* saw Lee capable of this. He's a kind and big-hearted man, but he's suffering from a mental disorder. Dementia is part of it. But, still." And then he thought of it and mentioned that he'd found that knife in Lee's room a few times and kept taking it back out.

"And that never struck you as bizarre or foreboding? It never struck you as a safety risk for others, or Lee himself?" The constable scribbled hurried little words as they talked.

"No, because it was one of many random things I'd find in his bedroom. I found a corkscrew on his nightstand one day. He doesn't drink wine. I'd ask him about the knife and he'd get confrontational, and it's just not worth upsetting the guy. We were in the process of finding suitable long-term care for Lee—"

"By *we*, whom do you mean?"

"By we, I mean Allie and myself. As I mentioned, Allie and I, we were...together. In the past. For years. Lee was a family friend of hers. So Lee and I got close, developed a friendship separate from me and Allie. Recently, she called needing help looking after Lee until she could secure long-term care. I was in a position where I could work from Lee's until she'd done so. I was happy to help. As a friend of Lee's." He was starting to feel like he was lying.

"How long have you been looking after Lee?"

"Not quite three months?"

"Is that six weeks? Seven?"

"I don't know. I'd need a calendar. Jesus." And the officer flipped to the back of his notepad and stuck a calendar in Cohen's face. "Going on eight weeks, I guess."

"And has his condition been the same or has it worsened or improved in that time?"

"Worsened."

"And were you advised by a medical professional to seek a proper care regime for the man? Meaning a facility with trained professionals?"

"Well, yes, more or less—"

"I ask that because the phone call I just took confirmed that Lee appears to be unaware of the consequences of what he's done. This indicates severe mental impairment. It may be construed as negligence on your and Allie's behalf to have not sought the proper medical assistance. As a result, a man has been stabbed."

"No one can predict something like—Honestly, no one would have guessed Lee was capable of violence."

"And yet Keith Stone has told police that Lee recently punched Allie Crosbie in the face, just weeks after nearly breaking her hand in a doorframe, on purpose. And you yourself told me he's thrown flower pots at Keith in the past, correct? That he's been carrying a knife on his person?" Cohen had no retort. His jaw lowered, shocked by the truth of the statement, but no words came out. The officer nodded and said, "He hits a woman and keeps a knife on his bedside table, and you tell me he never struck you as violent?"

"You've got to understand. I still think of Lee as the man he was before this disease—"

"I need to ask if you've been having sexual relations with Keith Stone's partner, Allie Crosbie, since moving into Lee's, as his makeshift caregiver."

"Does that really matter?"

"Yes. It may."

"How so?"

"Motive. I'm told that Keith Stone, the victim—"

"*Motive?*"

"I'm told that Keith Stone, the victim, says it felt like you were part of it. That you were distracting Keith so that Lee could sneak up on him, from behind, and stab him. Or, at best, that you had to have seen Mr. Brown coming, given the length of the kitchen, but that you didn't warn him at all—"

"Did Keith leave out the part that I just saved his life? Lee knew what he was doing with that knife. I stopped Lee from hauling the knife up through the man's organs and he's telling you I, what, put a hit out on him?"

"Second thoughts, perhaps? You changed your mind about a criminal plan?"

"Cold feet, yeah, that's it! Are you kidding?"

"Sir, I should advise you I'm officially taking your statement, and sarcasm will not come across to those who read it. Sarcasm will not help anyone and certainly not you. I've written here now that you've said, *Cold feet, yeah, that's it.* Do you understand?"

"Do I need a lawyer?"

"At this point, I'd like you to come down to the station with me. You're entitled to a lawyer's presence, yes, and I'm to make that perfectly clear. Not that anyone is accusing anyone other than Lee Brown of anything here. Mr. Stone is understandably in shock, but has, yes, implied you were negligent, at best, in this incident. And that you may have a reason or two to have wanted him hurt. It's my job to explore that notion while the incident is still fresh in all of our minds. Understood?"

"So how does this work? I'm more than willing to be truthful and detailed, but I want a lawyer."

THE INTERROGATION ROOM was a small, cold rectangle. Cement walls. No windows. One long strip of fluorescent lightning buzzed above them. There was a steel table welded to the floor with a single handcuff chained to the tabletop. They didn't use it on Cohen.

Cohen didn't know his lawyer. He chose one from a list an officer offered him, and not too long after the phone call, a tired-looking man with a tan briefcase had shown up and introduced himself. His limp handshake and his baggy black eyes said, *I don't give a shit.* They said, *I'm too tired for this.*

Cohen had too many questions of his own to care about answering theirs, paired with visions of Keith in critical condition, Lee in a prison cell, Allie, five or six years ago, pregnant. He had no idea what Allie knew about any of this. How much of it was true, how serious it all was. And he had no idea Zack's father had officially placed a complaint with the police, just two nights back, stating that Cohen had threatened him, in public, and not for the first time. The words the police used: slander, assault, and uttering threats. The quote, "Maybe I should stick a knife in your hand to teach you a lesson."

Cohen shouted, "I never said that! I never said *to teach you a lesson*, and the quote is out of context. He's a negligent father, and because of that negligence, his son cut his hand on a knife! So I was only referring back to the child's hand injury, by a knife!"

"So the *to teach you a lesson* was implied in the threat?"

"I didn't *threaten* the man. I was making a point. I was referring to his parental negligence by referring to Zack's bandaged hand."

And Cohen's lawyer intervened. "We're not here about—"

But Cohen, overtaken with emotion, silenced his lawyer. "You're taking out-of-context paraphrases, from negligent fathers and from jealous fiancés, to concoct what theory exactly?"

Looking over a file, smugly, like a man in control, "You do have a history of violence and questionable behaviour. Keith Stone has told us about your role in Allie's father's death. It means, you can rationalize devious action the way criminals can."

"Whatever Keith told you about Allie's father is only half true. I'd talked him out of...what he did. And then he did it anyway. And it was fucking horrible, for me more than anyone!"

"Your name also surfaced from an incident in Halifax. In which you jabbed a key into a kid's face."

"That's. Different. It didn't even go to court. It was self-defense. They had my goddamn arm stuck—" Cohen paused, looked at the man. "Keith and Allie are the only two people on earth who'd know that. Are you even allowed to take sides like this? To take their comments and use them against me?"

Cohen's appointed lawyer was staring at Cohen like he didn't know what he'd walked in on, and he started rummaging through papers, frantically.

"It was uncontrolled retaliation and speaks to an inability to contain your anger."

Cohen turned to his lawyer, "Can he cite something not on a criminal record?"

The lawyer looked like his allegiance to Cohen was shifting. He went to say something but the cop cut him off. "This I do have on file. Last week you threatened to stab a man in the hand, in front of *many* witnesses. You were fired on the spot for an act of aggression. It doesn't bode well, Mr. Davies. You said what you

EVERY
LITTLE
THING

said in front of a child, no less, which by anyone's standards shows an inability to control your own anger. When we visited your employer yesterday, he reluctantly informed us that you did, unquestionably, have a troublesome vendetta against this child's father and that you uttered threats involving a knife. Tonight you allowed a mentally impaired man to stab your former lover's fiancé."

The lawyer intervened, finally, "*That's* unfounded speculation—" But Cohen shouted over him, "*Allowed?* I *allowed* Lee to stab Keith?"

"The location of Lee's bedroom, and the length of the kitchen, suggests that if you didn't *know* what Lee Brown's intentions were, you at least had to have seen him coming. This assumption can be verified by your and Keith's statements of where you were standing when the stabbing occurred. We have statements, photos, and measurements of the kitchen, and you *must* have seen Lee coming with the knife. An old man like that."

"I didn't see him coming because I had my head down, quite in shock, on account of some very big news Keith had just told me. He—He's implied I have a—" Cohen's lawyer put a hand on Cohen's hand and said, "This is a bunch of speculation and nothing more. There's nothing solid here. And unless you have a charge to lay against my client, we're going to leave now."

The officer looked at Cohen. "No one is saying you didn't stop him. Once the knife was in. But we have police officers, myself included, who heard Lee openly state he did this *for* you and Allie. We have a witness who has seen you and Allie out in public, alone. We have Allie Crosbie's confession of recent sexual relations with you, and, I'm told, Lee is in his holding cell right now, incoherently yelling about how we've all sabotaged his last chance to make a difference. A statement that means his actions were premeditated. A plan was formed. You understand now? There's clearly a lot of pent up anger in that man, which, of course, you *could've* used to your advantage. You seem remarkably indifferent to the fact a man has been stabbed. Chillingly so."

"And you seem remarkably intent on making the stabbing about something more than one man's dementia. You expect me to show concern for a man who's telling you I had him stabbed?" Cohen's lawyer kept trying to tell him something. "And I might be a little more concerned about Keith's well-being if I hadn't of witnessed him being well enough to stick around and punch me in the face four or five times before calling his own ambulance." Both the officer and the lawyer stared at Cohen's fat lip—the crusty scabbing—and the black mounds rising along his cheekbones.

The constable turned his attention to the lawyer now. "Your client has a bit of an attitude. I must say."

And his lawyer said, "I think we're all done here."

Cohen and his lawyer walked to their cars together. Cohen apologized for cutting him off so many times in the interrogation and asked him, "I haven't done anything wrong, right? They don't have any charges or grounds for any further investigation or anything?"

He wasn't overly convincing as he said softly, "We've got nothing substantial to worry about here. Rest easy." He took his keys out of his coat pocket. "This is me." He pointed to his black sedan. It beeped, flashing lights as he pressed a door opener on his keychain. "We'll be in touch."

A yawn.

COHEN HADN'T BEEN home for weeks; when he plucked his keychain from his coat, he had to take a second look at his house key to be sure it was the right one. His mail slot was in his door, and enough mail had piled up behind the door to obstruct its swing as he pushed it open. His house was so quiet he pressed play on a stereo before picking up the mail. Sorting it. Nothing but junk mail and bills. He leaned against a hallway table. Looked around his house like he was searching for something. Something that should be filling the house with more life, sound.

He went upstairs. Turned his shower on, like maybe a shower could help. He ran the water, but took a second before taking his clothes off, leaning back against the bathroom counter—arms folded, head down—until the shower had been running so long, he could feel spongy moisture in the air. Breathe it in like smoke. He undressed, almost tripped in tugging his underwear free from an ankle it had caught on.

With the shower curtain drawn, and the temperature that high, he was standing in a hot cloud of steam. The free massage of hovering condensation. He put his head against the wall. Under the showerhead. Little bits of conversation coming to him. What Lee had done, what Keith had said, what the police had said. He'd

EVERY
LITTLE
THING

227

left the police station opening and closing his cellphone. No calls from Allie. He couldn't call her. It'd play right into the cop's fantasy.

His guess was Allie couldn't possibly call him from Keith's hospital room. *Who are you calling?* And she had to be torn: the stabbing would force her to bar Lee from her life. It was that black and white now, how she'd have to forget about a twenty-year kinship with the man.

She was pregnant when she left you to live with Lee.

He turned the water up higher. The sting was soothing after the first few branding jabs of water. He pictured Allie in the hospital room with Keith, playing the concerned fiancé. A hamster in a shaking cage. Her actions limited to what she *ought* to be saying and what she *ought* to be doing. But Cohen deserved an explanation, and he'd get it. He couldn't call her, and yet the whole drive home he was opening and closing his cellphone, dialling the first few numbers and hanging up. He got out of the shower and checked his phone again, and there was nothing. Again.

He brought the towel to his face. Pressed hard, scouring the water from his cheeks and eyes. A sigh. He thought about the day Allie had come by and found his computer open to the adoption website. She looked nothing like a woman who'd given his child away. She looked exactly like a woman who wanted him to have a child. She'd said it, and her face had been glowing. *I'm so excited for you.*

Keith had said, shouted, *Might not have even been yours* in a crass way that marred Allie more as a slut than a mother of a child. *Her and I started in long before she left you.* Keith always spoke about Allie as if Cohen and Keith knew her to be a different woman.

And through their eyes, she was: how Keith saw her and how Cohen saw her was a reflection of themselves. It was a reflection of what they wanted from life and what they needed from her to get it. He ran his towel through his hair, wondering what she might have needed from him, from Keith, and the kinds of things she might not have gotten from either of them.

She wanted kids. But she'd given that child away.

Cohen checked his phone again. Nothing. Finished drying himself off. Caught himself in the mirror. Stared. He put two hands on his vanity and stared at himself. Brushed his teeth. He saw the scar above his heart and thought of Zack. Clarence's comments, *He's got ARVC, Cohen. He's been diagnosed...He's got what you got. And he's got it bad.*

He was connecting dots now, from the flashes of conversation. How Zack had his genetic heart flaw. How Zack was roughly the same age his and Allie's child would be. *Would be*, if Allie's child was his. It was unlikely Keith had been telling the truth, but if he had been, it was unlikely Allie's child had been Cohen's. Birth control couldn't have failed them because they didn't use it. She found the pill *too unnatural* and Cohen hated five different things about wearing a condom. Allie simply insisted his two-second warning be twenty seconds.

All that stung now was *Her and I started in long before she left you.* The fact of her infidelity, back then, shouldn't have mattered. Not six years later. But it deflated something about how much he revered Allie. Shook the pedestal she was on.

He walked down over his stairs, to fetch a bottle of wine, and thought: Zack is around six and has ARVC. Less than a hundred thousand people lived in his city, and it's a genetic disorder.

He grabbed a bottle of wine from his rack. A bold, peppery shiraz that could burn a hole in his mouth, and he stuck the corkscrew in. He needed to hear that it had been a girl she'd given away. Or a boy with red hair, or Down Syndrome, or some other trait Zack never had, so Cohen could be certain Allie's child was in no way Zack.

He poured the glass of wine, turned his propane fire place on, and checked his phone again. Watched the fire flicker in time to music in the background. He closed his eyes, and the backs of his eyelids were immediately movie screens projecting memories: he and Allie in the car that night, her hair in his face, blocking out everything but her. Zack's father swinging that door like a bat into Zack's little face: all the blood there that night. And the tears.

He blinked. Saw the look in Lee's eyes as he ran across the kitchen with that knife. He looked like one of those bulls, in Spain, stuck full of spears: desperate, angry, and unable to communicate his pain.

Cohen opened his eyes, grabbed the handful of bills and mail beside him. For his bedframe and mattress on credit he owed $48.57 in interest. He owed $108.88 to Visa. Simple little

EVERY
LITTLE
THING

229

reminders of his trivial life back at home: paying bills, keeping the fridge stocked, cooking for one. Here, in this house, a knock on the door would never be Allie.

He picked up his phone and he called her. *Boy or a girl.* It was all he needed to know for now. So he picked up his phone, and he called her. Fuck what the police thought, because it was understandable that the question was gnawing at him, the way it would anyone. *Boy or girl.* He dialled her number, and she didn't answer, and he dialled it again. He took two steps towards the porch and stopped. Reconsidered. Pulled his jacket on.

The closer he got to her place, the more agitated and angry he felt. It was a long drive, and his thoughts, the memories that came, weren't the best reflection of Allie. The red lights were too long. And he hit every one of them. They'd chain him there, like a dog on a leash, two inches from the bone wanted. When he pulled into her driveway, it was after midnight and he'd seen the kaleidoscoping of TV lights on her living-room walls. She was home, awake, and not answering his calls.

He knocked. Keith could have been home or still in the hospital, and he didn't care. He knocked and no one answered. The doorbell had two strips of duct tape, X-ing out the option to use it. He knocked again and nobody answered.

But the TV was blaring. Somebody was home. And he turned the handle. It was a simple question, and he'd go. She could have picked up her goddamn phone.

Allie was on her couch, clicking through TV channels. Puffy eyes and crumpled tissues in her hands. She saw him come up over the stairs and took on the shocked posture of a frightened cat. "Cohen, you *can't* be here!" She got up and threw her hands out like she was trying to stop a train. "You just can't!" She put a finger to her lips, *Shh!* "Keith is upstairs, livid, on the phone with his lawyer! You really can't be here. You don't...*get* that?"

"He's okay then? His back, the wound?"

"*He's* all right. A clean cut. But *we're* not. And lower your voice!"

He didn't know who she meant by that *we*. Whispering now, to calm her at least that much, "What did Keith tell you about tonight? Did he mention what he said to me?"

She wasn't listening. She ran to the base of a second set of stairs to make sure Keith was still puttering around upstairs. "Get in your car and go!" She pushed him, one hand in his chest.

"Did he tell you—"

"There's no point in us talking right now!"

"Keith told me about the kid, Allie, the baby you gave away." A look like fingernails across a chalkboard. She went chalkwhite. "He *what?*" She stumbled towards the couch without looking where she was going. The backs of her knees hit the edge and she fell into the cushions. "He what?"

He stood over her, looking down. "Was it a boy or a girl, Allie. I need to know—"

She brought her shushing gesture to her lips again, "What did he say to you, exactly?"

"That you were pregnant when you moved into Lee's. That it might've been mine."

She needed a second. Didn't have it. "This isn't a conversation to have in a rush. I'll call you. I will. But...Go! *Now.*" She pointed to the door.

"I'm not in a rush. And Keith's welcome to join us since he started the conversation."

She went to the bottom of the staircase again, more panicked this time, flapping her hands like, *Go, go, now.*

"Was it a boy or a girl, Allie? Then I'll go. Not before. Simple question."

"I don't know anything! I'm not even legally allowed to know the name until the kid is eighteen!"

"You must know if it was a boy or a girl—"

"What difference does that make! You need to go!"

He looked at the front door. "The boy, Allie, at the Avian-Dome. The one I told you all about. The one that got me thinking adoption. The one with the shitty dad sending him off to Florida?" He waited for her to nod, but she only looked at him, wild-eyed and jittery, her head twitching around to scan the whole 360 of the room. "He'd be the age our child is. And he has ARVC, Allie." He touched his heart. "I just need my head clear of this wild notion." He walked to the top of the stairs leading down to the porch. Allie was still across the room at the base of the other stairs. He turned to face her. "Was it a boy or a girl, Allie, and then I'll go."

She came across the room to avoid yelling. "It'd be a slim chance, Cohen."

"Not really. Are you saying it was a boy?"

She looked at her hands, vibrating in panic. "No, Cohen, it was a girl. And she was gorgeous. What I'm *saying* is you need to leave. What I'm saying is there's too much to this story to tell you right now." And she pointed to the door.

Cohen's bones rang with disappointment when she'd said, *It was a girl.* And he pictured Zack, laying in a hospital bed, alone.

Keith's voice was loud but distant. "This is *perfect*," he said. "This is perfect." He walked to the living-room window, peered out like he was waiting for someone. He pulled his phone from his pocket and looked at it.

"Put the phone down, Keith. I had one question, about the kid, and now I'm going."

"Oh, I'm not calling anyone. I already did. I'm just checking how long ago it was, when I called our new friend, Constable MacDonald." He peered at the screen on his phone. "He should be here any minute now to pick you up again." Keith had his cellphone pinched between his thumb and middle finger, twirling it around in circles. A smug look on his face.

"I came over to ask about the kid, as anyone would, considering." He sized Keith up. "So you're alright then? The wound, your back?"

Keith simply stood there, looked Cohen up and down, laughed. "Pretending to give a shit, are you?" He grabbed the curtains and pulled them all the way open. The curtain rings rang like thunder. "Constable MacDonald calls *letting yourself in* trespassing, by the way."

Allie retreated too, to the centre of the room. "Just let him go, Keith. He came over to yell about the kid. You told him about the adoption. He had questions. That was all. Honestly."

"What, let him go, so you two can squirrel off again, behind my back?" He turned to her, his face a mouthful of lemon. "I can't even look at you. *Still.*" And he spat at her feet. He spat at her and she fell into the couch, crying so hard it didn't even make a sound. He picked up a pillow and threw it at her, hard, in a way that said she disgusted him. That he'd punch her if he could.

Cohen took the pillow off Allie's chest. "You should head upstairs and give her some space. I'll let myself out."

"Don't you fucking talk either! You hear me?" And he took two lunges at Cohen and swung, and Cohen swayed out of the way.

Cohen walked behind the coffee table, to put a barrier between him and Keith, and said, "You *can't*! Your back, your stitches!"

Keith grabbed a TV remote off the top of the television and threw it at Cohen. Cohen ducked and it put a small dent in the wall behind him. It hit Allie's shins as it fell onto the couch. She shot up, yelped more in fright than pain, but rubbed out the throbbing with her hand. Cohen took his eyes off Keith, and Keith laid the butt of his foot into the coffee table and drove the table into Cohen's shins, hard. Cohen jerked forward in pain, and Keith swung a fist into the bruise he'd left on Cohen's cheek earlier that night. A thick needle into his face. The after-sting was worse than the blow, and his whole face buzzed.

Allie was curled into a ball on the couch. "Keith *don't*! Just let him go. What are you *doing*?" She had a pillow clutched into her belly with both arms, and Keith put his foot on the pillow. He laid his foot there gently at first, and then he pushed down hard, like a man slamming on the brakes. She let out a horrific, pained exhale.

So Cohen swung at him, hard as he could, instinctively. He caught Keith in the side of the head and busted his earlobe. Perfect little drops of blood trickling onto his shoulder. Allie was shouting out *No!* endlessly and aimlessly, and Cohen and Keith were grappling like wrestlers, arms locked over each other's shoulders. They fell and broke apart like a shattered vase. But Keith jumped back up in time to kick Cohen in the ribs. He went for a second kick, but Cohen grabbed his leg and swept his other foot out from under him; a gut-deep howl of pain as Keith landed on his stitched-up knife wound. Keith laid there, on his side, his elbows stuck to his ribs; body struck like a gong.

A yellow glow of headlights swirled through the living room like one turn of a lighthouse. Slamming car doors. Two. An officer and the officer passenger side. Cohen got up, went to the window, and felt panicked when he saw they'd left their red and blue lights on. One of them jotting down Cohen's license plate, photographing the car with a landmark in the background. Keith grabbed Cohen from behind, hooking an arm around his throat, squeezing hard enough for Cohen's face to tingle and burn. So he put a foot against the wall and thrust hard, hoping to spring Keith into something and break the grip. But they stumbled back and back, gaining momentum as their feet entangled, and struggled to right themselves, and then there was nothing underfoot as Cohen saw the staircase railing. They tumbled together, but Cohen managed to grab the railing and Keith didn't. He'd gone down over the steps loud and hard and awkwardly. Cracked his head off a telephone stand at the base of the stairs. Shrieked about it. But it was his wrist he was clutching and howling about as the police walked in. Constable MacDonald. A satisfied look on his face like, *I was right about you, boy.*

Keith was still on the ground, like a picked-on school kid, clutching his wrist, then the back of his head, in alternating motions. But he was doing it like a bad actor, so everyone would know he was hurting head to toe. "He burst right into our house! Allie told him to leave! Isn't that trespassing? The...next thing I know he's punching me. He's thrown me over the stairs, and you've walked in to see it for yourselves! He's physically assaulted me in my own home, and he's verbally harassing his ex," he pointed up to Allie. "He called her, four times, back to back, before coming over and barrelling in! It's in her call history, his number." He looked down at his wrist. It was a balloon that needed air. "I think he's broken my wrist!" Keith stood up, turning his back to them all, to haul his shirt up. "I think he's torn my stitches open?" There was a single drop of blood trickling out from the tip of the wound. "I've been reasonable, 'til now. But I think I'd like to press charges. Assault, trespassing, whatever. And I'd like to revisit his role in my stabbing. Mostly, I'd like him out of my house, immediately." Keith pointed to Cohen like he owned the police and they'd do whatever he said.

Constable MacDonald walked up the stairs, glaring at Cohen, but he walked right passed him to Allie. "Are you all right, ma'am, physically anyway?" And she nodded. "Can you confirm what your fiancé has said?"

Keith shouted as he climbed the stairs, "As a witness, you mean?"

Allie looked at Cohen and said nothing to the officer. She looked over to Keith and Keith was glaring at her.

"Yes or no, Ms. Crosbie. That's all I need to hear, nothing else. Did Cohen Davies enter your home without your consent and knowledge of his entry?"

She looked at Cohen again, her head held sideways, curious.

"Don't look at him, ma'am. Look at me. Did he?"

She nodded and a new pattern of whimpering came out of her. She nodded yes and looked at Cohen immediately, crying as apology.

"I need you to say it, ma'am. A nod won't do. Yes or no?"

Keith was nodding his head up and down. Ravenous. Thrilled the police were taking sides.

"Ye—yes."

"And did you, at any point in your conversation, ask Cohen Davies to leave your premises?"

"Yes, but only—Only to prevent all of this!"

"Again, simply a yes or no, at this point."

Keith was glaring at her. She said, "Yes."

"And is this the man who caused bodily harm to your fiancé, Keith Stone?"

The officer stuck his fat hand in Cohen's direction. Close enough that Cohen could see the dirt under than man's nails and the scratch on his wedding band. Allie nodded.

"Ma'am, we need you to say it, not nod it."

"Yes. But—This didn't happen like. You—" Keith knifed her answer with the shake of his head. *Choose sides.* He had the posture of an angry father let down by his daughter. And then he stepped in front of the officers, "He started punching me, before he pushed me over the stairs. He did this to my ear!" Keith tilted his head and pointed to his bloody ear. "Look!" He pointed to the blood dried into his shirt.

Cohen didn't defend himself. He looked at Allie, gutted, and he said, "You're going to marry this man." It wasn't a question. He was proving a point as two hands clenched around the tops of his arms, to guide him down over the stairs. A hot whisper in his ear. "We've got charges this time, hotshot."

The officers held him stiff and straight; he couldn't turn to look at Allie. But he could hear her crying, bawling, as the police handled him like a criminal in front of her. Constable MacDonald didn't let go of Cohen's arm when Cohen bent to put his shoes on. They stepped out into the cold night. His lungs filling with it. The moon full, low, in a way he'd never seen before.

They tugged Cohen down over the cement staircase towards the car, and he almost lost his footing, tripped. There were no sirens going off, but the car's lights were on, and they were harsh on the eyes. Especially the white glare between the red and blue. There were nosey neighbours.

He looked over his shoulder, saw Allie and Keith getting in their car to head to the hospital. Keith clutching that limp wrist like it might win him an Oscar. Allie wouldn't look at Cohen—it'd be a sign of support or remorse, and Keith would hold it against her—but there was a kink in her neck, or an awkward posture, as she fought not to look.

He saw it then, for the first time, that she had a life built before he stumbled back into her world that second time. Joint mortgages, co-owned cars, a career tangled up in it all. He'd forgotten love was all those things too.

He watched her in the rear-view mirror of the police car, the lights off her face: white, blue, red, white, blue, red. He thought of a time, a decade ago, when he sat in the passenger seat of their car, and she scrapped ice from the window. Little green mitts on. She hauled the windshield wipers up, to do a thorough job. He watched thick snowflakes fall on her face, and the way they glistened and lingered, before melting into her, was a crushing sort of beauty. A weight that only she could pin him under.

FOCUS

LEE'S TRIAL HAD come much sooner than Cohen's. He'd been deemed mentally unfit—by two psychiatrists—to be tried and serve time in prison for attempted murder. He was court-ordered to live in a special wing at River Crest Hospital. It was the same place he'd been staying since the night he stabbed Keith.

River Crest was bleaker than a prison. Lee's wing was silent or it was filled with creepy, desperate moans. It stank of piss or something like it. Javex; sterile and depressing. It violated Cohen's nose the three times he'd gone to visit Lee.

They had him doped up beyond reason. Cohen could lift Lee's arm and drop it, like Lee was a doll. He could stick him with a pin and not expect Lee to react. By the second visit, Lee never recognized him anymore. One nurse had said, *He's adjusting to medication*, and on the third visit, the same nurse told him, *He's having more bad days now than good ones.* And she asked him who Allie was.

"A daughter maybe?"

At Lee's trial, Cohen had sat in the back of the courtroom. He'd watch Lee's head jerking around, with those owlish movements, like he was trying to figure out where he was. Or why Allie wasn't there. He'd called her name out one day, out of nowhere, cutting off the judge's answer to a lawyer's question. Everybody jumped. Spooked.

The judge made her ruling, and a caretaker, or a legal escort of some kind, called his name to come with him. Lee never responded. The escort had said *Lee?* and the word had no meaning for him anymore. His own name. Something even a dog responds to.

COHEN'S TRIAL CAME seven weeks after Lee's. Allie in the hot seat. A judge staring down on her. Shame kept her eyes glued to her bony little hands, fidgeting on her lap; the crown of her head pointing at the courthouse pews.

No, he didn't knock. Yes, I asked him to leave. Yes, it was this man who fought with my fiancé.

She shot looks at Cohen, *I'm so fucking sorry*, but he couldn't take her torment on top of his own. It was too much weight. And the sound of his mother, sniffling behind him, watching Allie squirm. The sight of his father on the edge of his seat; a hand on his mother's shoulder like a strong wind was coming.

Cohen was sunken in his chair, arms crossed, looking angry, and his lawyer nudged him. *Pay attention.* He'd lectured Cohen on the importance of looking repentant and wrong, not aloof. *This judge, she's judging your character. Impressions matter.*

Keith took the stand, and his mother growled after all his statements. Cohen's lawyer tried shutting it down, with objections and frustrated posturing, but Keith's lawyer found a way to let Keith share things unrelated to Cohen's trial. So everyone heard that he'd threatened Zack's father...*with a knife.* That he'd jabbed a kid in the face with a key. "I guess *I* got off easy," he'd said, like a victim.

Cohen's father had to take his mother out of the courtroom. He'd walked back in, alone. Glaring at Keith in the stand.

She was blonde, the judge, and had a look on her face like it was going to be a long day of trials no different than this one. Black bags under her eyes, and she'd been yawning. She'd been fair during the trial, professional, but detached, unmoved, unengaged. She struck the gavel down that day, and the base she'd struck with the gavel recoiled; it spun like a spintop. He watched it twirl as she'd said, *Six months in prison.* It felt like he was in a car, flying down a hill, and the brakes were gone, and there was nothing down there but traffic and trees and kids on crosswalks, and there was nowhere to swerve his car, and he was going to hit it all, hard, and he couldn't stop.

They'd expected him to just get up and carry on, walk out of there like everything hadn't just changed. He looked over to his father, and his father was glaring at Allie so she'd hurt. He had his glasses off, in one hand, biting one of the arms between his teeth. Staring at her.

Cohen's lawyer was shocked, promising things, but Cohen was still in that car, barrelling towards something. Until a man in a uniform insisted Cohen get up. Clear the area. So they could all move on. Start another trial.

The man let Cohen hug his father goodbye and walked Cohen to a holding cell in the courthouse basement. Throughout the day, more people were added to the cell. They weren't hard men, not all of them. They were nervous, kind. Pacing, sighing. One man had sat on a bench, with a hand clenched around a jail bar, like he was riding a subway. His foot bouncing up and down; laid on a nerve. He'd sat like that, staring, barely blinking, for hours.

At the end of the day, a van took Cohen and a fat black man named Curt to jail.

IT WAS A highly ordered process. Cohen and Curt were shipped and extensively catalogued. The man from the courtroom, in the brown uniform, drove through a series of computerized gates at the prison. He'd wink and nod and make small talk with people he knew, but he still had to go through formalities with them. He had a way of whistling between tasks and drumming his forefingers against the steering wheel in time to his whistling. A black cap over a full head of hair. A decent guy.

He popped the back of his van open, for Cohen and Curt to climb out, and handed them off to two new officers in black uniforms. More signatures and they were walked inside. Curt had a chinstrap beard and clipped hair. He was very tall, very fat, but had stumpy, bowed legs, and they couldn't take his weight. His crooked legs bent backwards at the kneecap and made him walk in a way that had his pants swooshing.

Once inside, the officers explained that they each had to be searched. In what was called a dirty cell. They explained everything they were about to do, right before they'd do it—like where they were going to put their hands and fingers and why they'd be doing that, and Cohen was naked in front of two strangers and it was all still impossible, what was happening. They'd finished searching Cohen first, and he had to wait in a hall while they finished checking Curt. And then Curt came out of the dirty cell with the same look on his face he'd been wearing since two o'clock that afternoon. Eyes wide and mouth agape, like he couldn't believe something was about to happen to him. They'd proven they were not smuggling anything in, and

239

then they had to prove, to a man at a computer, that they were who they said they were. ID wasn't enough, and they'd taken his wallet anyway, before the strip search. And they documented it all with tags, the way a curator at a museum would, treating it all like specimens. Right down to the coins Cohen had in his pockets. Cohen finally heard Curt's voice for the first time that day. *It's my daughter*, he said, *can I hang on to this picture?* He held the photo with such grace that Cohen was rooting for him. But they took the photo and sealed it in an envelope. Like a time capsule. His daughter, she'd look a little different, she'd change a little, she'd get a little smarter before he'd get out of this place. Curt had been caught selling pot to high-school kids, and it had been the fourth time.

The man sealed Cohen's belongings in an envelope and there was an option to mail it all home. His watch and his wallet, some coins. But he liked the idea of it being in the same building as him. He associated his wallet, and all those cards in it, with his identity, and he wanted that near him.

More forms: *Next of Kin? Dietary restrictions?* He was filling out the forms, looked up to Curt, and realized they hadn't spoken a word to each other all day. Curt nodded, and Cohen nodded back and finished up his form.

It all ended with a mandatory health check from a male nurse with bad breath. *Open your mouth and say aww*, and Cohen had to breathe it in. They'd waited forty-five minutes for that nurse. And it was another forty-five minutes Curt and Cohen hadn't said a word to each other. That look still on Curt's face. Cohen wondered, if he saw Curt in a week, in the cafeteria or the shower, if the look would be gone by then.

His jailroom was more of a box than a cage, but it was all his: no bunk bed or cellmate. And that was good. Things started off better than he'd envisioned. He spent his first day pacing back and forth in his cell. It only took six steps to get across the room. And then he'd turn and do it again. Pacing out the room had a way of making it feel bigger, more familiar. The front of his cell was all metal bars, floor to ceiling, like in the movies, but the other three walls were cold, porous cement. They trapped noise. Sounds ricocheted around in there: the guard's footsteps like racket balls bouncing off his walls.

At first, the worst wasn't where he was, but how he got there.

Allie's betrayal, or Keith's devious bullshit had festered in him. A maggot, agitated, disgusting, and clawing its way to the surface, so he could think about it again: every little thing that had landed him in jail. The way he met Allie, because his kid brother drowned. The way his kid brother drowned because his family happened to own a cabin on a pond. Or because his mother was the type who needed a weekend getaway to wrap her head around things.

Allie: if she'd never taken that job with Keith; if she never had the *qualifications* for that job; if she'd never befriended the likeable old war vet who'd sold her photos at a vendor's table in her town; or even if she'd answered her phone the night he called to ask her *boy or girl.* He wouldn't be in jail.

Zack: if Jamie had been a better father; if Zack hadn't reminded him of Ryan; if Jamie had put Zack in a different day-care; if another couple, elsewhere, had of adopted Zack first. The kid wouldn't have cost him so much.

Lee: if Lee had moved anywhere but Grayton in the years after the war; if he'd died in the war; if he'd come back a mechanic or doctor or grocery store bagger then Allie would have never met him.

Every day, every hour, really, it was a new name and a new suite of scenarios that could've gone differently, so he could've been a hundred places other than prison. Still at the Avian-Dome, taking kids on hikes. Maybe in love with Jenny Lane this time. Or teaching biology somewhere in Europe, had he gone along with those friends from university—Tommy and Cane—who'd done just that.

It was a game his mind played with or without him, and it kept him up at night. That and the other inmates snoring. Or the insects buzzing around the light down the hall. Or the ache of hunger in his belly for a thousand things they didn't feed him in there. So he'd go to his window and stare. Let the cold from the floor rise up through his feet and lull him.

GETTING NAKED AND getting showered with all those other men had only been weird the first couple of times. And there were things a biologist couldn't help but observe and mentally catalogue: the linked traits. How bald men tend to be hairy. Short men hung. Fat men would scrub longer, as if they felt dirtier.

There was an effeminate man who shaved his whole body

every day, like he was going on a date. No one gave him a hard time for it because his brother was Truck Drake, and Truck Drake wanted a reason to punch a hole in someone's face. Anyone's. Truck was the guy who'd lay one hand flat against a wall, wrap the other around his cock, and be loud about it. Not caring who was looking or where anything went. The guards kept their backs turned, stood at the door. It meant they'd never see anything happening until it was too late.

Truck had been two stalls down one morning, and he'd thrown three quick punches at the guy next to him, for no reason. It was a fat, bald, moustached guy, and it was terrifying to stand so close to it—so close Cohen should've been the one to break it up. The violence itself wasn't the terrifying part: Truck's pleasure in it was. And the way the poor man squealed as Truck attacked him. Cowering. He lay on the ground, curled in a ball, yelling, *Guard, guard, guard!* And everyone laughed, and it was the first blast of violence Cohen had seen. It was over before it started, but frightening for its senselessness and spontaneity. The way violence happened, like rain, wherever it wanted, meant Cohen wouldn't always see it coming. The poor man had been on Cohen's toes, yelling *guard!* and Cohen knew, looking down on the guy, that it would've arbitrarily been him had Cohen chosen the wrong stall that day.

The dull thudding of those punches had stayed with Cohen a week. He'd showered as close to the entrance as he could. To not feel trapped in there.

HIS FATHER HAD come to visit him, the first visitation hour he could. There was a rule that Cohen had to be there a week before his first visitation hour. He was still being catalogued and kept clear of certain areas: the visitation rooms, the cafeteria, the yard, the group sessions.

"Your mother," he'd said, "has written a letter to abolish this *one week rule*, and I've been stuck with the task of reading every new draft." He smiled, rolled his eyes. He grabbed Cohen's hand quickly and let go just as quickly, looking around as if someone might judge Cohen for the show of affection. "How ya' holding up?" There was a loud bang, like a book being slammed on a table, and his father jumped. Since sitting down, his father's eyes hadn't stopped scanning the room like everyone was out to get him.

"Your mother couldn't come. She just couldn't do it. She's afraid she'll break down and that'll make you seem...weak."

"It's a low security prison," he swept his arm around the room to men holding wives' hands, drawing kittens with their daughters, "I'm not in Alcatraz."

"We're talking about your mother, Cohen."

"Fine, but tell her to lay off the emails. I get thirty minutes a day on the web, if that. I'd need three hours to get through her circular, thousand-word essays on *hanging in there*." He laughed so that his father would. He looked painfully ill at ease. "And you guys should *not* have sold the boat!"

"*Cohen*," he waved his hand to dismiss Cohen's worry. "It's been sitting in the garage forever now. I haven't had a membership at the marina in two years. We never take it out anymore. Boating was a...brief infatuation."

"I've got enough in RRSPs and a tax-free savings account to get through six months of bills and mortgage payments."

His father's face said, *And then what?* "Just...remember this, when we're old and need a favour of our own." He sat back in his chair, looking happy to have helped.

Another bang and his father jumped again. Higher this time. "You know, it's still surreal. You being here. It's like I'm strapped in a car going two hundred." He looked to a man with bruises on his face, and his eyes stuck there. Cohen followed his father's gaze and saw that he'd been staring at the man who'd been beaten in the shower that week. "You know that guy or something?"

"No. Just. His daughter. He's very patient with her."

"Drunk driver," Cohen filled him in. "I saw the man get his face punched in a few days ago." The man's daughter pointed at the bruises, *How come, Daddy?*

Cohen lowered his voice, "The man seemed like he needed some company that day at lunch. I caught his story. He'd ploughed into two university kids at a *crosswalk* and only got a year in here. His second DUI. The fact he can even share the story, you know? If I was him, I'd just—I'd make up another story."

His father nodded. "So. How are *you* doing? How are you getting along, all things considered? Are you getting roughed up, like that guy, or did he have it coming, or what?"

"It's not good. But it's really not that bad either, for me, anyway. Honestly. I spent the first three days curled up in a ball in my bed, livid, infuriated." He looked up at his father, confessed, "I could have let Lee kill him, you know? One morning, I...actually thought about that."

"Jesus, Cohen!"

"I know. But I was furious—"

"Not so you could be with Allie? Not *that* way."

"No. Just, pure anger. This is low, even for him. Me in jail. It's absurd." He waited a second, worried it would sound pathetic. "She hasn't even come by. Sent a letter."

"What d'you expect from her? She's engaged. And then all of this?" He swooped a hand across the room. "She can hardly pop by and say hello after that shit she pulled? I mean, her apology, that's not going to change a goddamn thing now, is it?" He shook his head, angry. "Or at least, I hope it wouldn't. I can't believe you're thinking on her, to be honest."

Cohen put his hands up, smiled, *Okay, settle down.*

"So listen, anything I can do for you?"

"What, on *the outside?*" He laughed.

"I dunno. In general? C'mon?"

"Take back half the money Mom transferred me from selling your boat."

"I'm serious."

Cohen had been leaning back in his chair; had it back on two legs. He brought it forward, back onto the ground. Laid two elbows on the table. "The kid. The one I got fired because of." He watched his father's eyes pinch tight. "Can you get me an update. About his heart?"

An alarm sounded off: three long blares like transport truck horns. Visitation hour was over.

"Cohen, I'm sorry but. Between Allie and the boy from work. You've got to cut your losses, don't you think?" His father picked his hat up off the table. Put it on. "You've tried enough, with those two, and we can agree it didn't end well."

"There's a journal, in your breast pocket, right?"

His father tapped it. "Yeah." He smirked.

"Take it out."

His father leaned forward, laid his elbows on the table. "All due respect. To the boy and his troubles. But we've got our own, don't you think? You've poked your nose in far enough."

"Zack Janes." He nodded to his father's breast pocket. "*Janes. Zack Janes.* Dr. Jennings would know the boy, from the ARVC clinics. Just want an update. That's it. He'd been waiting on a goddamn heart, Dad. A *transplant.* I think about him sometimes. If you tell me's alright, I'll stop asking about him."

His father rolled his eyes. Fetched his pen. Bit the cap off, leaving it clamped between teeth. "James?"

"*Janes.* N. *Janes.*"

A guard approached them both. "Sir. It's time to leave."

His father stood, gave the guard a look, *Yes, I'm leaving,* and Cohen said, "Check on Zack. Remember."

BUT HIS FATHER never did check in on Zack. *Looking into it,* his father would say. Or two weeks later, *I can't just…roam around the hospital wings, calling out his name.* And finally, *I can't ask our doctor about some kid I don't know. There's probably rules against it.*

Cohen was at his cell window, his breath fogging it up. It was too dark to see anything, between eleven at night and one in the morning. He tried picturing Zack in Florida. The kid had always been ecstatic when he spoke of his grandmother. Zack would show Cohen the things she'd mail him—books about owls and all the right kinds of toys—and Zack would act all, *What's mine is yours* in sharing the goods with Cohen. *You can borrow this book anytime, I'll share!*

Cohen had been sitting at the desk in the daycare room one day. The kids drawing puffins and razorbills. He had his head down, reading a paper about bioremediation for a project he'd been assigned, and Zack's fist banged down on the surface of the desk. He took it away and a blue Tyrannosaurs figurine wobbled to a stop. *I've got two, so you can have that one! Keep it in your pocket. We'll have fights all the time!*

EVERY
LITTLE
THING

245

VISITATION HOUR

COHEN WAS A little late coming into the visitation room to see his father, and when he walked into the visitation room, it had been the first time he saw Truck in there with a visitor. It was his brother or something. Maybe a friend. Hulk Hogan-ish, but with brown hair. They were sitting two tables over from Cohen and his father, being loud and crass in a way that made Cohen's father sheepish.

His father covered his mouth, spoke through his hands. "An arm wrestle, really?" But they watched, entertained. "Five bucks on Blue Shirt," his father joked, yet he didn't laugh from the gut. The way he normally would, at his own jokes. So Cohen dropped the good news he'd been holding back for almost an hour. "Clarence, he sent me a link. Claymore University is looking for first-year biology instructors. Per-course, but it's something to try for." He'd served half his sentence now, and there was reason to think he'd not serve it all. "I've submitted an application, and Clarence knows a guy who knows a guy, or whatever. Hopefully they don't trace the IP address of my email back to a prison." He laughed but his father didn't. "The job would start the spring semester."

"That's good, son, that's good to hear. You'd like that, yeah? Teaching?"

"Teaching ecology courses to people who give a shit? Yes. Teaching first-year to kids who have to take it? No. But it'll pay the bills and beats a lot of jobs."

"Yeah. Yeah, for sure." His father was so obviously distracted and had been the full hour. It was like there was a TV screen behind Cohen, thieving his attention: a ballgame and his favourite team about to win. "And your sentence. Terrific news you'll be out—"

"Dad, what's up? You're a little...I don't know."

"Your mother. She's. She, you know. She thinks it's enough that you're in here. I don't know. Never mind." An awkward posture, an awkward shrugging of his shoulders. Truth had a way of wanting to bust out of his father. "She doesn't want you getting worked up about anything else until you're out of here, you know? And she's probably right, you know?"

The shrilling visitation-is-over bell rang.

His father got up to leave, and Cohen said it like, *Sit Down!* "What do you mean, Dad? I can see it on your face. Something's up."

"Nothing, just, keep looking for a job. That's priority one." His father stood up. "I hope you get the teaching position. That's your first priority. Focus on that, on getting a job, for now. That's the best use of your time, now. Your thoughts."

"*What* is wrong with you, babbling like that?"

His father put his hat on, "See you...I'll come by the weekend." He scurried off like the timid man he was. Secrets had a way of bouncing around in his body, and Cohen knew the signs, the junky posturing.

COHEN WAS ALLOWED three one-hour visits a week, and to prevent wasting one of those precious hours, he had the right to ask who it was and refuse the visit. But Cohen had yet to use all three in one week. So he'd get buzzed and he'd go. Expecting his father. The first few times he was told he had a visitor, he rounded the corner, and every time it wasn't Allie, he'd hit a wall that wasn't there: his father could read the disappointment on his face. The way Keith must've read the *shock* on Cohen's face the day he made a surprise visit. He'd been expecting his father, but he'd been expecting him at three o'clock. Cohen was reading in his cell, heard footsteps, heard humming, heard *Davies, your visitor is here*. He thought nothing of it, dog-eared a page in his novel, and laid it on his windowsill. Looked at the guard, *Lemme out, then*.

EVERY
LITTLE
THING

247

When Cohen saw Keith sitting at that table, he'd stopped walking so abruptly his sneaker squeaked off the floor. Two inmates behind him had bumped into him and pushed their way past him. Looks of disdain on their face because jail was no place to be bumping into people. Cohen wanted to turn and walk back to his cell, or he wanted to flip the table on Keith. Pin him under it and yell. But he was drawn to the look of anger on Keith's face. "Are you fucking *kidding* me?"

"Don't act shocked to see me, you son of a bitch."

"Shocked?"

"Allie's gone missing, and you know it. You're crazy mother's probably behind it, harbouring her?"

"What do you mean, *gone?*"

"Piss off, Cohen. I just want to know she's okay. I want to know where she's been sleeping, and if she's coming back to work or what?"

"What makes you think I give a shit where she'd be?"

Keith stopped talking and squinted his eyes at Cohen, like Cohen was out of focus. He tilted his head, curious, like maybe Cohen wasn't lying. "It's been...weeks. Maybe three, I don't know. Too long."

Cohen sat back in his chair. "You're not exaggerating?" and his concern for Allie sidetracked his anger.

"Un-clench your fists, tough guy. I think your temper's gotten you in enough shit this year?" Cohen looked down at his hands, and Keith said, "If you really don't know where she is, I'll just go."

"So, what, she hasn't called you, didn't leave a note?"

Keith slapped the table, pointed. People looked over at them, briefly, but got back to their own conversations just as fast. "*Don't* play dumb. She was here. She's a registered visitor for you! I saw her name when I signed in on your file as a visitor!"

"I'm not gonna argue about this, Keith. I'm gonna get up and go if this is all we're going to do!"

"You fucked her up. About the kid. How she lied." Cohen stared, waiting for more words. "The last thing she said to me was she needed to come here and tell you it was a boy she gave away, not a girl. And I haven't seen her since."

"A *boy*? It was a boy?" And his skin was crawling with invisible insects. He got up to leave again, and Keith muttered, "And what do you mean, *it was a boy* that me and Allie had? Your goddamn mother's been—"

"What do you mean, *that me and Allie had?* Why'd you tell me about her child that night, man, if it was yours."

He raised his shoulders in a slow shrug and made a dumb face that Cohen wanted to punch. "Logically, it was mine. If you're smart enough to do the math. But you, you're not even smart enough to lie, you piece of shit. Your mother's been by my house a dozen times. She barges in whenever she wants, tearing into Allie for whatever details she needs. She acts like I'm not there, in my own goddamn house. The two of them. And now Allie's run off."

Cohen put two hands on the table and stared at them. "Your mother's acting like a vigilante cop—"

"Just, back up! The whole story, when did this start?"

"This is *bullshit!* I'm not going to sit here and guess if you're pulling my leg or if your mother's batshit crazy or what?" Keith stayed sitting in his chair, but started pulling his jacket on. "If you don't know what she's up to, you should! Because someone needs to reel her in. She's out there fucking up peoples' lives. Ping Ponging around from my house to Zack's house to the police to Adoption Services—"

"What do you mean, *Adoption Services?*"

Keith sat back in his chair like a man with an upper hand. "She wants them to administer a paternity test. Before Zack's sent back into foster care."

"*Foster care?*"

"Fuck. You're way out of the loop, aren't you? I can see it in your eyes now." Keith sat up in his chair, grinning, about to get up and leave. The table they were sitting in was constructed the way a picnic table is built. It meant Keith's legs were trapped under the table, and Cohen wanted to thrust the table up and pin Keith to the floor. He wanted to drive the edge of the table into Keith's ribs, and he wanted to hear the fucker wheeze, cry, apologize. Keith stood up, looked left to right like he couldn't remember the way he'd come in.

Cohen went back to his cell and sat on the edge of his bed, rocking his legs back and forth; his cheeks puffed out from an everlasting sigh. The four walls of his cell meant there were no outlets for the kinds of questions that could wreck a man. He didn't have ten minutes to himself before the burly counsellor from corrections staff was at his cell door to fetch him, for another seminar, as required by his *Offender Plan*. The man had an impossible thick moustache and, always, a coffee in one hand, a file and pen in the other. And he smelled like waking up in a wet tent.

"My father's coming in an hour and a half."

"Well, this'll only take an hour," and the man had said it like Cohen didn't have a choice anyway. It had been another VHS tape. There was dust in the grooves of the cassette; Cohen could see it as the man slid it into the VCR. It was a two-hour video, about respecting peoples' boundaries, narrated by women with bad perms and men in acid-washed jeans. The counsellor at his desk, in the rehabilitation centre, clipped his nails through the movie. The sound of it was worse than fingernails across a chalkboard or a fork missing food on a plate.

COHEN'S FATHER WAS smiling at him as Cohen sat at the table that afternoon. *Smiling.* So Cohen's words came like cold water. "You fucked up, Dad, as a parent, as anything...I mean...do you have *any* idea what an absolute mental...like..." He clenched his teeth, shook his head. Looked around the room and back at his father's shocked face. "*Keith's* been here. And I can't make sense of what he was talking about!"

His father, deflating like a balloon, "Your mother, she—"

"I don't even want to hear an excuse for her. She's crossed a line this time, even for her. I just want the facts. Where's Allie? What does Mom have to do with it? Why is she talking to Zack's father, and the—"

"Your mother," he stuck his hands up to stop Cohen's words, "just wanted you to worry about getting through your sentence. She wanted you to focus on finding a job, while she tended to—"

"A *job*." He shook his head.

"You asked me to look in on this boy, didn't you?"

"There's a *huge* difference, don't you think? Between finding out if he's dead or alive and busting in on his life and doing whatever the fuck *Keith* just blurted out in bits and pieces!"

His father nodded, caught. "We'll start with the boy, then?"

"Just...start somewhere. We've got fifty minutes. And Allie. Is she really missing?"

"I honestly don't know anything about Allie. To be blunt, I don't care. That's your mother, dealing with her. I've stayed out of what your mother's been up to until she started needing my help. We fought long and hard about how much she's stuck her nose in. I mean, the both of you: look where sticking *your* nose into the kid's business landed you!"

"The boy. You said you'd start with the boy. So start!"

"I know you're mad, Cohen, but—"

"I am. I'm mad. And I'm sorry if I'm being horrible, but I'm exactly that, mad."

"I don't know what you know of the boy's adoptive situation. In a nutshell, the boy's father got stuck with the kid after his partner took off..." He paused and his face held still while he searched for a word. "I can never think of the boy's father's name?"

"Jamie."

"Jamie spent two years thinking of what to do about Zack. He got offered a *dream job*, his words, *dream job*, in Alaska. But there's no major hospital anywhere *near* the resort he'll be cooking in."

Cohen motioned his hand like he was trying to fast-forward his father. "Okay, so what? Jamie stuck Zack back in foster care and left for Alaska?"

"I'm getting there. Let me get there. The boy's name comes up and you get your back up!" They both sat back in their chairs. "ARVC is pretty much endemic to families in Atlantic Canada or something. There's specialists here. Zack's living in a top-notch pediatric cardiac care unit, and he's getting their absolute attention. Jamie couldn't take him away from the care he can get here and couldn't get in Alaska or Florida, and those places don't have free healthcare."

"So, he's still waiting on a heart transplant then?"

"Yes, and..." his father snapped his fingers, "What's his name again?"

"Jamie!" Cohen leaned forward in his chair.

"Jamie had been looking into putting Zack back into foster care long before the job opportunity in Alaska. And with the heart condition, well, that's that. Jamie's gone. The boy's here."

"All right, but I still don't understand the trouble with the boy's heart. He has what we have: a rhythm defect. It's not making any sense."

"His heart's failing, Cohen. His tissues are filling with fluid. He's swelling up. He's lethargic and confused. It's a hard thing to look at, I'll tell you that."

"So you've *seen* him then?"

"I'm getting to that. Yes."

"What you're describing is congestive heart failure. Like old people get. Not ARVC." He shook his head, "Has he *officially* been diagnosed with ARVC, with the DNA test?"

"Dr. Jennings explained it to me in analogies. Whatever's wrong with our heart gene, that causes ARVC, he's got that same thing wrong with his gene too, but he's also got other issues, with his heart gene, and all those issues are interacting negatively. Like gas on a fire."

"I—There's no such thing as a *heart gene*, Dad. It's a little more complicated than that."

"Well then I guess that's why he spoke to me in analogies? We're not all fluent in genetic-speak, are we?" His father put his hands up, *settle down*. "I didn't say I understood it. That's the best I can get my head around it. *Something* is exasperating the ARVC problem. There's virtually nothing on the internet about what's happening with Zack because cases like his have only been treated a dozen times in Canada."

"Who said that, Jennings, or the internet?"

"Jennings."

"So his heart is officially failing?"

"The heart is a muscle, Jennings said, and bits of the boy's heart are turning to fat, and fat can't pump like muscle can. Most days someone from the government comes by and sits with him, but your mother and I. We've been looking in too. They're watching his urine output. I don't know why, but I know it's a bad thing that it's getting lower and lower. Your mother sits with him a lot. Staring at the bag. Waiting for yellow."

"So, you're both looking in on the kid, yet you've been lying to me about not having any updates on the boy—"

"I got your mother involved in helping me gather news on the kid. I guess I should've seen this all coming, once she started poking her nose in. But, just to finish up on how Zack is doing, there's an upside to how bad off he is. It's bumped him up in queue on the transplant list."

Cohen blinked long and hard. His father said, "Do you know what an RVAD is?" And Cohen nodded yes.

"The RVAD is doing the pumping work his right ventricle can't do anymore. He's come around some since they hooked him up to it. The swelling is down, and he's breathing better. It's made the newspapers, Zack's plight. Heart transplants in children aren't common, and kids on VACs are even rarer." And he stopped there. Looked at his watch. Looked at Cohen. Looked at his watch again.

"Now listen. I'm going to leave you with that. That's enough for right now. Then I'm going to tell you the rest, with updates, on my next visit."

"Finish the story, Dad."

His father looked at his watch again. Tapped it this time." I can't blurt this next bit out in ten minutes, I'm sorry. And there's really nothing to say until your mother...gets through a few more tasks."

"Call me then, tonight?"

His father looked at him. "Like I said, there's nothing more to say until your mother clews up a few things.

"*Dad?*"

His father put his hat on. Twirled a scarf around his neck. Left.

THE PRISON LIBRARY had a horrible selection of books. Or it had been curated by someone with bad taste. Or they took whatever they could get in donations. There were nothing but trashy paperbacks with no substance or variation on *noble lawyer turned hero*. There was a whole wall of non-fiction, but he'd never read non-fiction because nothing seemed interesting enough to read three hundred pages about. So he stuck with the crime novels. There wasn't much else to do in there, other than read, but since his father's abrupt departure earlier that week, since his father's dangling *more to come*, Cohen had become too distracted to lose himself in the novels. His attention span would get punctured by isolated sentences from his father's visit. *There's really nothing to say until your mother...gets through a few more tasks.*

He went to the hack squat in the yard. Put on more weights than usual. Up and down, up and down. He closed his eyes, kept going. Felt the throb of a kick in the shin, *Get up*. It was Truck. For months, Cohen had skillfully managed to avoid a confrontation with the Truck—how to look at the man, how to not look at the man, where not to sit. But here it was. Cohen had let avoiding Truck slip his mind, and now Truck was kicking him in the shin, *Get up*.

Cohen stopped the up and down motion. Opened his eyes. He was taking his hands off the bar, and he knew what he did next mattered. If he cowered, Truck would hit him out of instinct, and if he challenged Truck, Truck would do the same. There was a middle ground, and Cohen had to find it—yield, give him the machine, but a solid look too, and not a word. But Cohen stood up, and Truck said, "Thanks, man," and slid in around him, onto the hack squat machine. And that was it.

Cohen walked off, afraid to turn around and see Truck there, swinging at him. He pictured a dumbbell into his mouth, the pain of cracked teeth and exposed nerve endings; the sight of his teeth bobbing in a pool of his own blood, and the guards not seeing it happen before another blow. He was afraid to turn around and see it coming, and he was afraid if he didn't turn around, he'd not see it coming.

There were weathered bleachers, not far from the exercise equipment. They used to be blue, but time had chipped and muted the colour. He sat there and watched Truck be calmed by the up and down motion of the hack squat. He heard a voice he recognized behind him. "That was close," the man said. Cohen turned around, and it was the drunk driver Truck had beaten up in the shower that day. "Thought you were a goner." Cohen felt wedged between enjoying the camaraderie and not wanting to talk to a man who'd run two kids down on a crosswalk instead of spending ten bucks on a cab. He said he had a book to get back to. A book he couldn't stop thinking about, and he went inside, willing the clock to spin faster so his father would arrive.

Visitation hours were his only real access to the outside world, and that meant he knew nothing of his life, but what visitors told him. His house could've burn down or Zack could've died or the town could've been rioting, and Cohen would only know it if his father chose to tell him, on one of those visits. It meant news came abruptly, like a rock thrown, with no warning. His father came by that day, and they were immediately arguing. Cohen was so painfully confused and overwhelmed, his panic came out caustic.

"This is *waaay* too much to orchestrate without a man's knowledge, his consent, I mean, Jesus, Jesus *fucking* Christ, Dad. Think about it!"

"She only wanted everything set up, so that all she'd need was your green light, your okay, and the child would come into our family. *If* that's what you wanted. *If* he turns out to be yours. *If* you want Zack in your life, then she'd have it all lined up, all the complicated mechanics of it. It's taken her two months to get to where we are now."

Cohen's shock had worn away after twenty or thirty minutes of circular yelling and invective retorts. *You're fucking kidding me! You've got to be kidding me! Are you goddamn crazy?* His father spent the first third of the visitation hour calming Cohen down. He'd gotten up from the table at one point, circled it, and the guards warned him. *Sit down, Davies, or it's back to your cell!* One of the guards had his hand wrapped around the club tied to his waist.

"It was Keith's child, Dad. Not mine. He all but told me that on his last visit."

"Let's not take the man's word over Allie's, who, no surprise at this point, really doesn't know the paternity. Your mother would *not* have made the headway she's made if there wasn't a significant chance this child is yours. So let's stick to working through your feelings about how to handle this, if he's yours."

"I can't even request a paternity test. I know I can't. For a fact."

"The immediate issue is when Allie gave her boy up for adoption, she said the paternity was uncertain, so your name isn't on your boy's adoption file. *If* your name *had been* on an adoption file, you could register with Post-Adoption Services, and maybe, given the circumstances, rules could be bent and things could be sped up. But your name isn't on the file associated with your boy. Understand? You have no way of tracking your son because Allie checked a box on her adoption file that said, paternity uncertain. Which means your name is nowhere on file associated with her child."

He waited for Cohen's nod. "But that's where the ARVC comes in, and what your mother's been up to. Allie's name *is* on a child's original adoption file. Is it Zack? Is it some other boy or girl? Who knows? No one but Adoption Services. But if we can get a court order to see the file for Allie's child, and that child is Zack. Well, Zack has *your* rare genetic heart disorder. Basically, logically, it'd make the boy yours. And then we could assess our next steps. Your feelings about adopting the boy, and the barriers we'd have to knock down to make that happen."

He'd had fifty minutes to calm down, but it was still surreal. His lungs still wouldn't fill, and he had more questions than he

EVERY
LITTLE
THING

255

could ask in the next ten minutes. He still felt hot and cold at the same time, and he desperately needed his father to better understand the absurdity of asking a man what he was asking Cohen. His father had been far too calm as he sat there relaying concrete details about a plan long in the works. The dizzying anger, and the jangling in his bones, was identical to the feeling of being stuck in traffic, late for something important—a flight, a wedding—and wanting to slam his hand on the horn or use the sidewalk as a passing lane. Like he had to get somewhere. It felt like that and felt like being accused of something too. And the latter didn't make sense.

"Your mother has gotten a lawyer. The lawyer is working on getting our eyes on Allie's adoption file. And if Zack is Allie's son, it's only a matter of a court-ordered DNA test to prove he's yours and Allie's."

"It's the wrong order, isn't it? It's not like I've be sitting around deciding to adopt the boy! It's not an overnight. Like. You're sitting there so calm, like you're doing me a favour I didn't ask for. And I can't imagine a bigger. Fucking. *Thing*. We're not talking about getting a dog or buying a car or something here, Dad."

"Were you not…looking into adoption? You seemed serious about it—"

"*Thinking* about it and setting off *court-ordered* courses of action—it's night and day."

"So we'll back off then?"

"That's not what I said." His father said nothing; he nodded his head like he understood. "Slow down, that's all I'm saying. I need to catch up, mentally. Slow down with the lawyer and everything."

"All we're doing right now, with our lawyer, is to determine paternity for Zack. Not his guardianship. One thing at a time. One decision at a time."

Cohen let out a long sigh, like he was blowing out fire in his father's words. "This is…" He shook his head.

"I know, Cohen. It's why your mother's handling it. Right or wrong, she had good intentions here. This is a *very* tricky and complicated situation, and she spent months on it."

"What about if he's *not* mine? Will it matter to Adoption Services that I know the kid? That we've bonded. Gotten…close?

It's an exceptional circumstance, like you said. The kid's waiting on a goddamn *heart*."

His father looked at him, curious. "I—I don't think that can happen, Cohen. If the boy's not yours. For now, let's stick with matters at hand. I need to know—"

Three loud blares, like transport truck horns, signalled the end of visitation hour, but Cohen felt like he'd just rounded that corner to greet his father. When the alarm rang, it frightened him for the first time. Cohen had grabbed the sides of his chair and ducked down like a raid was about to happen.

"I've got to know, Cohen. I—I need to relay to your mother, so that she'll know how to proceed. If we can arrange for it, do you want a paternity test done?"

All the other visitors had left. An officer approached, motioning his father to leave. "*Sir, now!*" The officer threw a hitch-hiker's thumb at the exit. "Time's long over."

NINE DAYS LATER, he was escorted to a small room in the medical wing of the prison. There was a nurse telling him to roll up his sleeve. She was wearing a purple top and a black pencil skirt instead of a hospital or prison uniform. A subtle hint of perfume, like wet grass and honey. Her shiny black hair swooping like a C around each ear; the soft wind her hair made when she'd move her head. He'd spent more than four months barred away from female grace, and that made this woman a cathedral.

She was asking him to make a fist as she wrapped a rubber string around his bicep. But no one could ever find his veins, and most nurses punctured his arm a few times, apologetically, in search of blood. But not this woman. She was having a hard time finding a vein, but she didn't feel the need for small talk and apologies. She hadn't even answered his, *How are you?* She had every reason to be curt, judgemental, to the point, and assume he was another prick trying to dodge child support or the kind of guy who has kids he doesn't know about.

Cohen had learned to spot fake courage in men in jail, so he knew hers was feigned. And he was sorry she'd had to take blood from a prisoner on account of him. He looked her in the eye, "I knew a man who had framed photos of his daughter's DNA in his house," he told her. "You can get cameras that work at that level of magnification. It struck me as an odd thing to frame, as artwork, but they'd framed it on their fifth wedding anniversary. It was a testament to how they loved each other enough to swirl themselves into one person. That whole new batch of DNA on their wall, it existed solely because they met and fell in love."

"Almost done," she said, not quite understanding his rambling.

"Those two twisted-ladders of DNA in his photo, they housed the personal histories of that kid's parents. And their parents and their parents, way back through time. And you think, *My God if our DNA could talk, you know?* About our ancestors, who clubbed sabre-tooths and mastodons for supper, then left themselves behind, somewhere, in that kid's DNA."

She raised an eyebrow, *Never thought about that before*, but she didn't say anything to him. She hit a vein, and they watched his blood fill another vial.

He tried again to break the silence, "This end of it is amazing too. How you can match a child's DNA to its parents', like holding up two sides of a torn piece of paper."

"It's really not that simple."

"No, nothing is, is it?"

"Sir, I—" and she never finished her sentence.

"What?"

"Nothing."

"Did you know that a child's mitochondrial DNA comes exclusively from their mother? So, technically, a child really *is* a little bit more of their mother than their father. It's not just nine months of pregnancy—and *that* bond—that a mother can hold over the father. It's the mitochondrial DNA too, which means every cell in a child's body has an exclusive bit of its mother in it. Fittingly, the mitochondria is basically the life force of a cell."

Surprised now, grinning a little, even, "I have to confess I graduated twelve years ago, and I can't even remember what mitochondria do, in a cell. All I remember is that there is the kidney-bean-shaped thing, in a diagram of a human cell."

"It's the cell's power plant, really."

She pulled the vial from the needle, capped it, and motioned for him to apply pressure to the tissue she'd placed over the needle hole in his arm. A little circle of red ballooned into the fabric of the tissue.

Rooting through her work kit, she said, "Can I ask you how

you know all of this stuff?"

"Would it be cliché of me to say I don't belong in here?"
She shrugged her shoulders. "We all make mistakes, I guess.
Open up and say Aw. We take cheek cells too. For comparison."
He opened his mouth, said, *Aww*, but then closed it to add,
"Sometimes people make mistakes for us." She hadn't seen the
second sentence coming, and he almost bit the swab as she
brought it to his mouth. "Sorry," he said, and she smiled, *That's
fine.*

He opened his mouth again and she took a swab. She bagged
the Q-tip-looking thing and handed him a pamphlet as she was
leaving. Paragraphs and paragraphs about how to deal with the
outcome of a paternity test, no matter what the result. There were
counselling options, and frequently asked questions, as if anyone
had ever been in Cohen's exact situation.

HE WOKE UP hungry and read the shade of orange falling
through his window as 6:30 at best. His door wouldn't slide open
for breakfast until 7:00, and by then the sunlight would be piss
yellow. Like it always was when those doors slid open.

Waiting out the hunger had been the most uncomfortable
part of his sentence. Or the most desperate ache he couldn't
distract himself from in there. He paced his room that morning:
six feet one way, then six feet the next. He went to his window,
stared. There were two crows on the ground, excited about
something they'd found, but he couldn't see what with them
hopping around. And the glass in the window was so thick that
the sunlight burned his eyes in a warm, refreshing way.

He laid back in bed. Held his stomach. Pushed a fist into
the hunger pang like he could numb it. Waking up that morning,
he thought about what kind of man, in a situation like his, would
not adopt his own child. He thought about the camping trips he
and his father had taken, alone, before Ryan had been born.
Though scant, they'd made him a biologist, and he knew it.
The impression they'd left. The way those nights were the only
nights from his childhood his memory had kept intact as a whole.
The wet smell of a rain-soaked tent. The distinct sound of a tent
zipper. The texture of smores in his mouth; how a third or fourth
marshmallow could make his teeth hurt, and how, ever since, a
toothache had made him think of his father. On those nights he'd

EVERY
LITTLE
THING

259

step out of the tent at 3 a.m. to pee, a life-affirming fear of black bears and coyotes had punched into his genetic makeup and re-wired his personality.

One morning there'd been bees buzzing around their campsite. *They're only here to pollinate flowers*, his father had promised him. *They've got no interest in stinging you if you leave them beeee.* And he pinched Cohen, but that pinch, that fact, that every animal on earth serves a concrete ecological role, amazed him. The way it amazed Zack. And what Zack deserved was a man making the world more accessible or amazing for him too.

He pictured Band-Aids in his medicine cabinet with cartoony images on them.

He pictured packing a lunchbox—sandwiches in little baggies with the crusts cut off—and wondered if Zack was that kind of picky-eater. It was one of too many things Cohen didn't know about Zack. What he liked to eat. What he liked to drink. Real orange juice or the cheap, tooth-zapping, concentrated stuff. Questions like those were the reasons he resented the notion of getting a *second chance* with his son because a *second chance* implied that starting from scratch was possible. It implied that Zack could be one day old again. Instead, Cohen would be parachuting down into a life in progress. He'd be learning a hundred things about a seven year old—all at once—that he should have gathered slowly, one clue at a time, over a period of seven years. *Loves chocolate milk, hates grapes. Likes bicycles or can't ride one and needs to be taught.*

The light in his room was going yellow now, and he tried to picture how bad off Zack was. There were some mornings the hunger in his stomach would crawl up into his chest and burn.

The doors opened, and Cohen weaved his way to the cafeteria. He was getting his ladleful of eggs, but the person spooning them onto his tray dropped the ladle as everyone jumped from a sudden guttural scream, somewhere in the cafeteria. The man dropped the ladle, and the ladle knocked over Cohen's tray, and the man said, "I'm sorry," as they both looked at Cohen's tray on the ground. "But you'll have to get back in line." And there were forty people in line now.

The howling had been from Curt, the big black man Cohen had been checked into prison with. It was the first time Cohen had seen him in there, and Truck had his head pressed into a table—one side of Curt's face pancaked hard against the surface and the other side covered by Truck's big hand; the folds of his big jowly cheek had smeared across his face so that his mouth and an eye had disappeared. Truck was twisting Curt's arm up behind his back, as far as it would go, and the guards were taking their time. Curt howled every time Truck bent that arm, and he howled in a way that begged sympathy from everyone in the room. And on that day, unlike any other time Truck had put a hand on a man, Curt had somehow managed get that sympathy put to action. He swept Truck's foot out from under him, and Truck went down hard. Five or six men got to stomping Truck, finally, and the lockdown alarm went off before Cohen could get his food. It was an hour before they let everyone back into the kitchen, and that meant going right from eating to the visitation room to see his father.

He'd learned to read people's facial expressions before rounding the corner to greet them. Bad news and anger held themselves in the jaw. A rigid jaw, or a closed mouth, was a bad sign. A smile was an obviously good sign, or it meant no news. Crossed arms meant the person was still wording things in their head, concentrating.

He rounded the corner, and his father had a posture he'd never seen before. He was already shaking his head like he didn't want to have to say whatever he was thinking. "Even if a heart does come now..." his father stopped shaking his head and stared at his knees. He looked like he hadn't slept or even showered in days, and he'd kept his hat on for the first time. The bags under his eyes were the colour of angry rain. With every visitation hour, it was clear his father was growing more and more attached to Zack. And it was more in his tone than his haggard appearance that day.

"Even if a heart *does* come. The doctors are saying we need to be prepared for...causality. Death. It's septic shock." He swirled his hands together to connote, *everything*. "Multiple organ failure. The tube, running from one of his bedside machines, into his abdomen—it rendered his body open to infection. There's a big abscess there. *E. Coli, Staph*. And his immune system's shot."

Cohen fell back in his chair. Breathed in and in and in.

"...One minute he's sweating, next minute he's shivering. Throwing up. It's everything at once. And we're back to watching his urine bag again. Waiting for yellow."

HE KNEW, FROM the return address on the envelope, that he was holding the paternity test results. He kept the envelope, folded in half, in his pant pocket, sometimes running a finger along its edges through the fabric of his pants.

The envelope was un-sealed—the prison scanned all incoming mail—so all he had to do was peer down into it because it wasn't a full piece of paper folded three times to hide its message: the results were printed on something the size of a cue card, one third the size of a piece of paper. He sat on the edge of his bed the day it came. He squinted his eyes, to blur the words, and he looked down into the envelope. There were two or three lines at the most. In isolation, he'd seen the word *negative*, out of context, like it could have been in reference to his blood type, or it could have meant a hundred things, so he shut the envelope.

He'd been romanticizing the idea of stepping on toy dinosaurs and dinkies scattered all around his house. He'd been picturing it now, him and Zack. A tent pitched in the living room, a flashlight pointing up, *once upon a time* stories.

It was Sunday. He was being released that Friday.

He had five days left in that place, and that could be dangerous. He'd seen men act out on others about to be released, but rumours had spread—from nosey listeners in the visitation room—that Cohen had a sick child. *His son is dying*, and Cohen never corrected what might be true. He'd seen the hardest men in there go soft for their children in the visitation room. And he'd caught their sympathetic nods—in the cafeteria, in the resource room—since the word had gotten around about Zack.

Cohen had five days left, four if Sunday didn't count because it *was* Sunday, and maybe Friday didn't count because it was the day he'd get out. And he'd be getting out early too: seven weeks shy of his six month sentence.

CHAD
PELLEY

WEIGHTING

FRIDAY CAME, HIS official release from prison, and his mother and father picked him up. Other than his mother's bear hug in the parking lot—her tears cold against his neck—there was nothing ceremonious about it. It was about getting out of that place and getting to the hospital. He'd asked them to take a change of clothes, a fresh one, so he wouldn't have to wear what the prison had given him back. He changed in a Tim Horton's washroom and threw the old clothes in the garbage—the garbage can was there and the old jeans were in his hand and he threw them in the garbage. Stared at them. One leg hanging out the side.

Before throwing his old clothes in the trash, he'd taken out the paternity test results. He had the envelope in his hand now, still folded in half, and he thought about opening it there and then, in a bathroom stall. But he pictured it saying: *No.* Saying: *Negative, not yours*, and that would affect how he *looked* at the boy, in ten minutes time, at the hospital. It would affect how he felt about the kid, and Zack deserved someone there now, anyone, immediately. It was that, and it was because he was afraid of the answer either way. He was too close to seeing the kid, and he had too many questions, and opening the envelope would only cause more, *Do I really want this child?* More panic and anxiety, more, *Can I adopt him anyway?* A man in a trench coat walked in. A heavy breather, and he'd said hello. He was distracting in every way, slurping his iced cappuccino through a seemingly faulty straw, before setting it down to hum as he stood in front of the urinal. Cohen put the results back in his pocket.

At a red light his father said, "You should've gotten the paternity results by now?" and Cohen said, "Do you know if they've put Zack on dialysis?"

"I can't keep the machines straight anymore," he confessed. "Or what tube does what. Why?"

"Because dialysis wouldn't be good."

"We were there Wednesday night, Cohen, and you should prepare yourself. He's in and out of consciousness now. He's not a pretty sight. It's hard to look at."

His mother said, "Keith came by our house last night. Looking for Allie again. Have you spoken to her?" and Cohen said nothing, and his father shot a look at his mother, *Don't meddle.*

Zack was in the pediatric intensive care unit. His bed surrounded by machines instead of people. A dialysis machine meant his kidneys were failing, and the thick, rippled tubing jammed down his throat meant his lungs were wilted. The RVAD machine, the source of Zack's infection, was still hooked up because his heart wouldn't pump without it. All those tubes, like a den of snakes, latched on.

Cohen walked into the room, and his mother grabbed his father's wrist; they both stayed in the doorway, so Cohen could be alone with Zack. He sat at the chair with a book he'd bought in the gift shop just in case, *The Mesozoic: Age of the Dinosaurs.* But Zack wasn't awake. There was a purple Tupperware container on the table beside Zack's bed, the lid off, exposing a half-eaten bran muffin, and Cohen wondered who'd owned it. He turned to his mother, tapping the Tupperware, "Is this yours?"

"There's a nurse here," she said, "And God love that woman's big red heart. Sits with him whenever she's not busy. Bends the rules for visitor hours." Cohen saw a pamphlet under the Tupperware container, pulled it out. *When Your Loved One is in a Coma: Frequently Asked Questions.* Someone had laid it there because there hadn't been a *loved one* by Zack's side to hand it to. He held the pamphlet up to his mother, and her knees bent low. His father put an arm around her and guided her down the hallway, saying, "We'll find out what's happening here. We'll find out what's happening."

Cohen stayed in the chair, and he tried to piece it all together. What the machines were doing. The clear fluids in IV bags would be antibiotics. A few drops per second would have to find and kill the million invisible bacteria poisoning every inch of the kid, and all it took was a few resistant bacteria, or a few well-hidden ones, and they'd spread and conquer again. There was something like a vertical accordion inside one of the machines, and Cohen watched it. Up and down. A sucking noise, a demon breathing, and it lulled Cohen's lungs into breathing in sync with it.

None of these machines were getting at the root cause. They weren't *curing* anything. Dialysis, because his kidneys were failing. Intubation, and a mainline of oxygen, because his lungs were compromised. It was putting up cardboard as a storm broke windows and punched holes in a roof. It was hoping the storm wouldn't be so bad. *All we can do now is assist each compromised organ*, and they did until Zack himself was a machine. If Cohen unplugged any one of those cords, Zack would be dead in hours.

He heard his mother watching him. Looked back at the doorway. His father closed his eyes, nodded his head. *Comatose.* His mother, "Five a.m., on Thursday." He looked at her hands, and she had that same *When Your Loved One is in a Coma* pamphlet buckled up in her grip.

He looked back to Zack. His chest up and down in an unnaturally perfect rhythm. A thin plastic tube in each nostril. *Oxygen.* Even that, his body couldn't get enough of, and yet the room was full of it. His blood was a polluted river, crashing off banks of bone and splashing over every organ, soaking them with infected blood. His lungs were taking it the hardest, so they had him ventilated. His mouth taped open to accommodate the thick, ribbed tubing. It was hard to look at and then it wasn't.

He'd sat there for hours, talking with his parents about everything: the job at the university he'd applied for, the *ginger nurse* who kept a steady supply of baked goods at Zack's bedside table for visitors. A new show on HBO that Cohen's father thought Cohen would love. For thirty minutes, they talked about the funny new things their crazy neighbour had been up to because they'd had the same neighbour since Cohen was nine or ten, and that neighbour was unpredictable and off the wall. He'd take up anything, but only for a month or two: ice sculpting, a backyard bread oven. One week, he'd put fliers in everyone's mailbox about a croquet tournament he was hosting in his backyard.

"...His latest venture is going around to yard sales on Saturdays, buying anything he deems a good deal, and selling it all, for a buck more than he bought it for, at his own yard sales on Sundays."

EVERY
LITTLE
THING

265

His mother laughed, "Yes, and your poor father. Jim insists, every Saturday around supper, that your father come over and see the day's best deals."

It'd been nice, catching up, laughing, talking about something other than how everything had gone wrong. His mother ran across the street and picked up a pizza; snuck wine in, in a thermos. They left him there just after nine o'clock, and shortly after they left, he went and got a tea. He hadn't been in a hospital cafeteria since Halifax: Allie in her room, not wanting to see him. Him pouring cashews into yogurt for Keith to bring to her.

His tea was too hot to sip. He sat at a table, alone, watching steam rise up and out of his cup, dangling there, until there was no more steam to watch. He took the envelope out of his pocket, unfolded it. Took out the slip of paper. He laid it print-side down on the table and threw the envelope into a recycling bin behind him. He folded the slip of paper, three times, took out his wallet, and tucked the test result into the clear plastic picture frame, where most men kept a photo of their child.

MONDAY NIGHT HE sat beside Zack, and Zack hadn't woken yet. Not for a minute. The wind and rain were drumming on the window, and the window was huge, thin—he thought back to the thick, boxy window in his cell. The one he'd perched at and peered through for months. And the duck pond in the far right corner. He thought about Curt, howling, as Truck pressed his face into that table, twisting his arm. The desperate look that Curt had on his face, the day they were both checked into prison, had always stayed with Cohen, in a haunting sort of way. It had been a look that said, *But life can just change.*

He'd been sitting at Zack's bedside for ten hours and only ate one meal that day, breakfast, and he planned to sit there another ten. He'd comb Zack's hair with his fingers whenever Zack looked too hopeless or defeated or dishevelled. A year ago the kid had been a wound-up, animated, fact-filled toy, tugging on his pants, *Do you know what I know about snowy owls?*

Zack opened his eyes at one point, but didn't move his head. His pupils tumbling around like clothes in a dryer. Cohen stood up, smiling, but Zack couldn't talk with the tubes down his throat. And he looked confused anyway. He took Zack's hand, rubbing a thumb up and down Zack's dry, red knuckles. "Can you hear me, buddy? Squeeze my hand if you can hear me?" But Zack's eyes closed again. As fast as that.

Cohen started reading aloud from the dinosaur book. Just in case. Or to amuse himself. Twelve hours in that room. Ten at night. A book of crossword puzzles half-filled out on the table next to him. A magazine that couldn't hold his interest.

A nurse strolled in on her final rounds, surprised to find someone there. A look of sympathy on her face. She had a red tin can in her hands and popped the lid off. "Double chocolate with cream cheese filling," she'd said. "Unless you're lactose-intolerant, you're going to enjoy these immensely."

"Thanks," he said, and he liked that the bottom of the muffin hadn't been wrapped in a muffin wrapper he'd have to contend with, discard. "You must be the *wonderful ginger nurse* I've been hearing about, who's been looking in on Zack?"

"Oh, just doing my job."

"Really?" he said, chewing the muffin she'd baked. "Baking and distributing these tasty muffins to everyone in your wing is part of your job?"

She'd smiled as he'd said *tasty*. "You're Anne's boy, then? Corey or Conan or something?"

"Cohen."

"Oh, good," she laughed. "Conan's not a good name for anyone."

"Unless you're a barbarian." She looked at him like she'd never seen the Schwarzenegger film. "It's a movie, never mind. A bad one, too."

She rubbed Zack's toes, through the white blanket draped over him, in a way that implied familiarity with the boy. "Visitation hours are over," she started pulling the curtain around them, "so I'm going to have to ask you to be super quiet for me and hide out behind this curtain?"

He nodded with appreciation and told her that Zack had opened his eyes for a while. "Not too long ago, actually. That's a good thing, right?"

"Well, it's certainly not a bad thing, is it? I can tell you what though. You being here for this little slugger. That's a good thing." She patted his toes again. "I've been with him, looking in on him, since day one. Stole my heart over a glass of apple juice, he did. A

EVERY
LITTLE
THING

267

charmer. Knows more about owls than anyone could possibly need to." She smiled, and Cohen didn't want her to leave the room. She had a textbook under her arm, and he asked her about it. "Med School," she said. "I'm studying to be a doctor."

"What, *and* working as a nurse?"

"I haven't had a life in three point five years. When I get a chance, a break, or after a shift, I slip in here, with this little slugger, and study a while."

"Feel free," he said, "to sit down. I was just about to leave, actually. I don't want to displace you, or steal away your study spot, and be personally responsible for your failing out of med school."

"You really don't mind?"

"No. And certainly not if you're going to bring muffins when you come."

She'd laughed that night, a lot. She was easy to figure out, and talk with, and want around. She'd laugh into a closed fist, as if coughing, and there was something about the gesture Cohen liked. Something about her tiny hands, her face, the copper mess of curls she never did much to restrain.

Two or three times a week, for two weeks, they'd crossed paths in Zack's room. He'd take her textbook and ask her questions about differential diagnosis and vaccinations, and one night, she'd asked him to help her recite the proper ways to tell a person their loved one had died. There was a checklist. It seemed callous until she'd explained the way hope—when not deflated by *short, clear, declarative sentences*—will soar into denial. "Hope and denial can be harder on a person than anything," she'd said, like she knew it for a fact.

Every time she slipped away for the night, she'd step to the other side of the curtain she'd drawn and poke her head back in. "I need you to really keep it down in here." Finger to her lips. *Shh.* "It's after visiting hours." He'd nod, smiling, and she'd cast one more sympathetic look at Zack and bow out.

He slept a lot in that room, but he could never spend the night, or the morning shift nurse would find him in violation of visitation hours and it would come back on Cassie. The more time he'd spend there, the more it felt like he had to spend time there. He'd invested so much time there, to be present when Zack woke up, that his conviction to be there when Zack woke up strengthened with every passing hour. Cassie would pop in and joke he was narcoleptic—*You're always asleep when I pop in!* She'd read him the symptoms of narcolepsy from one of her textbooks the night she'd come in with red velvet cupcakes. He'd fall asleep in there to the beeps and pulls and hums of all that machinery, and when he'd wake up, Cassie would have a muffin laid in wait, on the table beside *the little slugger.* He helped her bathe Zack one night, and she'd taken her nurse gown off to do so. Handed it to him, to lay over a chair. It felt like the start of something.

One night he'd gone to sleep there, and instead of waking to a muffin or cupcake, he'd woken up to a note beside him, pinned under Allie's engagement ring, like a paperweight holding it down.

Cohen,

It's not like I ever saw this day coming. Me walking into a hospital room, afraid to wake you. Afraid you'd yell at me and be right to yell. The boy I never told you about: I still believe it was Keith's. And I wasn't ready for a baby with Keith. And I couldn't deal with what it meant to not want a baby with Keith. To want a child, but not with the man I was with.

And if it was your son, that was wrong too. Because he should have been <u>ours</u>, not yours, not mine. We were going to have a little boy, and he was going to spill juice on our couch cushions and demand pets that pissed on our rugs and shat all over our yard, and he'd need our advice, and his fingernails clipped, and we were going to raise him. Together. The both of us. Vacations and parent-teacher interviews. Together. That's how it was supposed to be. Not this. Not all this confusion and court-intervention. Not you, here, at this boy's bedside anyway, because he might have been yours.

This is not an apology for all I've put you through. This situation is beyond forgiveness. But not understanding, I hope. And I need you to understand one thing: the day I revoked my parental rights to a little boy, I never imagined you in a hospital room and me afraid to wake you.

What I did was inexcusable. What I went along with in that courtroom even more so. But it took sitting in court six months ago, and turning on you, to realize how upside down my life's become. I stared at my engagement ring the whole time I was

EVERY LITTLE THING

269

on that stand, twisting it around and around my finger, until my finger was sore.

Sorry I'm saying sorry in a note, like a high-school girl—but I don't deserve the face time. Nor should you be put in a position of having to decide if you should grant me a dignified conversation. You're here with this boy. For this boy. Not for me. Not right now. But I do want to talk. This can't be like Dad again, where we don't address it, and drift apart. I want to talk with you, and you have my number, but you haven't called. Just know that I want you to. And please do, when your head is clear and you think I deserve a minute.

I bought you a muffin. It's all they had left down there in the cafeteria.

My deepest sinceriities, Cohen.

– Allie. Allie Crosbie. Remember her?

HE READ HER note two or three times that morning, inspecting it, the way a cat bats at a mouse to try and understand it. Or to understand its own reaction to it.

His mother showed up around noon. A bag of bagels. Some orange juice. "You have your interview at the university today, don't you?"

He threw Allie's note in the garbage. "Yeah," he said, looking in the garbage like the note didn't belong there. "At three thirty."

"It's twelve now. You should go on home, have a shower to clear your head. Think about some answers, to some questions they might ask you."

But he didn't go straight home. He stopped in to visit Lee on his way home, like he did every time he left the hospital. Lee was a statue now, unresponsive, but Cohen liked that. He felt bad about liking it, but Lee had become the perfect confessional booth. He could be viscerally honest with an old friend, but free of judgment. He could say, *I still love her.* He could say, *I fucking hate her, Lee,* and Lee wouldn't even look up.

That day, he found himself telling Lee about how he didn't want to teach university biology. And maybe he'd skip the interview. Move far away. A fresh start. A clean pair of eyes. In

Iceland. Montreal. Somewhere in Italy where he didn't know a goddamn thing, not even the language. Touching down in Italy and being forced to learn how to talk again, meet new people, find a career in something other than birds. There'd be a house there, and he'd have to get familiar with it: where the cutlery tray was, the AC dial, what the postal code was, the phone number. He'd have to find the delis, cafés, bookstores, and pick favourites. He liked not even knowing what the currency was.

"Euros?" he asked Lee. And Lee said nothing in return.

EVERY
LITTLE
THING

A CLEAN
FLAME

JULY 18TH. RYAN'S birthday. There was a bench not five paces away from Ryan's grave, and Cohen had been sitting there, sipping coffee from a Styrofoam cup. The coffee was cold now, but it tasted fine, or at least acidic enough to keep him from slipping into another daydream. He watched his parents standing at Ryan's headstone, doing whatever silent ceremony it was they did every year, in the last ten minutes of their visit: face-to-face, foreheads pressed together, and all four of their hands bound and balled up into a dangling pendulum. Eyes closed.

Cohen sat alone on the bench and thought back to the hospital. To Zack. To the month he'd spent by the kid's bedside, falling asleep to the pulls and hums of his machinery. The nurse there. Cassie. The muffins she'd bake for them, at home, and bring in *just for him*. He thought of the day Cassie came in with carrot cake muffins. A long sliver of carrot had gotten stuck between her two front teeth. She couldn't get it out and had to do her rounds anyway. The two of them laughing about it. She'd tried a piece of paper, as floss, torn from a magazine; licked the taste of print from her teeth and tried again. Cohen had gone to a vending machine and bought her a pack of gum, but nothing worked. "Could you," she wrestled a handful of coins from a pocket, "run across the street and grab me a toothpick or something?" She had a hand on his shoulder. That bone-softening look of hers in her eye. "There's a pharmacy there."

Cassie had been the one to get Cohen to read the test results. On a park bench, outside the hospital, under her umbrella. It wasn't raining, but she liked the shade when they'd go out for some fresh air together. He took the test result from his wallet, rolled it up between his fingers like a paper cigarette. He held it straight up, like a candle, between his thumb and forefinger. *Maybe I should just burn it?* She took it from him and read it, and Cohen tried to read her face. She'd looked let down. "It's between me now and this garbage can," and she laid it in with the trash, results facing up. "So you better decide, in the next few minutes, if you really want to know. Or the answer dies with me." She walked inside. Left him there. Worried a wind would blow. Worried everyone passing by, eating hot dogs and drinking lattes, was headed for that bin. He peered into the garbage, and the answer was resting on a dozen Tim Horton's cups. It had said, *Negative DNA Match for Cohen Davies and Zack Janes.* That was it. Short and official, no room for denial.

But the hospital wasn't the last place he'd seen the boy. The wake was. The funeral. A little casket, the small crowd there to watch it lowered into the ground. The grass was soggy and puddled, and there'd been a wet *suck* at his feet as he got up to walk away. The priest read from the bible, about God's good plan for children like Zack, and Cohen walked away from the words, back to his car, and slammed his door shut, hard, because his lungs couldn't take it, and his eyes, and if it couldn't be someone's fault, he could at least hate what the priest was reducing Zack's sad life to.

Shortly after Zack died, Cohen went out and bought an alarm clock that didn't sound like the hospital machines that had failed the boy. That long sustained beep. There was a crosswalk by the university, and it blared to let blind people know they could cross, but it blared a long, sustained beep, far too similar to the machine that pronounced Zack dead.

He didn't like the way the hospital staff threw a blanket over Zack and walked away like their job was done. And he hated the packs of students, and their clipboards, and questions about what had gone wrong with Zack. He was still there, in his bed, under a sheet, and the residents and interns were full of intrigue, scratching lessons into their notebooks about what had gone wrong. Cohen had to wait in the hallway, wait out their rotation, and he'd catch stray words, *I've never seen an RVAD before, pretty cool.*

That nurse, Cassie. She'd waited with him in the hallway. She bought him a water. Gave him her phone number. *Keep in touch?* She walked him out into the daylight, hugged him, rubbing his shoulders, as the sun burned in his eyes.

EVERY
LITTLE
THING

ANOTHER SIP OF that acidic coffee to fend off the memory. He looked up and his parents were still in their ritual, staring at Ryan's headstone, feigning telepathic communication with their dead son. It worked for them but never for Cohen. If he couldn't see something, if he couldn't touch it, it wasn't there.

They were alone in the graveyard that day. Anything louder than the faint drone of a passing car caught Cohen's attention: an empty chip bag, blowing around, slapping off headstones. A scratchy and irritating noise.

He heard footsteps, but he didn't turn around. The footsteps stopped. He saw his parents looking behind him, before he turned himself and saw Allie standing there. She had a bouquet of yellow flowers in her hands. Her nose in them like a bee. Cohen's mother and father excused themselves immediately. His mother looked at Allie smiling; his father wouldn't look at her.

"We'll wait in the car," his mother said, and his father was already in it.

Allie had a look on her face, *Smile, please*. A bit lip, glassy eyes, the tips of her shoes together like the top of a triangle, and she was staring down at it. Vulnerable, standing her ground. The wind lifting her hair every few gusts; billowing her skirt. Her eyes fighting off a finger of sunlight.

Cohen faced forward again, leaving her standing there behind him.

"I—I shouldn't have come. I'm sorry." She brought the flowers to Ryan's grave, laid them there, took a minute with the headstone. Cohen watched her, the way he always could watch her: like fire, satisfied to stare. When she looked up at Cohen, he had no words, no urge to say anything, and she said nothing. She started pacing back to her car, and as she passed him, her head was down, but her eyes were in his. He stuck his hand out. A palm against her belly. Allie Catherine Crosbie: he used to call her *Allie Cat*, for short. And for the way she'd come crawling into his life that night on the rooftop. Like a stray. Never quite his and always around.

ACKNOWLEDGEMENTS

THANKS FIRST AND foremost to this hip new reincarnation of Breakwater Books. Quite frankly, their President, Rebecca Rose, is the patron saint of my writing career. A book, and therefore a writer, cannot exist without a publisher, and four years ago, Rebecca took a chance on me with my debut, *Away from Everywhere*, when few others would. I owe all the literary thrills I've had to her—there have been movies deals, awards, time spent on bestseller tables, my book's been taught in university courses, and I've shared the stage with writers I cut my teeth on. I owe every fond memory and sense of accomplishment to Rebecca Rose for giving me a shot, my books a home, and my style a chance. Also, Breakwater's Managing Editor, James Langer, and their Marketing Coordinator, Elisabeth de Mariaffi, are both talented, award-winning writers I admire, and to me, it only makes sense the people I deal with at a publishing house are writers themselves. They *get it.* Where they had every right to tell me I was bonkers, and to shut up, and to hurry up, they did quite the opposite. What a fine bunch of people to publish with. And to Rhonda Molloy, thanks for another book design as flashy as your shoe collection.

To my editor, Mark Anthony Jarman, thanks for not only bettering the book, but for bettering me as a writer as well. By eradicating two tics I had as an author, I'm now twice the writer I used to be. Jessica Grant and Trish Osuch—two terrific, careful readers—lent me their patience and grace as first-draft readers. Subsequent drafts were much richer because of their two cents. Countless gracious friends and writers read passages from this book to answer questions I had. High fives to you. The kind that make your hand sting. And certainly to Kim Pelley, Ashley MacDonald, and Samuel Thomas Martin, for reading the first 50 pages, in 2010, and saying, *Yeah, keep writing this book.* And to Katie Guy-Knee for reading a bad draft at a crucial time. And to Mom, God love her, for always wanting to be part of the process and reading every draft, of this, and every little thing I write.

The authors who endorsed this novel—Lisa Moore, Russell Wangersky, and Billie Livingston. I write and write and write, in hopes of catching up to your talents. Your time and kind words meant as much to me as anything that will come of this novel. *(Everybody: go read their books!)* Thanks as well to Chris Bucci for his efforts with this novel, and for tolerating a client who can write novel-length emails about his novel.

And to you readers who bought this book: I really appreciate that my novel is in your hands. I'm figuring out this writing thing as I go, and your support and feedback along the way has meant more than I can articulate in an acknowledgements section.

Thanks to the Newfoundland & Labrador Arts Council for a grant that let me take a few months off to complete a tricky portion of this book.

CHAD PELLEY IS an award-winning author, songwriter, and photographer from St. John's. His debut novel, *Away from Everywhere*, was a Coles bestseller, won or was shortlisted for several awards, has been adopted by university courses, and a film adaptation is underway. His short fiction has been published in journals, textbooks, anthologies, and recognized by several awards. Chad is the founder of Salty Ink, President of the Writers Alliance of Newfoundland & Labrador, and has written for a variety of publications, such as *Quill & Quire*, *The National Post*, and *Atlantic Books Today*. As a result, he rarely sees more of the world than his computer screen, and his hottest one-night stands happen in his own bed, with books of Canadian fiction.